DELETED

BETRAYALS

Further Titles by Brian Freemantle from Severn House

BETRAYALS
DIRTY WHITE
O'FARRELL'S LAW

BETRAYALS

Brian Freemantle

This title first published in Great Britain 1996 by
SEVERN HOUSE PUBLISHERS LTD of
9–15 High Street, Sutton, Surrey SM1 1DF.

British Library Cataloguing in Publication Data

Freemantle, Brian, 1936–
  Betrayals
  1. English fiction – 20th century
  I. Title
  823.9'14 [F]

  ISBN 0-7278-4952-2

Typeset by Palimpsest Book Production Limited,
Polmont, Stirlingshire, Scotland.
Printed and bound in Great Britain by
Hartnolls Ltd, Bodmin, Cornwall.

To Alb and Gwen, with affection

Widow'd Wife and married maid,
Betrothed, betrayer and betray'd,

Sir Walter Scott—*The Betrothed*

BETRAYALS

·1·

Wrong.

Janet Stone let the word echo in her mind the way Hank had always said it when they'd made a mistake: deep down and echoing, like the sound of a bell, with all the emphasis at the end. And then let it chime again and reverberate again, waiting for the memory to hurt. There was a pang but not a bad one and she was grateful. It had taken too long—far too long—for her to get this far, being able positively to think about it without breaking down, without actually having to leave a room. So it was getting better: a necessary test.

She'd soon have to leave this room, though: she was ready for a lot of things, but not quite yet for Harriet Andrew's ritual assemblage of Washington glitterati, a melee of teeth-flashing gabble and spilled drinks and furtive hands. She should have known better, of course. She and Hank had nearly always found an excuse to avoid coming. Testing herself against the pain of memories, Janet forced another recollection. Hank hadn't called them melees. Menagerie had been his word. Janet thought the description was fitting; she was in a menagerie of performing human animals being watered and fed: doubtless, as she understood inhabitants of menageries did, they'd further perform by mating before the night was out. It was an impromptu intrusion and Janet thrust it irritably away. She could never allow herself reflections about sex: the subject—the very thought— was more tightly locked out and forbidden from her mind than anything else. How could it be otherwise? What could there be—who could there be—after Hank?

Janet gazed around, seeking a doorway from the cage in which she felt incarcerated. It was not Harriet's house. It was a four-story brownstone on Dumbarton Street that Harriet's father had bought when he was seconded from the Bank of England in London to the World Bank in Washington and had afterwards retained as the undoubted investment it was. The main living room area stretched the entire length of the book-lined, low-lighted first level and there were ornately metaled and overhanging balconies at either end, reached through floor-to-ceiling windows. Both were open and Janet began to maneuver through the crush towards the one directly overlooking the street, but she halted almost at once. This wasn't the way to escape: this was scurrying into an even smaller cage where she would be isolated in a more restricted area among people interested only in their own audiences, which were audiences she had no wish to join, and their own voices, which were voices she had no wish to hear.

From her hostess's command post near the bar, a permanent mahogany bunker where a hired-in black-tied waiter plied gallon jugs of booze, Harriet caught Janet's eye. Harriet was wearing a designer skirt tight enough to have revealed her underwear if she had been wearing any, which she wasn't, and a low silk blouse which her nipples puckered to show she was not wearing a bra, either. The makeup had not started to melt yet and the naturally blonde hair was still in comparative order, bubbled like fairground candyfloss around a fine-nosed face that was too long to make the style successful. Harriet shone an enameled smile and made a circular motion with an extended finger, as if she were stirring something, and Janet nodded and stirred in the opposite direction in a sign-language promise to circulate. Maybe someone would have talked to her if she'd bothered with as much makeup as Harriet or left her knickers in the underwear drawer or made an effort to get her hair professionally fixed before coming tonight instead of relying upon that morning's shampoo in the shower. More things forbidden to reflect upon, she thought.

Janet, who knew Harriet to be the closest friend she had in Washington—perhaps in the world—angrily stopped the drift of her thoughts. Harriet had simply tried to help by inviting her, like a lot of other people not as close had tried to help, in other ways, to get her out of the pit of despair in which she'd buried herself. Now she was struggling to emerge. And it was important to avoid self-pity. What had happened hadn't been anyone's fault: hadn't been avoidable or preventable. Dear God, how she wished so much had been avoidable or preventable! Self-pity again: careful, she warned herself.

She really did have to get away: find a quieter part of the cage at least. Claustrophobia was beginning to tighten around her, so that it was physically difficult to breathe, the first stirring of familiar panic she'd hoped to be over.

The gap was near the door, which was what she wanted anyway, a tiny oasis (were there oases in menageries?) kept vacant by the passing inrush of new arrivals. Cradling her barely sipped drink, a sweet punch Janet suspected might be too strongly laced with something like tasteless vodka from the gallon-bottle on the mahogany bar, she set out on her escape, turning and twisting and smiling her apologies through the crowd in between. Twice as she moved through she felt an apparently solicitous hand on her ass and once someone openly groped her left breast before she could get by.

Janet concentrated entirely upon reaching the space she'd identified and ignored the fondling, so it only took seconds to get through, but when she looked up the empty space wasn't empty any more. It wasn't possible so late to change direction; besides which, there wasn't anywhere else to go: The entrance now was jammed with a group of new arrivals, kissing greetings and discarding coats and dispensing presents and gesturing with booze contributions to prove their right of entry.

"Oh!" said Janet.

"I'm sorry?"

So was Janet, at her gauche reaction to his getting there ahead of her. "It was just that . . . nothing . . . I'm sorry," she stumbled, still awkward.

He smiled, unflustered, and said: "We can't both be sorry. Not when neither of us know what we're apologizing for."

"I didn't think you were apologizing," she said. It had been so long! She felt lost.

"I wasn't," he said. "But you seem disconcerted, so if I've done something wrong I will."

Janet knew she was flushed, red-faced. "It was just that I thought this part of the room, so near the door, wasn't occupied." She wished everything wasn't coming out so badly.

The smile stayed, a reassuring expression. "You too?" he said.

"I don't understand," Janet said, thinking in relief that she did, but didn't want to make any more mistakes.

"I was looking for somewhere to hide," he said. "Well, not hide exactly: to get out of the way."

Janet smiled herself, feeling further relief. "Me, too," she admitted.

"You didn't come with anyone either?"

"No."

"Or know anyone?"

"I know the girl whose party it is, Harriet Andrew," conceded Janet. "She's a close friend."

He looked beyond her, unhurriedly and appearing really to look, not just shift his attention casually. "Quite a bunch of people," he said.

"Harriet gives these sorts of parties often: gets her name in the social columns even."

He didn't seemed impressed. "You come to them all?"

"Oh no!" said Janet at once. "I haven't been to one for a long time." The last occasion she had been with . . . she started to remember and then stopped, blocking off the reminiscence.

"I don't think I fit particularly well here," he said, coming back to her and smiling again.

"I don't think I do, either," she said.

"You caught me."

"Caught you?"

"I wasn't trying to steal your space." He grinned. "I was making a break for it."

Without being aware of it happening, Janet realized she had relaxed: the words were coming easily and the claustrophobic girdle wasn't tight around her any more. She said: "I guess I was doing the same thing."

"That was before I found someone to talk to, of course."

"Me, too," she said again. Janet assured herself that this wasn't flirtation or anything like the sort of conversational foreplay going on everywhere else: it was simply nice—relaxing like she had already decided—just to talk and come back to some sort of social normalcy she had for so long denied herself.

With noise battling noise all around there was a moment of silence between them. He said: "So as we're talking I could stay."

"I don't want to keep you," she said, immediately retreating into the pit where she felt at home.

"OK," he said at once, going backwards himself.

"I'll probably leave as well," she said.

"Why don't we leave together?" He shrugged a no-big-deal shrug.

"Why not?" she said, answering the shrug as well as the question.

"My name's John," he said. "John Sheridan."

"Janet," she responded. "Janet Stone."

·2·

Dumbarton was jammed, as it nearly always was, cars tight against each other: some were even pulled in off the road, between the trees and parked halfway into driveways, completely blocking the pavement. The thunderclaps of party noise came out above them through the open balcony windows.

Sheridan said: "Being a neighbor of Harriet Andrew could seriously damage your peace of mind."

"She's a very good person," said Janet, defensively.

"I'm sure," he said. "You friends from England?"

"You're very observant."

"The accent is pretty obvious," said Sheridan.

"Yes," said Janet, answering the question. "We read at Oxford together." She hesitated, feeling as uncomfortable as she had back at the house. "I came by cab: there's a rank on Wisconsin."

"My car's that way," he said, falling into step beside her.

They had to maneuver around several obstructing vehicles. Always he politely stood back, deferring for her to go first, and never once reached for her hand or her arm on the pretense of helping her, not even when they had to go over a cross street. Wisconsin Avenue was brightly lit compared to the side roads and very busy, cars and people ebbing and flowing in both directions and with shops and bars and cafes open on either side. Sheridan turned towards M Street and announced: "No cabs."

Jane looked towards the deserted rank and said: "They're along here all the time."

She started down towards the intersection and again he went with her. At the junction they looked both ways along M Street: there wasn't anywhere a taxi showing a for hire light.

"Not really your night," he said.

"It won't take long, really."

"Would you like a drink?"

Janet had been expecting such an approach from the moment he began walking with her and had the polite refusal already rehearsed, work she had to do at home, which wasn't actually a lie because Monday's lecture—the slide of the Lebanon into utter anarchy— was still only half written. She saw from the clock in the bank window behind him that it wasn't yet eight. She said: "Thank you," not knowing why she'd accepted.

"I don't know Georgetown particularly well," he said.

"There's Nathan's," she said, nodding across the road.

He stood away from her while they waited for the lights and made no move to cup her arm when they went over. As he held back for her to enter the bar Janet saw three cabs in convoy coming from the city, their flags lit. Nathan's was crowded, but as they entered two people got up from a table near the door, so they were seated immediately. She asked for scotch and he said he'd have the same. When he came back with the drinks he said: "Cheers." Janet said "Cheers" back, unsure what would happen next.

"Where's your husband?" he asked, abruptly.

"How . . . ?" she began and then stopped, following his look towards her hand. Janet steeled herself to utter the word. Gazing directly across the table she blurted: "Dead." She paused and then said: "He's dead." She'd confronted it before, of course: to herself at first, staring into mirrors in their empty apartment, needing to convince herself it was true and not a bad dream, saying: "Dead, dead, dead . . . Hank's dead," but this was the first time to a complete stranger. Something else that did not hurt as much as she'd expected.

Janet waited for an insincere "I'm sorry," but instead he said: "How long?"

This was going beyond anything for which Janet had prepared herself. Clip-voiced, gazing down into her untouched drink, she said: "Ten months . . . ten months and two weeks . . ." There was another pause. ". . . And four days. It was a Friday."

"How did he die?"

Janet swallowed, deeply, and said: "I don't think I want to talk about it."

"Why not?"

She shrugged, lost. She said: "I just don't."

"You should," he said.

Suddenly angry, Janet said: "Don't give me any of that 'you'll feel better if you talk about it' amateur psychology . . ." She leveled her hand beneath her chin. "I've had that sort of crap up to here!"

"I wasn't going to give you any sort of amateur psychology crap."

Deflated, Janet demanded: "What then?"

Now he shrugged. "It just seems odd that if you loved a guy that much you want to lock everything away. You might as well take the rings off and pretend it never happened."

"It's not like that at all!" she said, still angry.

"If you say so."

"What sort of remark is that!"

"A backing-off sort of remark," he said. "I was out of order and now I'm embarrassed. Would you like another drink?"

"No!" she said. Then, quickly, "No, thank you."

"You want me to say I'm sorry?"

"That's up to you."

"I'm sorry."

It sounded as if he meant it. She said: "What about you? Wife, I mean?"

"There isn't one."

"Why not?" Janet said, trying to hit back with the unsettling sort of directness that he had shown earlier.

The shoulders rose and fell once more. "Never the right person in the right place at the right time."

"For the moment I can't remember the movie that line came from," said Janet.

Sheridan lowered and raised his head in acknowledgment. He said: "It just never happened, I guess. You sure about that drink?"

On the street outside the For Hire lights bobbed and dipped like leaves in a stream. Janet said: "Just one more."

Janet watched as Sheridan made his way to the bar, properly

studying him for the first time, deciding he was a difficult person about whom to form an instant impression. He was inconspicuous in stature and in demeanour and in the way he dressed—abruptly she realized he was wearing a collar and a tie and a muted suit while everyone else at the party had been laid-back casual—but he appeared in no way nervous or uncertain. Rather, the reverse. People parted at the bar and he was served almost at once, despite louder shouted demands, and people parted again for him when he turned away. Janet stayed intent upon him as he returned, concentrating upon detail now. He was a lean man, the skin almost taut over high cheekbones and a sharp, aquiline nose and there was some hint of discoloration to his face, as if he had spent a lot of time in the sun. She could not discern any beardline and wondered if he'd shaved a second time before going to the party. There was a slight sag of puffiness beneath his eyes, which had no positive color but seemed to her like a tweed, a mixture of browns and greens, and his brown hair was just lightening into gray at the sides and oddly at just one temple, the left. On the small finger of his left hand—the hand with which he proffered her drink—he wore a ruby-stoned ring and because his arm was extended she could see a thick, heavily calibrated Rolex watch. He repeated: "Cheers," and she raised her glass back to him in response.

"You were leading the inquisition," he said.

Janet was glad of the lightness. "So?" she asked.

"I work for the government."

"Saying that in Washington is like declaring you're a coalminer in Pennsylvania or brew beer in Milwaukee," said Janet. She allowed the pause. "Or maybe hinting at something sinister."

Sheridan smiled, unevenly because he did not appear to have bothered with any dental correction, and said: "Nothing spooky about me . . ." He gestured vaguely over his shoulder, towards the city, and said: "State Department. You know Foggy Bottom?"

Janet nodded, thinking how close the State Department headquarters were to a Georgetown he'd earlier said he didn't know very well. Whether or not he visited Georgetown was hardly any business of hers, she thought. "Must be interesting," she said, wishing as she spoke she had managed to avoid the cliche.

He shook his head. "Not at my lowly level," he said. "General analysis. Long reports that take weeks to prepare and weeks to print for nobody to read."

"Why bother in the first place?"

"Paperwork is the lifeblood of bureaucracy," said Sheridan, self-mocking. "I'm just one of the billions of bureaucrats who write billions of unread reports that need huge forests of trees cut down to make the paper to print them on. It's people like me who make cities possible in the cleared spaces."

"Thank you," laughed Janet, trying to respond. She decided, guiltily, that she was enjoying herself and because of that guilt made an immediate qualification. Not actually enjoying herself: relaxing, she thought again. More than she had for a very long time. There was nothing wrong in that: nothing disrespectful to Hank's memory. Just coming out of seclusion.

"Your turn," Sheridan said. And then at once, conscious of her slight stiffening, he said: "No! Forget it. Let's just drink our drinks . . . damned sight safer than that punch back there. By now they'll be swinging from the chandeliers."

She said, "You're very considerate."

"And you're very vulnerable."

"Does it show that much?"

"Is the Grand Canyon a ditch?"

"It was just . . ." she set out, stopping almost at once because the words weren't there. ". . . So complete," she started again. "I didn't want . . . didn't need anybody else. Neither did he. Which is what makes it worse because now he isn't here any more there's nothing. Just emptiness, like a hole I can't climb out of . . ." *Exactly* that, she thought: she had buried herself.

"Don't," said Sheridan, gently. "Leave it."

"Let me."

"You sure?"

Janet nodded, jerkily, eyes down on her drink again. She started to tell him, stumbling again at the beginning until the surroundings receded, going right back to Oxford where they'd met, she reading Modern History and Hank—whom she called Henry now, as she had in those early days—was studying law. Strangely there was no embarrassment telling this calm, unmoving stranger how Hank had moved in with her after four months and how she'd followed him back to America after they'd both graduated. She talked of the luck they'd had in his getting a position with the downtown law firm on 13th Street and of her own matching good fortune in getting a place—low in the pecking order at first—in the Middle East division at Georgetown University where she was now a senior lecturer in Middle Eastern Studies.

"There was no warning," she said, bitterly. "Nothing. And he'd always been so fit. He'd always worked out in England and he jogged when we came back here and we played tennis most weekends in the summer. It was just tiredness at first and we didn't think anything of it because he was working so hard, trying to prove himself in a new job. But it got worse and then he started to lose a lot of weight . . ." Janet gulped at her drink, needing a break in the narrative. "Did you know there isn't any pain, with cancer of the liver?"

Sheridan shook his head.

"That was another obscenity, along with so much else," she said. "He just faded away. Literally. Every day he seemed to get smaller, like he was collapsing inside. Which he was, I guess. We tried everything, of course: went to all the experts about a transplant which they said wasn't possible because it had been discovered too late to prevent the spread. I said I still wanted it done and they said he was too weak by then: that he could not withstand the shock of surgery . . ." She drank again. "So we just waited. That was the worst part, the thing I couldn't take. The helplessness. Just having to wait and accept there was nothing I could do . . . nothing that anyone could do. My mother came across towards the end and we just sat around and watched . . . that was all we could do. Can you imagine what that was like . . ."

"No," said the man. "I don't think I can."

"Do you want to hear something ridiculous?" Janet stretched out both hands, palms upwards, and said: "When he was so wasted away that I could pick him up like this, like a baby, I decided it wasn't going to happen. I convinced myself that it was going to go away, as quickly as it had come, and that he was going to get better again and we were going to go on just like we were before. Have the baby we'd talked about and that he would start his own law firm, which was another plan: make a lot of money so we could move to Chevy Chase . . ." Janet laughed, bitterly. "Can you imagine that! On the day he died, the Friday, I couldn't cry because I was too angry: I told my mother there'd been a mistake . . ." She gave another humorless, head-shaking laugh, unable to believe it herself.

"But you didn't go back to England?"

Janet looked up at the man, caught by how quick he was, how direct. She nodded and said: "My family wanted me to. Wanted me to get a job at a university or an institute there; put America behind me. I almost went but then I thought about it and somehow it seemed like giving up. Does that sound funny?"

"Maybe," Sheridan said. "Maybe not."

"Anyway!" she said, with forced briskness. "I didn't go and here I am. And that's it, the story of Janet Stone."

They looked at each other for several moments and then Sheridan said: "I can't think of anything to say that wouldn't sound trite."

"Thanks for not trying," said Janet. She was abruptly astonished at herself. She hadn't talked to anyone like this, not to Harriet and not even, she didn't think, to her mother. Was it *because* he was a stranger, someone completely uninvolved and unaffected? She felt embarrassed. But not, she realized in further surprise, anything else. No ache at the memories, no pain. The feeling of embarrassment worsened.

"Do you want another drink?" asked Sheridan.

"No, thank you," she said at once. Was that why she'd talked so much, because of the whisky? Of course not. She said: "You go ahead, if you want one."

"No," he said. "I'm fine." He looked around them and then out into the street. "Have you eaten? Georgetown seems to have cornered the market in restaurants."

"No, thank you." She'd done enough, said enough. This was an early outing, after all.

"OK." He smiled his crooked smile at her, open-faced, and said: "I guess it's time to go then?"

"I guess so," she said.

Outside the street was again completely devoid of taxis.

"Isn't it always the way?" He shrugged.

"Like I said, it won't take long to pick one up."

"My car really is close," said Sheridan. "Practically at the junction of Dumbarton and Wisconsin."

Janet looked unsuccessfully in every direction and then said: "That would be kind."

It was a Volkswagen, a Beetle, an inconspicuous gray car matching the inconspicuous man. Although it was dark there was sufficient light from the Wisconsin Avenue illumination for Janet to see the interior was immaculate and very clean.

"Where to?" he said.

"Rosslyn."

Janet began worrying as they drove over Key Bridge, trying to push the concern away by the reassurance of the evening so far. There had not been any furtive hand-on-the-knee, my-place-or-yours nonsense. He'd actually held back, at every opportunity. So it would be overreacting to become frightened now. Janet recognized, in a further revelation of the evening, she was in a situation she didn't know how to handle: had forgotten how to handle. For as long as she seemed able to remember Hank had always been with her, always there, controlling everything and keeping her safe. But Hank wasn't here any more. And she was being driven back to an obviously empty apartment by a man she knew only by name—if that was his real name—and a vague reference to the State Department. The apprehension began to burn through her and she felt the perspiration wet on her face and wetter still on her back. She shifted in her seat, edging closer to the passenger door.

"What's the matter?" Sheridan asked, conscious of her movement.

"Nothing." Janet felt stupid, childlike.

"You'll have to guide me," he said, as they crossed the parkway into Rosslyn.

She directed him to the apartments at Radnor Heights. Her uncertainty increased when he opened his door as he turned off the engine, walking around the front of the Volkswagen to let her out. Momentarily Janet hesitated and then swung herself from the vehicle. Her apartment was in the first of a matching block of three, each with its wide, open-planned vestibule before the elevator bank screened first by the doorman and then by a security clerk-cum-telephonist behind the mail counter. Janet walked with her hands tight beside her, knowing what she was expected to say but unsure whether she could bring herself to say it.

She stopped just before the main entrance, turning to face him, making him stop too. Sheridan kept a distance between them.

"Would you like to come in for a drink?" she said, with great effort.

"No thank you," he said at once.

Janet just stopped herself from blurting out her surprise. Instead she said: "I enjoyed the evening: the last part, anyway. Thanks for saving me from the party."

"I enjoyed it as well: I think we saved each other."

"Good night then," she said, hoping he would not try to kiss her.

"Good night," he said, making no move. "I'll stay here until you're safely inside."

Which he did. Janet looked back as she entered the elevator and he was still there, and when she entered her fifth-floor apartment, at the front of the building, she went immediately to the window and

stared down. There was no sign of the unobtrusive man or his unobtrusive car, neither in the parking lot nor in either direction on the
passing road: John Sheridan seemed able to disappear as easily as he
materialized.

He had not asked for her telephone number, Janet realized. Or if
he could see her again. She did not know what she would have said
if he'd suggested either.

·3·

It was an established ritual—one of the few outings she allowed herself—for them to have Sunday brunch at the American Cafe on the Hill, but Janet half expected Harriet to call off, pleading the previous night's party but she didn't. She was late, though, as usual. She flustered in fast enough to create a breeze in her wake, not pausing to be shown her seat because she was confident Janet would have gotten their customary table, close to the wall at the back. Harriet was wearing button-fly 501 jeans and loafers and a poncho, and her hair was still bubbled as it had been the previous night. Her face was scrubbed completely clean of makeup. Harrriet was talking before she actually sat down, a breathless litany of who'd screwed whom and who hadn't screwed whom and who'd been caught and who'd got away with it. She complained that someone called Jake or Geoff, she wasn't sure which, had been a disaster and couldn't get it up and tried to blame the booze but said she didn't think it was booze at all but that he'd been a momentarily reluctant gay trying to pretend that he wasn't.

"Can you imagine it, an experiment to prove his fucking manhood! Literally! At my own party!"

"I think you're silly, taking the risks you do."

They both ordered eggs Benedict and Bloody Marys and Harriet said: "I don't."

"Too many," insisted Janet. "You don't even know his name, for Christ's sake! What if he *is* gay? Or bisexual?"

"Believe me, darling," said Harriet. "The only thing I risked catching last night was a cold, hanging around waiting for something to happen that never did."

"I still think you're mad."

"You should see the house! It looks like the Red Army went through in a hurry, without saying excuse me."

"Would you like me to come back to help this afternoon?" asked Janet. The lecture was still only half-written, she remembered.

"Forget it," Harriet said. "Mrs. Barrett comes in tomorrow: I'll slip her an extra ten dollars."

Harriet worked as a senior administrative assistant for a Virginia senator who thought an Englishwoman on his staff conveyed the impression of European culture and indicated an awareness of international affairs. Janet wondered if her friend's brittleness were necessary for the job. Politely she said: "I thought it was a great party."

They held back for the drinks to be replaced and Harriet said: "You ducked it, without saying goodbye!"

"I didn't think you'd miss me. And I didn't duck it. I was there for over an hour."

"Well?"

"Well what?"

"What happened, that's well what?"

Janet was conscious of blushing, positively red-faced. She hadn't thought Harriet had seen her leave. "We had a drink, that's all."

Harriet reached across the table, covering Janet's hand with hers. "Darling!" she said. "This isn't headmistress's question time. I think it's wonderful you found a guy and had a drink. It's about time. There's no reason to get embarrassed."

Janet smiled and said: "I just don't find it easy."

"You're going to have to learn, my love. Life goes on. But yours hasn't, for far too long. You're so vulnerable—so innocent—it almost hurts. You're like a virgin in a whorehouse: I worry about you crossing roads!"

How recently would remarks like that have irritated her, wondered Janet, unperturbed. She said: "How well do you know him?"

"Not at all. He mean anything to you?"

"Of course not!" said Janet.

"OK, so I can be honest. I thought he was a boring asshole. He spent all night propping up the wall with one drink in his hand, talking to no one."

Like me, thought Janet: did Harriet Andrew secretly think she was a boring asshole, too? Janet said: "His name's John Sheridan."

"That much I know."

"And he's not really boring," Janet added, defensively.

"Sorry!" said Harriet, archly, stretching the word like elastic. "Why did you invite him, if you don't like him?"

"A research assistant on the senator's staff knows him: they belong to some racquet club or something," said Harriet, staring into her glass as if she were surprised to find its contents gone. "I wanted to make the numbers match and told this guy to bring another man. His choice was Sheridan: a mistake that won't be repeated." She smiled. "Celibate women like us need alternatives: I'm going to have another. How about you?"

Janet shook her head. "I'll pass. He said he worked in State."

Harriet was screwed around in her seat, trying to catch the waitress's eye. "Something like that," she said, succeeding in her attempt and turning back to the table. "And don't ask because I don't know if he's married or not."

"He said he's not," Janet remembered. "But it doesn't matter whether he is or he isn't, does it?"

"That's what they all say, darling," Harriet said cynically. "But no, if it doesn't matter it doesn't matter. Cheers."

Janet consciously let the conversation move away from John Sheridan. Harriet was organizing part of the senator's staff to visit NATO headquarters in Brussels, and she gabbled on about the clothes she was having to buy and of the hoped-for sideways trip to Paris and said wouldn't it be terrific if they could meet up in London when Janet made her twice-yearly visit to her parents and Janet agreed it would but warned she had not made any definite travel plans at the moment. She joined Harriet with another Bloody Mary and offered again to help clean up the Dumbarton Street house and Harriet waved away the suggestion as she had before.

It was almost three o'clock before they got up to leave, Harriet snatching up the bill and refusing any contribution from Janet. Outside they walked without any intentional direction towards the Capitol Building.

"What are you going to do for the rest of the day?" asked Harriet.

"I've got a lecture to finish off for tomorrow."

"Much?"

"An hour or two, maybe."

"You can always make up a couple of hours," urged Harriet. "Why don't we take in a movie? Maybe a drink afterwards? You can work later."

Janet shook her head. "You know how it is."

Her friend sighed in reply. "The dedicated Janet Stone, pillar of Washington academia!"

"I like always being on top of things," said Janet, defensive again. "You know that."

"You sure you get sufficient recognition for all you do at that damned university?"

"Yes," said Janet. "And it isn't a damned university. It's got very high standards." She'd worked as determinedly when Hank was alive—anxious then for the promotion and extra money that was so important for their plans—and now she needed the time-consuming, after-hours preparation work and the difficulty with students and being imposed upon for opinions by other Middle East lecturers to block out the sterility of the other parts of her life.

The Capitol dome was very clear now, starkly white and almost artificial in its perfection, more like a decoration than the seat of the most powerful legislature in the world.

"With your ability and qualifications you could get a hell of a job there," Harriet said, gesturing towards the administration building. "Ever thought about it?"

"No," said Janet.

"Why don't you? You'd probably double your salary."

"I'm happy enough where I am," said Janet. And safe, she thought. No longer being safe—no longer having someone she could completely rely on to protect and take care of her—had been one of Janet's worst and most persistent fears after Hank's death. And secretly—so secretly that she'd admitted it to no one—it still was. She kept the Rosslyn apartment despite its painful memories because she felt safe and cocooned in it and it was the need for such a feeling that had been her major reason for resisting her parents' demands that she return to England. She wanted always now to be with things and in places that were familiar. Safe: like hideaway holes.

Harriet smiled sideways. "You want me to ask around?"

"Ask about what?"

"John Sheridan, who props up walls and nurses one drink."

"Don't be ridiculous!" Janet said as forcefully as she could. "I had a drink with a shy man, a lonely man . . . lonely like me. OK? No drama. No nothing. Just that."

"What happened after the drink?"

"Less than happened with your starch-free gay."

"He didn't make a pass?"

"No."

"Ask for your number?"

"No."

"Ask if he could see you again?"

"No."

Harriet sighed, heavily. "Isn't life sometimes a bucket of shit?"

"Yes," Janet agreed. "More often than not life is a bucket of shit."

They stopped by the side of the enormous building, able from the top of the hill to gaze out over Washington and its orderly patterns of grassed malls and reflecting pools and museums and monolithic monuments to past presidents.

"I really could get you fixed up with a terrific job," Harriet said.

"I'll stay where I am." For how long? Janet wondered. Forever? Why not? There was nothing else for her to do.

"You sure about that movie?"

"Positive."

"Call me during the week?"

"You know I will."

It took Janet little over an hour to complete the Lebanese lecture, and she was pleased with the way it went the following day. A teaching assistant named Barnett who'd come close to making a pass several times asked her to go over his master's thesis, which she agreed to do although she knew it was a ploy giving them time together. The thesis was weak and badly argued—he actually predicted the Israelis might agree to surrender the occupied bank and the Gaza Strip, which Janet dismissed as ridiculously naive—and she told him so, hoping the rejection would go beyond the academic paper.

That week a letter arrived from her parents, who lived in Sussex, asking when she intended to visit. They planned to take a long tour through Egypt and the Sudan and Saudi Arabia, in each of which her father had served, and they did not want the dates to clash. She replied that she wasn't sure yet so why didn't they make their arrangements and she would fit in, whenever.

She had dinner with Harriet one night and brunch with her as usual the following Sunday, and the week after that went with

Harriet to Garfinkels and to the Georgetown Mall, setting up for Harriet's trip to Europe. Prompted by the shopping expedition, she thought about buying a winter coat in the sales but decided against it, because it was too soon in the year and she'd be gettting the previous autumn's style anyway. Her cat, George, developed a dry cough and she had to take it to the vet, who said it was easily treated this time but warned her that it was six years old. Sundays were lonely, like all the other days in the week, with Harriet away. She got cards from Bonn ("dullsville") and Berlin ("super").

Janet was marking papers in the Rosslyn apartment on a Wednesday evening when the telephone rang and momentarily she frowned at it, curiously, because she got so few calls.

"I don't know if you remember me," the voice said. "It's John Sheridan."

"I remember," Janet said.

· 4 ·

Janet's collapse into complete and abject despondency had come the day after the funeral, when she'd finally accepted Hank's death. She'd refused to get out of bed or to bathe—wash, even—or to eat. Most of all she had refused to eat, and when her mother warned that unless she did she would cause herself harm the idea of committing suicide settled in Janet's mind. For several days she lay curled beneath the covers, with her knees up under her chin, very calmly planning how to do it. She'd bought a lot of painkillers when Hank's cancer had first been diagnosed, scouring magazines for every brand name and every formula to find the maximum strength she thought would be necessary, not realizing there would be no pain and stupidly imagining she might find something better than the doctors would prescribe if there were. And they were all still in the bathroom cabinet. She'd been very confident about how easy it would be. She planned to respond to her mother's urging to take a bath, actually letting it run while she started swallowing the pills, slowly and carefully because she did not want to vomit and spoil everything. When the bath was ready she was going to get in with the bottles where she just had to reach out to go on, willing herself to fight against the initial sensation of unconsciousness and to continue swallowing to ensure she took enough to die and not just lapse into a drugged sleep from which she could be resuscitated if they got to her in time.

Her mother had smiled gratefully and helped her from her disheveled bed and Janet had forced herself not to think of the anguish she was going to cause the woman, sure her own anguish was greater. She said she felt a lot better and was going to take a long soak, to avoid her mother becoming alarmed and forcing her way in before the pills had time to work. Immediately inside the bathroom Janet had pressed back against the locked door, not frightened at all, her feeling rather one of impatience to get started, in a hurry to die. From outside her mother asked if she was all right and Janet called back that she was, turning the taps on in further reassurance.

And then she'd opened the bathroom cabinet to find every pill bottle gone. The frustration had whimpered through her as she scrabbled through what remained, thinking they might be hidden by something else, and then whimpered again at the awareness that her mother had cleared them out. Her mother called again and Janet made a sound back, slumping on the bath edge, emptied so completely she was unable even to think.

The bathroom was small and mirrored, to make it seem bigger, and when Janet had finally looked up, to turn off the water before it overflowed the bath edge, her instant and absurd reaction had been to wonder whose reflection she was seeing. The shock at realizing it was herself actually made her gasp.

Janet had always been fastidious, even at boarding school, before going up to Oxford: the girl whose dormitory place was never disarranged and whose drawers were always allocated, item for item, and whose shoes were always clean and whose hair was always neatly held and clipped and whose uniform was never stained or torn or borrowed or lost. She was—or had been until that moment—physically uncomfortable with untidiness and dirt and neglect.

Her first thought was that Hank would have been disgusted with her, because he had been as meticulous as she was: that she was letting him down. Her hair—which was naturally red and which she'd hated at boarding school, because it was so different from the other girls', and which she'd only really come to like after Hank had told her it was beautiful—was matted and tangled, straggled around her face. Which looked appalling. She was gaunt from not eating and not sleeping, the sallow skin strained over her high cheekbones and her green but now blank eyes deeply sunk into blackened surrounds. It was already the face of a dead person. And then she thought again that she was letting Hank down and determined abruptly, at that moment, not to give up: not to die.

Inherent though it already was, taking care of herself became privately something she did for Hank, for his memory, like other private and secret things: like sometimes, when she was sure she was quite alone, talking aloud as if he could hear her, imagining what he would say back.

She did it now, when she was almost ready. "You don't mind, do you?" she said, staring at her own reflection in the full length mirror, knowing what the answer would be. He hadn't known how to be jealous, not from the moment they'd first met, and not because he didn't care but because he trusted her, completely. "Only going out for the evening," she said. "That's all: just dinner. You know that, don't you? Of course you do."

The fuller, looser shirt with the jacket on top was better, Janet concluded: she'd matched a sweater with the checked skirt first but when she'd examined herself, half turning sideways, she thought it looked as if she was trying to make her breasts obvious and she didn't want to do that. She considered wearing her hair loose, the way Hank had liked it best, but quickly corrected that, too, pulling it back away from her face and twisting it into a chignon. The style meant she had to wear earrings. She chose gold studs to accompany the single gold chain but no other jewelry. She wore her engagement and wedding rings, of course.

Promptly at six, the time they'd agreed, the security clerk buzzed to say Sheridan was in the foyer and Janet said she would be down at once. She'd considered inviting him up for a drink, remaining unsure even while she was dressing, before dismissing the idea as a mistake, like wearing the sweater.

Sheridan asked if there was any place she would like to go and Janet said no, she'd leave it up to him, expecting he'd choose somewhere in town. Instead he drove out into Virginia to a beamed and rough-stone inn proudly proclaiming its one hundred and twenty year history. There was a log fire in the open hearth and they ate oysters and fresh trout and drank a French-bottled Sancerre. Janet found it as easy to talk to him as she had the night of their escape from the party. When he said he had worked for a while out of the American embassy in Cairo she asked if he'd known her father, who had been Third Secretary at the British legation there, but the postings had not been contemporary. Because it was her subject and from the talk of Egypt she thought he might have an interest she asked him what he thought about the Lebanon and he said it seemed a completely lost and collapsed country. About Iran, Sheridan said he didn't have any positive idea, either, but he thought another sort of revolution was possible after the death of the Ayatollah Khomeini. She asked how it had been possible for America to have been so wrong-footed about the overthrow of the Shah and then so helpless after the seizure of the U.S. embassy hostages in Teheran and he said he didn't know but agreed with her that it had been incredibly inept.

On the way back towards Washington Sheridan said he'd enjoyed the evening and Janet agreed that she had too, considering and once more dismissing the idea of inviting him in for a drink. When he stopped the car outside the apartment he asked if he could call her again and she said of course and he let her out as he had before but made no attempt to kiss her. When she looked down from her apartment window, he'd vanished again.

Sheridan called the same week to invite her to a performance of *The Taming of the Shrew* that the touring English Shakespearean Company was giving at the Kennedy Center. That evening she did suggest his coming in when they got back to Rosslyn. Sheridan drank coffee and brandy and looked at her bookshelves and said Paul Scott and Graham Greene were two of his favorite English authors, too. He enquired if she liked Updike and Janet said not much and asked him if he'd ever read anything by le Carré or Deighton. Sheridan replied that he didn't enjoy espionage fiction. Again he left without trying to kiss her.

Janet confessed the outings to Harriet at that Sunday's brunch and Harriet said why the hell not, and when they met later in the week Harriet admitted quizzing her friend on the senator's staff who'd originally invited Sheridan to the party. The man knew nothing at all about Sheridan except that he was a higher than average squash player, generous without being stupid in the clubhouse afterwards, never made passes at other guys' wives or girlfriends and never talked about himself. Janet remarked, unthinkingly, that Sheridan hadn't made a pass at her either and Harriet suggested that maybe he was gay, to which Janet replied that was more Harriet's problem than hers because she wasn't interested anyway. Harriet said: "Oh yeah!"

Janet felt a jump of excitement in immediately recognizing Sheridan's voice on the next call, which she answered hoping it would be him. That time they went to the National Theater, downtown. Afterwards they had drinks at the restored Willard where he recounted the names of the presidents who'd used it in the past and how the word "lobbying" had originated there to describe the favor-seekers waylaying President Grant, and later still they ate in Chinatown, Janet deferring to Sheridan's obvious knowledge of a Sichuan menu. He seemed to expect to come up to the apartment that night and the conversation was almost stilted. There developed an odd difficulty— an unspoken anticipation—between them and Janet became apprehensive. Which she needn't have been. When he got up to go after finishing the brandy he merely leaned forward and kissed her cheek, which she offered, and this time she watched from the window as he drove off in the Volkswagen.

Confidently alone in the apartment, she said: "Don't think badly, darling. It's just that I feel so very alone."

Once-a-week meetings became twice a week, and when the weather got better he took her to the yacht basin on the Alexandria side of the Potomac and they went sailing in his boat, which was not white fiberglass and gleaming chrome like most of the others, but fat-bellied and clinker-built, in wood. Sheridan sailed as he appeared to do everything else, with quiet, undemonstrative competence. That first time Janet was uncertain, because sailing had never been something she did, but with Sheridan she immediately felt safe. They started sailing every weekend, he the patient instructor, Janet the eager student. She was apprehensive again when he suggested going away for an entire weekend, casting off on Saturday and tying up overnight somewhere on the Chesapeake Bay: he kissed her differently now but had not suggested—or attempted to do—anything more and Janet was unsure how she would feel if he did. Yet again her fears were unfounded. There was only one cabin, the bunks on either side and when she went below she saw there were single sleeping bags laid out on each. That night, without any discussion, he let her go in first to undress and get into bed before he followed.

The season was right, and so one Sunday Sheridan took her to a crab feast in a weathered, unprepossessing wooden restaurant, where the waitress tore brown paper from a roll to form a tablecloth and Sheridan warned her they were expected to eat with their fingers. They drank beer from a pitcher and Sheridan taught her how to dismember the small crabs. Her fingers and face became sticky from the flavoring salt and Janet realized, surprised, that she was thinking of nothing beyond what she was doing and the person with whom she was doing it. She couldn't remember being so happy for a very long time.

Afterwards, after the disaster, when she reflected upon everything that had happened between them, Janet calculated that to be the precise moment she had fallen in love with John Sheridan, although of course that was not her awareness then.

It was a month after the crab feast that they made love. It was a Friday night and they had been out to the Virginia restaurant to which he had taken her on their first date. Afterwards he'd come up to the apartment for brandy, which had become the custom. He had one drink, which was all he ever allowed himself and then he said: "I suppose I should be going?" posing it as a question, which he never had before.

"I suppose you should," Janet said, making it sound like a question too, not knowing whether she had intended it that way or not.

Sheridan remained sitting across from her, gazing at her, and Janet held his eyes, unmoving as well. Sheridan said: "I don't want to."

"No," said Janet, as if she were agreeing to something they had already discussed. She waited for the nervousness that she expected but nothing came.

She tried not to be so stiff and awkward, embarrassed at herself, but he was gentle and kind, coaxing her to relax. And eventually she did relax although not, on that first occasion, as much as she was able to later. Sheridan was as competent as a lover as he appeared to be about everything else, despite her tenseness bringing her to a climax as he climaxed himself and then slowly leading her down from the peak of her excitement. They lay entwined for a long time afterwards, unspeaking, Sheridan soothing his hand along her face.

Eventually he said: "I don't want this to spoil how it was before with us."

"It won't."

"You sure?"

Janet wasn't, not then. "I don't think so."

"Sorry?"

"I don't know," she answered honestly. "Not yet."

Janet soon became sure.

There were nights when they did not see each other, but increasingly few. It was several weeks after that first occasion before they slept at his apartment, a conversion in an old building off Columbus

Circle. Janet went curiously, unsure what to expect, immediately conscious of his extreme neatness. One wall of the main room and three of a spare room were lined with books, a lot in French and Italian, languages which she had not known until then that he could speak. There were some ornaments which she recognized to be Egyptian, and a lot of other foreign souvenirs. Sheridan identified some as Aztec, from a posting to Mexico, and there were some Inca figures from a period he'd spent in Peru and which he said obviously weren't originals but copies about two hundred years old. Janet was intrigued by a crossbow and a heavily decorated knife which did not seem to fit. Sheridan told her they were Montagnard, and she learned for the first time that he had been attached to the American embassy in Saigon, "but before it really became the mess that it ended."

It was on that initial visit to Columbus Circle that Janet discovered he could cook. Sheridan prepared Chinese food better than she had tasted in any Washington restaurant, even the Beijing-government supported one in midtown, and Janet said: "Don't tell me you've worked in China as well!"

Sheridan laughed and said: "No. And I don't intend to. My days of overseas postings are over. I'm strictly a headquarters guy now."

Janet told Harriet, of course, and was apprehensive of the first meal the three of them had together, but Sheridan made a particular effort, obviously charming Harriet, maintaining a stream of anecdotes some of which were amusing and others hilarious. That Sunday, when they brunched together, Harriet said: "Darling, I'm abject! I take back everything I ever said. He's wonderful. When you get fed up with him, give him my number."

"I'm not going to get fed up with him," replied Janet.

Her parents' letters to her outnumbered Janet's to them. There were repeated assurances of how pleased they were and how much they wanted to meet "him" and demands to know all about him, which Janet tried to satisfy, but her answers always seemed to prompt fresh questions.

The Virginia inn became their favorite, their special place, and it was there, just over a year after their first meal, that Sheridan said: "I've got something to ask you."

"What?"

"Will you marry me?"

Janet sat unmoving, unthinking, aware only of a bizarre sensation of hollowness, and Sheridan misunderstood her silence. He blurted "I'm sorry . . . I shouldn't have asked . . ." but she spoke at last, cutting him off.

"Oh yes, darling," she said. "Yes please."

The following evening was one of the nights they did not spend together and abruptly, without consciously imagining Hank, Janet embarked on one of her lonely conversations with her dead husband, something she had not done for a long time.

"Don't hate me, darling," she said. "I'll always love you, of course. But I so much need someone to care. To love: to be safe with."

·5·

It was inevitable, of course, that Janet should compare the preparations for her wedding to John Sheridan with those for her wedding to Hank, and she was secretly uncomfortable that this time there seemed to be more excitement and anticipation. Her memories of the first relationship and the first marriage were that everything had happened gradually, almost without planning or arrangement. Her recollection was that they paired up at university without any positive decision to go together, and that it had then seemed natural but not overly dramatic to move in with Hank in Oxford and natural again when he suggested she come over to America to visit his now-dead parents, by which time the eventual marriage was an obvious and unavoidable culmination of everything. Everyone—their friends and their families—would have been shocked if it hadn't happened, as they themselves would have been. Janet could not actually recall Hank *asking* her to be his wife. Without her being able to pinpoint the moment, their conversation had suddenly become about what they would do and how they would do it and where they would do it *when* they were married, almost as if the actual nuptial had been decided upon by other people who knew best, and all they had to do was comply.

This time was quite different.

Harriet was the first person she told—ahead of her parents—and Harriet whooped her instant agreement to be Janet's maid of honor and immediately bustled in to take over the arrangements. Together they bought every fashion book and wedding magazine they could find, to choose the absolutely right gown for Janet and the absolutely right gown for Harriet. Still undecided about either, they extended their reading to house publications after Sheridan said he wanted to sell both their apartments and buy a house whose location and furnishing and fittings were to be entirely her choice. The day after Sheridan told her that, Janet put her name on the mailing list of every agent in Washington and the immediate suburbs. Sheridan had laid the boat up for the winter, so every weekend they scurried around Maryland and Virginia in the Volkswagen, assessing distances and convenience and prices.

Her parents foreshortened their trip to the Middle East and flew directly from Cairo to Washington to meet Sheridan. Janet was more nervous of that encounter than she had been about the meeting with Harriet, but once again, as they always seemed to be, her fears were unfounded. Sheridan's effort was not so obvious to Janet as it had been with Harriet, but the impression upon her parents was the same, if not better.

Janet's mother was clearly surprised and delighted that until their marriage they were maintaining separate homes, a reaction which Janet found curious, since her openly living with Hank had brought no criticism. The fact meant, of course, that her parents could stay with her, and on the night of their arrival she introduced Sheridan simply over early evening drinks, to enable the elderly couple to recover from their jet lag. The following night Sheridan took them out to the Virginia inn. When they went to the restroom, Janet's mother said she thought he was an extremely pleasant man—which for Janet's mother was a high accolade—and much later, after Sheridan left the Rosslyn apartment after his usual solitary brandy, her mother said she was very happy that Janet was getting together with such a nice man, and her father admitted to being impressed with Sheridan in every way. He added that Sheridan appeared extremely knowledgeable about a wide spectrum of international affairs, including the Middle East. From his career her father regarded himself as something of a Middle East specialist. Janet remarked that it was hardly surprising, considering that Sheridan was a State Department analyst, and her father said he'd met dozens of State Depart-

ment personnel, including supposed analysts, whose grasp was very
weak. He'd tried hard to find people who knew Sheridan at various
embassy postings but there hadn't been a single one, which the old
man regretted. He told his daughter he intended asking around at
the next reunion.

"They like you," Janet reported to Sheridan, when they were by
themselves.

"I like them," Sheridan said.

"Mother's campaigning for the wedding to be in England."

"Why not?"

"What about your friends? Won't it be difficult for them?"

Sheridan shrugged. "There are none close enough to worry
about. And there's no family to ferry across."

"You're sure?"

"Tell her it's fine."

"I love you," said Janet.

"I love you," he said.

Her parents' visit lasted a week, and by the end Janet believed
Sheridan and her father to be firm friends. Before they left they'd
agreed on having the ceremony in England in March, which gave
Janet and Sheridan five months to decide upon a house, dispose of
their own apartments, and make the purchase.

Throughout Janet remained working at Georgetown University
from which she called him most days because it was difficult for him
to get her when she was in class. It was often a problem for her to
reach him at the State Department, too: there was usually a connection delay. When she mentioned it to him, Sheridan agreed it was a
nuisance but explained he spent more time in committee meetings,
verbally analyzing situations and events, than at his desk, working
on papers and reports.

"Their concentration span is limited," he said, mockingly.
"They'd rather hear opinions than be forced to read an assessment. I
think it's all the fault of television: a hundred years from now no one
will be able to read."

At Christmas, during the university break, Sheridan had time
owing for a holiday. When Janet suggested it, he said he thought it
would be terrific to spend the time in England with her parents.
Janet wrote suggesting it and her mother was so excited that she
telephoned.

"I never thought I could be like this again," Janet said, to Harriet.
"Not this happy."

They were having an early dinner in Chinatown, so it was still only ten o'clock when Janet got back to Rosslyn.

Sheridan, who had had a key to her apartment for several months, was waiting as she entered, sitting forward on a couch, grave-faced.

Janet was stopped by his expression, remaining just inside the door. "Darling!" she said. "What is it?"

"I've been posted," said Sheridan. "Overseas."

"But . . ." started Janet, confused. "Where overseas?" she managed.

"Beirut," he announced, simply.

Janet stayed where she was, her mind and body frozen into incomprehension. The images and the thoughts flustered through her head, all half-formed and refusing to become whole. Not Beirut! That was inconceivable! There'd been U.S. embassy bombings by suicide squads and the kidnapping of U.S. embassy staff and Reagan's Irangate fiasco, and the apparently insoluble conflict between Christian and Moslem formed part of practically every lecture that she gave at the university. John Sheridan—*her* John Sheridan— couldn't go there; couldn't become involved in a situation like that! It was murderous, for God's sake! People *had* been murdered! Janet shook her head, disbelieving despite having heard him say it. She said: "No . . . no it's got to be a mistake."

Sheridan stood and came to her, holding her to him. Without knowing why, Janet was rigid, almost resisting. Sheridan said: "I don't want to go . . . you know that. Who would? I've tried to get out of it but I can't."

Janet pulled back from his embrace. "But you told me . . . a long time ago . . . that you weren't going to travel any more . . . that you were always going to be here, in Washington . . ."

"I know," he agreed. "I thought I was. They think I might be some use there."

"NO!" she wailed, finally confronting what he was saying.

Sheridan led her into the room and sat her where he had been sitting, kneeling at her feet. "Shush now," he said. "Now listen. There's no way I can get out of it: like I said, I've tried. No way. But it won't be for a long time. Six months; a year at most . . ."

Janet sat shaking her head, consciously—determinedly—refusing to absorb the words.

"It's an unaccompanied posting, obviously. I couldn't take you with me, even if we rushed the marriage through," Sheridan pushed on. "But we won't be apart all the time. We can spend our vacations together. Cyprus. Anywhere you like in the Mediterranean."

"But we've made plans," she said, in weak protest.

"It'll only mean delaying things a few months," assured Sheridan. "I promise. As soon as I'm reassigned—and don't worry, the time limit is a firm commitment—we'll get married. That's all it means, really. Putting the wedding back a month or two."

"That's not all it means!" Janet argued, recovering further. "You're going to Beirut, for Christ's sake! Beirut! You hear the name I'm saying?"

"We keep everything there as safe as it can be now," Sheridan tried to placate her. "No one takes any chances."

"Bullshit!" yelled Janet. "And you know it's bullshit. How can you be safe in a place where there's no law, no government! Beirut is a bunch of rival gangs, everyone fighting everyone else and stealing and kidnapping and killing. It's not religion any more: hasn't been for a long time. It's gang warfare: I've taught little else, for years, and I know!" She had to stop, breathless, but then blurted off again, extending her fingers and then collapsing them as she counted. "William Buckley, American, murdered. Peter Kilburn, American, murdered. Alec Collet, Briton, murdered."

"I know . . ." he tried to stop her but she wouldn't stop.

". . . Seven slaughtered, in all," she said. "Four Russsians, too. At least seventeen still held. Nothing's been heard of Terry Anderson, the AP bureau chief, since 1985. Terry Waite, the Archbishop of Canterbury's envoy, has been missing almost two years."

"I've got to go," he said, simply.

"No way of refusing!" she pleaded.

"None."

"When?" she said, dully.

"Two weeks."

"Two weeks!"

"Everything is being done in panic."

"That's not fair . . . not enough time . . ."

"It gives me an edge, to get back."

"Why, when everything was so good!" Janet demanded, allowing herself the briefly forgotten self-pity.

"It'll be all right," Sheridan said. "Everything will be all right."

They changed their vacation dates so they could spend the final week completely together, which they did at the Rosslyn apartment. They stored what furniture and effects he wanted to retain from the

Columbus Circle flat and sold the rest and Sheridan assigned Janet power of attorney to act on his behalf to dispose of the property. They drove again out into Virginia and Maryland, house-hunting but it was impossible in the circumstances so they abandoned the pretence. They made love every night but anxiously, as if it might be the last time, and when he suggested a farewell dinner at their Virginia inn Janet said no, because that was a place to celebrate good times, not bad.

"There's something we haven't done," Sheridan announced, the night before he was due to leave.

"What?"

"I haven't bought you a ring," he said.

Janet looked down at the hand where she still wore what Hank had bought her. "No," she agreed. "It isn't right to go on like this, is it?" As she spoke Janet realized that to remove the rings would be the final cutting off, the final parting from one to another.

They only had time to get to two shops but in the second Janet saw a sapphire surrounded by diamonds and said it was beautiful, then tried to pull back when she learned the price. Sheridan insisted on buying it and she sat for their final lunch with her hand before them, proudly displaying it.

"I love you," said Sheridan.

"I love you, too."

"You mustn't worry. Everything is going to be fine," he said. "Trust me."

"I do," said Janet.

·6·

Janet had forgotten the aching loneliness and when it immediately returned, that positive physical feeling she'd never wanted to know, ever again, she was surprised—and vaguely embarrassed—how easy it had been to put from her mind. The first echoing night she came close to embarking on one of her private conversations but quickly and determinedly stopped herself. That indulgence—that need—was over, she thought, gazing down at the new engagement ring. It was John now, not Hank; wrong then to talk about one to the other, even secretly when no one else would ever know. Everything was different now: like the loss was different. With Hank, when she'd eventually confronted reality, it had been absolute. Final. Finish. But not this time. This time it was only a separation—an unwanted, intrusive, resented, irritating separation—but no more than that. A separation. John could come back: would come back. A lot of women temporarily lost their men in situations like this, although perhaps not in places as dangerous as Beirut. She had to be logical about it: logical and sensible. She had to stop behaving like a spoiled child.

Janet tried hard. Work was still the obvious blanket and she wrapped herself in it beyond her customary dedication. And studied beyond that dedication, reading everything and watching everything and listening to everything connected with the Lebanon as a whole and Beirut in particular. Her assessment was that it was as lawless and as ungoverned and dangerous as she'd declared it to be, the night of Sheridan's announcement that he was going there, but Janet consciously opposed the depression. Separation, nothing more.

Before he'd left Sheridan had explained the correspondence procedure, providing her with the specific State Department address in Washington through which their letters could be channeled in the embassy's diplomatic bag, which resulted always in an unusually quick and reassuring exchange, better than any normal mail service. His letters touched upon the destruction of the city and the difficulty of civil control but never in detail, an attempt not to avoid the obvious but not to worry her, either. Janet out-wrote Sheridan, sometimes despatching as many as three letters a week. She related a great deal from what she was studying with increased interest about the Lebanon and she recounted the gossip of Washington and she gave practically an hour-by-hour account of what she did and how she felt, every day. Always, repeatedly, she told Sheridan how much she loved him. There was never a letter from Sheridan without the same assurance.

Apart from her Sunday brunches with Harriet, househunting occupied much of her weekends and provided more material for the letters. After two months Janet was shown a brick colonial she instantly adored, just over the D.C. border into Maryland, with a Chevy Chase address. It had only been on the agent's books for three days and Janet was frightened of losing it so she took a chance and on the spot handed over a nonreturnable deposit. That night she sent Sheridan all the photographs and the brochure together with her own excited plea that it was the best house she had ever seen in her entire life and could they have it, please. Because of the diplomatic routing, his reply came within the week. Sheridan thought the agent's house looked great and was sure that if she liked it he would too and said he wanted her to go ahead and secure the property, contingent on the sale of his apartment, and included an authorization notarized by an embassy lawyer giving her similar attorney power to take to his bank, for the mortgage to be arranged.

Janet at once secured the contract. The sellers were a charming, Pentagon-retiring colonel and his wife, fleeing the East Coast winters to California, who said she could come in any time, irrespective of the legal exchanges, to measure and to plan her own fittings. Two couples were interested in Sheridan's apartment; she asked the agent to put pressure on them to act.

Janet made two visits to the Chevy Chase house, on each of which Harriet accompanied her. Janet did not intend any major structural alterations, not even in the kitchen, so there was no need for any extensive measuring, but at Harriet's urging Janet decided upon color changes in practically every room, which meant some tape measure work where she decided to recarpet and again at the windows where she was going to hang new drapes. The activity occupied Janet—an inner lining to the work blanket—and her late shopping evenings and weekends were filled with visits to furnishing departments and making comparisons between the best deals that each offered. Although it was never demanded—never hinted at—by Sheridan, Janet determined to get the best for the least, to prove to him that she was not profligate, despite her reaction to the too-expensive sapphire and diamond ring.

Sheridan's apartment was sold. Then lawyers at Sheridan's bank wanted to check directly with Sheridan about his power of attorney for the house purchase, despite already having the legally sworn deposition from the Lebanon. Janet said of course, and by using the diplomatic channel the confirmation came back from Beirut in five days.

"I'm sorry," the bank executive said. "We want always to be sure."

"I understand," assured Janet.

That night, in the third letter of that week, Janet wrote that everything had been finalized and that the purchase was expected to be completed in six weeks, which was perfect timing for the carpet fitters and curtain hangers to move in to get everything ready. Sheridan's letter by return—just four days—was the one for which Janet had been waiting, from the moment of his going to the Middle East. It began beguilingly, responding to what she had written and saying that he was delighted and that he was sure the house was going to be wonderful. He could hardly wait, Sheridan said. And then wrote that he was not going to have to wait much longer—neither of them were—because he'd been officially notified that the date of his return was May 24. Which was just three and a half months away: or put another way, not more than six weeks beyond the originally chosen wedding date. Why didn't she, Sheridan demanded, start sending out the invitations and warn her parents to rearrange the wedding for some convenient date after the twenty-fourth?

Janet called Harriet and then her parents in London, and that night sat with a celebration glass of brandy in one hand, cradling George with her other, watching the evening news, which it had become her unthinking habit to do since Sheridan's assignment.

"There is a top-of-the-hour development which we will update during the course of this program," announced anchorman Tom Brokaw. "There has been another American embassy kidnap in Beirut. The victim has been confirmed as John Patrick Sheridan, aged 38 . . ." The screen was filled with a stilted, full-faced photograph. "Tonight NBC has confirmed through Washington sources that Sheridan was the CIA officer in charge . . ."

"Oh no!" said Janet. "Dear God no!"

· 7 ·

Janet's immediate, crowded impression was that she had been betrayed: cheated. That for all these months she had gone with a man and slept with a man and learned to love a man whom she thought she knew and now realized she knew not at all. As always she found it easy to remember words and phrases in the tone in which they had been uttered and Sheridan's remark forced its way mockingly into her mind, the plea he'd made the night he'd told her of the Beirut posting. *Trust me*, he'd said. And she had, not just then but before: trusted him completely. Believed that he was a senior but otherwise run-of-the-mill analyst in the anthill of the State Department, unimportant, uninvolved. With that reflection came more taunting words. *Nothing spooky about me*. Not much, she thought bitterly: not bloody much.

Janet blinked against her fogged vision, aware of library footage of the shell-cratered streets of West Beirut being put up on the screen, with Brokaw's voice commenting over.

". . . no official confirmation of his CIA position," intoned the anchorman. "But the official diplomatic listing records Sheridan to be a political officer . . ."

Janet sucked the breath into her body, conscious of the significance before it was made obvious as another picture was flashed on to the screen, a still photograph this time of a hollow-faced, bearded man.

". . . Political officer was the designation of William Buckley," recounted the newscaster. "Buckley, it will be recalled, was the CIA station chief in Beirut who was kidnapped and murdered by the Islamic Jihad in March, 1984. . . ."

The very name she'd identified to John, the night he'd made the Beirut announcement! Janet knew about the Buckley case: knew how a tape of Buckley's agonizing, screaming torture had been made and sent to the CIA in direct challenge to the Agency. Who had taken it as a challenge. There had never been a denial from the CIA headquarters at Langley or the Reagan administration that the Buckley tape had so disgusted and frightened CIA Director William Casey that he had personally urged upon the President the hostage freeing attempts that were later to emerge as Irangate.

The photographs were side by side on the screen now, Sheridan and Buckley, and illogically Janet thought how ordinary they both looked: just ordinary, open, American faces. Run-of-the-mill, she reflected again. It was the briefest of considerations because abruptly, horrifyingly, there was another, too vivid intrusion. Janet pictured what had happened to Buckley and imagined it happening now, at this moment, to Sheridan in some cellar or cell or lonely house. She physically squeezed her eyes shut against the mental picture and the mental sounds and clamped her mouth closed, too, until she could keep her lips together no longer.

"Don't let him be hurt!" she begged. "Dear God don't let him be hurt!"

Janet was distantly aware of a sound, beyond the television, and recognized the telephone but could not move herself to respond to it. Almost at once there was another bell, the downstairs summons this time, and Janet shifted at last, momentarily unsure which to answer. She chose the intercom and at once Harriet's voice babbled into her ear, demanding to be let in. Automatically Janet pressed the release button and unlatched the door, careless of leaving it open. She turned back to the strident telephone but as she moved towards it, the ringing stopped. Janet remained gazing down at it, wondering who it had been.

Harriet burst into the apartment in her usual flurry, throwing her arms around Janet and said: "I came as soon as I heard."

"Thanks," said Janet, dully. Harriet's was the sort of remark people made after a bad accident or a bereavement. Maybe, she thought, it was fitting.

"What have you been told!" demanded Harriet.

Janet indicated the television, now showing some baby cream commercial. "Just that."

"No one's called?"

Janet had not until now considered any official notification. She looked again to the telephone and said: "I didn't get to it in time."

"How long have you known!" pressed Harriet.

"I just told you . . ." began Janet but the other woman talked over her, impatiently.

"About John being in the CIA, I mean!"

"I didn't," she admitted, simply.

"Not a clue!"

"Nothing. I thought he worked in the State Department, like I told you." Another recollection came to Janet as she talked, of the invariable delay in reaching Sheridan when she'd called the office number he'd given her. She supposed it would have been some complicated switching device, transferring the calls from Foggy Bottom to . . . to where? Something else she didn't know, she accepted: even where he worked. His voice came into her mind once more, the glib, easy explanation when she'd complained of the difficulty in reaching him. *I spend more time verbally analyzing situations than working at my desk.*

"I'd heard that's the way it was but I never really believed it," said Harriet.

"The way it was?"

"Wives and girlfriends never ever being told . . . always a secret," said Harriet.

Janet realized, annoyed, that her friend was excited, enjoying it all. Would Sheridan have told her, after their marriage? Janet supposed officially he *would* have been forbidden to tell her anything. Janet said: "It's very serious."

"You don't have to tell me that, darling!" assured Harriet. "Don't you think I don't know what you're going through!"

No, thought Janet. Despite trying so hard Harriet had not been able to begin to imagine what it had been like with Hank slowly dying, and she would not be able to begin to imagine what it was like now. No one could. More to herself than to her friend Janet said: "If I had known it might have been better: I might have been more prepared."

"What are you going to do?"

"I don't know," admitted Janet, confronting her helplessness for the first time.

"No," said Harriet, an admission of her own, seeming embarrassed now by her question. "It's difficult to think of anything to do, isn't it?"

"I suppose I'll call tomorrow, to see what they can tell me," she said. Who? Janet demanded of herself. The only number she had was one she now suspected to be some clever telephone system. And who were "they"?

The telephone rang again and Janet jumped at the noise, realizing how already strained her nerves were. She recognized her mother's voice at once, although it was a difficult connection, one that made the words echo from the English end.

"I've been trying to reach you for hours," announced her mother, with typical exaggeration.

"When did you ring?" asked Janet.

"About half an hour ago."

The call she hadn't reached in time, decided Janet. So it had not been some official notification. She said: "I was here. You should have waited."

"What are you going to do?"

It seemed to be a repetitive question, thought Janet. She said: "I don't know yet. It's late here now: I'll start trying to do something tomorrow." What? she asked herself again.

"Did you know he was a spy?"

Janet could not respond at once. Her mind had not gone on to the actual description of what he did. The concept of the polite, cultured, quiet-talking John Sheridan actually being a spy seemed preposterous: *was* preposterous. She said: "No, I didn't know."

"How could he not have told you!" Her mother sounded outraged over the hollow line.

"He couldn't have told me, could he?" said Janet. Already she was making excuses. Almost irritably she said: "Did Daddy tell you everything he did at the embassies!"

Now the older woman hesitated. "No," she conceded, finally.

"So it's just the same, isn't it?"

"I suppose so," said her mother, doubtfully. "They'll get him out, won't they? The government—Washington—I mean."

Something else her mind had not gone on to, conceded Janet. Not quite true, she corrected: something she had refused to let herself think about. Janet said: "Of course," conscious as she spoke of the lack of conviction in her own voice.

"Do you want us to come over?"

"Why?" asked Janet, surprised.

"I don't know," admitted her mother. "I just feel that we should."

"There's not really a lot of point, is there?" said Janet. "There's nothing you can do."

"I suppose not," accepted the older woman.

"I'll let you know as soon as I hear anything," promised Janet.

There was a moment of silence on the telephone that seemed to go on for a long time. Janet said: "Hello! Are you still there?"

"I'm here," said her mother. "I just don't know what else to say."

"There's nothing much *to* say, is there?" pointed out Janet.

"Everything seemed so wonderful. After what happened to Hank your father and I were so happy for you . . . you didn't deserve this . . ." The voice trailed off, lost.

"I've thought about that, Mother," said Janet, tightly.

"He should have told you: warned you," blurted the woman, abruptly. "It wasn't fair."

"We've discussed that," reminded Janet, tighter still.

"Are you sure there is nothing we can do?"

The problem, thought Janet, was that she was sure about very little: nothing, in fact. She said: "No, but thank you."

"Keep in touch," urged her mother.

Janet thought it was a stupid remark to make and at once curbed her increasing irritation: her mother was only trying to be sympathetically helpful. She said: "Of course I will. The moment I hear anything."

"It's all going to turn out fine," insisted the woman, with forced enthusiasm. "Your father and I have talked about it and we know everything is going to be fine."

"I know you're right," said Janet, emptily. Now she was reassuring her mother instead of it being the other way around.

"Call if there's anything you need," said her mother, reluctant to sever the connection.

"I will."

"Promise?"

"Promise."

"Goodbye then."

"Goodbye."

"Sure you don't want us to come over?"

"Quite sure."

When she turned around from the telephone Janet saw that Harriet had overfilled two brandy snifters and was offering her one. Her immediate thought was that it was a cliched reaction to a personal drama, like a scene from one of the interminable soap operas, and then, just as quickly, that the glass being held out to her was the one in which Sheridan usually had his nightcap. Janet accepted the drink, although she didn't want it, and said: "Thanks."

"Now!" said Harriet, briskly. "What would you like me to do?"

Every conversation appeared limited to the same questions and answers, reflected Janet. She shrugged and said: "There's nothing any of us can do, not until tomorrow, is there?"

"Would you like me to stay over: sleep here?" Harriet asked.

Again Janet was surprised. "Whatever for!"

It became Harriet's turn to shrug. "I don't know: thought you might like some company."

"I'll be OK," Janet said.

"It's a bastard, isn't it?" Harriet said.

"Yes," Janet agreed. "A complete bastard."

·8·

The number rang twice before it was picked up and a voice Janet thought she recognized from her previous calls said: "State."

"Is it?" asked Janet.

There was a pause and the voice said: "Ma'am?"

"My name is Janet Stone," she said, carefully prepared. "I am the fiancée of John Sheridan, who gave me this number. I've reached him on it, several times. I want to speak to somebody to find out what's happened to him in Beirut."

There was a further hesitation before the voice said: "Will you hold a moment, ma'am?"

Janet did not time the delay but it seemed to last for several minutes. When the line opened again it was a different voice. The man said: "Who is this, please?"

Janet repeated her earlier statement, which she had rehearsed, just as she had written down questions she wanted answered, while she waited for eight-thirty to show on the clock, the time she imagined they might start work. She finished by saying: "Who am I talking to?"

He didn't answer her question. Instead he said: "How did you get this number?"

"I already told you, from my fiancé, John Sheridan," reiterated Janet. "I want to find somebody who can help me. Can you help me?"

"Ma'am, I'm sorry," he said. "I think you've got a misconnection. No John Sheridan works here."

Janet felt a hollowness begin to form deep down in her stomach, but there was anger, too. She tried to control the anger, knowing it would not help and believing, too, that this number and this unknown man was the only link she had to people who might know what was going on in Beirut. With forced calmness she said: "I have not got a misconnection and I know I did not misdial, either. I have used this number to speak to John Sheridan on a number of occasions during the past year. I want to know what's happened to him: what's going to be done to get him released."

"Ma'am, I've told you, I'm sorry. I really can't help you."

"Who are you?" demanded Janet. "What CIA department am I speaking to?"

"Ma'am, I really don't know what you're talking about. I genuinely can't assist you."

Janet's anger lapped over. She said: "For God's sake stop patronizing me and certainly stop talking about genuineness when you're not showing any! I want to know what's happened to my fiancé!"

"Ma'am, I've told you . . ."

". . . I know what you've told me," cut off Janet. "And I know you're lying. I'm not interested or concerned in any secrecy rubbish. I just want to speak to someone who can help me . . . who knows more than I've seen on the newscasts . . ." She felt her control begin to waver and fought against the collapse. ". . . Please!" she said. "Please help me!"

"Ma'am, there really isn't any point in continuing this conversation," said the man.

"I want . . ." began Janet and then stopped because she heard the click of disconnection and knew it was pointless. She sat crouched in the Rosslyn apartment, the telephone off its rest and purring in her hand, engulfed in a fury that physically burned through her, so that she felt hot. But it was not all fury. There was a frightening helplessness, too, the all-alone feeling she'd known in the coming-to-terms period after Hank's death. It was an emotion she'd never wanted to experience again. Janet realized she was crying, not from the wetness of any tears but from the shaking of her shoulders. She sniffed, angry at herself now, and tried to stop. She was surprised she still held the telephone and put it hurriedly down. She had to go into her bedroom for a Kleenex and returned blowing her nose hard, as if making a noise would help her control.

Back in the living room she stared down at the piece of paper upon which 648-3291 was written, suffused by a fresh wave of helplessness and striving to suppress it. *Wouldn't* give in; *couldn't* give in, she mentally recited to herself. What then? She didn't know; couldn't think. Janet, who had no religion, thought: Dear God, someone, something, please help me think! She reached out, intending to dial it again, and then stopped, willing herself to concentrate. And did. That wasn't the entire number! In the habit of Americans, which Janet had actually found curious when she first arrived in the United States, Sheridan had prefixed the number with the area code, 202. Which was Washington, D.C., Janet knew: just as she knew that the CIA headquarters were at Langley. Which was in Virginia.

She picked up the D.C. directory and found the State Department under the government heading. The main number was 655-4000. Janet carefully ran her finger through the subsidiary listings, seeking the number Sheridan had given her. It wasn't there. She dialed 655-4000 and when the switchboard answered asked as expectantly as she could to be put through to 648-3291.

"That's not a State Department extension," said the operator.

"I didn't think it was an extension," said Janet. "It was given to me as a State Department number."

"Let me check," said the operator. The line went dead but only briefly. "Sorry," said the woman, coming back. "That's not registered in any of our directories."

While she waited Janet had already changed telephone books and located two numbers for the Central Intelligence Agency, 482-1100 or 7676, both with a 703 area code.

She called the first and on impulse, when there was a reply, asked for Personnel.

The operator said: "In connection with what, ma'am?"

Christ, how she wished everyone would stop calling her "ma'am," Janet thought. She recited her practiced request and was asked to wait and again another unidentified male voice came on to the line and asked who she was and again Janet mouthed the ritual.

"We are aware of reports that have appeared in newspapers and on television," said the man. "The Central Intelligence Agency can neither deny or confirm that John Patrick Sheridan is in any way connected with the Agency."

The bloody man was reading from some written statement, Janet realized, frustration making her hot again. She hadn't known Sheridan's second name was Patrick: but then she hadn't known much about him at all, had she? She said: "I am not asking you to deny or confirm anything. I am going to marry the man, for Christ's sake! I want to speak to someone to find out what's going on."

"I am afraid I am not empowered to say anything more than I've already told you. Certainly not over the telephone."

"Wait, please!" said Janet, urgently. Fearing another disconnection Janet hurried on: "Listen to me! I've tried the 648-3291 number, which John gave me. And I've checked with the State Department and know it's not one of theirs, although that was John's cover. I can prove I am his fiancée because I have the power of attorney to dispose of his Columbus Circle apartment and also of some of the effects. I can prove he bought me my engagement ring. I've got about a hundred letters in his handwriting, to me, from Beirut. I've also lodged with our bank a notorized authorization in the name of a U.S. embassy lawyer in Beirut, for access to funds in his account, to secure the mortgage on a house in Chevy Chase . . ."

". . . . What's the point you're trying to make, Ms. Stone?" interrupted the anonymous spokesman, flat-voiced.

Janet supposed "Ms." was slightly better than "Ma'am," but not much. She said: "Very simple, really. Like I told you, I tried the 648-3291 number and got the runaround: just like you've been giving me the runaround so far. I don't want that. I want to be able to meet and to talk to someone who'll tell me what has happened to someone I love and intend to marry. And what's being done to get him back to safety. So I *can* marry him."

"You appear to have given a lot of thought to how provably connected you are."

The remark briefly confused Janet. In her anxiety she had set out her links with Sheridan without any conscious attempt at detail but able to think upon them now she acknowledged that the list had been comprehensive. But then why shouldn't it have been? She was going to marry him, wasn't she? Most wives-to-be could have recounted a hundred more things than she had done. She was still about to query the man's remark but then understood. Janet said:

"I've already spoken this morning to someone in the Agency, on the 3291 number. And I'll tell you what I told him: I'm not interested in what you are doing or what John is doing or in any of this espionage crap that you all seem to think is a normal way of life. I don't intend causing any trouble or any difficulty. All I want is someone to tell me how everything is going to be made all right. Have I made myself clear?"

"I think you have, Ms. Stone."

"So?" demanded Janet. She was unsure where the determination was coming from—maybe from the frustrated anger—but whatever the source she was grateful: oddly—gratefully again—she no longer felt in danger of collapsing into pleading tears.

"You have somewhere we could get back to?"

There wasn't any longer the insincere politeness, Janet recognized, relieved. She dictated her number and when he'd read it back she said: "How long until you get back to me?"

"I've no way of knowing that, ma'am."

It hadn't taken long for the bullshit to seep back into the exchange. She said: "I'm very anxious. I'd like to hear very soon."

"I've got your number."

Then dial the fucking thing! Janet thought, in a fresh surge of frustration. Her voice betrayed no indication of what she was thinking. "I'll wait then."

"Yes," agreed the man. "Wait."

Janet did just that, wandering aimlessly around the apartment and then, irritated at herself, remembered the continuous news broadcasts on CNN. Hurriedly she turned on the television. Sheridan's kidnap retained its place as lead item and Janet sat through two top-of-the-hour repeats, each time grimacing as the fatuous CIA refusal to deny or confirm Sheridan's connection with the Agency was parroted, as it had been parroted to her that morning. The library footage was similar to that of the previous night, and once more there were comparison still photographs of Sheridan and William Buckley. On one segment the Beirut situation was augmented by a live studio interview with a supposed intelligence expert whose name Janet had never heard before. Hands clenched, she sat as the man recounted brief details of the obscene torture the earlier CIA station chief had undergone. Before the expert finished Janet found herself saying: "No, please don't let it happen. Don't let him be hurt," like she had the previous night.

Janet snapped off the television, impatient at no fresh news development. She looked at her watch and then at the telephone—three hours since her contact with Langley. What was it that took so long! she thought, exasperated.

Realizing it was lunchtime and that she had taken nothing other than coffee that morning, Janet went into the kitchen and stood looking at the refrigerator and the cupboards, wondering why she bothered. She wasn't hungry and did not want to eat anything anyway. There were the remains of a bottle of wine she and Harriet had failed to finish last night, and Janet considered it and then decided against that, too. She'd never found solace from disaster in booze.

Although she was expecting it, she started when the telephone sounded, snatching it off the kitchen extension to hear Harriet's voice.

"What is it?" demanded Harriet, discerning the disappointment.

"I thought it would be someone else."

"From the Agency?"

"Yes."

"What have they said?"

"Nothing yet: that's why I'm waiting."

"It's all over the newspapers."

"Yes, of course," said Janet, trying to curb her anxiety. "Darling, I really am waiting on this call. Can I get back to you?"

"I'll come by, direct from work," announced her friend.

"Do that," Janet said at once, eager to clear the line, even though her telephone was equipped with call waiting, which had not registered during Harriet's interruption. Still, Janet rang the switchboard operator downstairs who confirmed there had been no other incoming call in the preceding ten minutes.

She tried CNN once more and saw a replay of the previous newscast and the intelligence expert's account of what had happened to the last CIA officer snatched in Beirut, with no additional information, and turned it off. She walked from the main room to the kitchen and from the kitchen to the bedroom and then back into the main room. There were some magazines disordered on a small table and so she tidied them. All over the newspapers, she remembered, as she did so. How could she have been so stupid?

Janet called the switchboard operator in the lobby and explained she was expecting an extremely important call: she was turning her telephone to answer and if the call came the operator was to ask whoever it was to hold as she was only going into the basement shopping area for a moment.

She moved impatiently from foot to foot waiting for the elevator to arrive and darted immediately inside when it did, emerging before the doors were fully open into the basement. She snatched up all the newspapers available in the 7-11 store and was able to catch the elevator she had left before it was summoned to another floor. On the way back to her apartment Janet tried to read the account in one of the smaller-sized newspapers, *Newsday*, but the bundle was too clumsy and she abandoned the attempt.

Inside she dumped the newspapers onto a pile, crossing directly to the telephone. The message light was not on but she spoke to the operator anyway. There hadn't been a call.

Janet had bought the *New York Times*, the *Washington Post*, *Newsday*, the *New York Daily News*, and the *New York Post*. She spread them all out over the floor, at first only scanning each. Harriet had been right: every paper had led with Sheridan's kidnapping. The *Times* and the *Washington Post* reports carried the byline of staff correspondents, rather than AP or UPI. Because their accounts appeared longer she read them first. Both reported that Sheridan had been waylaid in West Beirut as he drove, just after 9 A.M. the previous morning, from his apartment block to the fortified U.S. embassy, less than two miles away in the Yarzy district. Eyewitnesses talked of his vehicle being blocked front and back by two other cars and of Sheridan being bundled out at gunpoint. No responsibility had so far been claimed, but informed opinion was that the kidnap had been carried out by members of the Islamic Jihad. The *Times* pointed out that the warring factions in the Lebanon were so fragmented that it could have been the work of a splinter group of what they referred to as the Iran-backed Hezbollah, the Party of God, or simply a ransom-inspired snatch by any one of a dozen gangs running crime syndicates in the lawless city. The *Washington Post* speculated similarly but their correspondent doubted it was a gangland seizure because all U.S. embassy personnel followed a strict security pattern, alternating routes and arrival and departure times at the American compound, indicating that the kidnap was carefully planned.

The *Washington Post* story continued inside the paper and when she got to the continuation page Janet saw a biography of John Sheridan running alongside the news story. At once she abandoned the Beirut account.

There were three photographs of Sheridan, none of which Janet considered very good. Inevitably there was comparison again with

William Buckley, and part of Sheridan's supposed background was intermingled with information about Buckley, so Janet had to read carefully to differentiate between the two.

She learned for the first time that Sheridan had been born in Billings, Montana, had attended university there, and majored in law. His dead parents had been farmers and there was another photograph of a stiffly upright couple, both Sunday-best-dressed at what appeared to be an agricultural show. He'd run middle distance in his university athletics team and according to university contemporaries whom the newspaper had interviewed Sheridan had moved east almost directly after graduation. Those same unnamed sources described him as a serious, studious person who at school had not appeared to attract many friends.

The biography repeated the absurd, noncommittal statement from the CIA at Langley and then recounted Sheridan's postings in Mexico and Peru and Egypt. He was variously described as a political officer or a cultural attaché. There was a personal anecdote from a *Washington Post* staff writer who had worked in Saigon during Sheridan's period there, and who claimed to know the man. Sheridan had not been a mixer or a party-goer, the journalist remembered. He had played chess and enjoyed studying the culture of the country: during his two-year posting he had acquired a reasonable fluency in Vietnamese.

The biography concluded by saying that Sheridan was unmarried and had few friends in the Washington area, where he had been based for the previous three years, after his reassignment from Mexico.

What about me? thought Janet at once. Wasn't she a friend? More than a friend?

She went carefully through the biography a second time, feeling cheated and betrayed, as she had the previous night, stunned before the television set, hearing of the kidnap. It wasn't right—wasn't fair—that she should learn about the man she was going to marry from some dry newspaper account. Why hadn't he told her about Montana and his family? Of being an athlete? Of liking chess and being able to speak Vietnamese? They weren't things that needed to be hidden: things likely to impinge upon whatever ridiculous oath of secrecy or silence or whatever it was she imagined they swore to uphold, like members of some cloaked and closed society. Janet felt she was sharing him now with however many thousands or millions of readers read that morning's newspapers: that he wasn't hers any more.

The *New York Times* had also printed a profile. It included everything published in the *Washington Post*—although not so many photographs—but reported additionally that despite what the CIA was publicly saying Sheridan had for the past three years held the rank of supervisor in the Middle East analysis section and was regarded as one of the top three Middle East experts in the Agency. His loss, said the newspaper, was viewed extremely seriously both at Langley and at the White House. Determined to avoid another assassination, like that of Buckley, the State Department had already made a formal diplomatic approach to Damascus asking Syria to bring all possible pressure upon whatever group had seized Sheridan. In addition, informal contact had been made to every friendly or neutral embassy in the Lebanese capital, seeking information from their sources on the CIA man's whereabouts.

Janet had read the newspapers kneeling on the floor upon which they were laid. She slumped back now on her heels, wanting to feel relieved at learning that some effort was being made to get Sheridan released, but finding that reaction difficult. She told herself that the word "loss" in the *Times* report was just a journalistic usage and carried no special significance, but it made her uneasy. Like the account of the diplomatic efforts made her uneasy. Again, she tried to convince herself that it was exactly what the U.S. government should be doing—what she would have expected them to be doing and been angry if they hadn't—but it seemed to hint at panic. And if the government and the Agency were panicking, they clearly feared Sheridan would be treated *exactly* like the previous CIA hostage. Janet fought against the conclusion, recognizing there was no reason whatsoever to speculate like that, but she was unable completely to remove it from her mind.

It was a physical as well as mental agony to wait until four o'clock in the afternoon—the skin on her arms and legs began to itch, and became sore at her scratching—but she delayed until then to avoid annoyance at Langley. At four she decided she had every reason to go back to them.

She went through the morning's explanation to the switchboard operator, and when she was transferred, realized at once that she was not speaking to the same secondary spokesman. It meant a further repetition which she gave as calmly as possible, even when the man began reciting the official statement and she had to cut him off by insisting she had been promised a call back by the person to whom she had earlier spoken.

The man asked her to hold and then returned to say: "Your earlier call has been logged, Ms. Stone."

"What's that mean?" demanded Janet.

"That it's been logged," repeated the man, doggedly.

"I heard the words," Janet said. "Logging something is just recording the fact. I'm waiting to speak to someone . . . hopefully meet with someone."

"I'm afraid I don't know anything beyond what I've told you, ma'am."

Stop calling me ma'am! Janet almost screamed. She said: "You haven't told me anything yet. Can I speak to whoever it was I had the conversation with this morning?"

"I'm afraid that isn't possible, ma'am."

"Why not?"

There was a pause, as if the person at the other end were undecided whether he was risking an unauthorized disclosure. Then he said: "That person is no longer on duty today."

"So when can I expect to hear from whoever is going to talk to me!"

"I'm afraid I have no knowledge of that, ma'am."

For several moments Janet had to clamp her mouth shut against a yell of frustration. Tightly she said: "Can you find out for me? Find out and call me back? I've been sitting by this telephone all day expecting some contact from you."

"I'm afraid that would not be proper, Ms. Stone," said the man, at least varying his politeness.

"Why the hell wouldn't it be proper!" demanded Janet.

"I've no way of knowing what my colleague might have already done," said the man. "Wires could get crossed."

Janet pressed her knuckles against her mouth, creating a physical barrier. "How long?" she said, her words distorted.

"I'm sorry?" prompted the man.

Janet took her hand from her mouth and said, slowly and distinctly: "How long is it going to be before I hear from someone at the Central Intelligence Agency about what's happening here and what's happening in Beirut after the kidnap yesterday of John Sheridan!"

There was a hesitation. Then the man said: "I'm afraid I can't answer that, ma'am."

"Is this the way dependents of CIA officers are normally treated?" said Janet, regretting the anger as she spoke.

"Ma'am," said the spokesman. "I've told you your earlier call has been logged and that a colleague is working on it. But from what you've explained to me, it would seem that you are not legally a dependent."

The words had a chilling effect, cooling Janet's anger as if icy water had been thrown in her face. "You're telling me that I haven't the *right* to know!"

"I don't wish to get into a dispute with you over this," said the spokesman. "I was just expressing a personal point of view."

She was being blocked out, Janet decided. As she'd been blocked out when she called the supposed State Department number and when she made that first approach to Langley. She said: "No one is going to try to help me, are they?"

"Ma'am, I've already tried to make it clear how little I can assist you."

"Poor bugger," said Janet.

"Ma'am?"

"I was feeling sorry for John Sheridan, for ever getting involved," she said, quietly now.

"I really don't think there is anything further I can help you with," said the man.

"Don't forget to log the call, will you?" urged Janet, slamming down the telephone.

The gesture didn't help and she sat there, the renewed frustration trembling through her. Gradually she focused on the spread-apart *Washington Post*. During that morning's conversations, she'd said she didn't want to cause difficulties. It wasn't she who had imposed those difficulties, Janet decided: they had.

She picked up the telephone again. She explained yet again, to the *Washington Post* operator, and was connected at once to a voice that said, simply: "City."

"My name is Janet Stone," she said. "I am engaged to be married to John Sheridan."

"Would you talk to us about that, Ms. Stone?" asked the man, at once.

"I want to, very much," said Janet. "I'm being shoved aside by the Agency."

"Where are you?"

When Janet gave her address, the deskman said: "We can have a writer and photographer there in forty-five minutes."

They arrived in thirty. The writer was a thin, bony woman with prematurely gray-streaked hair, and the male photographer wore jeans and a T-shirt and round, metal-framed granny glasses.

"What can you tell us about John Sheridan and yourself?" asked the woman, as soon as she was inside the apartment.

"Everything," promised Janet.

·9·

Janet had little experience of newspapers or the other media, and the reaction to her interview with the *Washington Post* overwhelmed her. It was only eleven o'clock that night, and Harriet was still with her, when the telephone first rang. It was the staff correspondent for the BBC who had read the piece in the first edition of the following morning's paper and wanted an interview at their Washington studio, to be transmitted by a satellite link-up with London for their breakfast program. Knowing there would be no contact from the CIA that late at night, she agreed. Harrriet offered to remain in the apartment just in case, and it was Harriet who relayed to her at the studio the calls from American bureaus of five London newspapers, CBS, NBC, and ABC, the *New York Times*, *Newsday*, *Newsweek*, and Reuters news agency. She agreed to the American television interviews and spoke to the *London Times*, the *Daily Telegraph*, and the *Daily Mail* but then, exhausted, asked the others to wait until the following morning. It was three-thirty before she got to bed. The Reuters reporter and photographer called from the downstairs lobby at seven.

Their interview and picture session was just finishing when the delayed contact of the previous night started to be made, not by telephone now but by journalists coming personally to Rosslyn. Janet posed and talked to them all and agreed to fresh interviews for different programs with the three main American television networks, with ITN in London, and with CNN.

It was late afternoon before she was able properly to read the *Washington Post* interview which had started it all. Although there was a story datelined from Beirut, it was immediately obvious that there had been no developments in Beirut, and her story was given the emphasis. The *Post* had divided it into two parts. That on the front page, turning later on to page nine, focused upon her anger at the lack of help from the CIA, and Janet was glad—it was to force some response from the Agency that she had approached the newspaper in the first place and then agreed to the media onslaught that followed. There were photographs of the legal documents she had made available to them, proving that she was Sheridan's fiancée, including the document from the U.S. embassy in Beirut giving her control of his bank account, which was reproduced in full. The second, inside-page story was a personality profile and Janet was surprised at its depth. There was reference to her diplomat father and a quote from her department head at Georgetown University describing her as a brilliant academic and there were lengthy quotes from the letters that had passed between her and Sheridan, always concerning some remark about their impending wedding. There were three photographs of herself and Janet was disappointed. She thought they made her look fuller-faced than she really was, and in each she appeared strained, which she supposed she was, and she was obviously not made up, which had been her fault, not that of the photographer. It had been a mistake, too, not to change from the jeans and shirt she had been wearing when they arrived. She was reading with the television tuned to the continuous CNN news program, as she had the previous day, and was much happier with her appearance there. It had been right to wear her hair pulled back from her face and the formal business suit. She thought she looked concerned but not haggard. When she had responded to a question about their engagement the camera closed in upon her ring. She had been worriedly intertwining and then releasing her fingers, which she couldn't remember having done.

The next telephone call was from her mother. She said she had been out specially to buy all the English newspapers and there were stories and photographs in every one. They had not expected her to appear on BBC television that morning and would have liked to have been told; as it was they had only caught it by accident.

"Sorry," said Janet.

"You didn't smile," her mother said. "You've got a nice smile, too."

"I don't really think there's a lot to smile about, do you?"

"You still haven't heard anything?"

"Nothing."

"It can't be easy for them."

"It's not easy for me, either."

"We could still come across."

"There's no point."

"You going to be on television here again?"

Janet frowned at the thought that her mother was enjoying it, like she'd earlier imagined Harriet was enjoying it. Remembering the ITN interview, she said: "Probably. I don't know. You'll just have to watch the various channels."

"Your father sends his love and says you're not to worry."

"That's a . . ." Janet began, irritably, and then stopped. She said: "Give my love to him."

"You looked very pretty on television, even though you didn't smile."

Janet didn't know what to say. "Thanks," she managed.

"Call us the minute you hear something?" ended her mother, predictably.

"Of course," promised Janet, just as predictably.

Janet's hand was still on the telephone, in the act of replacing it, when it sounded again, startling her. Hopefully she picked it up, disappointed at Harriet's voice.

"Anything?" asked her friend.

"A lot more interviews. Nothing from the Agency."

"You're the most famous girl in town."

"Bugger being the most famous girl in town."

"The boss wants to help."

"The boss?" Janet asked, not understanding.

"Senator Willard J. Blackstone."

Until that moment Janet had not considered the possibility of political pressure from anyone in Congress. "How?" she said, cautiously.

"I don't know exactly," said Harriet. "But he wants you to come up to the Hill, to see him. He asked me to fix a time."

"It will mean leaving the telephone."

"Darling," said Harriet. "Do you really think you raise the chances of their calling by sitting next to the damned thing! You've got a switchboard downstairs. Use it. You set out to throw stones in pools; let's make as many ripples as we can."

Janet paused. It would be wrong to lose the impetus she appeared to have created but she had not anticipated the effect of approaching the *Washington Post* and still had no proof it would achieve anything anyway. At once came the balancing reflection. Even more reason to meet with an American senator then. She said: "All right."

"What time?"

"That's a matter for you, really."

"How about an hour?" suggested Harriet.

Janet looked down to her sweater and jeans and remembered the mistake of the *Washington Post* photographs and said: "An hour and a half."

"I'll be waiting," assured her friend.

Which she was when Janet, wearing the same suit she'd worn for the CNN interview, arrived at the Dirksen Building housing the Senate offices. Harriet greeted Janet at the entrance and cupped her elbow with her hand to guide her familiarly along the high-ceilinged corridors to Blackstone's suite. Blackstone was a senior, four-term senator with an office to match that seniority. There was a cluster of outer rooms accommodating secretaries and aides, a more expansive paneled chamber for his personal assistant, and beyond that Blackstone's sanctum itself. It was at the corner of the building, with a view of Constitution Avenue and the Capitol beyond. The walls were lined with photographs showing Blackstone with every domestic and international political figure Janet could remember over the preceding ten years. Beneath the pictures there were enough leather couches and chairs for a large, informal conference and to one side a conference table itself, hedged by about a dozen upright chairs. Blackstone's desk was against the windows: occupying the wall space in between was a furled but staffed American flag held up by a special support.

Blackstone rose as the women entered. He was an impressive but carefully cultivated man. He had a thick mane of completely white hair, which he wore long and swept back and he was tall enough, well over six feet, to be able to wear suits tailored practically in the style of the frock coats of an earlier age, waisted and then full again over his hips.

He came forward with both hands outstretched, encompassed

Janet's fingers between them, and said welcome and how sorry he was and how he was determined to help as, still holding her hand, he led her to one of the side couches. He pulled one of the easy chairs around to face her but sat forward, elbows on his knees, face between his hands, in the well-practiced attitude of a politician giving someone their undivided attention, and told her to tell him all about it, from the very beginning. The voice was Southern drawl, tailored like the clothes.

After recounting the story of herself and John Sheridan so often in the past twenty-four hours, Janet was able to do so automatically, actually able to recall dates and places and even quote the official phrasing of the legal documents that had passed between herself in Washington and Sheridan in Beirut.

"And the Agency refused to see you?"

"Not actually refused," qualified Janet, carefully. "I keep asking to be told something and all they say is that my original request has been logged."

Blackstone made a vague gesture in the direction of his desk upon which Janet saw for the first time marked and annotated newspaper clippings. He said: "What makes you fear you're not being considered a proper, legal dependent then?"

"The last man I spoke to at Langley, yesterday," said Janet. "He said in his opinion I did not appear to be."

"I don't have any difficulty considering you precisely that," said Blackstone.

"I want to hear that they don't, either," said Janet.

"You know what I'm going to do, little lady?" asked Blackstone, rhetorically. "I'm going to poke a stick into the hornets' nest. I'm going to ask questions and keep asking questions until I get some goddamned answers. For you and for myself. I think you're being treated badly and I think Americans are being treated badly. I don't think we should sit back and let our guys out there in the field get pushed around by a bunch of fanatics and do nothing about it. I think we've put up with just about enough humiliation there. I think it's time we kicked ass, if you'll forgive me the expression."

"Thank you," said Janet, not knowing what else to say. She supposed little lady ranked with ma'am and ms.

"Starting right now," Blackstone announced, standing abruptly and crossing to his desk. He snapped down an intercom and said: "Ready, Ray?"

"Ready, senator," replied a disembodied voice.

"Let's go," urged Blackstone, returning to where Janet sat and offering his hand.

She stood without his assistance, following uncomprehendingly as the politician led the way into the paneled outer office but turned right through a door leading to the conference room. She hesitated at the entrance, conscious that the room into which she was being taken was already crowded and that the harsh lights she could now recognize as television illumination were burning, in readiness. She felt a push from Harriet, behind, and continued on into the room.

At Blackstone's bidding she sat beside him on a raised dais, unable because of the lights to see if any of the assembled journalists were those she had met before. She heard Blackstone insist that she had approached him for help and that he was going to give it. He described her as a tragic little lady and talked about fanatics and good American boys in the field and too much humiliation which had to stop and how he intended asking questions until he got answers and Janet realized Blackstone's earlier remarks in his office had been a rehearsed and prepared speech, for this press conference. She heard herself being questioned and replied that she was grateful for the senator's assistance and that she still had not been told anything officially and thought, illogically, how glad she was she'd worn her suit and not stayed in her jeans.

"Well!" demanded Harriet, excitedly, as they drove back across the river towards Rossyln, listening already over the car radio to a report of what had taken place. "What did you think of that?"

That she'd been used by a publicity-conscious politician anxious to clamber aboard a bandwagon, Janet replied, mentally. Aloud she said: "Let's hope it works."

The switchboard had one message when they went into the apartment. There was no name or identification, just a number but with a 703 area code. When she called it and identified herself a man said: "I think it's time we met, don't you?"

"See!" exclaimed Harriet. "It worked!"

·10·

It was a typical office building on 13th Street near Franklin Park. Janet had been surprised at receiving an address in Washington rather than being asked to go out to Langley, which was what she had expected. She supposed, upon reflection, that it was obvious the Agency would have places away from their headquarters complex for meetings like this. As the elevator ascended to the sixth floor Janet wondered if it were in just such an office that Sheridan had worked or whether he'd been based at Langley. If he were the senior analyst the newspapers had described him as being, she guessed he would have been out in Virginia.

The suite number she had been given—6223—confronted her when the lift doors opened. There was no identification plate. The door, without any apparent security lock or device, opened into an expansive area dominated by wide-leafed plants in a selection of wood-chipped pots. There were magazines on several small tables centered among low-backed easy chairs, and Janet thought it was just like every doctor's or dentist's waiting room she'd ever visited. The receptionist was black and very pretty, her hair braided and all the braids capped off with different-colored beads which rattled at her every movement. From a chain around her neck hung the sort of identification badge, complete with picture, that everyone in Washington appeared to wear. Behind the receptionist two closed-circuit television cameras were positioned to encompass the entire room.

When Janet identified herself the receptionist said: "Of course," as if she personally recognized her. The woman passed the name on through the intercom box on her desk and immediately a fresh-faced, bespectacled man emerged from a cubicle behind. He wore a waistcoated gray checked suit with a club-striped tie pinned into place by a metal bar which stretched from each collar tip. He, too, recited her name as if he recognized her and asked her politely to follow him into the rear of the building.

The office into which he led her was very small, a partitioned box among a lot of other partitioned boxes. It was bare of any personal photographs or mementos. There was nothing on the desk apart from a single telephone and a blotter pad: the pad was crisply white and unmarked. There was another closed-circuit camera high in the left corner. Janet guessed the size of the room made more than one camera unnecessary.

The man gestured her to a seat and politely remained standing until Janet sat. He left his jacket fastened when he lowered himself into his seat, so that the material strained around him, but did not appear discomfited. Through the gape of the jacket Janet saw he had an identification badge on a chain, as well.

"Thank you for coming," he said.

"It was hardly likely that I wouldn't, surely?" said Janet. She hadn't intended to sound rude but realized her reply could be construed that way.

He did not appear offended. He said: "We think all the publicity has been unfortunate."

"I think it is unfortunate I have been treated as I have," replied Janet.

"On occasions like this the Agency receives a lot of crank calls," he said.

"You thought I was a crank!"

"We had to be sure."

"You mean you checked on me?"

"Of course."

Janet looked directly at the camera, wondering the purpose of whatever it was recording. She said: "I could have been told. That there would be a delay, I mean."

The man nodded and said: "Our people didn't handle it well."

"Am I to know your name?" asked Janet.

The man hesitated, appearing reluctant, then said: "Willsher. Robert Willsher."

"So now that we've at last met, Mr. Willsher, what can you tell me about John?"

"Very little, I'm afraid," said the CIA man. "Through an allied embassy in Beirut we've got some guidance that the kidnappers are Fundamentalists but there's been no direct contact. Or demand."

"So what's the purpose of the kidnap in the first place?"

Willsher shrugged. "Humiliation of Americans is usually sufficient. There are a lot of our people held."

"Too many," said Janet, accusingly. "What's the policy to be when there is contact? Is there to be a bargained deal?"

"Official policy is not to surrender to terrorism," said Willsher.

"Rubbish," rejected Janet, at once. "What was Irangate all about! And it failed."

"I'm authorized to say that every avenue will be explored, to secure Sheridan's release," said the man.

"What, precisely, does that mean!"

"What it says. It's impossible for us to be any more specific than that until we know who's got him and what they want."

"You looked into my background?"

"Yes," frowned Willsher.

"So you know my university subject. And from it will be aware I study the area," reminded Janet.

Willsher nodded again, understanding. He said: "And because of your subject you should be able to appreciate how difficult it is for us."

"Do you just intend to wait?" asked Janet. "Or are you trying to make contact from your side?"

"You must believe we're doing everything we can."

"That isn't an answer to my question."

"Through Arab governments with whom we have dialogue we have made it clear we want contact," conceded Willsher. "That's why your courting publicity didn't help."

"Would this meeting be taking place if I had not made some sort of protest?"

"I told you we had to be sure," repeated Willsher.

"What harm has the publicity done?"

"From the outset the aim has been damage limitation," said

Willsher, pedantically. He looked away from her, appearing almost embarrassed, then continued: "The CIA, as an organization, is a particular target among these people. We wanted as much as possible to minimize Sheridan's position."

Janet felt the familiar anger begin to build up. The man was discussing John as if he were some disembodied awkwardness, not a human being going through God knows what sort of torment. She said: "I did not disclose John's position in the CIA. I didn't even *know* he was connected to the CIA until I heard it on a television newscast. If you'd been so goddamned anxious to deny any connection with the CIA you could have done so by doing just that: telling a lie and denying it. That ridiculous statement saying neither one thing or the other was practically an out-and-out admission!"

"Something else that wasn't handled particularly well," conceded the man.

"I know about William Buckley," said Janet, flatly.

"So do we, ma'am," said Willsher, more forcefully than he had so far spoken. "And we don't want anything like it to happen again."

"There must be *something* the government can do, other than just sit around and wait!" said Janet. "Why not issue a public warning about retribution if any harm comes to him!"

Willsher shook his head. "You must believe me, Ms. Stone. A lot of discussion and consideration has already gone into this. The combined view of the Agency and the State Department is that a confrontational stance is not the right one to adopt."

What the hell was a confrontational stance? thought Janet. Ma'am and Ms. had re-entered the conversation, too, she realized. She said: "What is, then?"

"It has been decided to wait until the demand."

"Then what?"

"We can't answer that until we know what the demand is."

Around and around on the carousel, thought Janet. She said: "That could take weeks . . . months . . ."

"We're prepared for it to take as long as necessary, if it means getting John safely back."

Janet supposed it was the right attitude—the only attitude—but she was impatient with it. She wanted to be told that something positive was being done, like offering a definite ransom or assembling some sort of gung-ho rescue squad. She said: "Just sit back and wait!"

"No," said Willsher, patiently. "I told you everything that can be done is being done, and it is. The State Department has made approaches to every Arab country, saying that the government will react in the strongest possible way . . . without being specific what that might be . . . if any harm befalls him."

"I thought you were pulling back from confrontation!"

"These are diplomatic messages, not press statements getting headlines," Willsher said. "And I think it's important they remain that way. I don't think what I've just told you should get to the newspapers."

"The *New York Times* has already come pretty close."

Willsher shook his head. "No one has reported how we might react."

Remembering her earlier impatience, Janet said: "What about when there is contact? What about sending in some sort of snatch squad?"

"I thought I'd already made it clear, Ms. Stone, that every sort of contingency is being explored."

"Including some sort of commando assault?"

"I don't think I can be as specific as that."

"You don't trust me, do you?"

"I don't think trust comes into it, Ms. Stone. I don't know the specific proposals myself."

"And if you did you wouldn't tell me?"

"Probably not," admitted Willsher, at once. "That wouldn't be particularly good security, would it?"

"Did you know John?" Janet asked abruptly. "Personally, I mean?"

Willsher hesitated and then said: "We were on station together once, some time ago. But not together here, in Washington."

"Were you a friend?"

Willsher frowned once more, head to one side. "We saw each other occasionally," he said. "It wasn't really friendship."

"Will he be able to stand it?" asked Janet, urgently. "The imprisonment . . . and . . . and . . ." She stumbled to a halt and then blurted out. "Whatever else there might be . . . ?"

For the first time Willsher's reserved formality wavered. He said: "John's a very strong man. Very tough."

Janet laughed, without humor. "That's the strangest part, since all this happened. I realize I never thought of him as someone with strength . . . with resilience. Isn't that odd?"

"I'm not going to say anything ridiculous, like don't worry, but he's able to sustain hardship," Willsher said.

"I hope you're right," said Janet. "Dear God, I hope you're right."

"You must leave things with us now," Willsher said. "No more media hype. Or protests from senators."

"For how long?"

"For as long as it takes, Ms. Stone."

"Gagged, you mean?"

"I mean there's only one consideration, for both of us. Which is getting John out. And we think that means low profile."

"You wouldn't abandon him, would you?" Janet demanded.

"I don't understand that question, ma'am."

"I mean that it wouldn't be considered wise politics in a region in which America has already made a whole bunch of mistakes to consider John Sheridan as being disposable . . ." Janet paused. Remembering the phrase, she said: "Someone who's plausibly deniable."

"No, Ms. Stone. I can assure you that isn't the way we're thinking."

"I'd like to believe you, Mr. Willsher."

"All I can do is repeat that it isn't so."

"Are you going to remain in contact?"

"Of course."

"How?"

Willsher paused and said: "You shouldn't have disclosed the telephone number that John gave you: we've had to close it down."

"And I shouldn't have been given the bum's rush when I asked for help," came back Janet. "I thought we'd cleared the decks on that."

"I hope we have," agreed the CIA officer.

"So how?"

"I've got your number."

"No!" refused Janet, shaking her head. "I want something better than that!"

Willsher sighed, looking down at his pristine blotter. He said: "There are going to be more media approaches."

Every conversation reverted to their sensitivity about publicity, Janet recognized. She said: "I understand what you're saying: I really do. To refuse to talk would be as wrong as saying too much. How about if I said there had been a meeting with an official of the Agency who assured me that everything possible was being done?"

Willsher smiled, suddenly, an unexpected expression. He said: "I think that sounds fine."

"In return for which I get a number where I can reach you whenever I want," insisted Janet.

The smile died. Willsher said: "You have my word I will call as soon as there is news."

"I want a number, damn it!"

Willsher blinked at the outburst. He said: "For you only."

"I told you I understand!"

There was the briefest of hesitations and the man scrawled out a number on a scratch pad and offered it to her across the table. Janet took it and saw at once, relieved, that it was prefixed by the 703 Langley area code. Willsher said: "We're going to stay on top with this one. You must believe me on that."

"I'll try," said Janet.

She rigidly maintained her side of the bargain, confining herself to what they had agreed when the renewed newspaper and television inquiries came, until after three days the only regular callers were news agencies. The *Washington Post* tried to keep the story alive by publishing in their Sunday "Style" section more of the letters between herself and Sheridan that she had made available that first day, and Janet spent an uncomfortable twenty-four hours until Monday, when she could reach Willsher to explain. The CIA man said he understood and that there the feature hadn't caused any problems.

In the first few days Janet rang Willsher morning and night. Never once did he react impatiently. By the end of the second week Janet herself recognized the pointlessness and reduced her calls to one a day.

For his part, Willsher kept the terms on behalf of the Agency, as well, reaching her, at the beginning of the third week before any news outlet to tell her of the photographs released by the Islamic Jihad. Harriet hurried over, in response to Janet's call, and together they sat, hands linked, in front of the television.

Janet whimpered aloud when the picture flashed up, shocked by Sheridan's appearance. There was no identifiable background and she guessed it had been taken against the wall of the cell in which he was being held. He had not been allowed to shave and the beard growth was very white, making him look much older. His hair was unkempt and straggled in places almost to his collar and it was grayer than she remembered, too, adding to the impression of age. The sports shirt was open at the neck and his thinness, almost a frailty, was more obvious to her from the bony ridges around his neck and chest than the hollow, sunken cheeks. Sheridan's eyes were sunken, as well. Janet thought how similar he appeared around the eyes to how she had looked that day of the intended bathroom suicide.

Beside her Harriet said: "Jesus!" and then at once, embarrassed at the unthinking reaction, tried to correct it by saying "I'm sorry . . . I didn't mean that . . ." and finally, "Oh shit!"

The commentary said the photograph had been accompanied by demands for the release of ten members of the group with whom the kidnappers were linked and who were currently being held in custody in Kuwait. If the Kuwaiti prisoners were not released, the American would be executed. The still photograph of Sheridan faded, to be replaced by live footage of a State Department spokesman in front of a map of the world, saying that the demands were being considered and discussed with friendly countries. Janet took the first two calls herself but after that relayed her reaction through Harriet, saying that she was relieved at the evidence that Sheridan was still alive and that she hoped negotiations could now be opened leading to his freedom. So busy was her telephone that it was difficult to get a call out but she finally did. Willsher seemed to be expecting her.

"Kuwait normally refuses to be pressured," Janet said at once.

"Yes," agreed the CIA official, just as quickly.

"Will they on this occasion?"

"The liaison is through the State Department," Willsher said vaguely.

"Is Kuwait being asked to concede?"

"It's delicate," Willsher said. "There's a limit to the requests and demands we can make."

Janet paused, needing to force herself to ask the question. "So John is going to die?"

"No, Ms. Stone," said the man, always patient. "Everything that can be done is being done: I keep telling you that. And you've overlooked something in their demand."

"What!" asked Janet.

"They haven't imposed a time limit for compliance."

Janet was annoyed at herself for not having spotted the fact, which was important. Probing to see if the official view were the same as her own, Janet said: "How do you see the significance of that?"

"A concession, before we even start," said Willsher, encouragingly. "They know a time limit would have boxed us in. So they've already accepted that persuasion can take a while. We've got room to move."

"Yes," agreed Janet, feeling a sweep of hope.

"So let's not get too depressed too quickly," Willsher said encouragingly.

"I'll try not to let it happen," Janet said.

It was not an easy undertaking to keep. Two days later Kuwait officially announced that it saw no reason to abandon its established policy of resisting terrorist pressure and that they would not comply with the demand involving the American citizen, John Sheridan. The State Department immediately summoned the Kuwaiti ambassador to Foggy Bottom for talks with the Secretary of State, who was photographed bidding the diplomat farewell. On the steps of the Kuwait embassy the ambassador allowed himself to be interviewed. He said that while his country sympathized with the hostage taking of a U.S. national there had been nothing in his conversation with the Secretary of State to make him think his country would alter its stance. Concessions to terrorism encouraged further and worse acts of terrorism.

Three days after the Kuwaiti rejection, Sheridan's kidnappers issued another photograph of him, this time apparently manacled to a metal bed or platform, with a second statement threatening to send to the U.S. embassy in Beirut severed parts of the CIA man's body, to convince Washington and Kuwait of the seriousness of their demands.

The White House in turn issued a statement of its own deploring the threat as bestial, insisting that any such act would be treated as common criminality to be prosecuted in any country in the world and called upon civilized governments to impose their combined efforts to resolve the situation. In an unprecedented demonstration of cooperation between Mikhail Gorbachev and Ronald Reagan, Moscow published a condemnation of hostage taking and promised to liaise with Western governments to bring about its cessation.

Janet was inundated by fresh press inquiries, invitations to television appearances and offers, one as high as $10,000, to write her own account of her romance with John Sheridan and the pressure to which she felt subjected by the kidnap. A talk-show agency in Atlanta asked to represent her, suggesting a country-wide lecture tour at $5,000 an address with an assurance of a minimum of ten lec-

tures. Senator Blackstone tried to persuade her to appear with him
on a televised evangelical church service when he intended asking
watching worshippers to link hands across the entire United States in
a silent vigil for the safe release of John Sehridan. Janet refused them
all, sticking to the agreement she had made with Willsher, although
she believed that continued publicity would have maintained the
U.S. public concern she regarded as necessary. She did, however,
insist upon another personal meeting, and Willsher set it up at the
Franklin Park office block.

The day before the appointment the university authorities gratefully agreed to her taking an unspecified leave of absence. After
being besieged for so long in her apartment, Janet sneaked out the
basement garbage entrance to hide in Harriet's Georgetown house.

The next day, with Willsher, Janet carefully enumerated all approaches, wanting to impress upon the CIA officer that she was
observing her side of the pact. Willsher said: "I think you've been
very wise."

"I don't, particularly," said Janet. "I made a deal and I've kept to
it. So what have you got to offer in return?"

"You wouldn't believe the background pressure that's being imposed," said Willsher.

"I won't, unless it's spelled out to me in detail," agreed Janet,
relentlessly.

The neat, precise man coughed. "It's unheard of for Moscow to
come out, like they did. It means that between us there isn't an Arab
government, pro-East or pro-West, that isn't involved."

"Doing what?" persisted Janet.

"We've positive assurances from Syria of the cooperation of their
troops on the ground and their intelligence service actively to try to
find him," Willsher said. "In addition, the President has been personally assured by Israel that the Mossad are pulling out all the
stops."

"You haven't mentioned Iran," reminded Janet, pointedly. "And
the only lead the Islamic Jihad and the Fundamentalists follow
comes from Teheran and the ayatollahs."

"Who would you say has closest links?"

Janet considered the question and said: "France."

Willsher smiled. "Another President to President promise, from
Paris. In adddition the British have made available to us all their
electronic eavesdropping facilities on Cyprus and we're flying overhead intercepts the length and breadth of the Lebanon, from the

NATO bases in Turkey. A fortnight ago NSA shifted one of its Mediterranean satellites and put it in permanent geo-stationary orbit directly over Beirut. No one speaks on the telephone or the radio without us hearing what's said: we can count the bricks in the walls."

"All very impressive," said Janet.

"I'm glad you think so," said Willsher, misunderatanding.

"So what's it achieved?"

"Ms. Stone," said Willsher, gently. "Some hostages have been held in the Lebanon for years."

"Seventeen hostages," enumerated Janet, just as controlled. "And if we're going to go on quoting statistics, seven more have been tortured and killed. All of which frightens the hell out of me because I don't want John Sheridan achieving some kidnap endurance record or being tortured or dismembered or killed."

"Tell me!" demanded Willsher, holding his hands out towards her. "Tell me what else or what more you'd have us do! Tell me something we haven't thought of!"

"You know why no other Russians have been kidnapped, after October, 1985?"

"Yes I do, Ms. Stone," Willsher responded at once. "I know the KGB sent in hit squads and I know that fifteen Shia fanatics were killed as a warning to leave Soviet personnel alone. But I also know that one of the four Russians kidnapped in October, 1985, was murdered before the rescue squads got to him."

"There must be some way you can force the Kuwaitis to give in!" pleaded Janet, desperately.

"We can't," said the CIA officer. "We know we can't because we've tried that, too."

That night, in Harriet's Georgetown house where she'd first met John Sheridan, Janet drank more than she normally did, agreeing to brandy after the wine, but the idea, when it came, was in no way a drunken one, although that was Harriet's immediate thought.

When she belatedly realized that Janet was quite serious, Harriet said: "That's absurd: absolutely absurd."

"Why?"

"Jesus Christ, darling! For every reason!"

"I'm going to do it," said Janet, feeling positively excited.

"What if John dies?"

Janet gazed for several moments across the dinner table at her friend and then said: "That's almost inevitable, the way it's being handled so far. Which is what I'm trying to prevent. The last time there wasn't anything I could even try to do to prevent the inevitable, remember?"

"Darling!" exclaimed her mother, when Janet telephoned five minutes later. "It would be wonderful to have you home!"

"Not for long, Mother," warned Janet. "Not for long."

·11·

I t was an overnight flight from America, landing in London early in the morning. Janet had been unable to sleep at all and arrived feeling unwashed and gritty-eyed. It was not until she got through Immigration and was waiting by the carousel for her luggage that Janet remembered the original plan: to be here with John, for the wedding. She half turned, as if expecting him to be by her side, an unthinking reaction of tiredness. She blinked, feeling stupid, relieved that her bag came up almost at once so she could grab it and move away.

Her parents were waiting right by the exit, behind the barrier, and the moment Janet emerged her mother waved to attract attention. The woman hugged her and released her and hugged her again while her father waited patiently for his turn and just hugged her and kissed her once when it came.

From the first kiss her mother began a non-stop jabber of questions without ever waiting for answers and over the woman's head her father smiled and Janet smiled back. Janet thought her mother twittered and decided the word was apposite: she was a thin, small-boned woman with jerky movements, like a twittering bird. Her father was a complete contrast, a quiet, unemotional man who she

doubted had ever done anything or said anything without considering it first. From their time on postings together Janet always
thought of him as someone in black because he really had worn a
kind of uniform, dark subdued suits when it had not been striped
trousers with black formal jacket. Now the suit was a retired country
tweed but the sharp trouser crease and the waistcoat still gave a
vague formality to it. He seemed fuller in the face than Janet remembered from her last visit, but it was his hair that registered with
her most. Although he had to be twenty-five years older than John,
her father's hair was still almost completely black: from those awful
pictures that remained so vivid in her mind Janet decided it was John
who could be this man's father rather than the other way around.

Responding minimally to her mother's back-seat chatter Janet
agreed that she was tired and that it was nice to be back and that it
had been a reasonable flight—although already she could scarcely
recall it—and that it was awful what had happened to John and that
she was managing to cope and that Harriet had been wonderful and
that everyone else had been wonderful, too. Her mother proudly
announced she had kept a scrapbook of all the newspaper stories and
features, knowing Janet would want one. Janet, who considered it
the last thing she wanted, thanked the other woman and said it was a
kind thought.

Her father picked the orbital motorway and as they drove south he
looked sideways across the car and said: "You all right?"

"I don't know, not really. I suppose so."

"Was the pressure bad in Washington?"

"Not after I moved in with Harriet."

"We had the press camped at the bottom of the lane for a week."

"I'm sorry," said Janet, not sure what she was apologizing for.

"They wanted photographs of you when you were a child," intruded her mother from the back seat. "I let them have that one of
you at the Necropolis of Thebes, on a camel."

She'd been terrified and it had shown, Janet remembered. She
said: "I don't mind, whatever you did."

"One or two papers have kept in touch, but we haven't said anything about your coming home," assured her father.

"I'm glad you haven't."

"I'm sure everything is going to work out all right," said her
mother.

Janet was surprised it had taken so long: it had usually been her

mother's second or third remark in every conversation since the kidnap. She said she hoped so, wanting her mother to stop talking. It
was a gray, pressed-down day with the clouds low against the beginning of the Sussex hills. An uncertain mist kept the windows damp
and the tires sounded sticky on the road beneath them. The motorway was jammed, far more crowded than the Washington Beltway,
and dirt sprayed up from the stream of cars ahead of them. The
traffic did not improve when they left the motorway to head further
south, into Sussex, on a lesser-used road. Although it was not cold
inside the car Janet shivered and guessed it was another reaction to
her tiredness.

Her parents lived in a hamlet just outside Cuckfield and it was still
only midmorning when they arrived. Her father carried her case and
her mother ran a bath and turned down her bed. When she went
into the bedroom Janet was sorry for the impatience she appeared
constantly to feel towards the woman. It was, she acknowledged,
quite unfair: her mother was doing her best, in her way, to help and
to be supportive. Janet further acknowledged that impatience had
been her predominant feeling about everything and towards everybody since John had been taken hostage. And that it wasn't, either, a
constructive or useful attitude, whatever that might be.

Janet wanted to sleep and tried hard to do so but it was not the
proper sort of rest, more a submission to exhaustion. She was suspended in a conscious sort of a dream, one she knew to be a dream,
from which she would awaken: mental images of John Sheridan and
William Buckley kept being confused and she could recall whole
tracts of commentary from television and newspaper coverage.
Willsher featured prominently although not in the Franklin Park
office but in the sort of lecture hall she used at the university, and he
was at the podium in the manner of an instructor, admonishing her
for not listening or understanding and making mistakes through lack
of concentration.

When she did awake Janet lay in bed, although not balled up as
she had when Hank died, but fully outstretched and reflective, with
her hands cupped behind her head. So what the hell did she imagine she was doing by coming here and intending to go on, as she did
intend to go on! What *could* she do that wasn't already being done,
with more expertise and more resources than she could ever have?
Unanswerable questions. So she stopped trying to answer them.
Janet accepted that a lot of the rationale—if rationale were the right

word—lay in her response to Harriet, that night of the decision in
the Georgetown house. She had felt—and still felt—guilt at not
being able to do anything to combat Hank's cancer. She knew it to
be an illogical—even absurd—feeling because she wasn't a doctor
or a surgeon or a specialist and so there was nothing she could have
done, during those last few months. But it still remained an impression that she could not lose: would never lose. She was determined
that she would not feel guilty about John. Now there was something
she believed she could do, some physical movement it was possible
for her to make. Was that all it would be, just moving around to give
herself the impression of some sort of useful activity? Janet closed
her mind against the inrush of questions: she was going to *do*, not
think.

Janet got up in the late afternoon and agreed to tea she didn't want
and looked at the cuttings book her mother had assembled. She was
surprised at the British media coverage engendered by the kidnap
and hoped it would help. She wished her mother hadn't given away
the photograph of herself on a camel.

It was not until the early evening, when her mother was busying
herself over supper, that Janet was alone with her father. It was he
who initiated the conversation.

He poured drinks—sherry for her and whisky for himself—and as
he handed the glass to her said: "What does 'not for long' mean?"

"I'm sorry?" Janet frowned, momentarily not remembering.

"That's what your mother said you told her on the telephone: that
you were coming home but not for long."

Janet sipped her drink, unsure how to say it and then decided
there was only one way. "I'm going there," she announced.

Now it was her father's turn momentarily not to understand.
"Going where?"

"Beirut."

For a long time her father stared across the room at her, unmoving, his face expressionless, and when he responded his voice, predictably, was just as controlled. He said: "That's ridiculous: you
wouldn't even get a visa."

"Cyprus then," insisted Janet. "Since the war there's been as
much Lebanese activity there as in Beirut anyway."

"To do what?" asked the man.

"A bloody sight more than is being done at the moment to find
John!"

Her father shook his head, still talking evenly. "It's a fantasy, darling. There's nothing you *can* do."

"I can, if you'll help me!"

"Me?"

"You've still got friends in the Foreign Office. And in the area."

He shrugged. "A few, I suppose."

"Introduce me," demanded Janet. "Personally in London: by letter where you can in the Middle East."

"For *what!*" repeated the man.

"They could make inquiries, couldn't they? Isn't that how it was done, in the embassies where you served: questions from London relayed to you and in turn taken up with the authorities?"

"There isn't any authority in the Lebanon any more: not the sort of authority you're talking about," argued her father. "You should know that better than most!"

"There is still diplomatic representation in Beirut, nominal though it might be," Janet argued back. "John's not the only person being held: there must be some contact with these groups! *Some* links!"

"Darling," said the man, gently. "Don't you think the Americans will have explored every possibility like that?"

"I think they're just sitting around, doing bugger all."

Her father hesitated, as if he were surprised at her swearing. He said: "That isn't true: can't be true. And you know it."

"*I* want to do something!"

"OK," he said, a diplomat whose entire career had involved patient argument and inevitable compromise. "What happens if people I know do have contacts with friends in Beirut? And those friends have the sort of links you think must exist? And through the chain you do get some sort of information about John? What then?"

Now it was Janet who hesitated, not having thought that far ahead. "Tell the Americans," she said. She indicated the scrapbook that lay on the settee between them and went on: "Tell them and let them know that if they don't try to do something to get him out I'll ask why, through the newspapers."

"Get into a public slanging match, you mean?"

"If that's what it takes."

"Haven't you thought of an inherent danger?"

"I don't care what happens to me," said Janet, thoughtlessly.

"I wasn't thinking about you at that moment," said her father, still gentle. "I was thinking of what could happen to John if some suggestion were given as to his whereabouts and demands made that America do something to get him out. Do you imagine whoever's got him would just sit around and wait for it to happen?"

Janet bit her lip, uncomfortably. "Threaten," she said, retreating. "Just threaten to go to the newspapers unless they did something."

"As you mentioned it," said the man. "What about you?"

"I said I didn't care."

"That's stupid, which is something else you know," her father said, still not raising his voice. "And again you've misunderstood. Let's not think of physical danger for a moment, although of course we should. You're a woman. What sort of chance do you really think a woman—any woman—would stand of achieving anything in any sort of Middle East situation?"

"I know the area and I know the language and I know the dangers and the likely difficulties," insisted Janet.

"You're still a woman."

"A very determined one."

He shook his head, more in sadness than refusal. "I do care," he said. "I care and I feel sorry—desperately sorry—for what's happened. Your mother and I liked John enormously and hoped, really hoped, that you were going to get a second chance. But this isn't the way, darling. Leave it to the people who know what they're doing: you really could do more harm—harm to John, I mean—than good by trying to get involved like this."

Janet's eyes clouded with anger. "You know what you've just done!" she said. "You've just talked of John in the past tense, like he's already dead and there's no possibility of our ever marrying: that I've lost the second chance. And you've lectured me like Willsher, the CIA man. Patronized me and patted me on the head and told me to go home and be a good girl and stop making a nuisance of myself. I haven't had to wait until I got to the Middle East to be treated like a second-class person. From you, of all people, I didn't expect that: neither attitude!"

Her father went to the drinks tray and refilled his glass, without inviting her to have another. Still standing by it, he said: "I'm sorry. I did not intend to talk of John as if he were dead. I didn't intend to patronize, either."

"I *will* go," insisted Janet. "Whether you help me or not, I will go."

"Yes," accepted her father, shortly. "You will, won't you?"

"So?"

"So what?"

"Do I get help or do I get patronized?"

"Do you really have to ask a question like that?"

"After tonight I'm not sure."

"What's this sort of conversation going to achieve?"

Janet shrugged, regretting the outburst. "I'm fed up, Daddy: so fed up! I love John and I really do think of it as a second chance and I want it so very much. So I'm fed up being told to go away: being told that everyone else knows better than me. That I haven't the right to know anything, even!"

Her father moved from where he stood, coming to her and pulling her to him. "You know I'll do everything I can."

Janet twisted, to look up at him. "I'm sorry," she said.

He shook his head, dismissing her apology. "Don't regard it as anything more than it is," he cautioned. "I don't know yet whether anyone I know personally is in any position to help. Or if they will, if they are."

"It's good just to have someone on my side," she said.

"I'll always be that," her father said.

Janet was further encouraged the following day, when her father emerged from his study after an entire morning's telephoning, to announce that he had located two old diplomatic acquaintances, one in London, the other working out of the British embassy in Nicosia.

"Cyprus!" exclaimed Janet.

"It isn't significant," warned her father. "We don't know yet if he'll be prepared to do anything."

"It's wonderful!" insisted Janet, refusing to be disheartened.

Depression was, however, a feeling that was quick to come. Her father's friend in London was named McDermott, and he'd served under her father at the British embassy in Cairo. They met not at Whitehall but over lunch at Lockett's, nearby. He was a tall, thin, pink-cheeked man with the habit of looking reprovingly, like some schoolmaster, over half-rimmed spectacles. The frames had grooved the bridge of his nose and the sides of his head, where his hair was white. He said he remembered Janet from her Cairo visits during school vacations and she smiled, unable to remember him, and agreed that Egypt had been a fascinating country. He'd read of Sheridan's kidnap but had not realized her association, because she had been referred to in all the newspaper stories by her previously married name. He was sorry. He said the situation in the Lebanon appeared, regrettably, quite intractable and ordered gulls' eggs, with lemon sole to follow.

McDermott seemed genuinely surprised at the request for assistance, which her father introduced into the conversation and which Janet at once took up and expanded upon, elaborating the early, first-night debate with her father.

When she finished McDermott said at once and again apparently genuinely: "Why are you asking me to do this?"

"I would have thought that was obvious," said Janet.

McDermott put down his knife and fork, not immediately looking up, assembling his words. When he did speak, it was to her father rather than to Janet, and Janet thought again that she didn't have to wait until the Middle East to encounter the dismissive relegation of her sex.

"You should know better than to ask me!" said McDermott. "John Sheridan is a foreign national, an American. What right has the Foreign Office to interfere!"

The same rejection, only reversed, that she'd encountered on her first approaches to the State Department and the CIA, remembered Janet: it was like being on a roundabout with a forwards-and-backwards control, but always in the same direction.

"We were thinking of it more as a personal favor," said her father. "A discreet sort of inquiry."

"There is no such thing in the Lebanese hostage situation," lectured McDermott. "We've had the special envoy of the Archbishop of Canterbury held for over a year! A British television journalist for two. How on earth can I get involved, risk tangling up whatever negotiation might be going on to gain the freedom of Britons, by intruding into the affairs of another country? It's unthinkable!"

"It wasn't our intention to embarrass you," said Janet's father, diplomat soothing diplomat.

McDermott retrieved his knife and fork. "This is a social occasion," he said. "Nothing official. So there is no embarrassment." He looked at last to Janet. "Please don't think I'm not sympathetic. I am. I recognize very well the predicament in which you find yourself: that you're in a kind of limbo. But there is nothing I can do, either officially or unofficially."

"You've made that very clear," said Janet, tightly.

"Can I give you some advice?" asked the man.

"Of course," said Janet, knowing he would whether she agreed or not.

"Leave it to the experts who know what they are doing," smiled McDermott.

"Like your experts know what they are doing, with an Arch-bishop's enjoy still held after one year! And a TV journalist for two!" snapped Janet.

Red spots of irritation pricked out on McDermott's face, but his voice was completely even when he spoke. He said: "I understand your distress. I wish there were something I could do. I really do."

What did it take to get men like McDermott and her father to lose control, Janet wondered. Perhaps their lives were too well cocooned for the risk ever to arise. Striving for politeness, Janet said: "Thank you, for agreeing to meet me at least."

McDermott's attention was back to the other man. "Always a plea-sure to meet old and respected friends," he said. "The food here is always very good, don't you think?"

"Very good," echoed her father.

It was an absurd, esoteric game with no written rules, thought Janet, the exasperation burning through her. She wondered what John thought of the food he was getting, in whatever shithole he was tethered.

"I warned you," her father said as they traveled back to Sussex.

"You warned me," agreed Janet. An additional avenue had oc-curred to her, so perhaps the lunch had not been a complete waste of time.

"Still want to go on?"

Janet turned sideways in the passenger seat, to look directly at the man. "I want you to understand something," she said, trying to match his unemotional tone of voice. "I shall go on until one of two things happens. Until John is freed and we're able to marry. Or until I go to the funeral of someone whose body is said to be his."

Her father chanced looking briefly away from the road, towards her. "I'll write the letter tonight for you to take to Cyprus."

"I want to try something else, first," said Janet. "Something I'll arrange myself."

It took two days for Janet to fix an interview at Lambeth Palace. The priest, named Davidson, was younger than she had expected for a member of the personal staff of the Archbishop, a scrub-faced, spike-haired, eager man whose solicitousness showed in that he'd read all the cuttings concerning John Sheridan by the time they met. He said he was sorry, as everyone seemed to do, and Janet thanked him. When Janet asked directly, he replied he couldn't confirm or deny that any secret negotiations were taking place to free their envoy, Terry Waite, and Janet heard the CIA statement echo in her mind. Were negotiations to take place, asked Janet, could they be extended to include John? When the priest began to reiterate that he couldn't confirm or deny, Janet interrupted to say that she understood, but could he record her request anyway? Davidson promised he would but repeated again that he knew nothing about any such negotiations. In an obvious attempt to offer some comfort, the priest added that they had an assurance from the British government that every possible pressure was being exerted upon every other government who might be able to assist, not just for information about their own emissary and the British journalist but all other foreign nationals, as well. At the end of the interview Davidson suggested they pray together and Janet did, feeling self-conscious, because she had never been able to believe and therefore to pray, not even when Hank was dying.

"A wasted journey?" her father asked that night.

"I think he was sincere: that he would try to include John's name if there were any negotiations," said Janet. It had become a habit since her return from America for them to have pre-dinner drinks in his study, while her mother supervised in the kitchen.

"What now?"

"Because the airline office was convenient, in London, I bought a ticket to Cyprus."

"When?"

"The day after tomorrow."

Her father nodded. "I know it's a fatuous thing to say, but be careful."

"I will be: as careful as I can."

"I still wish you wouldn't go."

"Don't forget what I said in the car."

"I'm hardly likely to."

"I've got another favor."

"What?"

"I've an inheritance, right?"

Her father frowned across the rim of his whisky glass, nodding. "Yes."

"Can I have it now?"

He smiled, sadly. "Very biblical," he said.

"The parable of the Prodigal Son had a happy ending, remember?" Turning the word, she added: "And I don't intend being prodigal, believe me!"

"Don't you think the Americans have tried bribery? Or even straightforward ranson?" he said. "And offered far more money than we're likely to be able to afford?"

"We've had this sort of conversation before," said Janet. "I don't intend walking around with a satchel full of money. I just want to have some available, if it's necessary."

Her father gestured around the room, encompassing the house. "This is part of your inheritance, of course. All I could raise in cash at such short notice would be about £30,000."

It was more than Janet had expected. She said: "I love you very much," and then added, hurriedly, "I love both of you very much."

"I'll want to know where you are, all the time. And for us to be in regular touch."

"Of course."

He indicated the letter of introduction that lay on his study table and said: "And go beyond that. Register properly at the embassy, so that there is proof of your being on the island. I want an instant and official reaction if you get into any sort of difficulty."

"I promise."

Her mother's unremitting chatter had dried up, from the moment of her being told days before of Janet's intention to go to Cyprus and she became further subdued that night at dinner when Janet disclosed the airline booking. Everyone made an effort to find something else to talk about, and failed, so the evening became strained and clumsy and Janet excused herself early, pleading the need to get some rest before the impending flight.

The couple remained at the table and Janet's mother accepted brandy, which she rarely did.

"It's madness," she protested.

"I know," he agreed.

"She could get hurt."

"Yes."

"So you must stop her! Forbid her to go!"

"That wouldn't work. Not a direct confrontation."

"There must be something you can do!"

"I hope so," said Janet's father.

·12·

J anet had forgotten the Mediterranean heat of the near Middle East, just as, she was soon to realize, she had forgotten much else about an area in which she was supposed to be an expert. The heat engulfed her like oven breath as soon as she disembarked at Larnaca, dry and quite unlike the damp mugginess of summer Washington: by the time she reclaimed her luggage she was sweatingly wet. There was no air conditioning in the Mercedes taxi, so she traveled with the rear window fully down, for whatever breeze she could get. Against the dashboard the driver had a picture of a man in an elaborate frame made even more ornate by a bouquet of dyed straws and dried flowers in a small vase, making it into some sort of shrine, and Janet realized she had not carried a photograph of John with her. She wasn't sorry. She didn't need a reminder. Or a shrine: definitely not a shrine. The route inland from the airport, into Nicosia, took her near Larnaca marina and the harbor beyond and there were signs, faded and unrepaired, advertising ferries to Beirut. She strained to see the direction they indicated but the ochre and white buildings were jammed too close together, blocking her view.

The boundary of the town was quite abrupt, huddled-together

houses giving way to rolling, dun-colored scrubland. They began passing mules and donkeys almost completely obscured by their loads, cloth-wrapped bundles on legs, and the roadside was dotted with stick-framed lean-to shelters against the sun from which tiny children yelled and waved for them to stop to buy oranges or lemons or melons or carved souvenirs. Orienting herself, Janet looked south. The Troodos Mountains were too far away from her to make out but she imagined a rise in the scrubland, where it climbed towards them. The British had made their listening facilities on the island available in the hope of hearing some telephone or radio communication about John, she remembered from conversation with Willsher. Troodos was the highest point of the island and she supposed that was where the technology would be sited. Would anything have been heard? She doubted the CIA man would have told her, if it had.

The pale blue berets of the United Nations peacekeeping force were Janet's first physical reminder of the haphazard partition of the island after the Turkish invasion of 1974, and as they entered Nicosia she passed another indication, the Turkish-held enclave wired off and controlled by guard posts.

"Gangsters," said the driver, as they skirted the Turkish pocket.

Janet did not reply; she had gangsters of her own to worry about. She chose the Churchill Hotel, on Achaeans Street, not for its four-star luxury but because it was a place where telephones would be guaranteed to work. They did. She was connected without any delay to her father in England, to give him her address and room number and to assure him she was all right. He asked if she had contacted the British embassy yet and Janet said he'd been her first call, because that was the promise she'd made. He told her to be careful, which Janet expected, and she assured him she would be.

William Partington had served under her father in the same position as the unhelpful McDermott, although in Amman, not Cairo. He was not available when Janet called but a secretary promised he would be returning after lunch. Janet used the time to deposit her father's bank draft for £30,000 at a branch of Barclays International within walking distance of the hotel, although by the time she reached the bank she was bathed in perspiration again. The size of the transfer intimidated the counter clerk, who insisted upon her being greeted by an assistant manager. Janet patiently endured the ritual, arranging for the money to be held on deposit and maintained in a sterling account. The man presented her with a business

card and asked that she deal personally with him and Janet agreed
that she would.

She reached Partington on the second call. The attaché remembered her father at once and said he was delighted to hear from her,
and why didn't she come for supper with him and his wife the following evening? Janet said she wanted a more formal meeting, although dinner would be fine later. There was a pause from the other
end of the line and Partington said he was not particularly busy and
would she like to come to the embassy that afternoon. Janet said she
would, very much.

Janet showered and changed and managed to get an air-conditioned taxi to Alexander Pallis Street. She identified herself to the
reception clerk, and at once Partington hurried from the rear of the
building.

Partington was a contrast to her father's acquaintance McDermott, just as tall but a bluff, bulging man, face reddened beneath
the tan by the blood pressure of good living, a crumpled lightweight
suit strained by the effort of containing him all. He shook her hand
and said welcome and, still holding it, led her into the back of the
building where at once, gratefully, Janet felt the chill of better air
conditioning than in the outer vestibule.

"You in a spot of bother?" demanded the man.

"Something like that," agreed Janet, offering the man the letter of
introduction from her father.

Partington read the letter carefully, tapping a fingernail against his
teeth as he did so: from the movement of his head, Janet realized the
man was going through it twice.

At last Partington looked up, subdued now, and said: "I see."

"Please!" said Janet at once."Don't say you're sorry. Everyone
does."

"Then I won't." He gestured to the paper he had placed before
him on the desk. "Your father asks me to help, in any way I can.
Which of course I would if I could. But I don't see how. We're no
way involved. We can't be."

Remembering her reflection about the Troodos Mountains on her
way into Nicosia that morning Janet said: "I know that you're making British listening facilities here available to the CIA."

Partington sucked in his breath, shaking his head as he did so.
"Not my province, Mrs. Stone. That's an intelligence matter, quite
separate. I wouldn't know anything about that: wouldn't want to
know."

Janet felt the familiar rise of exasperation and tried to curb it. She said: "This close to the Lebanon there must be links, between the British presence there and you, here?"

"Some," Partington agreed, doubtfully.

"Before I left London I went to Lambeth Palace," Janet said. She hesitated, deciding upon an exaggeration, and went on: "I talked there with a member of the Archbishop's staff, about negotiations to free the Britons being held. Your people in Beirut must know of them, hear things about other hostages."

Partington moved his head again. "Something else about which I have no knowledge: you must believe me, Mrs. Stone. If there are any contacts, any negotiations, they'd be restricted to the smallest group of people. They'd have to be, wouldn't they?"

Janet sighed, wishing she could confront the logic. She said: "What about here, in Cyprus?"

"I don't understand the question."

"There's been a mass exodus from Beirut to this island," said Janet. "There must be a lot of information, passing back and forth. People I could talk to."

Partington leaned forward across the desk, his face serious. "There has been a mass exodus," he agreed. "I've heard areas of Nicosia and Larnaca likened to Berlin, in 1945, and it's a pretty good description. I mean there are people here in Cyprus doing what people always do, in a war situation. Profiting by it. We don't get involved and neither should you. It's crooked and it's dangerous and it won't do anything to help your fiancé."

"What areas?" demanded Janet. "What people?"

"Your father was a senior diplomatic officer to me in Jordan: someone I like and whom I consider a friend," said Partington. "I would be abusing that friendship by getting you involved with such people, such places."

"My father has asked you to help!" said Janet, jabbing her finger at the letter between them.

"That wouldn't be helping," Partington said. "It would be doing the reverse, exposing you to pointless danger. That I won't do."

Despite her efforts at control, Janet could not prevent the heat of frustration burning through her. This man was her only contact, her only hope, she realized, desperately. "There must be something!" she pleaded. Then, hurriedly, she added: "And don't advise me to leave it to people who know what they're doing: everyone tells me to do that, too."

"Mrs. Stone," said Partington, in a tone reminiscent of that frustrating lunch at Lockett's. "I know it's difficult: I can understand, I'd like to think, something of what you are going through. But what other advice can there be? Look at the situation objectively. What—possibly, sensibly—can you do? You're quite alone. You haven't any resources. You've no official backing . . ."

". . . and I'm a woman," cut off Janet.

Partington hesitated and then said: "And yes, you're a woman. There's no point or purpose in our getting into a sexist or women's liberation discussion about it, but the simple fact is that in this situation and in this area of the world, as a woman you're at a disadvantage . . ." He paused again but continued: "If it's any satisfaction—and I can't imagine that it will be—a man by himself, without any resources and with no official backing, would hardly be in an improved position anyway."

"Helpless, you mean!"

Partington considered the question. "Yes, I suppose that's exactly what I mean. Helpless."

Which was precisely how she felt, Janet realized, angry at herself because she thought of it as giving way. It had been another roundabout ride, backwards and forwards in the same circle, apparently moving but getting nowhere. Partington, as unresponsive as he was, remained her only contact, she thought again. She said: "It was kind of you, seeing me as you have."

"I wish, I really do wish, that there had been something more positive I could have done," said Partington. "I know you asked me not to say it, but I'm very sorry for what's happened."

"I'd like to accept your invitation," said Janet.

Partington's face creased in confusion, and then he remembered and said: "Oh yes."

"Is tomorrow night still convenient, or would you like to call, to confirm?"

"Maybe I should call, to confirm," the man said.

"I'm at the Churchill," Janet said. "And my father particularly asked me officially to register here, at the embassy."

"You intend staying, then?"

"Yes."

"Why?" the diplomat asked, just as direct.

"I'm near to where John is," ad-libbed Janet. Impulsively she added: "And I have been getting some help and guidance from the Americans. They've an embassy here, haven't they?"

Partington sat regarding her steadily for several moments before he said: "I'll see to it that you are officially registered. Will the Churchill be your permanent address here?"

"I think so."

"For how long?"

"I'm not sure," Janet said, matching his stare.

"Please don't do anything foolish, Mrs. Stone."

"I won't."

"This isn't fiction, you know? Not something in a novel you read by the pool or see in a cinema. This is reality."

Now it was Janet who came forward, to stress her seriousness. "Now you must believe me, Mr. Partington. I don't need reminding just how real it is having someone I love and hope to marry chained up as a hostage, like some animal."

Again, for several moments, there was a silence between them. Then Partington said: "I'll call, about tomorrow."

"You're very kind," said Janet, grateful at least that she had the tenuous link into the embassy although she was unsure after this encounter how much practical advantage it would give.

Partington accompanied her back to the entrance and waited with her until the summoned taxi—air-conditioned again—arrived to take her back to Achaeans Street. Janet slumped dejected in the back of the vehicle, going over in her mind the circular conversation she'd had with the man. Increasingly one word echoed in her mind, like another word that reverberated in her mind that night she'd met John for the first time, at Harriet's Georgetown party. Helpless. It came like a drumbeat, helpless, helpless, helpless, and then a second word intruded, making the connection. Helpless-woman, help-less-woman. Janet screwed her hands tight, into a fist, in renewed frustration. Suddenly, like an additional taunt, came the first snatch of a menstrual cramp and she felt even more frustrated.

She smiled her thanks to the clerk at the Churchill who handed her the room key and went automatically to the elevator, oblivious to her surroundings, punching her floor number automatically. She *was* helpless, Janet accepted. It was pointless—absurd—to try to think otherwise. Partington had been right, accusing her of romanticism. The whole episode was some personal fantasy, Superwoman against the Kidnappers, based on nothing more than the flimsy hope, God how flimsy, that she might have got some assistance from her father's former colleagues. But she hadn't, Janet recognized, forcing the objectivity. And now she didn't know—didn't have a clue—what to do next. There was a fresh wash of dejection and another menstrual taunt.

In her room Janet discarded the key on the bed and slumped into the only easy chair, gazing sightlessly at the slatted windows. Could she ask her father to intervene? Persuade him to call Partington from England to try to pressure the man into offering more? More of what? Where was the logic in imagining Partington had any more to offer anyway? Partington was a *bona fide* First Secretary, head of Chancery, not an embassy-concealed intelligence officer. Janet accepted that, as such, Partington would be shielded from contact with the legation's intelligence emplacement, a barrier against possible diplomatic embarrassment if any covert activity in a host country became public knowledge. What about the Lebanese enclaves the man had acknowledged to exist on the island? There was little pressure she could expect her father to bring in having them identified, Janet realized, in further defeat. Her father would side with Partington upon the possible dangers rather than trying to help her learn where such places were.

So unexpected was it that Janet jumped at the knock at her door, remaining still for several seconds so that the summons came again, louder the second time.

Her surprise increased at the sight of two policemen, their uniform English-style: she did not know how to designate rank but from the epaulet markings one appeared to be of high rank.

"Mrs. Stone?" enquired the senior officer.

"Yes," she said.

"Mrs. Janet Stone?"

"Yes."

"Detective Chief Inspector Zarpas," the man said.

Very high rank, thought Janet, through her bewilderment at their presence.

Zarpas nodded sideways. "Sergeant Kashianis."

"What do you want?" Janet asked.

"To talk," Zarpas said. "We'd like to come in."

Janet hesitated, confused and unsure. "What for?" she said.

"To talk," Zarpas repeated.

"What about?" Janet was refusing to move back from the door.

"Have you something to hide, Mrs. Stone?"

"I don't know what you mean."

"I'll explain, if you let us in."

Careful, she remembered; her father had warned her to be careful. She said: "What proof of identity do you have?"

Zarpas, a sallow-skinned man whose wilting moustache made his long face appear even more mournful, looked down at his uniform and then, sighing, extracted a warrant card from the left-hand breast pocket of his tunic and offered it to her. Janet stared uncomprehendingly at the Greek, but then saw that beneath his photograph the man was identified in English, by rank.

Still unsure, Janet stepped back, opening the door further. Inside the room both men remained standing. Janet regained the easy chair, hoping it put her in the most commanding position in the room, although not knowing why she needed it. Zarpas perched on the dressing table stool. The sergeant looked at the bed and apparently decided against it, remaining upright. He took a small pad from one pocket and a pen from another. He examined the tip intently, as if it were something he had not seen before.

"Why are you here on the island, Mrs. Stone?" demanded Zarpas, at once.

"What right have you to come to my room and ask me questions?" Janet said.

"The right of Cyprus law," Zarpas said easily. "So why are you here, on the island?"

Janet did not immediately reply, wanting the right answer. "Business," she replied, at last.

"Ah!" Zarpas exclaimed, as if the reply were important. He looked sideways at the sergeant. Kashianis was writing very quickly. Zarpas said: "What sort of business?"

"A friend of mine is missing in the Lebanon."

Again Zarpas looked at the sergeant, appearing to think the reply important, and said: "What is the name of this friend?"

There was no reason why she should not give it, she decided. "John Sheridan."

"Missing in the Bekaa, perhaps?"

"The what!" said Janet. What the hell was this stupidity all about!

"That's where the hashish comes from," Zarpas said. "But then you'd know that, wouldn't you?"

Janet shook her head, holding her hands briefly out towards the two men. "I haven't got the remotest idea what you're talking about. Why you're here. This conversation is completely unintelligible to me."

"Is it, Mrs. Stone?" Zarpas's disbelief was obvious. "Isn't the £30,000 with which you earlier today opened a deposit account for the purpose of buying drugs?"

"How . . . !" Janet began indignantly, but then laughed. "So that's what this is all about!" she said, relieved at last.

"You didn't answer my question."

Still smiling and shaking her head again, Janet said: "No, it is not to buy drugs!"

"What then?"

"Doesn't the name John Sheridan mean anything to you?"

For the first time Zarpas faltered. "No," he said.

"Think!" said Janet. "John Sheridan. An American."

The look to the sergeant this time was for assistance. Kashianis kept his head down over his notebook. "No," Zarpas had to concede again.

With forced patience Janet said: "He is the most recent American to be kidnapped in Beirut. Check with the U.S. embassy here in Beirut if you like."

"This still does not explain the £30,000. Or your presence here," refused Zarpas, stubbornly.

"I am John Sheridan's fiancée," said Janet. "I have come here to find out what's being done to get him out."

"With £30,000!"

"There may be expenses," said Janet. She realized, discomfited, that the explanation sounded unconvincing.

"John Sheridan is an American national?"

"Yes."

"His job?" Zarpas had recovered supremacy now.

"The embassy," said Janet, awkwardly. "He worked at the American embassy in Beirut."

"Wouldn't the responsibility . . . and any expense involved . . . in freeing this man if indeed he is held hostage by one of the religious groups . . . be that of the American government?" said Zarpas.

"Yes," Janet said. The awkwardness worsened.

"So why have you arrived in Cyprus with £30,000?"

To give herself time to think, Janet said: "How *did* you learn about the deposit?"

"It is a requirement, by law, that all large deposits are automatically reported to the authorities," said Zarpas, officiously. "Cyprus does not intend to become a financial center for drug trafficking. Or a conduit, either."

"I'm not trafficking in drugs!" erupted Janet. "I've answered every question honestly!"

"Can I tell you something, Mrs. Stone?"

"What?"

"Every criminal I have ever known has sometime or other told me he is being completely honest."

The "he" isolated Janet. Why did everything have to be divided, superior male, inferior female? What could a prick do that a cunt couldn't? They had to fit together to make something complete! At once she became irritated at herself. Male to female, female to male. What the fuck—wrong word—did it matter! She sighed— and wished she hadn't—and said: "I am *not* a drug trafficker. I am a . . ." She stopped short of saying "woman." Janet picked up: ". . . a person trying to find out about another person whom she loves!"

This time the sergeant looked up, to meet his superior's gaze. Zarpas responded but came immediately back to Janet. "So you've come to Cyprus with what you believe to be sufficient money to buy information of which no one else is aware?"

"Yes!" Janet shouted in fresh indignation. "Where's the illegality in that?"

Abruptly—and disconcertingly because the sad face was not made for such an expression—Zarpas smiled. "Poor lady!" he said.

Sex again, Janet thought immediately. "Where's the illegality in that!" she repeated.

Zarpas leaned back against the dressing table and said: "On your part, none."

"What then?"

"Don't you have people—friends or family—telling you that what you're trying to do is stupid?"

"Too many!" shot back Janet.

"Then you're doubly stupid, not to listen."

"It's my money!"

"It's your life," shouted back Zarpas.

"My choice," responded Janet, just as loud.

"Very good," the policeman said, abruptly soft-voiced. "You really are very good."

"Does that mean you don't believe me?"

"It means I'm making no decision." He paused and added heavily: "Not yet."

"That sounds like a warning."

"Take it to sound how you like."

"Can you help me?" Janet demanded suddenly.

"Help you?"

"Cyprus is crowded with Lebanese since the civil war," said Janet, eagerly. "You must have sources."

Zarpas made a sad gesture with his head, not immediately replying. "Yours is a marked account, Mrs. Stone."

"What does that mean?"

"That I'll know, if there's any abrupt withdrawals. Or deposits."

"I asked you for help."

"How about advice?"

"We've already talked about that."

"Go home, Mrs. Stone. Go to wherever home is before you get hurt . . ." The policeman hesitated. "Hurt by whoever, whatever."

"If that's meant to scare me, it doesn't!" Janet said with a defiance she secretly did not feel.

"It should do, Mrs. Stone. It's meant to scare you a lot."

"What about helping me!"

"Get out of Cyprus. We don't want you here. For whatever reason you are here."

Janet was suddenly overwhelmed by a feeling she could not immediately identify. It was an impression of sagging fatigue, but it had a form, as if she were in an enclosed room from which she was trying to escape by beating against walls which would not yield but were instead closing inexorably in upon her, ever tightening. She actually straightened in her chair, physically trying to slough off the attitude. She said: "All I want is someone to help."

"Go home," the policeman repeated, stone-faced.

"If I don't!"

"This isn't a bargaining situation."

"You can't just expel me, without reasonable grounds!"

"An unexplained deposit of £30,000 in a Cyprus bank account is sufficient reason."

"I *have* explained it!"

"Not to my satisfaction."

"No," Janet said, slowly. "Not by yourself: you can't make that decision by yourself."

Again, this time just momentarily, Zarpas faltered. Recovering, he said: "Do you imagine my recommendation would not be accepted?"

"I shall appeal to my embassy," Janet said. She added: "I'm already registered there: they know I'm here."

Zarpas rose, to look down upon her. He said: "You are a very stupid woman."

Janet looked up in reply, feeling oddly superior despite their positions, but said nothing.

For several moments Zarpas waited, expectantly, but she did not speak. "I—my government—will not have you cause any embarrassment to this island."

"I do not intend causing any embarrassment to anyone," Janet said.

"Don't!" Zarpas insisted, making the warning positive. "The slightest embarrassment would be the reason to expel you, wouldn't it?"

Janet intentionally did not stand to show them from the room and was distressed as soon as they closed the door behind themselves to find that she was physically shaking, from the stress of the encounter. There was no reason, she told herself: no reason at all. She'd fought back, as strongly as the policeman had attacked: won, to a degree. Definitely no reason, then, to react like this, like a . . . She stopped short of the word, refusing to acknowledge it even in her thoughts. Sexist bastard: they were all sexist bastards. . . . As positively as she had stopped one slide of thought Janet halted another, because it had no purpose, no point. What, actually, had emerged from the meeting? It all revolved around the money: the policeman's absurd suspicion that she was somehow involved in drug trafficking. *Yours is a marked account,* she remembered. She should have carried it from England in cash and put it in the hotel's safe deposit the moment she arrived: wise after the event, Janet told herself. What about drawing it out and doing that anyway? Too late. If Zarpas were monitoring the money the worse thing imaginable would be to close it with a cash withdrawal. Trapped, she accepted: she had no alternative but to leave it where it was, until she needed it for the real purpose for which she had brought it. *If* she needed it, Janet thought, in balancing, difficult realism.

The sound at the door did not startle her this time as much as the first because she imagined it to be Zarpas, returning for some reason. The surprise came when she opened the door. It was not the policeman but a slightly built, compact man with an out-of-date crew cut, rimless glasses, a multicolored check shirt, needle cords, and brown Topsider loafers.

"Well lookee here!" the man declared. The accent, as well as the expression, was clearly American.

Janet positioned her foot as firmly behind the door as she could, wishing the room were fitted with a safety chain. "What do you want?"

"A little talk, Ms. Stone."

"It's been a busy afternoon for little talks," said Janet, with genuine weariness.

"And you've been a busy girl. Langley is real worried."

A Southerner and proud of it, guessed Janet: the sort who sang rebel songs at parties and had a special recipe for mint juleps. With sudden hopefulness, irritated at herself, Janet said: "Have you heard something?"

"Heard a lot of things, Ms. Stone. A lot of things."

Careless of any identification this time, Janet opened the door wider, smiling in anticipation, and said: "Come in! Please come in!"

The American did so as if he had the right, almost strolling. He swiveled on his heel, examining the room, and said: "Pretty, real pretty."

Passingly Janet thought the man's affectation to repeat everything was irritating. She said: "What! What is it?"

"What's what, Ms. Stone?"

"The news, about John?"

The man reached the easy chair and sat, heavily. "That's the problem," he said. "There isn't any."

A rash of dizziness made Janet reach out to the dressing table for support. Momentarily she closed her eyes against the whirl. "Please!" she said. "Please don't play word games!"

"Don't intend to, ma'am. Don't intend to."

Ma'am. And Ms., earlier. She said: "Who are you?"

"Who do you think I am?"

"I think you're someone from the American embassy here in Nicosia attached to the CIA," Janet said, recovering. "I also think you're someone who watches too much American television. *Miami Vice* a favorite of yours?"

The man's face tightened and Janet knew she'd scored and was glad. She didn't feel dizzy any more. It was anger now. Again.

"What the hell do you think you're doing here?" he demanded.

"You didn't tell me your name."

"With the sort of shit you can stir, lady! You must be joking!"

Lady, to go with ma'am and Ms. She said: "Is that what you're frightened of? The shit I can stir?"

"We're frightened for John, Ms. Stone. We're frightened that you're going to do some dumb-assed thing and get him killed. Aren't you frightened of that?"

Janet swallowed. She said: "I'm frightened of his being killed, certainly. Like I'm frightened that you're doing fuck-all to stop it happening."

"You got a lot of help and guidance in Washington," said the man. "You got told things you really shouldn't have been told. So you know that isn't true."

"I know nothing of the sort," fought back Janet, glad now he was lower than her because she enjoyed being above him: enjoyed, too, letting her anger out because it needed to go. "I got assurances and I got platitudes and it's been over a month since he got snatched, so where is he? If the CIA is all-so-fucking powerful, why hasn't John Sheridan been found and got out of Beirut?"

The American blinked under the assault, clearly off balance. "You've got to understand . . ." he started, but Janet, furious now, interrupted.

"Cut it!" she said. "Cut the crap about the difficulties and the intricacies and how it should all be left to the experts. I've heard it: I've heard it until it's running out of my ears." Repetition seemed to be contagious, she thought.

"What do you think you can achieve by coming here?" demanded the man, trying to escape sideways from the attack.

"I don't know," answered Janet honestly. "I haven't been here a day yet."

"It's John's life you're playing with."

"It's John's life *you're* playing with," Janet said. "Tell me . . . convince me by telling me of something positive you've done to get him out . . . that you've made the right contacts and that there's a chance of his being released . . . that you know where he is!"

"Lady, you're a pain in the ass."

"That's exactly what I am,"agreed Janet. "And I'm going to remain a pain in your ass and everyone else's ass until I get some fucking action!"

"Am I supposed to be impressed because you know bad words?"

The offended Southerner, Janet thought. Furiously she said: "I don't give a fuck whether you're offended or not! There's only one person I want to impress. His name's John Sheridan."

The man brought his hands lightly together, in mocking applause. "So you're going to poke around Larnaca marina and the dives of Zenon Square and Kitieus Street and find out something we don't know and show us all how to do it!"

"I'm going to do whatever it takes, however it takes to get him back," said Janet.

"In a body bag."

Janet swallowed against the threat. Hopefully she said: "What's the point in our fighting? It's not going to achieve anything."

"Nor is your being here, getting in the way."

"Help me!" said Janet, hopeful still.

The American shook his head. He said: "Langley guessed you'd do something like this, when you suddenly left Washington: that's why we set up the arrival check, here at the airport. There was just one simple message, if you did come: for me to tell you to get out and stay out. Which I've done. Regard that as help: it's all you're going to get."

Janet straightened, irritated at herself now for pleading. "So you get out!" she said. "You've delivered your message."

The man was slow in standing, not wanting the departure to appear to be on her terms. "Remember what I've said, lady: remember what I've said."

"Get out, messenger boy!"

He left the room as slowly as he'd stood, but with his face burning. Janet almost slammed the door behind him, but instead she closed it as quietly as possible. She remained with her back pressed against it, staring into the room. She was shaking again, worse than she had after the encounter with the policeman. She hadn't known what to expect but certainly she hadn't considered this, a procession of men with a procession of threats. Why not? she demanded of herself. Wasn't that how Willsher had behaved in Washington and McDermott in London and Partington, earlier that day? Not so openly or so brutally, perhaps, but there wasn't any real difference. Damn them, she thought: damn them all.

She stared at the telephone when it rang, not at first moving to answer it. When she did, she instantly recognized Partington's voice.

"I'm most awfully sorry," the diplomat said. "Tomorrow isn't as convenient as I thought it might be. Could we leave it that I'll call you again?"

"Of course," Janet agreed, actually relieved. She had Larnaca marina to visit. And the dives of Zenon Square and Kitieus Street, as well. The repetitious American hadn't been as smart as he obviously thought he was.

As she replaced the receiver Janet realized, unhappily, that her period had started. A woman, she thought, bitterly.

·13·

It was raining, the storm hurling itself against her window and making black what should have been the squinting brightness of early morning. Something else—that this was not a place of perpetual sunshine—that she had forgotten. Oddly, the awareness upset her more than the previous day's confrontations: she'd imagined, at least, she'd remember the weather in an area where she'd spent so much time growing up. Her room overlooked the junction of Achaeans with Metokhi Street and Janet stood at the drip-splashed and trickling glass, gazing beyond towards the Turkish occupation in the center of Nicosia. On a clear day she supposed she could have actually seen the mountains separating Nicosia from Kyrenia but now everything was cloaked in bulge-bellied clouds, anxious to relieve themselves. Male or female clouds? she wondered. Female: they were squatting. At least, she thought, the heat would not be so bad today. And at once contradicted herself. If the rain didn't let up it could be positively worse: steamy and monsoon-like. What would a day such as this be like for John, wherever he was? No air conditioning: probably no window or vent, to provide even air, steamy or monsoon-like. Maybe not a hole in the ground or a bucket to pee into.

"Poor darling!" said Janet, aloud. "My poor darling!" She was talking to a different ghost, she realized, abruptly. No! Hank was the ghost: Hank was dead. John wasn't dead: she was sure he wasn't dead. *Knew* he wasn't dead. John was alive: alive and waiting to be rescued. "I'm here," she said, unashamedly, no longer seeing the darkened, rain-lashed view beyond the window. "I'm trying: please believe that I'm trying." John *would* believe her, she knew: would trust her. Not like everyone else.

Janet squeezed her eyes shut, against the rain and the imagery, not opening them until she turned back into the room. The weather didn't matter: nothing mattered more than finding the way—the link or the thread or whatever—to John. And she *would* find it. No threatening policeman with absurd moustaches or threatening American with no name or patronizing diplomat was going to frighten her away. "Beat you!" she said to them now, louder than the first time she'd talked to herself but still unashamed. "I'm going to beat the lot of you bastards!"

Around her the hotel stayed eerily quiet. The rain splattered noisily and insistently against the window. "Beat you," repeated Janet, quieter now and more to herself than before, a personal encouragement.

She put on jeans and a baggy workshirt and loafers. In the hotel coffee shop, where she ordered coffee with rolls, Janet tried to study everyone around her. Was she under surveillance, from Zarpas's people or from the Americans? Several times other customers answered her stare—two men hopefully—and very quickly Janet stopped trying. She was, she acknowledged, the amateur that she was constantly accused of being; so what chance did she have, if everyone else was professional? None, she answered herself: another fantasy exercise. Preposterous to attempt, then.

Unsure how the Cypriot policeman intended to monitor her movements—but knowing that hotel cab drivers would be an obvious source—Janet disdained a taxi, deciding instead to rent an Avis car. She drove towards Larnaca. Twice she stopped at lean-to souvenir stalls, to let traffic pass, and staged another more protracted halt, at Kosi, for more coffee that she did not want. By that time the clouds had pulled back to the mountains where they belonged and everywhere was drying out, the roads and the houses steaming under the displaced and disgruntled sun. Janet chose a table outside the cafe, which the waiter had to wipe dry, as he did the seat, and she sat at once and tried to memorize the cars that went by directly after her. There were so many that quickly she became confused. A feeling of impotence started to rise, but she refused to let it grip her. What was the point of becoming upset at an inability to do something for which she wasn't trained?

She entered Larnaca on Grivas Digenis Avenue and kept driving eastwards and by the time she passed the Zeno stadium she was getting snatches of the sea, silvered now by a white sun from an unclouded, uncluttered sky. She spotted one of the faded and bent direction signs to the Beirut ferries at Karaolis and Demetriou so she went to the left. There was a dog's-leg she was forced to follow and when Janet reached the T-junction she looked for some other marker and almost at once smiled at the sign for Kitieus Street. At last, she thought, something was becoming easy: it had taken long enough. She turned left because she could tell it to be the route into the center of the town, seeking somewhere to park the car and again, practically immediately, saw the Othello Cinema.

She drove into its car park and despite her previous resolution remained in the car after stopping it, alert for any car following her in. None did.

The asphalt was already baked hot underfoot when Janet stepped from the car. She hurried away from the vehicle and the cinema, apprehensive of some challenge against her parking there, but none came. On Kitieus Street she hesitated, unsure which direction to take until she saw a sign to the marina. Following it, she realized the street led directly into the square that the crew-cut, unnamed American of the previous afternoon had identified and, illogically, she felt further encouraged. She went down one side of Zenon Square to emerge on Athens Street and stopped, gazing out over the sea.

Beirut was in a direct line, she knew. Just over a hundred miles: only a hundred miles between her and John. Dear God, how she wished it were as easy as that, simply measured in distance! I'm trying, she thought, echoing in her mind her empty bedroom conversation of that morning: I'm trying, my darling.

The marina and pier were very obvious, behind the harbor groin. Janet walked unhurriedly past the hotel and apartment blocks, glancing up to the balconies and loggias where oiled people were already spreadeagled and relaxed, grilling themselves. No worries beyond diarrhea, incorrect camera exposure and forgetting to send holiday postcards to their mothers, thought Janet, enviously.

The bent arm of the pier and the furthest barrier of the marina created an almost enclosed square for the yachts and motorcraft to

be moored, against the spread-apart fingers of the floating pontoons.
Janet hesitated near the bar named appropriately the Marina Pub,
gazing down at the assembly. She'd found the marina and she'd
found Zenon Square and she'd found Kitieus Street. And what the
hell was she going to do now? How, from among all the innocent
yachtsmen and holidaymakers in the bars and restaurants, was she
supposed to isolate someone with links to religious fanatics or gangsters in Beirut? Janet fought against this new despair, forcing herself
forward into the marina, just needing the movement.

All around the boats' fittings tinkled and chimed, like chattering
birds, and the floating dock pontoons shifted just slightly but disconcertingly beneath her feet. Remembering, suddenly, John's fat-bellied boat in which they'd spent so much time the previous summer,
Janet stared about her, looking for something like it. She took her
time before giving up, resigned, unable to find anything even
vaguely resembling it. But this was hardly John's sort of place; this
was designer deckwear and remembering the ice for the drinks before casting off and getting back in time for cocktails. Janet continued slowly up and down the docks, gradually discerning a
pattern. The crafts were graded, the smaller boats assigned the area
near the pier but increasing in size finally to the large, oceangoing
vessels against the far edge of the marina, where the offices and
chandlers appeared to be.

Janet hesitated, trying to encompass the entire area. She supposed
the small boats to her right were capable of reaching the Lebanon,
those with sails certainly, but it would be an uncertain crossing.
From her limited sailing experience Janet guessed the middle pontoon, which she had not yet reached, was where the yachts began
which could comfortably make the journey. She went to it and
strolled casually seawards, head moving from side to side as she
studied each mooring. The yachts seemed roughly divided equally,
half open, either occupied or preparing to sail, half secured and
battened. Near the pontoon's end a yacht was open but with its sails
reefed and its fenders out. *Journey's End*, Janet read, from the stern
markings: registered at Falmouth. In the stern a woman lay prostrate
on an air-mattress, a bikini wisped over her nipples and crotch,
twice as much material employed in the hardscarf protecting her
blonde hair from bleaching further in the sun.

"Wonderful day," said Janet.

The woman's eyes opened, in apparent surprise. She remained
lying as she was.

'Wonderful day," repeated Janet.

The woman moved, but slowly, easing up on to her elbow and using her other hand to shield her eyes while she squinted up at the pontoon. "What?"

"You sail all the way here from England?" asked Janet, unwilling to repeat her fatuous opening for a third time.

"Two years ago," said the sunbather. "We leave it here now. You have a boat here on the marina?"

Janet squatted to take the sun from the other woman's eyes, shaking her head. "Just looking around and admiring," she said. "How often do you get out?"

The woman shifted, bringing her legs up in front of her and wrapping her arms around them. "Not as much as we should, unfortunately."

Janet hesitated, not knowing how to continue. "Ever get across there?" she said, clumsily, jerking her head seawards.

The woman actually looked beyond the marina and then back again, frowning. "Where?" she demanded.

"Lebanon," said Janet. She was handling it all very badly, she thought. But how *could* she handle it!

The woman snorted a laugh, incredulous. "Are you serious?" she demanded.

"I just wondered," said Janet, retreating.

"You'd have to be out of your mind to go anywhere near that coastline!" insisted the woman.

Maybe I am, thought Janet. She said: "Some people must."

The woman cocked her head curiously to one side and did not respond immediately. When she did the words came slowly. "Mad people, like I said."

Janet desperately searched for another way to phrase the question but could not find one. Directly she said: "Know any?"

The woman pulled herself tighter together on the mattress and stared at Janet. Janet guessed the woman was trying to memorize her features and thought, Oh shit! Abruptly the woman said: "What's going on!"

"Nothing's going on," insisted Janet. "Just chatting."

"Who are you?"

"English," tried Janet.

"That wasn't what I asked. I can tell you're English."

"Stone," she said, trapped. "Janet Stone."

"Why so much interest in the Lebanon?"

"No reason," shrugged Janet, deciding against telling the woman anything. "Just chatting, like I said." She straightened, to relieve the cramp from her legs.

"I don't know anyone who's mad enough to sail to Beirut," insisted the woman. "And if I did, I'd be suspicious of them, because there's only one reason to go there and that's to smuggle. And my husband and I are not smugglers."

A defense against an unvoiced accusation? wondered Janet. Or did the woman suspect her of being an *agent provocateur?* It was immaterial, either way. She said: "It was nice talking to you."

The woman did not reply but remained gazing at her intently.

Janet started to walk away, realizing at once she was going in the wrong direction, further along the pontoon towards the open sea. There appeared to be no more occupied boats—and if there had been Janet realized she could not have attempted another conversation of the sort she'd just had with the woman, whom she guessed would have hurried along immediately to inquire after she'd finished—and to retrace her steps meant passing directly in front of her. Janet guessed the woman would be staring at her and saw that she was, when she turned at the pontoon head to walk back.

At the yacht Janet hesitated and said: "Bye now."

The woman nodded, but didn't speak.

Janet continued on, tensed against a sensation going beyond helplessness, to hopelessness. Stop it! she demanded of herself. Stop it! stop it! stop it! She'd only just started . . . *hadn't* started . . . so it was infantile to become depressed because the first person to whom she'd tried to speak (and spoken to like some mental defective, at that) hadn't been the premier hostage-freeing tour operator of the Middle East. Worse than infantile: stupidly infantile. At the larger, linking pontoon Janet turned and looked back in the direction from which she'd just come: the bikini-clad woman on *Journey's End* was standing now, gazing towards her. For her own satisfaction—and not even sure what that satisfaction was—Janet slightly raised her hand and jiggled her fingers in the smallest of farewell waves before going consciously out of sight towards—and behind—the larger boats.

It was right that she should not become depressed so soon but just as important not to continue in the gauche manner in which she had just behaved. One more episode like that, coupled with the sort of gossip Janet guessed to be the glue that kept a marina like this bonded together, and her next encounter with the disbelieving Chief Inspector Zarpas would probably be in a police cell.

But how! Janet halted at the next out-thrust leg towards the sea, looking up along the larger boats but not making towards them yet. *Journey's End*, registered in Falmouth, she remembered: mistake upon mistake! It was always possible, of course, that an English-registered vessel with English-speaking occupants could have the sort of links she sought, but other registrations and other nationalities were far more likely. Such as? Cyprus, obviously. The Lebanon itself. Or Syrian. Or Greek. Turkish, too, although those would not be moored on this part of the island. Still too wide a spread, she thought, gazing generally over the marina: there had to be over a hundred yachts moored here at least. Janet tried to think of a way to narrow her search down to the most obvious choices, smiling when the idea came to her. Language, she decided. So what were the most likely languages? French had been the tongue of the Lebanon before the outbreak of the troubles, in the early 70s. But since then the country had been awash with Syrians and Iranians and Palestinians. Arabic, then, as a second choice: maybe no longer second, but equal. Janet felt a brief pop of encouraging relief: French and Arabic, and she spoke both of them.

Unwilling to be seen by the Englishwoman, Janet ignored the immediate pontoon, going on until the second before setting out along it behind the protective hedge of two sets of anchored and tethered vessels. As before she walked slowly, intent upon names and registrations. Up one side and down the other she walked, never once seeing a registration to fit her idea. Twice she heard French being spoken, both times from yachts identified from French ports, and Janet realized she had not reduced her search as effectively as she had imagined. Both vessels were crowded, with bathing-costumed groups already drunk, and she decided it was pointless attempting any sort of conversation.

On the last possible pontoon, three berths along, Janet saw a blue-and-white-hulled boat listing Latakia as its home port. The name, *Sea Mist*, was picked out in Arabic script below the title in Roman print, which Janet presumed was required by some international maritime agreement.

The sails were stowed but there was a man in the stern, hunched over what appeared to be an engine flap. He was balding and a sagging stomach hung over his belt, straining the T-shirt to contain it.

"*Marhaba*," said Janet.

The glance was barely perceptible but Janet knew he had seen her.

He gave no response. Her dismissal as a woman, Janet recognized. She said: *"Hather illak?"*

Without bothering to look up, the workman said: "No, it belongs to someone else."

"Heloo."

"It is adequate. How did a Western woman learn Arabic?" He looked up at last, curiosity winning, blatantly studying her body.

"I teach," she replied, in English also.

"But not Arab ways," he said, dismissive again. He moved to go back over the engine cowling.

"Syrian registered?" said Janet, stopping him.

"So?"

"Do you sail there often?"

"Of course." He was leaning against the flap but not bothering with the engine now.

"I am told it is dangerous."

"Not the Syrian coast."

"Lebanon then?"

"Awaih, bas meen fara'a ma-oh Lubnan?" he said, testing her by reverting to Arabic.

"Some care about the Lebanon," Janet answered him at once.

"Not enough."

"Do you ever sail there?"

The man lounged inside the yacht, looking at her for several moments, but not replying. Then he said: "The Lebanon, you mean?" Janet nodded.

Again there was a hesitation. The pontoon heaved beneath her feet and she saw that the T-shirt was stained, not just with engine oil but with sweat-marks under the arms. With intentional awkwardness the man said: "I wouldn't know."

Bastard, decided Janet. She thought of the word in Arabic, too, wondering how he would react if she openly called him *a'krout*. She said: "Some must."

"I suppose."

"You worked this dock long?"

There was a shoulder lift, the only response.

Janet could feel the perspiration making its own pathway down her back: a lot of it was not because of the sun. Trying to stir his obvious chauvinism, Janet said: "It would take a brave man, to risk sailing there."

"Or a fool," he said, not responding to the taunt, either.

"Do you know such people?" demanded Janet, direct once more.
The exaggerated shrug came again. He was playing with her,
Janet decided: acting out his own strange charade. "Perhaps you
know where such people gather?" persisted Janet.
The man looked beyond her, generally towards the town.
"Around," he said.
It was time to be even more direct, Janet guessed: she had nothing
to lose. She said: "I have £50, in sterling. I would give £50 to learn
the names of places where such people gather."
The man's lips parted, in a smile made unpleasant by two teeth
missing in the front. "I have heard things," he allowed.
"Like what?"
"You said £50?"
Janet took the money, two £20 notes and one £10, from her shoul-
der bag and folded them to make the amount look thicker. She did
not offer the small bundle to the man.
He held out his hand.
"The names," Janet insisted, keeping hers by her side.
The man said nothing, remaining with his palm outstretched.
Janet peeled one £20 note from the remainder and passed it over the
sliver of water separating them. The man just stopped himself
snatching at it.
"There's the Marina Pub," he said, jerking his head back towards
Athens Street. "A place called the Rainbow, on Kitieus Street. I've
heard another meeting place is the Archontissa restaurant, although
at night, not during the day. And at night there's the Byzantium
restaurant . . . it has a nightclub, too . . . and the Sanacosta. Mostly
around the center of town although the Byzantium is out a bit,
along Artemis Avenue."
"I can find them," said Janet, eagerly. She was about to pass over
the rest of the money and then hesitated. "What about the name of a
person?" she asked. "Do you know anyone?"
The man made a beckoning movement with his hand, for the
other £30. As Janet gave it to him, there was a head shake of refusal.
"Don't know any people," he said.
"Thank you for the places, at least," said Janet. It was actually
working, she thought excitedly as she climbed from the marina. At
last it was working, and she was getting somewhere! Not just one
place but several. Surely from all the names she had she was going
to be able to find somebody!
Because it was the nearest, Janet went first to the Marina Pub at

the end of the pier. It was just past mid-day when she got there. It was already jostled with a combination of sun-pink tourists and weather-tanned occupants of the marina. Through the expansive windows, Janet could make out the yacht of the hostile English-woman, although she was no longer on the air mattress. The work-man on the *Sea Mist* was back at the engine hatch.

Janet got a seat near one of the windows and ordered *kokkineli* rosé, gazing around. She wanted someone who was resident, on the marina at least, and Janet realized at once that at this time of the day the place was too crowded to make any guesses and certainly not any approaches. She made the wine last, finally ordering another, and—although she was not really hungry—justified her lingering occupa-tion of the table by choosing a sandwich of spitted lamb, in an en-velope of pita bread. It was almost three o'clock before the clientele thinned. She attempted to get into conversation with a group at the bar whom she overheard talking in both French and Arabic but was rebuffed. She got a friendlier reception from two men and a woman talking French but after half an hour of conversation discovered they were cruising from Cannes, had never been to the Lebanon and had no intention of attempting to do so.

Her hopes soared on her third approach. Almost at once the cou-ple talked of being Lebanese, actually residents of Beirut. Eagerly—although not showing it—she let them lead the conversation, only occasionally risking the intrusion of a question, not wanting to hear the story that gradually emerged and even more unwilling as it did so to confront the gradual descent of her hopes. The man had been a high-rise store owner whose premises had been situated literally be-tween the Maronite Christians and Sunni Moslems when the war broke out with those first shots in April, 1975, in the civil war which was not a civil war any longer because no one knew what it was any more. He had been cautious—a half-boastful smile at this stage of the history—although he had never imagined ("who could?") it would degenerate into what it had now become. But they'd been able to get out so little of their capital: far too little. They'd already had their yacht ("good fortune when there was so little") which was now their home. Their livelihood—the high-rise in the most desir-able district of Beirut—they'd seen destroyed by the successive ex-change of gunfire and mortar and artillery, until it had been cut from its multi-million ("multi-million in any currency you like") size as if some giant hand had been slicing pieces off a special cake. They'd fled before the anarchy, of course: risked just one return. The

formerly proud skyscraper had been a disappointing bump of concrete and steel, the girders and the rusting frames appropriately like
the bones of something long dead and picked clean, like things were
picked clean by vultures. They had two souvenirs: the front door
key, and a fish mold the vultures had somehow, inexplicably, missed
in the rubble. The woman said she'd never been able to use the
mold again: how could she? Both smiled and accepted Janet's offer
of more drinks, the woman *kokkineli* like Janet was drinking, the
man *ouzo* which he milked white, with water, with obvious
nostalgia.

Janet clung to the fact that she was establishing contact with Lebanese, and obstinately refused to accept the encounter as a failure.
She was met with shrugs when she asked if they maintained contacts
with anyone in Beirut. Still, deciding her sad story matched their
sad story, she volunteered an account of herself and Sheridan.

Exiles know everything about the country—and the city—from
which they were exiled, and the couple immediately recognized
Sheridan's name. The woman clutched Janet's hand and said she
was so sorry. Janet smiled her gratitude, as if it were the first time
anyone had ever expressed regret.

"It won't work, what you're trying to do," warned the man.

"I need guidance: a name," cut off Janet, unwilling to get back on
to the carousel.

"The only people who go back and forth are smugglers," said the
man. "There are a lot of shortages in Beirut: things people need.
And for which they are willing to pay."

"I'm looking for an intermediary, someone who knows. Not a
priest."

"I paid a man, once," conceded the Lebanese. "It was before we
went back ourselves. I wanted to know how badly damaged my block
was . . ." He sniggered an unamused laugh. "Actually had thoughts
of going back and trying to run it again! Can you believe that!"

"What man? Where?" demanded Janet, disinterested in rhetoric.

"Nicos," said the man. "He called himself Nicos.

"What family name!" said Janet, with intense urgency.

The Lebanese shook his head. "Just Nicos. Nothing more than
Nicos. He's careful, you see."

"Where?" persisted Janet.

The Lebanese gestured behind him, towards Athens Street.
"There is a hotel, the Four Lanterns," he said. "At night there is a
discothèque. He is often there."

Practically on Zenon Square, remembered Janet: on one of the side roads, leading towards the sea. "Will you take me to him?"

Uncertain looks passed between the couple. The man said: "It is not good: I don't think we should get involved."

"Just an introduction!" pleaded Janet. "Not even that: just point him out to me!"

Looks were exchanged again. The woman said: "Why not?"

"We'll point him out," conceded the man.

"Thank you," said Janet, swallowing. She felt full-up, ballooned, with satisfaction.

Janet offered more drinks but they chose coffee instead: Janet joined the woman with *glykos*, the sweetest of the Turkish preparations, but the man took *sketos*, without sugar. Janet sat patiently through the production of photographs, admiring the skycraper before its destruction and pictures of the couple's summer home, in the Lebanese mountains. The lack of formal introduction between them appeared to register at the same time. With some small ceremony the man took a card from his wallet identifying himself as Mohammed Kholi and Janet repeated her name, apologizing for not carrying cards: Kholi said he remembered her name, from the accounts of herself and Sheridan. At Kholi's suggestion they left the Marina bar and wandered along the harbor. Janet asked about their yacht and Kholi pointed to one of the furthest arms of the marina and said it was blue, with a white superstructure, and could she see it? The boats seemed to be predominantly blue but Janet thought she isolated it. Politely she said it looked very nice.

"So completely different from what I've always been accustomed," complained Mrs. Kholi. "Like living in a box. I hate it."

"You'd better become accustomed to it," remarked Kholi, realistically.

Kholi said they were too early for the discothèque and invited Janet to be their guest for the rest of the afternoon, and although she did not want to drink or eat anything more she said she'd be delighted to accept. Kholi bundled the two women into a taxi and sat beside the driver before giving a destination that Janet did not hear. They drove away from town, with the sea to their right, and at the junction with Timayia Avenue Janet saw the direction to Dhekelia.

"Best hotel in Larnaca," assured Kholi, when they arrived at the Palm Beach. The man chose their seats in the covered balcony overlooking the sea and insisted upon a bottle of Arsinoe white wine. Janet sipped it and said it was excellent, managing to control any facial reaction to its sweetness. On the second glass, Kholi pressed Janet upon what she hoped to achieve. Janet replied, honestly, that she was not sure.

"Just information," she said. "Anything more than the sort of silence—the not knowing—that there is now."

"Don't expect too much from this man Nicos," warned Kholi. "All he had to do in my case was walk along a street and look at a building, to see how badly damaged it was."

"I won't expect too much," promised Janet.

Kholi offered dinner but Janet refused, anxious to get to the club, and the other woman said she was not hungry either. Kholi said it was a pity, because he thought the Palm Beach did the best lamb on the island.

It was eight before they moved and Janet thought abruptly—wondering why it had taken so long—that she was still wearing the same jeans and flat shoes in which she'd left Nicosia that morning, and she had not even washed her face or repaired her minimal makeup since then. There was nothing she could do about it now, apart perhaps from rinsing her face in the lavatory. But that would mean making up again. So why bother?

Janet recognized the route on the return journey, deciding she had oriented Larnaca in her mind now. Kholi stopped the cab near the Sun Hall Hotel, waving away Janet's offer to settle the fare, and led them protectively into the nightclub entrance of the Four Lanterns, where again he insisted on paying.

It catered very much to tourists, realized Janet, the moment she entered. There was a disc jockey booth alongside a deserted stage. In front was a circular dance area over which hung the sort of multifaceted revolving glass dome that reflects light from variously aimed and colored spotlights. There were oases of tables, illuminated by candles in round pots and hedged by tub seats; and around the wall, which dipped and undulated into the room, were bench seats that met other tables around each of which, on the room side, were more tub seats. The bar was the brightest area in the discothèque, with more lights and more multifaceted reflecting glass. Behind the barmen bottles were racked directly in front of long, highly polished sheets of further reflecting glass. Kholi led the way to the bar and three adjoining stools. Janet examined herself in the bar mirror and decided that in this light the fact that she had been away from a wash basin and a makeup bag all day was not as noticeable as she had feared it would be.

Janet declined any more alcohol, grateful at seeing Perrier but wishing it had been iced when it was served. The club was only half full, but the music was stridently loud, more to attract waverers outside in the street than for the immediate enjoyment of those who'd already paid their entrance fee. Janet and the Kholis attempted conversation but the volume defeated them and eventually they abandoned the effort, remaining side by side and out-of-place in their surroundings. Janet felt distinctly uncomfortable.

It was ten o'clock when Kholi nudged and gestured towards the far end of the bar, nearest the door. The man standing there was young, not much older than twenty, Janet guessed, and very aware of himself, preening to the mirror's reflection. The deep and even suntan was accentuated by the way he was dressed, tight yellow shirt smooth around his flat waist, white trousers matchingly tight around hips moving in time to the music. His hair was very long and curled low over his neck, around which was looped a thin gold chain. When he gestured for a drink—Perrier, Janet noticed—the light struck off a stone in a ring on his left hand. The smile of thanks flashed almost as much as the ring stone.

"Nicos," whispered Kholi unnecessarily.

"Introduce me?" urged Janet, despite their earlier agreement.

The Lebanese hesitated, looking for guidance to his wife, who grimaced with the corners of her mouth down, in a "so-what" expression.

Kholi moved, cupping Janet's arm to move her with him. She followed the man around the crush of the bar and saw Nicos turn and look without any recognition at Kholi's touch to his arm. The man's face remained empty despite Kholi's mouth-to-ear explanation, only opening in recollection when Kholi took the earlier department store photograph from his pocket and offered it to the man.

"She wants something out of Beirut, too," said Kholi, indicating Janet.

For the first time Nicos looked at her. Janet's impression of being mentally undressed was strong. Closer, the self-assured smile was even brighter.

"What?" demanded the man.

"Somewhere quieter," Janet said.

The smile widened. "Sounds interesting."

Janet felt herself sweating with the sort of discomfort she'd known talking to the arrogant crewman. "You interested in a business deal?"

An explosion of music kept the answer from her. Realizing she had not heard, Nicos repeated: "I'm interested in everything."

"Business," Janet repeated, in further insistence.

"There's a quieter bar upstairs, in the hotel," the man suggested. "We can get a return ticket for here."

"I shan't be coming back," said Janet.

·14·

Nicos led the way into the upstairs bar and to a table over-looking the now-darkened sea and announced: "I will take *zivania*."

Janet order the brandy for him and another Perrier for herself, conscious of his changed attitude. There had been a swagger when he had left the downstairs club but here, without an audience, there was no pretense. She was glad.

As if in confirmation of her thoughts he said, seriously: "What is it, this business in Beirut?"

Janet talked intently, alert for his reaction. He sat with his hands around his glass but not drinking and not looking directly back at her, either, his eyes down to the table as if he were deep in thought. When she finished he did not speak immediately.

"Well!" she demanded. "Can you help?"

His eyes came up to her at last. "I don't know," he said, simply.

Janet frowned at the unexpected honesty. "You do have contacts in Beirut, don't you?"

"Some," he said. "I don't know if they could help on this, though."

"Will you try?"

Nicos shrugged and said: "Before it was just to look at a building: take a photograph. This is different."

"I accept that."

"Dangerous."

"How much?"

The smile flashed, briefly. "Just information, right? If he is OK? Whereabouts in Beirut he's being held?"

"The whereabouts particularly."

"Nothing," declared the man.

"Nothing!"

"Payment on results," he said, in another announcement. "I will try to find out where he is being held. See if I can get a photograph to prove it. If I do that, then I get £10,000. If I discover nothing, I get nothing."

Janet smiled tentatively. "I did not expect that," she admitted.

"It is fair?"

"Very fair."

"So we agree?"

"Oh yes!" Janet said, urgently. "Very much we agree. When can you go?"

Nicos held up his hand, stopping her. "There is more to discuss," he said. "I have to find someone to take me across. Make arrangements to get in."

"Yes," Janet said cautiously.

"There will be expense."

Janet hesitated. "How much?"

The shrug came again. "I do not know how much they will ask. There is always the risk of losing the boat: of getting shot even."

"You must have some idea."

Nicos's eyes were fixed on the table again. "I will need to make a deal on the spot: not be able to go back and forth to discuss it."

"Of course."

"How about this?" suggested the man. "I take £5,000. Trust me to be honest. I will tell you what the boat costs and what the bribes cost and what is left over comes off the £10,000 we've agreed. If I can't find out anything, I give you back what's left. Fair again?"

"Fair again," Janet agreed.

"How long, to get the money?"

"Tomorrow."

The man nodded. "Then tomorrow I start."

"I am very grateful," said Janet.

"I haven't achieved anything yet."

"For agreeing to try," said Janet.

They arranged for him to come to the hotel at ten the following morning and Janet left. She tried to think objectively—he was right, he hadn't achieved anything yet—but she found it difficult to control the euphoria. Everyone had sneered and laughed and dismissed her but she'd done it! She'd made a contact and he was going to go into Beirut and find something out about John. She just *knew* he would.

It was near midnight when she got back to the hotel and Janet sagged with tiredness. Despite which, she bathed, wanting to relax as much as remove the dirt of the day, but when she went to bed she still found it difficult to sleep, managing little more than to catnap throughout the night. She got up just after it was light, staring out over the gradually awakening city, impatient for the hours to pass until Nicos arrived.

She did not bother with breakfast and was down in the foyer, waiting for him, half an hour before the agreed meeting. He arrived promptly on time, subdued today in gray trousers and white shirt and once more without any swagger. He carried a briefcase, the sort that locked by coded numerals, adding to the businesslike impression.

They took a taxi to the bank and he waited while she sought out the assistant manager who had taken her deposit and arranged the withdrawal of the £5,000. Janet accepted the money in a thick manila envelope and handed it straight to Nicos, who put it in the briefcase and twirled the numbers.

"How long?" asked Janet, on the pavement outside the bank.

"I don't know," said Nicos. "You are going to remain at the Churchill?"

"Yes."

"I'll contact you there, as soon as there is something. Just wait. It might take time."

"Be as quick as you can," she urged.

"I'll be as quick as it is safe to be," he said.

Back at the hotel Janet realized, practically in surprise, that all she could now do was wait. She telephoned England to assure her father she was all right, holding back with difficulty the temptation to tell him about Nicos, saying merely that she thought she had made a useful contact and was hopeful of it leading to some sort of news about John. In the afternoon she sunbathed by the pool, managing to doze after her fitful night, and had just returned to her room when Partington called from the embassy, extending his delayed invitation for dinner the following night. Janet accepted, deciding she could always cancel if there were news from Nicos, and took care the following morning to tell both the reception desk clerk and the switchboard operator that she would be by the pool if anyone tried to get in touch with her. She became bored with sunbathing by lunchtime. She remained by the pool to eat but in the afternoon risked leaving the hotel briefly to walk to Laiki Yitonia to watch the lace makers at their open-air stalls and wander through the silk booths. After an hour she became worried that she might have missed contact from Nicos and hurried back to the Churchill. There were no messages.

Partington's wife was named Anne. She was a constantly moving, flustered woman who reminded Janet of her own mother and the evening became a further reminder of how fervently her mother had welcomed visitors from outside the insular, claustrophobic embassy enclaves in which they had served abroad. The beef was proudly served ("all there is here is lamb, you know") and Partington poured French wine. Anne Partington said she hoped Janet didn't mind, but William had told her about the kidnap and wasn't it awful but she was sure it would all be all right. When his wife was in the kitchen preparing the coffee the attaché asked how much longer she intended staying.

"I'm not sure," said Janet.

"Have you seen anyone from the American embassy?"

"Yes," Janet said. There did not seem any purpose in elaborating.

"What news was there?"

"None," said Janet. "They warned I was interfering: that I should get out."

"It's good advice."

Twenty-four hours earlier the repetitive attitude would have depressed her, but it didn't now. Janet said: "I've only just got here."

Partington looked towards the kitchen door and then back to Janet. He said: "There was a secure radio patch today, with Beirut."

Janet came forward across the table. "And!"

"I only talked generally: about Waite and the journalist and then I asked about any other nationals . . ." The man faltered. "I don't know why I began this conversation."

"What do you mean!" Janet demanded, anxiously.

"Just that: that there wasn't any point. There's no news."

"There was more than that!" Janet insisted, reacting to instinct.

"Everyone is very depressed there," Partington said, a grudging concession.

"What did they say!"

"That it was difficult to get the smallest scrap of reliable information."

"More than that!" Janet said again.

Partington shook his head, refusing to meet her eyes. "I'm sorry," he said.

"For Christ's sake, what is it!"

The diplomat's eyes came up to hers. "They said it was hopeless: absolutely hopeless. That there's no way to establish any sort of link. The whole place is a shambles. Lost."

I've made a contact, thought Janet, triumphantly. She said: "Thank you, for bothering to ask."

The conversation was at an end when Anne Partington returned with the coffee ("proper stuff, not this Turkish sugar water that rots your teeth"). The souvenir snapshots were produced, one of her parents with the Partingtons on some horseback expedition in Jordan: even then, Janet saw, her father appeared formal, in a very dark riding habit. Anne said they were wonderful people and Janet agreed that they were, and the woman said if she intended staying long she should come to supper again and Janet said that would be nice and that perhaps they could talk on the telephone.

Janet drove as fast as she felt safely able back to the hotel, hurrying anxiously to the concierge desk, trying to isolate her pigeonhole on the keyboard before she reached it. There were no messages.

The following morning, not wanting another day by the pool, Janet walked to Kyprianos Square and went around the Byzantine Museum, trying unsuccessfully to become interested in the icons. She was back at the Churchill by noon: the concierge smiled up at her approach, shaking his head before she reached the desk. After lunch she strolled to the old quarter and toured the sixteenth-century Venetian walls and bought a cheap red clay replica of a spouted oil lamp, deciding it would be something they could keep after John was released to remind themselves of the whole episode, when it was all over. There was nothing waiting for her when she got back to the hotel.

Janet ate dinner early because she became fed up with the four walls of her hotel room, protracted her coffee with an unwanted brandy, and was back in her room by nine. *Dallas* was on television, with Greek subtitles: she watched ten incomprehensible minutes and then turned it off. In bed, with the light out, she stared sightlessly at the ceiling, conscious as the hours passed of the hotel and then the city growing quiet around her. She finally slept, after a fashion, but there was always part of her consciousness alert so that when daylight came she felt as if she had not slept at all.

She was the first by the pool, with her choice of loungers and umbrellas. She lay on her back, then on her front, then on her back, then on her front again. She checked her watch, anxious for lunch to break the tedium, and was unable to believe it was only ten o'clock. When she checked with the pool attendant she found her watch was fast; it was only ten to the hour.

Janet was lying on her back again when the shadow came between herself and the sun, breaking the brightness despite her closed eyes. She lay waiting for it go as the person passed but it didn't and so she opened her eyes, initially unable to see who it was.

"The reception desk told me I would find you here: said you were waiting for a message."

Janet pulled herself into the shadows of her umbrella, raising the back of her lounger as she did so, better able to sit up. Detective Chief Inspector Zarpas was in civilian clothes today, a fawn summerweight suit already creased and with his shirt collar undone and stretched apart from the knot of his tie. Janet was surprised at the contrast from his smartness of their last encounter. She wondered where Sergeant Kashianis was, with his notebook.

"Hello," she said.

"Who are you expecting a message from, Mrs. Stone?"

Janet hesitated. "An embassy," she said, as the thought came to her. "Either the English or the American: I've talked with representatives of both."

"Who else have you talked with?"

"I don't understand the question."

Zarpas looked searchingly around him and smiled permission to take an upright chair from a nearby table. He brought it back, sat gratefully down and took a photograph from his pocket, offering it to her. "Not him, perhaps?"

Janet looked at the official, front-faced photograph of the man she knew as Nicos, thinking how similar it was to the official pictures of John Sheridan, as if they were all taken by the same photographer. A hollowness formed, deep in the pit of her stomach. "Why should I have expected to hear from him?"

"That's what I want you to tell me," said the policeman.

"I said I didn't understand," said Janet, desperately.

"Didn't he even give you a name?"

"Please!" pleaded Janet.

"Nicos," supplied Zarpas. "Nicos Kholi."

Janet closed her eyes, briefly, hoping the policeman would imagine it was a reaction to the sun: the hollow feeling grew worse, a gouging sensation. With difficulty, trying to convince herself she was clinging to a thread of truth, Janet said: "I do not know anyone named Nicos Kholi."

"How about Mohammed Kholi and his wife, who hang around Larnaca marina a lot?"

Stubbornly Janet shook her head.

Zarpas sighed, pulling at the ends of his drooped moustache with his right hand. He said: "Mrs. Stone, we know all about the £5,000 withdrawal. The assistant manager has made a near-positive identification from that photograph as being that of the man who was with you when you took the money, all in cash, from your account. Because it was such a large withdrawal the numbers of the notes were recorded. After we arrested Kholi in Larnaca this morning we went back to his apartment: we found £3,000, all in £20 notes. The numbers matched against those supplied by your bank."

"Oh Christ!" said Janet, despairingly.

"To go into Beirut, after your fiancé?"

"Yes," nodded Janet, tightly.

"After the mother and father told you a story of losing everything in the war? Showed you photographs?"

"Yes," said Janet again.

"They're very good at it," said Zarpas. "Done it twice before."

"Are they Lebanese?"

Zarpas snorted a laugh. "Greek Cypriots," he said. "They've never been to Beirut in their lives. His name is not Mohammed, either. He's a tour guide around the ruins at Paphos when he isn't conning drinks out of sympathetic tourists with his ruined refugee story."

"He bought a lot of drinks that night."

"It was an investment, wasn't it?"

"Why was Nicos arrested?"

Zarpas hesitated and said: "He picked up an Australian girl at a discothèque in Larnaca: slept with her. When she woke up all her money, travelers' checks, and jewelery were gone. So was he. Usually the girls are too embarrassed to complain and explain. She wasn't. Took us back to the discothèque and identified him. We found a necklace, most of her money and her travelers' checks, along with your stuff, at the place he shares with his parents."

"Lucky girl," said Janet, unthinkingly.

"Not really," said Zarpas, solemnly. "He's got syphilis. It'll take some time to see whether she has, too."

Janet tried to think of something to say and couldn't.

Zarpas said: "We'll need you to make out a formal complaint for a charge to be brought."

"What about the Australian girl?"

"She thinks she's contracted venereal disease," reminded the policeman. "She's making every accusation she can think of."

"So you've got a case?"

Zarpas stared pointedly at her. "Don't be stupid!"

"No," said Janet, determinedly. The publicity could be dangerous for John: and make her look naive, too. Stupid, like the man was already accusing her of being but for different reasons.

"It's £5000!"

Janet said nothing.

"If you don't make out a formal complaint you can't recover the £3000 we've got back!"

"What about the others who were tricked?"

"They wouldn't formally complain, either."

"Neither will I," said Janet, stubbornly.

"We'll try to spare you as much embarrassment as possible," Zarpas promised, probing for her reluctance.

"I won't do it."

"Whatever accusations the other woman makes, the maximum Nicos could get is a year. Which he won't: it'll be six months top, more likely three," set out Zarpas. "With a charge of willful deception in the sum of £5000, which we could bring if you complain, I could get the whole family off the streets for more than a year."

Janet shook her head, her mouth tight together.

The silence echoed between them. Zarpas broke it. "I felt sorry for you, the first time. Didn't like bullying you, although I had to. You know my feelings now? I despise you, Mrs. Stone. I think you are a spoiled, rich, stupid woman posturing like someone out of a cheap book."

"I'm not any of that," Janet tried, in weak defense.

"Get out of Cyprus. We don't want you here; won't have you here. Have you ever heard of an expression called stitching up?"

"No."

"It's what policemen do when they know someone is guilty but can't prove it: they arrange incontrovertible evidence to get a conviction on something else," elaborated Zarpas. "That's what I'm prepared to do with you. I'm prepared to fix a reason to get you expelled from this island if you don't leave under your own volition. I actually want to stitch you up."

"No!" Janet shouted, careless of the looks that came from around the pool. Thirty minutes later, after their hostile parting, Janet lay face down on her bed, weeping uncontrollably for the first time since Sheridan's kidnap, both hands clutching her pillow and pulling it into her face.

"How!" she said. "How!"

·15·

J anet was lying stiffly on her back, her eyes open, when
the maid came into the room in the morning and for
several moments the girl didn't realize the room—or the
bed—was occupied, so still was Janet. The maid gave a tiny mew of
surprise and backed away apologizing, giggling near the door in her
embarrassment. Janet remained where she was, scarcely aware of
the intrusion; scarcely, after another near-sleepless night, aware of
anything. She'd gone through all the emotions—anger and frustration and helplessness and despair and back to anger again—until
now she was used up, quite empty. Wrong to be that way, she told
herself. That was how she had collapsed when Hank had died.
When she'd given up. Wouldn't give up this time: it would be
weak—womanlike tried to intrude into her mind but she refused to
let it—to give up. So she'd been conned. Always a possibility: she'd
actually be warned against it. But it would be immature to accept
the first setback as a disaster and give up again, although in a different way. What, realistically, had she lost? Five thousand pounds. A
lot of money but not the end of the world: certainly not the end of
John Sheridan's life. Also, she supposed, she'd lost face and cred-
ibility in the eyes of a Cyprus policeman and about that she couldn't

give a shit, apart from the difficulty that his threat might cause her. She simply had to try again.

Janet got out of bed and spent a long time under the shower, trying to wash away the lingering disappointment. By ten she'd had another hire car delivered and by ten-thirty she was on the road to Larnaca, not bothering with the attempts of the previous journey to spot any cars which might be following her because she'd already accepted the futility of that.

In Larnaca, still unsure how to proceed, Janet decided upon more reconnaissance. Because the Arab boatworker had told her the Byzantium restaurant was away from the center of the town she drove on to locate Artemis Avenue and then the gathering spot that had been identified to her. Although it was nearly lunchtime it appeared practically deserted: the nightclub annex, obviously, was shuttered and unlit. Janet made a three-point turn, to drive back in the direction of the town center, but when she asked directions she discovered that the Sanacosta was even further away, on the Dhekelia Road along which the Kholi family had taken her to soften her up for the deception. As she passed the Palm Beach Hotel Janet became aware that she was actually blushing, embarrassed at how easily she'd been tricked. Practically deserved it, in fact. Right, then, to feel embarrassed, but the other feelings of that long night hadn't been necessary. The Sanacosta seemed even more deserted than the restaurant on Artemis Avenue and Janet reluctantly saw that if she were going to attempt contact in either she would have to wait until the evening.

She returned to the town center and left the vehicle as before in the Othello Cinema car park. The Rainbow was busy although not as crowded as the Marina Pub had been.

Janet ordered *kokkineli* and remained standing at the bar, gazing around. This was not really the way, she forced herself to admit. This was the way to get laughed at or conned again, maybe, but without a better sort of introduction—the proper sort of introduction, by someone who knew the right people—she was wasting her time. Imagining movement was productive activity, in fact.

Who then? She didn't know anyone apart from the hostile, unnamed American and he certainly wasn't going to provide any introductions. Yes, she did know someone!

Janet gulped at her drink and then decided she did not want to finish it anyway, leaving her glass half-filled on the bar. She hurried out into Kitieus Street and walked around the square, to the marina, not able from the level at which she was walking to establish whether the *Sea Mist* was still at its moorings. She glanced along the earlier pontoon as she hurried by and saw that the English yacht and its bikini-clad sunbather had gone. With two pontoons still to go Janet faltered and then stopped, able to see now the other mooring she was seeking. The space was occupied by a different vessel, a high-bridged motor-cruiser, big game lines upright in their prepared sockets, two fighting seats still with their belts and harnesses in the stern. She could not see anyone aboard but some sort of motor was running, pumping bilge water out in little spurts.

Disappointment rose within her. She remained where she was for several moments and then turned back towards the entrance to the marina. And saw him.

The Arab was just beyond the marina wire, looking away in the direction of the pier, as if he were searching for someone. He wore the same stained T-shirt as before. She hurried along the slatted, heaving pontoon, anxious he should not walk away before she reached him. Almost within hailing distance he looked into the marina and saw her, too. His face opened, in frowned recognition.

"*Marhaba*," she said, out of breath.

"The lady who speaks good Arabic."

"I thought you had gone."

"Gone?" He appeared apprehensive.

Janet nodded back towards the mooring. "The yacht you were on the other day. It's sailed."

"I fix engines," said the man.

"I misunderstood: I thought you were a crewman."

The man hitched himself on to a low wall, one leg swinging. "And you're still here, too?"

Janet nodded. "Still looking," she said, cautiously. No more mistakes, she promised herself.

He gestured generally in towards the town: they could both see the Marina bar. "What happened?"

"No luck," she said.

"Such people do get there, sometimes," said the man, urgently.

Janet abruptly gauged the cause of his uncertainty: the Arab thought she was going to demand her money back. Just as quickly she said: "I'm sure they do! I wasn't doubting you."

He relaxed, visibly. "Not easy to find," he said.

"That's why I'm glad I ran into you again."

He tensed again, slightly. "Why?"

Janet indicated the bar in which she had been tricked. "I am not going to get anywhere trying to find people by myself, am I? I need more than just places."

The man looked away from her, to the ground. Janet saw for the first time that he wasn't wearing shoes: his feet were horny and calloused, as if he never did. Very quietly, practically to himself, he said: "Maybe it is possible."

"What?" she demanded. "What may be possible?"

The Arab waved towards the marina and said: "Any idea how much those sorts of yachts cost?"

Janet forced herself to be patient, realizing it would have to be at his pace. "No," she said.

"Thousands," he said. "Half a million some of them, easily."

"A lot of money," Janet agreed, to keep the conversation going.

"Would you take a yacht costing that much somewhere where it might get damaged? Destroyed even?"

"Probably not." Dear God, what sort of game was the awkward bastard playing now!

"Always important, to consider the cost of things."

Awareness registered with her. Janet said: "I'm prepared to pay for help: for a proper introduction. Pay more than last time. But it's got to work."

The man looked back to her, smiling his gap-toothed smile. "Keep thinking about money," he suggested. "What sort of boats don't cost half a million and can sail much more safely in Lebanese waters?"

"I don't . . ." began Janet and then stopped. "Fishing boats," she said.

"Big industry here in Cyprus, fishing. Lot of boats."

"How much?" Janet asked directly, fed up with the constant pirouettte.

"What exactly do you want?"

"To meet a man . . . men . . . who go there. Who know people who can find out things."

"What sort of things?"

She would have to tell him. "There is a man, a hostage. I want to find out about him."

The Arab's face clouded. "That will not be easy."

"I understand that."

"Dangerous. Perhaps the people I am thinking about will not want to do it: will not be able to do it," he said.

"Ask!" Janet pleaded.

The man nodded, head bent again in apparent thought. He said: "I will ask."

"Now?"

He looked up, squinting against the sun in the cloudless sky. "Now the boats are out, not yet returned from the morning catch," he said, professionally.

"When?"

"Late afternoon maybe. If I can find them."

Janet guessed the vagueness was being intentionally introduced. She said: "One hundred pounds."

He shook his head, sadly. "For something like this! Two hundred."

"One hundred and fifty," countered Janet. "And that must be for an introduction to people who can really help. I won't pay for nothing."

"Two hundred," repeated the man.

She was in no position to bargain and he knew it, conceded Janet. She said: "Two hundred. But it's got to be for something definite. A positive, worthwhile introduction."

"I can't guarantee that they will agree. Not for something like this."

"I've accepted that," Janet reminded him.

"Tonight, in the square," said the Arab. "Seven."

"You'll know something by then?"

"You'll have the money?"

It would mean driving back to Nicosia, thought Janet. But she had nothing else to do until that night's appointment. She said: "I'll have the money."

"I'll try to have arranged something."

There was none of the euphoria during this journey back that there had been on the previous occasion when Janet thought she had made a contact. It looked promising, certainly. But then so had the encounter with someone who'd turned out to be a syphilitic thief. This time she'd want more, be less gullible. I'm learning, thought Janet: expensively but learning.

Janet did not bother to go through the assistant manager this time because the amount was so small, joining a line for an ordinary counter withdrawal. From the hotel she telephoned England, to give her parents assurance about her safety, dismissing her father's query about her hopefulness during the last call by quickly saying that the approach that had looked so good then had turned out to be nothing, which was not really a lie. She lunched by the pool and that afternoon lay by it, for the first time not feeling bored: right not to become euphoric or even excited, but borrowing a word from the telephone conversation to England she decided she was allowed to be hopeful.

Unsure what to expect that evening, Janet dressed once more in jeans and an evening shirt and flat shoes. She chose a handbag with a long strap which she could loop across her body and at the moment of departure stood looking at the money she had withdrawn from the bank. Impulsively she stuffed it into the rear pocket of her jeans, not her handbag: she'd made the withdrawal in £20 notes and it lay flat and unobtrusive.

The route now was very familiar to her. Cautiously she had allowed herself more than enough time but there were no traffic hold-ups, so she was early. She parked in her accustomed place and strolled along the front and cut up to the square from the seaward side.

She saw him at once. He was sitting on a bench near the tourist information office. He'd changed into a blue workshirt, faded but clean, light-colored baggy trousers that had long ago lost any crease, and open-toed, open-heeled sandals. Janet knew he had not seen her and so for a few moments she remained in the shadow of a large and unidentified building, watching him. He looked very relaxed, apparently quite content for her to seek him, not bothering himself to find her.

He saw her when she began to approach, smiling but not standing. When she reached the bench he patted it, for her to sit. She remained looking down at him for a few moments and then lowered herself on to it leaving a wide gap between them.

"Well?" she said at once.

He nodded, satisfied with himself. "I have found people who are prepared to talk to you."

"They can find something out?"

"That is for you to decide, when you meet them."

"Tonight?"

"Yes."

"Right away?"

"We had a deal."

"Which was for proper, useful contact," Janet said, remembering the lost £5,000. "You get nothing until I meet your people . . ." She paused, realizing that the bargaining positions could be tilting in her favor now. "*And* that they can do something," she added.

He looked steadily at her, not responding for a while. Then he said: "You have a car?"

"Yes."

"We'll need a car: it's out of town."

And she would be in it with him by herself, thought Janet, recalling the obvious sexual examination of their first encounter. "Where?" she asked, apprehensively.

"About five kilometers: on the road to Dhekelia."

Even the same route as before. Janet said: "What are the arrangements?"

"There are three men, who jointly own a boat," said the man. "They sail out of here although they live nearer to Dhekelia. They fish the mullet: it is better on the Lebanese coast. They say they know people."

"Do you believe them?"

The shoulders came up and down, expansively. "Who believes?" he said.

"Who indeed?" Janet agreed.

"Are you frightened to come with me?" the man asked.

"Should I be?" Janet asked, avoiding question with question.

"No."

"Why did you ask then?"

"You're a woman," he said, openly.

"That has no importance."

"If you are sure."

It was becoming pointlessly coquettish, on his part, decided Janet. Wanting to shift direction, she said: "How are you called?"

He hesitated and she waited, curiously. At last he said: "Haseeb."

"Haseeb what?"

"Just Haseeb."

First Nicos, now Haseeb: no family names, thought Janet. She said: "What are we waiting for, Haseeb?"

"I will get my money?"

"If I get what I want."

He rose, decisively, and Janet followed him up from the bench. "Which direction?" he asked.

Janet led away from the square and along Kitieus Street to the cinema car park. It had filled up by now with patrons' vehicles, many sloppily parked, so it was difficult for her to maneuver out.

Knowing the direction from her previous reconnaissance Janet turned left: even before she reached the square where they'd met she was conscious of his body odor permeating the car. Janet waited until they were running parallel with the sea, on Makarios Avenue, before slightly lowering the window on her side.

"Hot night?" he said, seeing what she had done.

"Very."

"It is not far," Haseeb said, as they got on to the Dhekelia Road. He shifted as he spoke, using the back of her seat as a hand-hold to turn in his own seat to look into the back of the vehicle.

Janet pulled away from any supposed accidental touch and said: "What are you looking for?"

"Nothing," he said, turning back.

It had been her handbag, she guessed. In those brief moments alone in the car in the cinema park she'd put it beneath her seat. They passed the Palm Hotel and the Sanacosta restaurant and night-club and all the other hotels necklacing the seafront road. The concentration of light began gradually to diminish, very quickly becoming just the occasional pinprick of a local house or the rickety, uncertain illumination of a shanty non-tourist bar.

"Not long now," Haseeb said.

It was so dark now it was difficult for Janet to distinguish him across the other side of the car. "Good," she said.

Although dark inside the car, it was a clear night outside, the moon so bright it marked a glittered reflection against the rolling sea to her right: through her open window Janet could just hear the hissed growl of its arrival against the shore.

"Engine's rough," he said, expertly.

Dear God, don't let the car break down, thought Janet. She said: "It goes."

"Tappets," Haseeb said.

Janet had no idea what he was talking about. She said: "How much further?"

Haseeb gestured vaguely ahead. "Just around the bend."

He'd said five kilometers, Janet remembered: they'd traveled much more than five kilometers. She'd been stupid not to register the mileage when they'd set out. "What time are they expecting us?"

"When we arrive," Haseeb said.

"I thought we'd be there by now."

"There!" the man said.

Janet could not at once make out the place to which he was pointing and then, on the seaward side of the road, she became aware of a cluster of dull lights around a roadside stop. Closer, she saw it was not directly against the road but down a short dirt track that dropped frighteningly downwards as soon as she left the road: dust billowed up around them and rocks and ruts jarred through the vehicle from beneath. There were no other cars in the clearing made for parking, just two motor scooters and some bicycles.

"This is it!" Haseeb announced, practically with the pride of ownership.

It was a low single-story building of maybe three rooms. There was a long rectangle which she could see, through uncurtained windows, forming the public, cafe part, with a kitchen adjoining. Alongside, in darkness, was what she presumed to be where the owner lived. Or maybe he lived somewhere else and it was a storage area. There was a door cut into the side of the cafe, leading out on to an open verandah. Beams extended from the main building and trellis had been linked to them, to make the foundation for a grape vine. The vines were already intertwined but they were thin and sparse and Janet couldn't imagined they provided much shade during the heat of the day. Cables had also been looped through and from them, at intervals, unshaded bulbs hung down. They were mostly ordinary white household bulbs but just occasionally an effort had been made with colors. There were several red and a few blue. The verandah was set with tables, half of which were covered with red checked table cloths to designate that they were for people who intended to eat. The rest were uncovered. All were set with metal-framed, canvas-backed and seated chairs.

As Janet got from the car she caught an overwhelming smell of long-used cooking oil, from the kitchen. As she followed Haseeb up slatted wooden steps to the verandah she saw a family of cats: several kittens were chasing and snatching at insects she could not see. From all around came the crackle and chirp of cicadas in the undergrowth beyond the cafe.

There were only locals, and less than a dozen of them, on the eating section of the verandah and Janet walked its length conscious of their absolute attention: two men actually stopped eating, with their forks suspended before them, to watch her pass.

Haseeb led the way to one of the unclothed tables at the very rear in a corner, so that walls blocked it on two sides. Three men sat at the table. Two wore shirts and trousers but Janet was intrigued that the third man wore a suit, dark although in the poor light she could not be positive of the true color, with a tie neatly knotted into a white shirt which appeared fresh and clean.

The three observed her approach and remained seated when she got to the table, as Haseeb had remained seated in the Larnaca square. With the sort of pride with which he'd identified the cafe, Haseeb announced to the three: "This is the woman."

The suited man nodded to a chair which would put her facing him. Unhelped, Janet withdrew it from the table and sat down. Haseeb hesitated and then, uninvited, sat down at another edge of the table.

Directly, unwilling to begin any more word games, Janet said: "I'm told you have contacts in Beirut."

"Perhaps," the suited man said.

He wore a drooped moustache, like Chief Inspector Zarpas. She wondered if the policeman had by now monitored the £200 withdrawal: she'd already decided it could be easily explained as living expenses, if he demanded an account. She said: "I'm looking for someone to make inquiries for me."

The man jerked his head towards Haseeb. "He explained."

"Can you do it?"

"Perhaps," he said again.

"Depending on what?"

"Being able to find the right people. And the money."

"How much money?"

"How much have you got?"

"I can pay," assured Janet. Quickly she added: "I can pay if the information is good."

"Ten thousand," said the moustached man.

Janet lowered her head, caught by the sensation of *déjà vu*—the same amount demanded by the cheating Nicos Kholi. Looking up, she said with odd formality: "If you can provide positive information about the man for whom I am looking I will pay you £10,000."

There was a stir from among the men around the table. Janet detected another odor, competing with the smell of cooking oil, and realized it was the stink of fish. Then she remembered that they were fishermen.

A young boy carrying an empty tray emerged from inside the restaurant, looking at them expectantly. Haseeb immediately ordered brandy and the three other men indicated their glasses for more: it was *ouzo*, Janet saw. She shook her head.

The man waited for the boy to go and said: "I think we can do a deal."

"What sort of deal?" demanded Janet.

The suited man looked to his two companions. Janet saw that one was younger than the other but both had long and very curly hair and long faces, with similar long aquiline noses, and wondered if they were father and son. The elder of the two moved his head in agreement and the younger, taking his lead from the gesture, did the same.

The moustached spokesman, whom Janet assumed to be the captain, said: "Today is Monday: we sail later tonight. You could come here again on Thursday?"

"Yes," said Janet, eagerly.

"By Thursday we will have spoken to people. We will know if we can help."

"People in Beirut, you mean?"

The man nodded and said: "You can have the money, by Thursday?"

"Yes," said Janet again.

"Then it is agreed," said the man, positively.

There was another pause while the drinks were served. When the waiter left for the second time she said: "What time Thursday?"

"Mid-day."

"Do you really think you will be able to discover something?"

"Not until you tell me the name," the man said.

"Sheridan," supplied Janet anxiously, irritated with herself. "John Sheridan."

"English?"

"American."

"When was he taken?"

"February."

"Anyone claim responsibility?"

"*Hezbollah.*"

"Any particular group?"

Janet shook her head. "No."

The man remained silent for several moments, then said: "We will try."

"I am grateful."

"You have no reason, not yet."

Janet pushed her chair away from the table, as if to stand up, and said: "I'll be here, on Thursday." If demands were going to be made for some money in advance they would come now, she knew.

"Wait!" the man said.

"What?" Janet asked.

"Money for the drinks," the man said. "Five pounds will cover it."

Janet led the way back to the car, aware of Haseeb watching her stow her handbag beneath her seat. As they regained the road, he said: "It is good?"

"I don't know: I think so," said Janet, cautiously. She was encouraged that no money request had been made: a small omen but important. There was still Thursday, of course. What precautions could she take against being cheated then, when she would have the money?

"I want to be paid," demanded the Arab, beside her.

Ahead Janet could see the brightness of the hotels along the Dhekelia Road. She wanted the safety of their surroundings before handing over the £200. She said: "Those men. How are they called?"

"The boss is named Stavos," said the man. "I've heard the older one called Dimitri. I don't know the other. I think they are related."

Greek, thought Janet. "What family name?"

"I don't know."

They were among the hotels now. Janet eased the money from her pocket and handed it across the car. As she continued driving she was conscious of the man slowly counting it.

"I could take you again, on Thursday?"

"No, really." She was aware of his shrug of acceptance. Aware, too, of the even brighter lights marking the approach to Larnaca.

Hopefully Haseeb said: "You would like a drink?"

"No," Janet said quickly again. "There are people expecting me, back in Nicosia." Had she answered his look across the car she wondered if his disbelief would have been obvious. Sure of her way through the town now she slowed at the junction with Grigoris Avxentiou Avenue, knowing she could cut down it to gain the Nicosia road. "This all right for you?"

"Fine." He made no immediate effort to get out of the car.

With the vehicle stationary Janet turned further towards him but pressed with her back against her door, as far away as possible. "Goodbye then," she said, pointedly. "And thank you."

Still he stayed, edging his arm along the back of his seat towards her.

"Get out of the car!" she said. She kept her voice calm. Inwardly fear was churning through her. She moved her hand towards the horn button.

Abruptly, unexpectedly, he smiled his ugly smile and said: "OK," opening the door as he did so. He slammed it behind him and walked away without once looking back.

Janet started the car and drove hurriedly off, the fear coming out now in the trembling that vibrated through her, so she had to grip the wheel more tightly. She was still aware of the stink of fish, mixed with the stronger smell of Haseeb's odor, and she wound her window competely down, trying to blow it—and her nervousness—away. It was ridiculous, an overreaction, to behave like an offended virgin. She'd known the danger and she'd confronted it and nothing had happened, anyway. There were far more important, more positive, things to think about. Like three men who had not sought money in advance and who should by now be at sea, heading towards the Lebanese coastline. How, in three days time, to decide if anything they might tell her was worth £10,000. Or whether once again people were trying to cheat her. And how to stop being cheated.

Three days, she calculated again; time to think and to plan.

·16·

For the first night, largely from the fatigue of her previous sleeplessness, Janet slept soundly and awoke the following morning absolutely refreshed, wishing there was something, some activity, she could use to fill in the intervening days.

She telephoned her father, who asked at once when she was coming home. Janet was off-balanced by the demand. She said she had what she thought was another hopeful lead and because of it had no plans whatsoever at that moment to return. He pressed: Did she genuinely think there was any purpose in remaining on the island? Janet replied that if there wasn't any purpose then obviously she wouldn't stay. So what was it then that was so promising? Remembering the first disappointment, Janet held back, saying she thought she'd met people who had contacts in Beirut.

"Your mother and I are worried: now we've had time to think about it, your being there doesn't seem very sensible at all."

"I'm all right."

"Hasn't Partington been able to help with anything?"

"No," said Janet, then added: "I had dinner with him and his wife. There had been some link with Beirut. The word was that it was hopeless."

"There!" pounced the man at once. "If people on the spot say it's hopeless, what chance do you stand!"

"Daddy, we've been through all this!"

"I think you should come home."

"I don't want to fight about this."

"Neither do I," said her father.

"Let's not then."

"Set yourself a time limit, at least."

"Why?" demanded Janet. "What's time got to do with it?"

"You can't stay there forever."

"I don't intend to," said Janet. "But I'm certainly not coming home yet."

The conversation depressed Janet, dampening the enthusiasm with which she had awoken. Trying to remain objective—and thinking, too, of their age—she supposed it was natural that her parents should become increasingly concerned the longer she stayed but she really hadn't been on Cyprus long, less than two weeks, and the change in their attitude seemed abrupt, disorienting.

To force the argument out of her mind, Janet tried to consider her other problem, how not to be cheated out of more money, remembering as she did so the policeman's threat to monitor the account. A £10,000 withdrawal could be the immediate trigger for that other, more worrying threat, of his manipulating something to get her expelled from the island. The timing would be crucial: she'd have to make the withdrawal on her way to the cafe on the Dhekelia Road, not giving Zarpas any time to intercept or question her. And then what? Uncomfortably Janet accepted yet again that she didn't know.

Although they had parted with half promises of meeting again, Partington's call was unexpected, and Janet responded at once and not just because she had time to occupy before the Thursday meeting. Partington remained her official link, the conduit she still might have to use.

They met at the Ekali, on St. Spyridon Street, and without Partington's wife this time. Janet let the diplomat guide her through the *meze*, the Cypriot way of eating fish and meat and vegetables ferried in practically continuous procession from the kitchen: it all came too quickly for her properly to enjoy.

"So how's it going?" asked Partington.

"I don't know, not really," said Janet, guardedly.

"You're wasting your time, you know?"

"Maybe," Janet said. She paused, revolving her wine glass between her fingers, and then said: "Let's talk hypothetically for a moment. Let's say—just say—that I was told something that looked good. Some sort of new information."

Partington was staring intently at her across the table and momentarily Janet wondered if she should not have delayed this conversation until after Thursday. "All right, let's just say that," agreed Partington.

"It would have to be properly assessed: judged whether it was accurate or not, wouldn't it?"

"Go on."

"So who would do it?"

"Why don't we stop talking hypothetically?" challenged the diplomat. "Why don't you tell me what you're really saying?"

"I'm not saying anything at the moment."

"At the moment!"

Damn, thought Janet. She said: "There might be a possibility of my learning something."

"Who from?"

"I can't say."

"Why can't you?"

"Won't say," Janet qualified.

"Why not?" Partington repeated.

"Because at the moment there's nothing *to* say. It's all too vague."

"Don't," Partington said.

"Don't what?"

"Don't go on . . . get any further inveigled . . . in whatever it is you're caught up in."

"This isn't what I want to hear."

"It's the only thing you need to hear."

"I'm not giving up! When the hell will people accept that!"

"I won't help you, Janet. Encourage you."

"I told you I'd seen the Americans?"

"Yes," Partington agreed, curiously.

"Actually, they saw me," the woman admitted. "Warned me off. If I tried to tell them anything, they wouldn't listen."

"I'm not sure I'm following."

"Would you listen?" Janet asked, openly.

"I told you before that we couldn't get mixed up in this."

"I'm not asking you to get mixed up in anything!" Janet pleaded. "I've told you the Americans wouldn't listen to me. But they would to you."

"Which would make it official."

"No!" Janet protested. "I know the way embassies work: all about the backdoor conversations."

Partington shook his head. "Not about something as sensitive as this: it's too important. Which you know it is. I couldn't become linked unofficially. It would have to be official."

"All right, then! Will you pass on anything officially?"

Partington leaned closer towards her, over the table. "Tell me what it is!" he insisted. "Tell me who you're dealing with, how they operate, where they operate. What they're doing: everything. Only when I know everything—and I really mean *everything*—will I ever begin to contemplate answering your question."

It was not an outright refusal. Janet knew she was seeking a supportive straw: in fact it was as firm an undertaking as she could have expected, from what she'd told him. "I can't, not yet."

"When!"

Janet opened her mouth to speak and then clamped it shut. "A few days," she said, instead.

"This week!"

"I'm not sure," said Janet, trying to escape the pressure. "I hope so but maybe not so soon."

"What guarantees have you got?"

Janet smiled, thinking the question naive and surprised the man posed it. "What sort of guarantees could I have?"

"Exactly," said the man, turning her answer against her. "Don't do it!" he repeated. "By yourself you *can't* do anything that is going to get John free!"

Janet sipped her neglected wine, refusing to get on the roundabout. "Thank you for listening," she said. "And for saying what you did: what you were able to say, that is."

"I haven't said anything: given any undertaking," Partington insisted at once.

Always the need for a diplomatic avenue of escape, thought Janet. She said: "I haven't inferred any undertaking."

For the first time for many minutes the man looked away from her. He said: "I feel I'm failing your father."

Don't sit with your hands between your legs then, thought Janet, irritably. She said: "If there is a need for us to talk . . . about what we've been discusing now . . . and it's out of office hours, can I call you at home?"

"Of course you can."

"I appreciate that."

"I can't say anything to stop you?"

"You know you can't."

"Then . . ." Partington began but Janet cut in.

". . . be careful," she completed.

"Yes," he said, seriously. "For God's sake be careful."

Janet returned unhurriedly to the hotel, quieted but not completely disheartened by the encounter. And when she entered the foyer her mood lifted abruptly at the sight of a group of American tourists crowded around the cashier's desk negotiating the exchange of travelers' checks. Briefly she stood, watching, realizing she knew the way to protect the money demand, wondering why it had taken her so long to think of it.

The last intervening day dragged boringly by and Janet was up once more at first light on Thursday, impatient to begin. She made herself eat and thought as carefully as she had before about how to dress and as before decided upon jeans and a shapeless shirt. She checked the car, the oil and the water as well as the fuel, and timed her arrival at the bank to give herself two hours to reach the meeting spot, without the need to return again to the hotel.

At the bank she insisted upon a bearer's letter of credit endorsed in her name, waiting while the official went through the procedure, alert to his using the telephone. He didn't, not that she saw, but Janet knew a message could have been passed to Zarpas through any of the clerks and lesser officials whom the man apparently felt it necessary to consult.

She left the bank imagining their continued concentration and was glad she had not parked the hire car where they could have identified it to record the number. The encouragement was short-lived: it would only take Zarpas minutes to find out at the hotel, she guessed.

The journey to Larnaca took Janet longer than she'd scheduled because there was a delay of nearly thirty minutes getting around a vegetable lorry which had overturned, shedding its load, on the outskirts of Markon. She drove fast afterwards, to catch up, and still reached Larnaca with forty-five minutes in hand. She headed directly out upon the hotel-lined road, seeing no reason why she should not get to the cafe ahead of time.

She did, by fifteen minutes, but the three men were already there, sitting proprietorially at the same outside table, drinking *ouzo* as they had been the night of the first encounter. As before they studied her approach across the open area, each quite expressionless. The smell of bad cooking oil was as bad as it had been on Monday and Janet wondered if that were why they occupied the verandah instead of the inside area. The captain identified to her as Stavos still wore his suit: when Janet got close she could see in the brighter daylight that it was very old, greasy with age.

"I'm glad to see you here," she said.

"There was an arrangement," the moustached man reminded her.

Janet pulled a chair away from the table so that she could sit directly opposite him and said: "Well?"

Instead of replying, the man looked slightly over her shoulder and Janet turned to the attentive boy with the tray. Impatiently she ordered beer, because it would come capped, and the men indicated three more *ouzos*. Turning back to Stavos, she said: "Have you found out anything!"

"Yes," said the man, simply. "Quite a lot."

Although Janet had rigidly controlled any hope during the intervening days, refusing to let herself imagine they would come back with anything at all, there had always lurked in that locked-away part of her mind the supposedly ignored faith that they would, in fact, be successful. She turned the opening key now on that optimism and it engulfed her, a dizzying burst of excitement. She had to close her eyes briefly against the sensation and was glad she was sitting down because inexplicably her legs began to tremble.

"Thank God!" she said, but quietly, to herself. "Oh, thank God!"

"We had an agreement," Stavos said, flat-voiced and unemotional.

"I have the money," Janet said anxiously.

"All of it!"

"Please tell me: what have you found out!"

"The money," insisted the man, monotone.

Janet began to take the bearer letter from her pocket but he raised his hand, stopping her. From the rear the waiter approached and set out the drinks. Janet remained unmoving until the man said: "All right," and then she completed the movement, handing him the document.

Stavos stared down, frowning with incomprehension. "What is this!"

Janet leaned across, indicating the amount. "A letter of credit for £10,000," she said.

"It is not money."

"It becomes money."

"How?"

Janet pointed again to the endorsement. "Once I sign it . . . once I'm satisfied with what you've got to tell me . . . any bank on the island will exchange it, for cash."

The elder of the other two men, Dimitri, leaned close to the captain and spoke so softly that Janet could not detect the words. Stavos nodded and looked back at her. He said: "You didn't trust us!"

"I was tricked before. I lost my money," replied Janet. She wondered if the medical tests had been completed upon the Australian girl.

Stavos turned it over in his hands, examining its blank back as if expecting to find something there. He said: "All you have to do is sign it?"

"That's all."

This time Janet discerned the nod of agreement, between the two older men.

Stavos added water to his drink, watching it whiten, and then said: "Sheridan worked for the CIA?"

"Yes." She hadn't told the man that, she remembered. Premature to believe it significant: it was fairly public knowledge, not difficult for him to have discovered.

"They were extremely indiscreet, the Americans," said the man. "It was commonly known what his position was within the embassy."

"I don't know about that," Janet conceded.

"They were very stupid, after what happened before."

Janet gauged that to be a clear reference to William Buckley. Would a Cypriot fisherman—all right, a Cypriot fishing boat captain—be that familiar with the circumstances without some informative links on the mainland? She said: "Please be honest with me! Have you found someone—anyone—who *knows*!"

Stavos did not reply at once. Then he said: "People who want a message passed."

"I don't understand."

"Beirut is very much divided now," said Stavos. "In East Beirut, it is difficult to believe there is any sort of conflict: it is practically like it was before 1975. The battleground is in the West, where the Shia, the Hezbollah, fanatics are."

Janet nodded her head in agreement, further impressed by his knowledge. "I know all this," she said.

"There is a particular district," continued Stavos, as if she had not interrupted. "The Basta area."

"What about it?"

"It is in the Basta district that Sheridan is being held," the man announced.

Once more Janet felt reality swim away from her: they could have been discussing the whereabouts of a casually met acquaintance, as she and Harriet used to talk about people after one of Harriet's Georgetown parties. She swallowed and said: "Where in Basta?"

There was the shrug that Janet had hoped not to see. "I don't know that," Stavos said.

It sounded convincing but it was not information worth £10,000, Janet decided: nothing, in fact, that was positive at all. She said: "What do you mean, about meeting people who want a message passed?"

"The group that are holding him want a public statement made, by the American government."

"What!"

"That's what I was told," Stavos insisted. "That if Washington publicly apologized for spying . . . for interfering in the area . . . then Sheridan would be set free."

This was something! The sensation—the excitement and the re-lief—flooding through Janet now was more intense than the initial optimism. "Where is it, this statement?"

There was another shrug. "I was not given it. They thought you would need proof."

"We talked about a photograph before," remembered Janet.

"More than that," said Stavos. "They are prepared to meet you. There were no promises, not undertakings, but I had the impression you might even be taken to see him. If you could bring back a photograph of the two of you together the authorities would know that you were speaking the truth, wouldn't they? Have to react."

Janet found it impossible initially to speak. Thoughts crowded her head and the words clogged in the back of her throat. She coughed. "See him . . . !" she said, incredulous. "A photograph together!"

"Nothing definite was said," the man repeated, cautiously. "Just an impression."

"How could I do this!" Janet demanded, recovering. "How could I get to West Beirut . . . meet these people!"

"With us," the man replied, as if he were surprised by the question. "How else?"

"You would take me?"

"How otherwise would you know who they were? How to meet them?"

"When?"

"You could go today? Now?"

She could, Janet realized: she even had her passport in her handbag, although she did not imagine their entry was going to be official. "Yes," she said, pressing her legs beneath the table in an effort to quieten their renewed trembling. "Yes, I can quite easily go now."

Dimitri turned sideways again, for another inaudible conversation. The captain listened, nodding in agreement. He looked over the table at Janet and said: "We have kept our side of the agreement?"

"I think so," said Janet.

"So we get the money?"

"When we get back," said Janet. "You can keep the letter and when we get back we can go to a bank together and it will be cashed." There was no way she could be cheated: the bearer document was non-negotiable without her signature.

Stavos looked down at the draft and then handed it sideways to Dimitri, who studied it for several moments, before returning it. Passingly Janet wondered if either of them could read English.

"Which bank?" demanded Stavos.

"Any bank," assured Janet.

"Here in Larnaca?"

"Yes."

The captain folded the letter carefully, so that the sides aligned, and just as carefully put it into a worn and scuffed wallet which he eased into a rear pocket of his trousers, making sure that the flap was buttoned over it. He looked up at her: "It is agreed. You are ready?"

"Yes," said Janet. "I am ready."

This time Stavos paid for the drinks. Janet filed out between the men, Dimitri and the younger man ahead, Stavos behind. Stavos said: "We will take your car."

Janet had imagined their boat would be nearby and was surprised they had to drive somewhere. Stavos got authoritatively into the front passenger seat and the other two men wedged themselves into the back. The smell of their work was stronger in the confined space and Janet wound her window fully down. "Which way?" she asked.

Stavos gestured: "On towards Dhekelia."

Janet jolted out of the car park and turned along the bay, driving with it to her right. The sweeping beach was crammed with oil-shiny tourists and technicolored umbrellas. The lowering sun was on the other side of the car and Janet was glad she had the shade. The men seemed untroubled by the heat and uninterested in anything around them: Stavos stared directly ahead, and in her rear-view mirror Janet saw the other two were doing the same. She passed the signs to Leivadie and Xylotymvou before Stavos gestured to his right and Janet saw a huddle of working boats in the fishing shelter. Closer, Janet saw, there was a public car park. Stavos said: "Leave the car there."

Janet did, locking it, and following Stavos's lead crossed the main road to walk parallel with the beach. At this part of the bay sheets of nets hung from their poles or were laid out on the sand, drying, and a lot of lobster pots lay in apparent disorder. Flocks of gulls screeched and argued overhead, suddenly dipping to scavenge what bits there were still among the netting. The smell was overwhelming and there were no holidaymakers or parasols for a long way. The working area was quieter than Janet had expected, too: practically deserted, in fact, with no one in any of the boats.

To Stavos she said: "Where is everybody?"

"This is the between time," he said. "The morning boats are back, with their catches . . ." He indicated the drying nets. "Those are theirs," he said. "The night boats won't go out for another three or four hours."

"When do you normally fish?"

"When it suits."

Janet look at her watch. It was 2 P.M. "What time will we get to Beirut?"

"Depends on the sea. The forecast is good so I would expect around midnight."

"They are expecting you?"

"I know a way to make contact."

"So I could be taken to see John tonight?" Janet asked, feeling another sweep of excitement.

"That will be for them to decide," Stavos said. He halted at the water's edge and said something in Greek. The younger man waded immediately out to a flat-bottom dory tethered to a buoy about five yards offshore. He did not bother to remove his shoes or roll his trousers up: by the time he reached the boat the sea was up to his thighs. He released the line and hauled it into shore. In the daylight Janet guessed he was younger than she'd first thought, probably little more than twenty.

To Dimitri she said: "Your son?"

"Cousin," said the older man. It was the first time Janet had heard him speak. The English was thickly accented.

The man halted the dinghy about a yard offshore and Stavos said: "I could carry you out?"

"No," Janet said, at once. She quickly took off her shoes and waded into the water without attempting to roll up the bottom of her jeans. Remembering Sheridan's teaching she got easily into the boat, wedging her behind over the gunwales first and then swinging her legs inboard.

Both men followed without bothering to remove their shoes. The youngest man rowed, pulling them out to the fishing boat anchored furthest from the shore. As they passed the stern Janet saw there was no name but a lettered number. She thought it was C-39 but the marking was worn by sea and weather so she could have been mistaken.

The younger man vaulted easily from the dinghy into the larger boat, while the other two steadied it against the side. He leaned over, reaching out to help her. Janet accepted his offer: after hauling her halfway out he changed his grip, cupping both hands beneath her arms finally to bring her into the boat. It meant his fingers brushed briefly against her breasts. Janet pulled away at once, deciding it was an accident. The man appeared unaware of what he'd done, paying her no overt attention, instead taking the line from Stavos to trail the dory to the stern, where it would be winched from the water into its davits.

Janet thought the condition of the fishing boat was appalling. She was accustomed to Sheridan's immaculately maintained vessel, with its neatly curled and stowed lines, tightly reefed sails, scrubbed and stoned deck and burnished metalwork.

This boat was squat and bulge-stemmed, lobster pots discarded where they'd clearly fallen, weed-clogged nets tangled and lumped in the stern. Amongst it all were bamboo-poled fishing lines and several ropes of cork floats. There was a central wheelhouse and alongside a minute cowl over steps leading below to what Janet supposed were cabins or at least some sort of sleeping accommodation. Directly behind, amidships, was the engine flap which Dimitri already had open, his body upended over the machinery. The working area where Janet presumed fish were gutted or prepared on homeward journeys was behind the engine area. There were actually knives in some kind of frame and the deck here was slimed with guts and scales which had not been washed down from the previous trip and which, inexplicably, had escaped the seabirds. Perhaps, thought Janet, even they had been unable to confront the stench. It was more than soured and rotting fish and their innards. There were exhaust fumes from the diesel engines which at that moment shuddered into life and the smell of the diesel itself and then something more for which she could find no comparison or identification: just a general odorous miasma of dirt and neglect.

"There's a bench in the wheelhouse," Stavos said.

Looking more intently Janet saw that a plank had been fixed along the bulkhead furthest from the wheel itself: it was padded with various pieces of sagging cloth and blanket, some of which hung down like lank hair to reach the decking. Pointing to her wet jeans bottoms Janet said: "I'll stay outside for these to dry."

"Please yourself," shrugged the man, going towards the bench himself.

Neglected though the boat might be, there was nevertheless an oddly disjointed sort of efficiency about the fashion in which the group got it underway. Janet never once saw Stavos give any obvious command but the other two men went through what appeared an established routine, slipping anchor and stowing things unstowed—although doing little to clear the mess, rather moving it from one jumbled area to another—and preparing themselves and the vessel for sea. Janet tried to find herself a convenient place on one of the clearer sections of the deck directly in the dropping sunlight; although it was still comparatively hot, her trouser hems clung uncomfortably wet and cold around her ankles, sometimes actually making her shiver and she was anxious to dry them as much as possible. The ship had a flat stern and she wedged herself into the corner it made with the starboard rail, stetching her foot out on top of a lobster pot to catch the warmth. Because she was thinking about her feet she turned to the two seamen and saw both had, unseen by her, discarded their footwear and rolled up their sodden trouser bottoms: they moved flat-footed and assuredly around the boat, their toes splayed almost like fingers as they felt their way.

Janet was not conscious of their clearing the lee of Larnaca Bay but realized they must have done so by the increased movement of the boat. It obviously had a shallow draft, and the square back made it even more vulnerable, so very quickly it began to pitch and roll, although the swell was comparatively small. Janet had to take her leg down from the pot for balance. In the wheelhouse the moustached man hung nonchalantly against the spoked steering, a spilling hand-made cigarette stuck precariously to his bottom lip. She decided against going there yet.

The sun was losing its heat, and the sea was becoming dulled from bright silver into soft gold. There were a lot of yachts and pleasure boats, both sail and engine driven: some, she thought, were too small to have ventured this far. Caught by the thought she looked back, surprised how low Cyprus was becoming on the sky-line: it was just a continuous black and vaguely undulating shape, from which it was difficult to pick out positive landmarks. From the direction she imagined they had come Janet guessed a hazed white area to be the pier and marina at Larnaca but she couldn't be sure. She wondered how Stavos navigated: there did not appear to be any aerials or electronic equipment but she knew there had to be: a radio, at least.

The younger man plodded wide-footed from the stem of the boat towards her. The other was bent over pots, finally putting them into some sort of order, on the opposite side of the stern. He saw her look and smiled, surprisingly white-teethed, and Janet smiled back, deciding it was ridiculous not being able to properly address him. She said: "How are you called?"

He hesitated, still smiling, and said: "Costas."

The other man continued working over the pots but said something in Greek. Costas responded and Dimitri spoke again, louder this time. The younger man's reply was just one word and Janet wondered if it were an obscenity.

Janet's jean bottoms were drier but not by much, and she acknowledged there was hardly enough heat left in the sun to make any further improvement. What did it matter? she asked herself, not knowing why she was even thinking of something so inconsequential. What did anything matter—this awful stinking ship or £10,000 or anything—beyond the fact that she was on her way to Beirut! To Beirut and people who might actually let her see John: people who certainly knew about him and wanted her to convey some message, back to America, to gain his freedom. And she could most definitely get any message conveyed, Janet knew, after her experience of publicity in Washington. She didn't give a damn what sort of crap it was—she'd get the Koran published if that were one of the demands—just as long as it got John out from wherever he was. She should, Janet supposed, be feeling some sort of "I told you so" satisfaction from what she'd achieved but she didn't. Just relief: excited relief. Any other emotion would have been an intrusion. Unnecessary. The only satisfaction she sought was that of having John back with her, safely.

It was the half-light of the Mediterranean now, Cyprus lost beyond the horizon from which night was proudly approaching in a tumble of black clouds. There was a wind coming, too, and the boat began to rise and fall more steeply as the swell increased. Janet shivered, tightening her arms around herself: the jeans were adequate, but the shirt was for the heat of mid-day, not the numb of an open boat at night. The smell was getting to her, as well, combining with the rise-and-fall movement. She swallowed deeply against what lumped in the back of her throat, tight-lipped against showing the slightest weakness.

"Here!"

Janet became conscious of Costas before her, offering a bottle. Janet could see that it was unlabeled but nothing else. "No, thank you."

"Make you feel better."

"I'm all right."

"It's brandy," he said, belatedly.

"No, really. Thank you all the same."

If her discomfort were that obvious it was ridiculous remaining any longer beyond whatever little protection the wheelhouse would give, Janet accepted: now that it was completely dark the excuse about drying her clothes didn't apply, either. Using the rail, greasy to her touch, for as much support as it would give, Janet groped amidships to the tiny hut. Nearer she saw that Stavos had lighted the red and green navigation lights and that there was also a dull white light in the place itself.

She got to the door and said: "I would like to come in now, please."

From his look it was almost as if he were startled to find her on his boat at all. He jerked his head towards the bench and said: "Of course."

Janet eased her way into the tiny hut and sat on the lumpy padding close to the open door. The door slid back and forth on runners, she saw. There was a matching entrance on the far side of the wheelhouse but it was secured by an inside bolt. In front of Stavos was a sloped chart table but there were no charts on it. What she could see was a magazine, well thumbed, with what appeared to be a naked girl on the front. It was partially concealed by pages of a newspaper, which Stavos was reading. There was also an empty tobacco tin, acting as an ashtray. And there was a radio, although not the type Janet expected. It looked like the sort of transistor those Larnaca Bay holidaymakers would have had: as the thought came she heard, very softly, a wailing pop song coming from it. The radio was taped against the side of the chart table and swung back and forth, like a pendulum, with the rocking of the boat. Beneath the table was a tangle of ropes and lines. Stavos had taken his shoes off, like the other two crewmen, and rolled his trousers up.

"How much longer?" Janet asked.

Stavos grunted away from his newspaper. He looked briefly through the salt-rimmed glass out into the completely empty blackness of the night, then at his watch, and said: "Maybe two hours: maybe less."

Janet checked her own watch and said: "Before midnight, then?"

"Maybe," said Stavos.

A man of definite opinions, thought Janet. She said: "Are you sure you will be able to find the people tonight?"

"I said I would come back with a decision: with something," said Stavos, abandoning his newspaper altogether and turning to her.

"So they are expecting you!"

"They said they would be ready."

Costas appeared at the doorway next to her. He still carried the bottle and in the better light Janet thought his face appeared flushed. He said something in Greek and offered it to the captain but Stavos shook his head in refusal. The young man then smiled at Janet, moving his outstretched arm so that the bottle was towards her.

"No thank you," she said again.

The doorway was completely blocked by the arrival of Dimitri. He spoke in Greek to Stavos who glanced briefly at his watch before replying and Janet guessed it was a query about an arrival time. The younger man remained looking at her, smiling. Janet smiled back. Costas took a swig from the bottle and said: "Good stuff. The best."

"I'm sure," Janet said.

Stavos said something, brief and sharp, and Costas's smile flickered off. He replied, equally brief, his face sullen. No one moved for several moments and then the younger man screwed the metal top back on to the bottle.

"Would you like to eat?" Stavos asked, suddenly. "There's some fish and bread. Olives, too. Wine, as well."

"I'm really not hungry," Janet said, swallowing against the sensation that came once more to the back of her throat at the very thought of consuming anything.

"It's going to be a long night."

"I'll ask, if I get hungry." Anxious to switch the conversation from food Janet gestured to what she thought was a gradual lightening ahead and said: "Is that it! Beirut!"

Without looking, Stavos said: "Yes."

Here! thought Janet; I'm here! She said: "How much longer now?"

"Maybe an hour."

Janet sat practically oblivious to anything and anyone around her, occupied only upon what was ahead. There was a definite break in the darkness now, an actual horizon line although she could not make out the shapes of buildings. She was surprised at so much light: without positively thinking about it she'd imagined it would be a place of enforced and protective darkness, like the Second World War blackouts in England that her parents had described. She strained to hear any sound, and realized that—ridiculously—she was listening for the sound of gunfire. All she could hear was the grating, reverberating throb of the engines, behind her. Soon, my darling, she thought: I'll be there soon.

Stavos broke into her reverie. He said: "There's a part of the harbor, to the west, where we can go alongside. You'll stay aboard, while I go to find them."

"Why can't I come with you?"

"West Beirut isn't a place for evening strolls," rejected the captain.
"It's safer this way."

"How far is it from the harbor to where you expect to meet them?"

"Not far."

"It can't be that dangerous, then?"

"This is how it is going to be done!" Stavos said loudly.

Janet winced, not wanting to alienate a man upon whom she was
so dependent. "I'm sorry," she said at once. "Of course."

Beirut was more discernible now and Janet saw that the brightness
was not as uniform as she had imagined it to be. The street lights
and house and building lights and even the lights of cars moving
along coastal highways were all to the east. Which Stavos had described as safe: *practically like it was before 1975*, Janet remembered.
It was much darker to the west and what she calculated to be the
south, the war areas. Street illumination was intermittent, over large
areas none existing at all, and there were hardly any building lights,
either. Nothing seemed to be moving on the roads; if there were cars
they were driving without headlights.

Stavos extinguished the dull white bulb inside the wheelhouse,
leaning forward in complete darkness against the glass, which he
scrubbed with his hand to remove something obstructing his view.
The harbor, like the city, was divided by light. To Janet's left a lot
of boats and ships showed themselves at anchor or against jetty or
harbor moorings but in the direction in which they were moving,
very slowly, hulls and outlines were black and indistinct, whatever was showing nothing more than the barest glimmer. Stavos
began to talk, in Greek, and Janet became aware that Dimitri
was between the wheelhouse and the front of the ship, as a relay,
and that Costas was in the actual V of the stem, guiding them
through the channels and past obstructions. A shout came louder
than the rest and Stavos jerked the gear lever into reverse but they
still came against the mooring hard, bouncing away from the wall so
the man had to go back and forth between the gears to maneuver
himself into position again. The two crewmen jumped onto the jetty
with securing lines and at once Stavos turned to her. He said: "You
must wait."

"Yes," Janet said. She added: "In the dark?"

"It is better."

"Why?"

"Just better."

"I can't see anything."

"It won't be long."

He brushed past her to get out of the tiny hut and there was a mumble of inaudible conversation near the shoreside rail where Janet assumed the other two men to be. Blackness was all around her, stifling, like a blanket that was too thick: she felt positively hot, despite the coldness of the night. She got up and groped to the other side of the wheelhouse, twitching her fingers until she located the bolt and tested it to ensure that it was locked. To be doubly sure, she found the opening handle and tugged against it: the door shifted but only slightly. Reassured, Janet returned to the bench and sat down.

It was getting easier to see, Janet decided. The blackness wasn't blackness any more but a kind of gray: her eyes had adjusted so that she was able to make out shapes and objects, able to differentiate. Black lumps, gray lumps, black lumps, gray lumps: boats and boat equipment she supposed (what else could they be?), but she could not definitely be sure. With her improving vision Janet tried to locate Dimitri and Costas but she couldn't: everything around was totally quiet and unmoving, just the lap of water and the creak of the boats. Black lump, creak creak, gray lump, creak creak. Maybe they'd all gone together. Which would mean that she was all alone on the boat. Janet wasn't hot now. Cold. She shivered, violently, and remembered that when she'd done that as a child her mother had invoked a folklore expression about someone walking over her grave.

"Drink?"

Janet yelped in surprise. She'd imagined herself deserted and had not heard Costas approach. "You frightened me," she said.

"I'm sorry: I saw you shiver."

"You were watching me?"

"Yes."

"I didn't know you were there."

"No."

"Where's Dimitri?"

"Somewhere."

"Has he gone with Stavos?"

"Maybe."

He was blocking the open door and through all the other smells Janet could detect the scent of brandy. She said: "They'll be back soon."

Fully adjusted to her surroundings now Janet saw the shoulder hump.

"Perhaps," he said. "Why not try a little drink? It's very good for the cold. Just a little drink."

Janet felt the bottle against her arm. "I don't want to drink," she said.

"You're very pretty."

"Thank you."

"You weren't upset by what I did when I helped you into the boat."

"I don't remember what you did helping me into the boat," lied Janet. Oh Christ, she thought.

"You're very firm. Big."

"I don't understand what you are saying."

"Big tits."

Janet's immediate impulse was properly to scream this time, to drive him away with the fear of someone intervening to arrest him. And then she remembered where she was and how she couldn't expect anyone to intervene: that more than at any time in her life she was completely and absolutely and utterly alone. Pressing control upon herself she said: "Don't talk like that."

"Why not?"

"I don't like it."

"I like it: like big tits."

"Please don't."

"Shouldn't wear baggy shirts like that, covering them up. Want to see them."

"Don't Costas. Please don't."

Janet cringed when she felt his hand. He missed at first, groping her waist, but at once moved up, cupping his hand beneath her breast and feeling for where he imagined her nipple to be, squeezing hard. He didn't have her nipple but it still hurt and Janet snatched a breath but refused to cry out in case that was what he wanted.

"Liked that," he said. "Feels good."

"So did I," Janet forced herself to say. "I liked it, too."

The man giggled and Janet was engulfed in more brandy breath: his hands moved over her breasts, kneading and squeezing, hurting her badly. He said: "Knew you would. Big tits."

Janet edged slightly away from him, further along the bench. "I'd like that drink now," she said.

Costas stumbled awkwardly into the wheelhouse entrance, colliding with either side. "Sure," he said. "Here."

It gave Janet the excuse to stand up and get further away. She reached out, toward him: one hand grabbed for her but she was able to evade it. "The bottle?" she said. "Where's the bottle?"

"Here," he said and this time the other hand connected and she felt the coldness of the glass.

Janet had edged backwards all the time, risking his inevitable entry into the tiny hut. She felt out, putting her hand against his chest and said: "Give me room to take a drink then!"

Costas stopped coming towards her and Janet raised the bottle to her lips, keeping them pressed tightly together, with her free hand reaching behind for the bolt to the other sliding door. She scraped her foot against the deck as loudly as she could to mask any other sound she made. Knowing where it was, she was able at once to locate the opening handle. She jerked sideways against it, anxiously, starting to turn to run through it.

Nothing happened.

It moved just slightly, as it had when she'd checked it earlier, but it remained rigid. Janet tried once more, harder this time, but it refused to budge, and she realized there were additional outside locks or securing bars. On top of one horrified realization tumbled others, all as terrifying: that she'd encouraged a drunken man intent upon rape into believing she wanted him sexually: that unquestionably he was stronger than she was, physically, and would succeed: that they were together, in the smallest of places; that she was trapped.

"Good stuff?" he mumbled.

"Very good."

"Have another drink."

Trying to delay what was inevitably to happen Janet raised the bottle again, feeling the cheap liquor burn her lips: a little got through, making her choke. He was against her, pressing her to the door through which she couldn't escape, one hand cruel against her breast, the other trying to work its way between her tight legs, fingers spidering through the cloth in what he believed would stimulate her sex. But worst of all he attempted to kiss her, smearing an open wet mouth against hers, trying to drive his tongue into her. Janet bit down against the inside of her lips, desperate to seal them, not caring if she bit herself to bleed. She was going to bleed anyway, elsewhere. His body ground into her thigh and she could feel his erection: it seemed huge. Bleed a lot, she thought.

"Not so tight," he mumbled. "Stop being so tight."

Janet pushed him away. "Not here," she said, short-breathed. "It won't be comfortable here. There's nowhere for me to lie."

Costas backed off slightly: she could see that his head was uncertainly to one side. He said: "Down below. There's down below."

"Bunks?"

"Sort of."

"Let's go below."

With absurd courtesy the man offered his hand, to guide her. Repelled, Janet still took it and allowed herself to be led from the restriction of the wheelhouse, actually gulping at the air the moment she got beyond the door. She stopped. He stopped with her, his free hand groping at her breast again, trying to get his fingers into the opening of her shirt to touch her flesh. Janet let him because it was not an immediate danger: the tiny cowl to her right, leading down into God knows where, was the immediate danger.

"I like a party," she said.

Costas sniggered, popping a button to make room for his hand, and said: "I'll give you a party: I'll give you a party you've never had before."

"Here," offered Janet, raising the bottle between them. "Have a drink yourself."

Still with one hand loosely inside her shirt Costas took the brandy with the other, tilting his head in a gesture of macho bravado to take a swig. Janet was perfectly able to see. She waited until his throat visibly started to move, to take the liquor, and then drove her hand upwards with all the fear-driven force she could manage. Which was a lot. The heel of her hand precisely caught the bottle at its very bottom, ramming the neck of the bottle fully up into the man's mouth. There was a snap, of breaking teeth, and a scream of agony, and still Janet kept thrusting, holding the bottle now and screwing it further into his mouth, wanting to drive it down his throat. Costas floundered backwards, gagging, and tripped over something littering the deck, going down. The bottle was jerked out of her hands, smashing as he threw his head sideways: the man lay on his side, choking. Janet looked desperately around, for some other weapon, whimpering with fresh fear as she was grabbed from behind. Dimitri's arms wrapped around her, trapping her own. It was not a sexual attack. He was restraining her, trying to pull her away. In front she saw Costas pushing himself from the planking, struggling to get up: he was still spitting the blood from his mouth. Janet strained outwards, to break the older man's grip, but couldn't.

Dimitri spoke, directly into her ear and not to her but to Costas and in Arabic now.

"Ya himar! Al-lak titrik-ha l'al ba-i-een!"

Briefly, for no more than secounds, Janet stopped struggling. Why should she have been left? What did it mean, that she was for the others? Her stopping deceived the man holding her. She was aware of his slight relaxation and she jerked suddenly, turning to bring Dimitri around between herself and the younger man. Dimitri moved with her and at once there was an angonized yell and the grip fell away, freeing her.

Janet turned, to face the man. He was hopping on one foot and in the heel of the other she could see embedded the jagged base of the broken brandy bottle, and Janet remembered their being barefoot during the voyage. Costas was almost upright now, crouched and about to run at her. Janet shoved out, driven by anger as well as fear. She caught Dimitri fully in the back and without any balance Dimitri hurtled into the other man. They both fell and there were fresh yells. She guessed they'd gone on to more broken glass and hoped they were pieces that hurt badly, like the base embedded in Dimitri's foot.

Janet gazed frantically around, not knowing what to do. There was scuffling, from behind, and she saw Costas pulling himself upright once more. She ran without thought to the stern, grunting as she hit against something. She felt out, not able to tell from the feel what it was, and then realized it was the frame holding the gutting knives she had seen when she boarded that afternoon. She grabbed at one, holding it outwards between both her hands, level with her waist, turning back towards Costas.

He was coming towards her cautiously, crab-like, bent and with his body half turned. His face appeared covered with something black and Janet guessed it was blood.

When he spoke the words were slurred by the damage she had caused to his mouth. "Hurt you," he said. "You can't believe how I'm going to hurt you. Break you in, that's what I'm going to do. Really break you in."

Dimitri's voice came from behind, still in Arabic: Janet couldn't see him and guessed he was lying where he'd fallen. "*Homme bidhum yaha. Ma bit-'oud tiswa.*"

Who wanted her for themselves? How would she be no good, split apart? Janet thought she knew and felt the vomit rise, to her throat.

"*Anna biddi ya-ha abil-il kill!*" Costas shouted back.

He wasn't going to have her first, Janet determined. No one was going to have her. She stood where the boat was darkest: she'd just be a black outline. So he wouldn't have seen the knife. Could she kill him: intentionally drive the knife into his body? Hurt her, he'd said: hurt her badly. Yes, she could kill him: stab him at least, to make him stop. He was very close now, no more than a yard or two: she was aware of his tensing, to jump at her.

"*Trickni. Hill 'anni!*"

Janet spoke—told him to stay away—in Arabic and he did stop, surprised she knew the language. The halt was only brief. She saw his crushed lips pull back, in the grimace of a smile, and he answered her in Arabic, calling her a whore. And then he came at her. He just rushed, arms stretched forward to grab her, and he actually had her shoulders before he ran on to the knife.

He gave a great gasp, sucking in his breath, in pain and in shock, and staggered backwards, looking down. The knife was in very deep: Janet was only able to see the handle, protruding from the left-hand side of his body. Costas sagged, as if he were about to collapse at the knees, tried to straighten but couldn't, not completely, and finally toppled over. His legs quivered upwards, forming his body into a ball, and a long groan gurgled from him.

Janet ran.

She used one of the mooring ropes as a hand-hold, balanced herself on the rail and then jumped over the narrow ditch of sea on to the jetty. After the hours on the ship Janet felt immediately unsteady on a solid footing and had to snatch out for a bollard for support. It gave her the opportunity to orientate herself.

She was about halfway along a narrow mooring finger maybe two hundred yards long and ten yards wide. Underfoot she detected cobbles and guessed it was a very old part of the harbor construction. There were bollards like the one she was holding, roughly twenty yards apart along either side, and every so often small sheds and buildings which she supposed accommodated the fishing tackle and equipment of boats permanently using the berths. The mooring on either side of where they had tied up was empty, which would have accounted for the noise of her struggling not being overhead: she doubted if anyone would have bothered to intrude if they had been detected.

Her mind was disjointed, thoughts only half forming before others presented themselves to get in the way. Janet tried to concentrate, to assess the situation she was in and to find a way out. Confronting literally the need to find a way out, she realized, abruptly, she was still trapped: she had to clear the jetty.

Feeling steadier at last she set out towards the port, the sea to her back, heading into the shadow of the first storage hut. It was fortunate she did because she was completely hidden when she saw the movement ahead. Three men, maybe four, walking in a group with their heads close in conversation. Janet stopped, easing slightly backwards and then around the tiny building, keeping it between herself and the group. The mumble of words came to her as they got closer: she strained, not sure at first, then definitely identified Stavos's voice. The talk was in Arabic. There was something about a problem and then she heard "taught" and the slap of a fist being driven into the palm of a hand and the splatter of laughter. She missed the beginning of a sentence but caught "morale of the men" and there was more laughter. Someone said they were very pleased and Stavos replied that he would like to be able to do more business.

When they reached the hut Janet edged around it, keeping it between herself and them. She'd actually reversed their positions— so that she was on the landside and they had passed, towards the sea—when she heard a muffled shout, in Arabic, and recognized Dimitri's voice.

"She's got away," he said.

Janet ran. She did so as quietly as possible and stayed in the shadows so that they would not see and reckoned she'd gained about thirty yards before she heard the shout behind and the slap of feet in pursuit. Uncaring about being heard or seen any more she fled headlong, legs pumping, arms jerking, leaping and dodging over ropes and boxes: there were dark movements of curiosity from some of the boats she went by, but no challenges. Behind she heard: "Stop. Stop her," and someone started to move from a boat to her left, but she ran faster and passed it before anyone could get in the way.

There were a few lights on the harbor wall, and she saw it was too high to clear in a single jump. She managed to get over by leaping onto its top and then dropping down. She still seemed to be in the port area. There were cranes and trucks with lifting gear, and offices, to her right. The clear area was to her left. She went in that direction, aware too late of an enclosing wire mesh fence. She changed direction, running parallel and looking for a break. There wasn't one. The men were over the wall now. She jerked to a halt, gazing around, seeing as she did so that they were fanning out from where they'd landed to entrap her from either side. They weren't even bothering to run any more, strolling quite confidently, enjoying an unexpected game.

Janet started off again, towards the offices which made up a continuation of the fence. They were lighted and she saw figures in two of them but knew from the assurance with which the men were closing in upon her that whoever the officials or clerks were they would not protect her. She snatched at the first door. It was locked and from the men close behind she heard a snigger and one shouted something to another. The second was locked too: she thought she could hear their footsteps now, so near were they. Then the third door gave.

She thrust through, hearing the outraged shout very close, but had the sense to turn as she slammed it, to seek the key. She twisted it in the lock as a body hit on the other side: the door lever flapped furiously but uselessly up and down.

Janet threw herself along the corridor, ready to thrust anyone aside, but no one emerged from any of the offices. Behind there was hammering and yelling and she heard thumps and grunts as someone tried to break the door in. The street exit was secured, but the key was in its hole. Janet opened it, began to go through and then halted as the idea came. She ducked back, extracted the key, and stopped outside long enough to lock it behind her. As she panted across the harbor road she heard the sound of someone rattling the metal of the fence in frustration. There was a shout but she didn't hear the words.

It was a long time before Janet stopped hurrying. She twisted and turned along the cratered and rubble-strewn streets, pulling into the shadows when she became aware of any movement around her, always trying to go eastwards to what she imagined would be safety.

Janet was shocked by the devastation. Whole streets were lined with humps of brickwork and concrete, no glass or windows remaining anywhere, although from the sounds—scratching and slithering and the occasional moving shadow—she recognized that people lived in the warrens formed by the debris. There were movements and shadows from the burned-out and sometimes overturned shells of vehicles, too, and she realized they made homes for more people. Several times there were calls of challenge: always Janet pulled deeper into whatever darkness she could find, never replying. Dogs barked and yapped, frequently. None came near.

The immediate danger receding, Janet felt increasingly weak— her knees actually threatening to give out more than once—from the delayed terror of what might have happened and the exhaustion of getting away. She had to stop several times just to lean against a rubble pile or sagging wall, pulling the breath into herself in the effort to stay calm. That's what she had to do: stay calm, not panic. Stay calm and cross whatever the dividing line was and go some-where—a hotel or an embassy or a Western airline office—where she could explain what she'd been through and get help. Get away. Christ, she'd been lucky: luckier probably than she'd ever know.

The shadows gradually stopped seeming so dark and during one of her stops—to rest again her quivering legs—Janet stared upwards and saw that the sky was lightening. Dawn, early dawn at last, could not be far off. Would it be more difficult to cross in daylight rather than darkness? Cross what? Was there an actual border, between the east and the rest of the city, like there was in Berlin? Or was it just an understood demarcation, one street devastation, the next street so-phistication? She pushed herself up from a concrete mound and groped on, finding it difficult to properly walk, managing little more than to get one foot in front of the other, trying not to scuff too loudly as she did so. The light increased, and the movement all around grew: a few people actually passed on an early errand or on the way to work. No one gave her more than the briefest passing attention.

The hotel appeared suddenly in front of her, like an oasis, and for the initial seconds Janet could not believe that it was there, staring at it as if it really were a mirage that would disappear. But it didn't. It was shell-pocked and there were some sandbags and a few of their windows were taped against bomb blast but it was definitely a hotel. There were people moving about inside and there were lights on, more lights than there had been in any other building she passed.

She dragged herself forward, stumbling on the steps up to the revolving doors, and stopped directly inside, to gather her strength against breaking down at reaching safety.

At the desk it seemed to be changeover time, from the night to day staff. They frowned, startled, as she approached and Janet looked down, shocked at the state of herself. Her jeans were tattered and her blouse was ripped and only held across her by one remaining button. There was lot of blood which must have come from Costas, changed brown by the dust in which she was caked.

"Please help me," she said. "I'm English. English-American. My name is Stone: Janet Stone."

"The fiancée of John Sheridan," said an American voice behind.

·17·

I t was not one man but several. Another—not the American who'd first spoken, because the voice was different—said: "Jesus, you're right!" and Janet looked blankly at all of them.

The first man came closer, smiling and with his hand outstretched: "Whelan, Jim Whelan. CBS. I did an interview with you in Washington when Sheridan first went missing. Just been posted here myself."

Limply Janet took his hand, not remembering, looking beyond him to the other men. Whelan said, "Welcome to the Summerland Hotel, home of the international press corps," he said.

The first man who had spoken came to her now. "Henry Black," he said. "*Washington Post.* And do you look as if you've got problems!"

Janet burst into tears.

She tried to stop but couldn't and they sat her in the foyer and got coffee she didn't drink and waited until she'd recovered. When she did, it seemed as if the group had grown larger. Other people introduced themselves. There were more Americans and three or maybe four Englishmen and an Englishwoman stringing for two London newspapers, as well as some French and Germans, far too many names for Janet to remember. She was aware of cameras going off and shunned away, wishing they wouldn't, and a soft-voiced argument began between the Americans she'd first met and the photographers. Janet said she wanted to wash, to try to clean herself up, and the CBS reporter arranged a room for her, and the Englishwoman, whose name she finally got as Ann, became a self-appointed guardian, telling the other reporters they would have to wait. Janet bathed and washed her hair, getting rid of her fatigue as well as the dirt and when she emerged from the bathroom found the other woman had set out some of her own clothes for her to borrow, a skirt and a shirt and a sweater. Everything was slightly too big but didn't appear so when Janet surveyed herself in the mirror.

While she'd bathed Janet had fully regained control. Now she assessed the problems. She was an illegal entrant, certainly. But that wasn't the most serious; the most serious had to be the stabbing aboard the fishing boat. Perhaps more than a stabbing: perhaps a killing. Her word against . . . against how many? She didn't know: but she'd definitely be outnumbered. Stavos and Dimitri would get the others to lie against her, to concoct any sort of story they wanted. So she needed protection: official, professional protection, before even surrendering herself to whatever Beirut authority existed. And public, outside protection, too. Which meant the waiting pressmen downstairs.

Janet cooperated with everyone and everything. She gave a combined press conference and then individual interviews and posed for still photographs and the television cameras. Because he had been the first to approach her she asked Whelan to take her to the British embassy, and there, even before she explained her situation, she set out the cooperation she had given to the world media, openly using it as a threat although she was not sure against what.

The embassy official's name was John Prescott: his position within the legation was never made clear to her. He was a precise, neat man and surprisingly slight. The word that came to Janet the moment they met was dainty. He listened without any outward reaction, small hand against his small face, making an occasional note in careful script. When she finished he asked her to wait in the office and was gone for more than an hour. He returned with another man whom he introduced as Robertson and identified as the embassy's legal advisor. The lawyer was a heavy, florid-faced man: he reminded Janet of Partington, in the Nicosia embassy. Robertson

asked her to repeat much of the story, which she did, and when she
finished he complained, red-faced, that it would have been much
more sensible for her to have come direct to the embassy instead of
announcing it in advance to the press. Janet didn't apologize.

Prescott pedantically explained that as her first marriage gave her
certain rights to American citizenship he had felt it right to involve
the U.S. embassy, as well as themselves. He had also been in communication with the British embassy in Beirut and had sent a full
account to the Foreign Office in London. It was all very difficult and
complicated, he said.

Janet wondered what they were waiting for until, thirty minutes
later, two other men were ushered into the rapidly overcrowding
room. Only one provided a name. It was William Burr and he described himself as an attaché at the U.S. embassy. He said: "You're
causing us all a lot of headaches, Ms. Stone: a whole lot of headaches. We're getting far too accustomed to hearing your name."

To the Englishmen, Burr said: "You arranged an interview?"

Robertson nodded and said: "Three o'clock."

"Where?"

"Here," said the lawyer. "Within British jurdisdiction: it gives her
the protection of the embassy."

"Very wise," agreed the American. Janet thought his hair was surprisingly long for a diplomat. He had a very freckled face and wore
the sort of heavy moustache she remembered being popular among
young people in the late '60s, when she'd first gone up to the university. The other, unnamed American was much younger, an open-
faced, bespectacled man who moved his head obviously between
every speaker. Janet wondered if he were a lawyer, like Robertson.
"Interview with whom?" she demanded.

"Police. And Immigration," said Robertson.

Five Lebanese arrived, so it was necessary to move into a larger
room. It was dominated by a conference table and Prescott carefully
sat her between himself and Robertson on one side, keeping the
Beirut officials on the other. The Americans sat at one end, like
referees.

Janet answered the questions from two of the Lebanese, one police, the other immigration. A third man bent constantly over his
pad, keeping verbatim notes. After an hour the policeman had a
whispered conversation with his companion, who nodded, and
asked for the use of a telephone. Prescott led one who had so far
taken no part in the questioning to the smaller office in which they'd

first been, and the interrogation resumed. It was not as demanding, as hostile even, as Janet had expected. Both questioners frequently smiled as they put their queries and the immigration inspector often nodded to her replies, as if he were in agreement with what she were saying.

When the Lebanese official returned to the room there was a muffled conversation between the group and the questioner produced a detailed map and asked Janet to identify the berth against which she believed the fishing boat had tied up the previous night. When Janet did so the man asked Robertson if they would agree to Janet accompanying them upon a launch, to point out the spot.

"Leave the embassy, you mean?" demanded the lawyer.

The Lebanese lowered his head, acknowledging the point of the question: "My colleague and I are happy to agree with the protection of the embassy extending with you: presumably one or all of you will wish to come too."

"Why?" intruded Janet. "Why do you want me to do this?" She was frightened of going near that stinking hulk again; of actually confronting Stavos and Dimitri and whoever—or whatever—else might be aboard.

"There is no fishing boat of the sort you have described anywhere in that part of the harbor: no Cyprus-registered vessel at all," announced the policeman, simply.

"Which means . . ." began the American, but the Lebanese cut him short, in agreement. ". . . that there is no incident involving a stabbing for us to become involved in," said the man.

The British lawyer and Burr accompanied Janet. They drove in a British embassy car to a different part of the harbor, in the east of the city, where there were police in uniform and as many sparkling and glittering yachts and boats at their moorings as there were in the Larnaca marina.

All four Lebanese crowded aboard the officially designated harbor launch, which looped out to sea and then came in at Janet's hesitant direction, as she tried to recall her approach the previous night. In the daylight she was better able to make out the division between the parts of the city and the port. When she became almost certain of the jetty she squinted shorewards, to locate the fenced-in part near the offices where she had been hounded by the pursuing men. She found it, running her eyes from it as a marker, and decided she was right.

"There!" she said.

"You're sure?" Robertson asked.

"Positive."

"It's the jetty you picked out on the map," said the Lebanese policeman. "As I said, we have no official record of any vessel from Cyprus having put in there during the night. And most definitely, as we can all see, there is no Cyprus fishing boat there now."

"So any stabbing inquiry ends?" Burr pressed, instantly.

The Lebanese gave an expansive shrug. "Of course."

"It happened!" Janet insisted.

"Nothing happened for me to investigate," the man said, with matching insistence.

Robertson waved his hands in a pressing-down gesture to Janet. As the launch turned to cut its way back across the harbor to the pier where they had boarded, the lawyer said: "Which just leaves the matter of illegal entry."

"I think I need to make telephone calls," said the immigration man, avoiding any immediate commitment.

More had happened ashore than at sea during the hour they had been absent from the embassy. There was a cluster of reporters and television cameramen actually around the building when they reached it. They surged forward in a glare of camera lights as they saw Janet in the car, yelling unheard questions, and it was difficult for the driver to edge by them and at the same time to negotiate the dogs' tooth barriers set up at the entrance to the British compound against any terrorist car suicide attack. The car managed it, but only just.

Prescott was waiting at the side entrance when the vehicle stopped. As they got out, Robertson demanded: "What the hell's that all about?"

Prescott waited until they had assembled back in the larger room before answering. Then he said: "Some developments, in Cyprus. A man was arrested in Larnaca today trying to negotiate at the Hellenic Bank a £10,000 bearer letter of credit made out in the name of Janet Stone."

She'd guessed Stavos had not understood, remembered Janet: served the bastard right. She said: "What about the one I stabbed?"

Prescott shook his head. "I've no information about that. I queried it and Nicosia say they don't know anything about a stabbing. The police have located the boat, apparently. There *is* a lot of blood, but as far as I can understand the story is that a crewman had an accident, with a bottle or some glass. And there's always a lot of fish blood around anyway on a boat like that."

The American who had so far not spoken said: "Apparently Ms. Stone's interviews have gotten a pretty big play, worldwide. And there's still tomorrow's papers to come. What's happened in Cyprus has added to the interest. The pressure for official statements and more interviews isn't just coming from those guys outside in the road. There's a whole bunch at our legation, too."

"I think too much has been publicly said already," Robertson complained with lawyer's caution.

"There is a legal situation," Prescott agreed. "There's been an official request from the Cyprus authorities, through our Nicosia embassy, for Mrs. Stone to be returned to help police inquiries there."

"That would seem to take care of the matter of illegal entry," the Lebanese immigration official said at once. "The Cyprus situation obviously takes precedence, in importance. And the most common resolution to illegal entry in any case is usually deportation to the port of origin. Which will be the outcome here."

Janet found herself only half listening to the quiet-voiced discussion going on around her. Could it only be hours—less than one whole day—since she'd stabbed a man trying to rape her? And fled in terror from other men intent on God knows what? She found it difficult—inconceivable—to believe it was all being settled as easily as this. To the Lebanese she said: "Can I ask you something?"

"Of course," smiled the immigration man.

"I came here for a reason, a purpose," said Janet, hurriedly, not wanting to lose what she saw as an opportunity. "I was trying to find out anything about my financé, John Sheridan? Do you know anything? Can you help me find him? Where the hell is he?"

The effect throughout the room was very obvious. A physical stiffness appeared to tighten each man and their faces went blank, except for that of Robertson, whose suffused features became even redder.

It was the lawyer who spoke. He started, in cliche, to say: "I really don't think this is either the time or the . . ." But Janet stopped him, erupting in frustrated disbelief.

"This is exactly the time and exactly the place, for Christ's sake!" she yelled. "This is Beirut! This is where he's held! So what the fuck is anyone doing about it!"

Janet hadn't meant to say "fuck" and as soon as she did she regretted it. Trying to recover—but at the same time refusing to back away from the stone-masked men—she said: "Well, isn't it? Isn't this where John and all those other poor bastards are held, with no one doing anything about it? Isn't it!"

The Lebanese shuffled awkwardly, appearing to move away from the general group to form a separate, muttered gathering: Janet was aware of a shoulder-humped, eyebrow-raised exchange between the British and American diplomats.

"Well!" she demanded, still not giving in. "Isn't it!"

"You're not helping, Ms. Stone," Burr said.

"Who is?" Janet pressed on. "Tell me just who—how—anyone in Beirut is helping John and all those others. Come on! Tell me!"

The immigration official emerged as the Lebanese spokesman. He said: "None of this is our business: our responsibility."

Janet sighed, focusing on the American whose name she knew. "What about you, Mr. Burr? You're a United States diplomatic officer officially assigned to a country in which Americans are being held hostage, for whatever reason God or Allah knows. Do you consider it your business; your responsibility?"

"You've had a traumatic time, Ms. Stone," soothed Burr, hopefully. "Let's not press it, shall we?"

"I'm not taking that cop out!" rejected Janet, in further refusal. "OK! I've had a traumatic time: I nearly got raped and I stuck a knife in somebody whom no one seems able to find any more and I don't know if the bastard is alive or dead. And despite what he tried to do and although he's a bastard I don't want him to be dead, although he deserves to be. But I'm still not hysterical: I'm not hysterical, and I haven't lost control. I've got here and I don't want to leave here until I get some idea what's happening—if anything *is* happening—to find John Sheridan."

It was the nameless American who spoke. He said: "Let's talk about this sometime else, Ms. Stone."

"Why!"

"Later, Ms. Stone!"

"Not later! Now!"

"There's nothing to say, not here, not now," came in Burr, defensively.

"We know nothing," said the Lebanese policeman who had not spoken for a long time. "There's nothing we can say to help you."

Janet experienced a familiar sensation, the feeling of having something that blocked out the light—a blanket maybe—pulled over her head, shutting out her access to everything and anything beyond, as she herself had literally pulled the blankets over her head when Hank died.

The American without a name spoke, not to Janet but to the British diplomats. He said: "We've got a helicopter going to Cyprus, later today. We'd be happy to offer transportation to Ms. Stone."

"That's very good of you," Prescott said in apparent acceptance.

"Wait a minute!" protested Janet. "Just wait a goddamned minute! Why isn't anyone answering me!" Directly to Prescott she said: "What the hell right have you got to make arrangements on my behalf?"

"Every right," the tiny man said at once and with a forcefulness strangely out of keeping with his stature. "You are a distressed person of original British nationality seeking the protection of this embassy. The Lebanese authorities have agreed—with exceptional understanding, for which we are extremely grateful—to take no action whatsoever against you. Which they clearly could have done, had they so seen fit. I am entirely and legally entitled to repatriate you to your port of origin in the most cost-effective and efficient way that presents itself. That way *has* presented itself."

"Absolutely and utterly correct," Robertson said.

The blanket was doing more now than just blocking out the light; there was the familiar stifling sensation, too. "Thanks!" Janet said, intending sarcasm.

"You know what I think, Ms. Stone?" Burr said, throwing it back at her. "I don't really think you've any idea just how much you've got to be thankful for."

The truth of the remark, pompous though it was, further punctured Janet's attitude. She felt weighed down and not just from the exhaustion of not having slept for longer than she was able to remember. Trying for a pebble to throw back against the boulders, she said: "I'd like to meet the press."

"No!" Robertson said at once.

"Why not?"

"For the reason that's already been made clear," said the lawyer. Continuing professionally, he went on: "There is in custody in Cyprus a man who is alleged to have fraudulently attempted to convert a money order in your name to his own benefit. Anything you might say could materially affect whatever evidence you might give at his trial: if you want the legal definition, it is *sub judice*."

"What evidence?" Janet said, fighting back.

"I don't wish to continue this discussion," Robertson said. "But if you are considering not supporting the charges that could be brought, then I would consider you a very stupid woman."

"And I consider you a very arrogant man . . ." Janet paused, encompassing everyone in the room. ". . . I consider you all very arrogant men, interested in only one thing: getting rid of a potential embarrassment as quickly and as easily as possible."

Janet waited for a reaction but there wasn't one, and their absolute dismissal was the most crushing part of the encounter.

To the Lebanese, Robertson said formally: "Do you entrust custody of Mrs. Stone to the British authorities?"

Appearing relieved, the man immediately said: "Yes."

To the Americans, Robertson said: "On behalf of the British government I would like to accept your offer of transportation."

"You're welcome," Burr said.

"I won't go!" Janet shouted, desperately and without thought. "I won't go until I have found out something about John!"

"You don't have any choice in the matter," said Robertson flatly. "You're being expelled. And in the circumstances in the best way possible: as I've just told you, you're a very fortunate woman."

There was another futile journalistic rush towards the departing car, which had to slow at the barriers and by doing so provided the opportunity for yet more photographs, and more unheard questions before it accelerated on the outside road to run parallel to the sea towards the American embassy. The sun was very low, half over the horizon, and Janet thought that at this time the previous night she had still only been approaching the Lebanese coastline. Burr was beside her, in the back, with the other American in the front but turned towards them: Janet had been conscious of the man hunching against the burst of camera bulbs and on impulse said: "You were with John, weren't you? With the Agency, I mean."

"I knew him," the man conceded.

"You never told me your name."

"The way you run to the newspapers it's dangerous even to tell you the time of day," said Burr, beside her.

"I know the lecture by heart," said Janet.

"People are supposed to learn from lectures," said Burr. "Why haven't you?"

"Because none of them have had any useful information."

"Smart!" Burr acknowledged. "Very smart."

Janet ignored Burr, concentrating upon the man in front of her. "OK, so don't tell me if you're in the Agency or not: I couldn't give a damn. But I know you are. So you must be involved in trying to find him! For God's sake tell me what's going on!"

"I . . ." the man started but Burr said: "No!," cutting him off. Then the man said: "I was only going to say that I would like to but I can't."

"Let's cut it, right there, shall we!" Burr said.

"No!" Janet protested. "Let's not cut anything! I want to know: I want to know anything!"

"There's nothing to know," Burr said. "It's a cold trail."

"I don't believe you!" Janet said. "It can't be!"

"Ms. Stone," Burr said. "We've got Americans somewhere in this asshole of a country who've been missing for years, not just weeks! There's nothing that hasn't been done that could not have been done to make contact, to negotiate or to plead or arrange their freedom. To normal people you can talk; discuss things. But these aren't normal people. They're fanatics, nuts."

"So what the hell's the answer!"

"We've got to wait," Burr said, fatalistically. "All the lines are out: they know we want to hear from them. All we can do is wait for them to come to us. Come to us and give us their terms and their demands so we can see where we go from there."

"Where *do* we go from there!" persisted Janet. "Do we deal? Or do we come up with the line that we won't condone terrorism, which is a load of crap after Irangate!"

"I don't make policy, Ms. Stone," said the diplomat, with sudden weariness. "I just try to interpret it. Sometimes it isn't easy."

The car had to make its way through another press throng at the U.S. legation, which was protected by more concreted antiterrorist barriers than the British building, and once more Janet was conscious of the American in the front seat moving to conceal himself as much as possible from the cameras. Inside the compound, Burr said: "I'm going to issue a very short statement. Just that you have cooperated with the authorities here in Beirut and that you are returning to Cyprus to help with some police matters there."

"Why don't I take Ms. Stone with me, until the helo gets here?" the other man suggested.

"Just as long as I know where to find you," Burr agreed.

Janet followed the younger man from the car, past a Marine-guarded, sandbagged pillbox and into the embassy through a side

door, not the main entrance. The man courteously opened doors
and stood back every time they had to move through one section of
the building to another. They did not stop until they reached what
had to be the very rear: the final door was operated by a combination
lock and Janet remembered the briefcase carried by the first man
who'd tricked her. Absurdly she could not immediately recall the
name. Nicos, she thought: Nicos Kholi.

She followed the man into an office harsh under fluorescent lighting, with no outside windows. Everything was practical and func-
tional, just a desk, three filing cabinets side by side and sealed by
thick iron bars which padlocked through the handles of each drawer,
and one chair for a visitor. He gestured her to it and Janet sat down.

"The name's Knox," he said. "George Knox. I'm glad there's the
chance for us to be alone for a few moments."

"I don't understand," said Janet.

"I've got something for you." The man reached into a side drawer
of the desk and then stretched out towards her.

It was not until she accepted what he was offering that Janet realized it was a photograph, and her eyes instantly blurred at the image
of Sheridan. It was a color print, obviously taken somewhere in
Beirut: there were palm trees in the background and the edge of a
swimming pool. Sheridan was wearing shorts and a shirt and Top-
siders without socks, and appeared to be smiling at someone beyond
the camera.

"John really was my friend," disclosed Knox. "He'd actually invited me to your wedding."

·18·

Janet had a strange feeling and in the initial few moments could not decide what it was. Then it flooded in upon her, an awareness that for the first time in too many days—weeks—she was being treated with understanding, actual friendship, and not as an irritant to be kept at arm's length and moved on to become someone else's problem. Her reaction was one of relief and something more: a brief sensation of actual relaxation. It became very obvious as Knox talked that he and John *had* been friends: close friends, in fact. The young CIA man knew about their boat and the house in Chevy Chase and even the circumstances of their meeting at Harriet's oppressive Georgetown party.

Janet listened to it all, waiting, and when Knox paused she demanded: "Why? Tell me how it happened! Why nothing appears to be going on to get him out!"

In this more confined space, Knox's habit of studying a speaker's face, almost as if he were lip-reading, was more pronounced than it had been at the earlier conference. He gazed intently at her, weighing his reply. Then he said: "It was what John was trying to do."

"A mission, you mean?"

"Very much a mission," said the man. "We've got a whole bunch of Americans caged up here somewhere . . ."

". . . I know the figures," stopped Janet, impatiently. "The names even. What was John trying to do?"

"Remember what Bill said in the car coming back here, about all the lines being out?"

"Of course," nodded Janet.

"That's what John was doing: what the mission was," Knox said. "He was trying to set up the contacts: to initiate the negotiations to get our guys out. And then the sons-of-bitches grabbed him!"

"Just like Terry Waite," said Janet.

"Probably one lot got the idea from the other," agreed Knox. "John had been working at it for months: reckoned he was making real progress. He'd disappear for days at a time: actually go into south or west Beirut. At times he went deep into south Lebanon, near the Israeli border. He'd come back covered in filth and with a beard this long and every time say he was getting just that bit closer."

"So they were cooperating, the Hezbollah!" Janet said.

Knox shook his head. "Some, not all," he qualified. "It's a mistake to think they're a cohesive group, by whatever name they call themselves, obeying just one ayatollah. There's dozens of cells, groups sometimes not much bigger than ten, twenty men. There's liaison between a few: communication, at least. But mostly it's fratricidal war. And some aren't even operating in the name of Allah. They're just gangs, out for a buck."

"Is that what you think happened to John? That he was seized by some group rivaling that with which he was dealing?"

"It's as good a guess as any," said Knox. "That and the fact that he was CIA in the first place."

"Wasn't it absurd to send another CIA officer out at all?" erupted Janet, regretting the outburst at once: it hadn't been Knox who initiated the assignment.

"Someone had to do it," said Knox, unoffended. "John was bureau chief here: considered it his responsibility."

"Yes," Janet agreed, distantly. "That was the sort of attitude John would have."

"There were reports, some files, of course," the American said. "We had leads to follow, but a lot of it was in John's head, personal relationships . . ." He hesitated, the sadness obvious on his open face. "So far, nothing." There was another pause. Then

Knox added: "You've no idea—really no idea—how it hurts to say that."

"Is there someone else?" Janet asked.

"Someone else?"

"Trying to pick up where John stopped?" Janet asked. "Putting out more lines?"

For several moments Knox gave no reaction. Then, bluntly, he said: "No."

"No one trying at all!"

"We're tapping all the sources we can," Knox tried to assure her. "Our liaison with all branches of Lebanese intelligence is good: through them we have a feed into some parts of Syrian intelligence, particularly the army. And a dialogue, of sorts, with a few of the Amal Shias themselves."

"But no one is out specifically looking and negotiating, not like John was out specifically looking and negotiating!"

"It's specifically forbidden."

"Since when?" Janet asked, anticipating the answer.

"Since John got snatched," Knox confirmed.

With anyone else Janet would have been outraged, disgusted, but she couldn't feel any anger at the man who had been John's friend. She sagged with fatigue. "What am I going to do?" she asked, limp-voiced. "I don't know what to do, not any more."

"No one does," said Knox. "That's the biggest bastard. And personally I think they're aware of it, and it gives them a buzz to know just how helpless great big Uncle Sam really is."

"Is he dead!" Janet blurted, abruptly. "Do you think they've killed him already?"

Knox hurried from behind the desk and put a comforting hand on Janet's shoulder. "Hey now!" he said. "Hold back a while!"

"I don't know how much longer I can hold back," said Janet, emptily. "I feel so lost. Far worse this time than when Hank died. Then, at least, I knew: knew when I forced myself to accept the truth. It's the . . . it's the not knowing . . ."

"Yes," agreed Knox. "That's what it is."

"Thank you," said Janet. "For being kind, I mean." Recalling her impression upon entering the room, she said: "It seems to have been a long time."

"I wish there were more I could do: a lot more."

Janet looked down at the photo which she still held in her hand.

She said: "This is something." She raised her eyes. "I don't know what's going to happen back in Cyprus, but I think I'll stay on for a while. At the Churchill. Will you get me there, if anything comes up?"

"If anything comes up, I'll get a message through if I have to bring it myself," Knox promised. He went back around the desk, checking his watch. "Al's late," he said.

"Al?" she queried.

"Al Hart, our guy in Nicosia. He's coming in on the helo, to escort you back. I thought you'd met already."

A name for the other anonymous American, Janet realized. She said: "Yes, we met. He told me to get out."

"Why don't you, Janet?" implored the man, gently. "When you've done whatever they want in Cyprus, why don't you go back to England or to America? Getting mixed up in what happened here isn't going to get John out. It's just going to get you hurt: maybe badly hurt."

"Maybe," she said, vaguely. "I don't know."

There was a summons from beyond the combination-locked door, and Janet started slightly at the unexpected intrusion. Knox pushed an unseen release button somewhere beyond the desk and Janet half turned, expecting to see the American with whom she had returned from the British embassy. Instead, it was the CIA officer who had confronted her within hours of her arrival in Cyprus.

"Here we are again!" he greeted. "The lady who knows bad words and can't take good advice!"

"I'm very tired," said Janet, wearily.

"You're goddamned lucky to be able to feel anything," said the American. He came into the room, seeking a chair. When he saw there wasn't one, he hitched himself on the corner of the desk and said to Knox: "How about this, George! Today I'm a baby minder!"

"Is this really necessary?" Knox asked, mildly.

"What are you talking about?"

"She's been through quite a lot," Knox said. "I don't think the Humphrey Bogart routine helps much."

Hart frowned and began to go red. Janet remembered how he'd left her room at the Churchill with his face burning. "What the hell's wrong with you?"

"Why don't we just leave it?" Knox said, disinterested in an argument.

Knox's dismissal appeared to anger the other American further. He looked from Knox to Janet and said: "Cosy times, eh!"

"Shut up, Al, for Christ's sake!" said Knox. "You're making yourself look like a jerk."

Hart said: "Not as much of a jerk as Mrs. Stone here made herself look. Oh no, siree!"

The hostility didn't frighten Janet. Rather it revitalized her. Janet decided the abrupt and unexpected kindness that Knox had shown—and for which she'd been so grateful—had lulled her and that she didn't need to be lulled. She needed to face antagonistic attitudes like Al Hart's, who unquestionably was a jerk, to fight back. She said: "What about the man I stabbed? Have you heard anything?"

"I've heard a whole bunch of things," Hart said. "A whole bunch of things. Like just what they had in mind for you, for instance."

"What?" Janet asked, sure she knew.

"Did you think—did you really think—that they had an inside track to some Fundamentalist group holding John?" Hart demanded, intent on conducting the conversation his way.

"Yes," Janet admitted. "I believed it. They were Cypriot fishermen who knew the area, so why couldn't they have had?"

"Cypriot fishermen!" Hart echoed, in artificial incredulity. "Oh Jesus, lady! Dear Jesus! They're scum Arabs: the best guess is from around Jablah or Baniyas, on the north Syrian coast. They're all members of the same family, uncles and cousins and stuff like that. The family name is said to be Fettal, although that could be so much bullshit, like whatever names they used with you. The nearest they've ever come to catching fish is buying some at the market to spread the guts and mess about their boat, to make it look like fishing is what they really do. But what they really do is smuggle. Anything . . ." Hart paused, looking down at her. ". . . or in your case, anybody. And did they have a market for you! Do you know where you were heading, little lady? They had you already sold as a whore. You were on your way to some Amal militia camp, in south Beirut. And we're not talking perfumed harems, with satin sheets and scented fountains. We're talking being tethered like the piece of meat they were going to use you as in some hovel while they stood in line to hump you, the next in line hauling the other guy off if he took too long . . . we're talking gang-bangs and open mouths and whatever other trick you had to perform . . ."

"For Christ's sake, Al, shut up!" Knox erupted. "What the fuck do you think you're proving!"

They had spoken Arabic, Janet remembered. Like she remembered some of the things that they'd said. *Break you in, that's what I'm going to do. Really break you in.* And then the protest. *She's no good split apart.* And the reply. *Going to have her first.* Janet spoke with conscious evenness, almost casually, determined not to give Hart the satisfaction of knowing how much he'd sickened her. She said: "So what about the man I stabbed? What happened to him?"

"Zarpas didn't say anything about a stabbing," Hart said, at last, visibly disappointed at her lack of reaction.

"How many are in custody?" Janet persisted.

"Two. The one who ran the boat and an old guy."

So where was the one she'd known as Costas? Had Haseeb, the Arab engineer from Larnaca marina, known she was going to be sold as a whore? Other less-formed questions tugged at Janet's mind. The American had spoken easily of the Cypriot policeman, as if he knew him. But then there was every reason why he should. And Zarpas would be handling the currency case, wouldn't he, because it was he who had continually warned her? They'd both warned her, in fact, practically within minutes of each other, that first day. Janet looked up at the lounging crew-cut man, her head to one side, and said curiously: "It was you, wasn't it?"

"You're not getting through to me, lady."

"That first day, in Nicosia," Janet said. "When you came to my hotel room and warned me off. It was you who mentioned Larnaca marina and Zenon Square and Kitieus Street."

"I'm hearing the words but I'm missing the meaning."

"I thought you'd made a slip at the time," Janet continued, in growing conviction. "But do you know what I think now? I don't think you made a slip at all. I think you knew I'd go there and you knew I'd get ripped off and then you thought I'd have to get out, like Langley told you to make me get out."

"Bullshit," Hart said, but there was just the slightest flush.

"Did you do that, Al?" demanded the other American. "Did you set her up, like she thinks you did?"

"Of course I damned well didn't!" protested Hart. "What sort of question's that?"

"The sort of question that needs an answer," Knox said.

"I told you no!"

"I know what you told me," Knox said. "What's the truth?"

"I didn't set her up." Hart was redder now. "It would have been hard, getting in ahead of everyone else."

"What's that supposed to mean?" Janet asked.

Hart stared directly down at her, a nerve in his left cheek twitching in his obvious anger. "Think about it, lady. Think about how Zarpas knew where you were and how much money you'd deposited, within hours of getting to Nicosia! And how I knew where you were, to come in heavy with a warning, right after him!"

"The bank was required to make a report," Janet said unsteadily. "You said you had a watch out at the airport."

"A bank report would have taken weeks to get through the system, even if such a requirement existed," dismissed Hart. "And I haven't the resources to run any sort of check on airport arrivals, not that quickly anyway."

"So how?" Janet asked.

"Partington," the American said. "He warned Zarpas that you were there and what you intended to do: all Zarpas had to do in turn was demand the banks call him immediately after you'd made the deposit."

"But you . . . ?" Janet asked, emptily.

"Partington again."

"Why?" Janet said. "I don't understand why . . ." She stumbled to a halt. "There was no reason, no purpose. And he didn't know where I'd put the money anyway."

Hart leaned slightly forward, to make his point. "Ms. Stone, I want you to understand something. I don't really give a damn whether you get taken for every penny you've got or whether you really do end up in an Arab outhouse, along with the rest of the animals. But I do care if anything you do causes one of my colleagues to get killed. That's why I want to see your ass out of here. But others are concerned about you, personally . . ."

"Partington didn't know about the money!" Janet insisted.

"Lady," Hart said. "Partington knew all about the money because your father called him from England before you even landed, told him what you were likely to do and asked him to pull every string he could think of to get you on the next available plane out of the island and back somewhere sensible."

"My father!" Janet said, disbelieving.

"Your father," Hart said. "He worries about you."

From behind the desk Knox said: "You know, Al, I always knew you were a shit. I just never knew until now exactly how much of a shit you are. It's something: it's really something!"

·19·

It was a military helicopter, attached to the base at Akrotiri, so the comforts were minimal. Conversation was impossible and Janet was grateful. She did not want any talk—any contact at all—with Al Hart. After takeoff from the American compound in Beirut Janet pulled as far away from him as possible on the continuous, port-to-starboard seat, and after they landed she tried to distance herself similarly in the back of the waiting police car. Hart seemed unaware of what she was doing: if he did notice it, he didn't appear to care, not wanting to talk any more to her, either.

There was still some heat in the day, and the vehicle had no air conditioning. Almost at once the interior became eye-droopingly hot: very shortly after picking up the motorway for the drive into the capital Janet felt her lids closing and let it happen.

Janet started, frightened, into bewildered wakefulness, her body aching, not immediately able to remember where she was or what she was doing, babbling ". . . What . . . ? No . . . !" before becoming properly aware of her surroundings. Someone was shaking her shoulder.

It was the notetaking Sergeant Kashianis who was leaning into the car to shake her: Zarpas stood behind him. Janet heard a slam, another noise that made her jump, and saw that Hart had left the car and closed his door.

"This way, please," said Kashianis.

Janet got unsteadily from the vehicle, needing the door edge for support until she became properly awake. She ached very badly, seemingly at every joint, and her eyes were sticky and still heavy: it would have been very easy for her to go back to sleep.

"This way, please," urged the sergeant, again.

Janet made an uncertain path into the police headquarters, aware of Zarpas and Hart ahead of her, their heads lowered and close together in intent conversation.

The air was heavy inside, but there was at least a desultory fan in Zarpas's office. It was a disordered, cluttered box of a place, files and dossiers haphazard on top of cabinets which supposedly should have contained them, others overflowing on to the floor. The police officer's desk was mountained with more paperwork, in peaks and foothills: in a glass vase were yellow, long-used water and a sad flower, head lolled to one side, already atrophying, and Janet wondered why he bothered.

Zarpas shifted dossiers from a chair for Janet to sit in. Kashianis took another chair alongside the desk and arranged his pad and pencils there. Zarpas sat behind the desk. Yet again Hart had nowhere to sit. There was no space in the disorder for him to perch on the desk, as he had in Beirut. Janet was childishly glad.

"So you didn't bother to listen," Zarpas began.

"I really am very tired," Janet said. She vaguely remembered saying something similar to Hart and wished she had thought of a better rejoiner.

"We're all very tired of it, Mrs. Stone," said the Cypriot.

"Do you normally share interviews with American intelligence personnel!" fought back Janet.

"When it pleases me to do so," replied Zarpas, unimpressed. "And for our mutual benefit—his and my own mutual benefit—at the moment it pleases me to do so." Zarpas paused, looking towards the American as if inviting the man to say something as well. Hart remained silent. The Cypriot announced, "We've found the man we think you stabbed."

"Dead!" demanded Janet, no longer lethargic.

"Not yet," said the policeman. "Someone—or maybe some people—this morning dumped him on the steps of the hospital in Homer Avenue. There was a deep stab wound to the stomach and a sepsis had developed because it had not been properly treated. There also seems a possibility of tetanus."

"Not dead!" accepted Janet, the relief sighing from her.

"Not yet," repeated Zarpas.

"What does the bastard say!"

Zarpas blinked, surprised at hearing a woman swear. He said: "It's not been possible yet to take a statement from him: he's in intensive care."

"What about the others?"

"They claim the idea of selling you to a Shia group in Beirut was that of the man found on the hospital steps this morning. I'd guess they abandoned him, expecting him to die. If he does die there's only the fraud involving that Letter of Credit to worry them, isn't there? Still serious but still a lesser charge."

"The captain went ashore to negotiate with whoever it was in Beirut," insisted Janet.

"Good," said Zarpas obtusely. "That's what I want. I want a full and complete statement: I want you to tell me everything."

"For a prosecution?" asked Janet, cautiously.

"Of course."

Janet tried to imagine how absurd she would appear in court, recounting the events, but found it difficult properly to encompass. She said: "They weren't able to cash the credit letter, were they? I haven't suffered any financial loss."

"Not this time!" said Zarpas, his voice loud. "I'm not letting you refuse this time."

"You can't force me to testify," rejected Janet.

"No one's trying to force you to do anything," came in Hart, speaking for the first time. "But you have the right of American residency, from your marriage. Washington likes American residents to cooperate, in matters of law and order. You own an apartment in Washington and have got a pretty high-powered job at a university there. It would all be very inconvenient if you couldn't live in the United States any more, wouldn't it?"

"What the hell are you saying!"

"I'm not saying anything," said the man, innocent-faced. "Just posing a thought."

"Why!" demanded Janet.

"Why what?" said Hart, playing word games.

"You want me to be publicly discredited, don't you!" discerned Janet, in awareness. "I've caused you a lot of awkwardness and you want me labeled in a court as an empty-headed fool who didn't have a clue what she was doing!"

"I don't know what you're talking about," said Hart.

"Then why make the threat?"

"What threat?"

It was a mental struggle for Janet to keep up. She said: "About my residency being revoked."

The American turned towards the policeman. "Did I say anything about Ms. Stone's residency?"

Zarpas shook his head. "Not that I heard."

Janet looked between the two men, moving her own head in understanding. To Zarpas she said: "So this is it, is it? This is what you call a stitch-up? Unless I make a statement and appear in court and end up looking a complete idiot—a laughingstock that no one is going to take seriously—I lose my right to remain in America?"

"I'm sorry," said the policeman. "I really don't understand what you're saying."

A feeling of being lost engulfed Janet: of being lost and too weary to fight and wanting to give up and actually do what they wanted, to go home. She said: "And you'd deny it, if I complained? Talked to the newspapers, for instance?"

"Ms. Stone!" said Hart, patronizingly. "What right do I have to threaten your right to live in America! Any complaint would be demonstrably untrue!"

"And this is why I was flown here by an American helicopter and why the CIA can take part in a Cypriot police interview!" said Janet. "You really have created a complicated little scenario to get rid of— or rather to ridicule—a nuisance, haven't you?"

"All I am asking is that you make a complete statement to enable a prosecution to be brought against men who tried to defraud you out of £10,000," said Zarpas, formally. "I am not going to comment upon the foolhardiness of preparing to give men you didn't even know £10,000. Or the wiseness of getting on a boat with them expecting to be introduced to more men you didn't know in the Lebanon."

From where he stood near the overflowing filing cabinets Hart made a snorting, laughing sound.

It did sound ridiculous now, conceded Janet: *would* sound ridiculous. It hadn't, though, at the time. To the patiently waiting Kashianis she said: "Why don't we get it over with?"

Zarpas only let her talk briefly before intruding with a question,

which became the way the statement was recorded, Janet's responses
to questions but written down in the form of a continuous narrative.
Zarpas was very particular, carefully bringing out every detail of the
voyage and stopped her briefly but completely while he issued telephone orders for the arrest of Hasseb as a possible accomplice.

When she finished her account Janet said: "What about if the
man dies? Won't I be guilty of something?"

Zarpas brought the corners of his mouth down, in a doubtful
expression. "I would have thought that could be considered justifiable self-defense," said the man. "And although if he does die it will
be on Cyprus territory the wound he suffered would appear to have
been inflicted outside Cyprus jurisdiction. And no accusation has
anyway been brought against you, has it? The other two *want* him to
die."

Janet supposed it was the tiredness but everything seemed very
difficult to comprehend: there were disorientating lapses in her concentration, so that sometimes Zarpas's words were quite clear but
other times what the man said seemed indistinct. Janet supposed she
should be grateful for the reassurance about the stabbing. She said:
"Have you finished with me now?"

"There will be the need for clarification: maybe more questions,"
Zarpas said. "I will want to know where you are going to be at all
times."

"House arrest?" Janet asked.

"Cooperation," contradicted Zarpas.

Hart said: "And let's not have any more nonsense, OK, lady?
You've caused an awful lot of flak and achieved absolutely zero. Let's
leave it at that: let us, the professionals, worry about getting John
out."

Janet was too exhausted to argue as she had in the past: couldn't
think how to argue, any more. She said: "I would like to go."

Zarpas provided a car and driver. Janet traveled with the window
down and the wind in her face, trying to revive herself, and when
she got to the hotel it was besieged with reporters. Janet let herself be
bustled into a side lounge and responded to the questions but insisted that the television and radio interviews be conducted at the
same time because she did not feel able to do them separately.

It still took a long time, more than an hour, and Janet was so
weary at the end that she had literally to force one foot in front of the
other to walk to the elevator and from the elevator to her room. She

let her borrowed clothes lie where they fell and burrowed into bed, scarcely aware of where she was, sinking immediately into sleep.

She thought at first that the sound was in a dream, not responding for several minutes to the ringing telephone, and even when she lifted it she had to struggle for consciousness. She did not completely succeed, so that she could not follow what the man was saying for several more minutes.

". . . An in-depth, long feature," the man was saying. "I was at the conference downstairs but I want much more. I would appreciate our being able to meet."

"Not today," mumbled Janet. "Far too tired. Tomorrow."

"Tomorrow will be fine," said the voice. "I'll call around ten."

Janet was asleep again and didn't hear the stipulated time.

·20·

Which was why she was bewildered when the call came, awakening her. She was aware of her surroundings but momentarily unsure whether it was the same day that she'd stumbled into bed or the following one. The forgotten man to whom she was talking spoke of yesterday's conversation, which gave Janet a guide. She lied and assured him she remembered but explained that she was running late and he asked how long and she said thirty minutes and he agreed that would be fine. He said he would recognize her when she came into the lobby area.

While she was showering Janet wondered how to get the borrowed clothes back to the journalist in Beirut and decided, pleased with the resolve, to entrust the chore to Al Hart. She wished there were more she could do to disturb the bastard.

As Janet emerged from the elevator, the man approached her. He thanked her for agreeing to the meeting and offered a card identifying himself as David Baxeter. She saw that the publication for which he wrote was based in Vancouver. He was a slight but wiry man with tightly curled hair that topped his head without any obvious attempt at style and the mannerism of gazing directly into her eyes, making her the only focus of his attention. Baxeter wore a gray sports jacket over gray trousers and the striped tie was predominantly gray, too. There was no identifiable accent in his voice at all, certainly not Canadian: he was very soft-spoken.

She welcomed the idea of coffee and they sat indoors but overlooking the pool: as she was seated, Janet supposed that sitting by the pool was the only way she would be able to occupy her time now, until whatever hearing or trial took place. It wasn't giving up or knuckling under to Partington and Hart and Zarpas—or to her father, whose actions she'd think about later—to abandon the idea of doing something personal, entirely by herself. It was, finally, confronting the common sense she had locked away and ignored from the moment the absurd idea first occurred to her in Washington. It had been stupid to imagine that alone she, Janet Stone, could do something—discover something—that the professional agencies couldn't. Maybe she actually deserved the sneers and humiliation that would come with the trial.

After the coffee was served Baxeter produced a small, pocket-sized tape recorder which he placed between them, hurriedly asking if she minded the interview being conducted that way. Janet, only half paying attention, shook her head and said it was fine, wishing it were over before it began. With difficulty Janet concentrated upon the interview: maintaining the publicity was probably the only way for her sensibly to help John, from now on.

Baxeter was a very patient and courteous interviewer. In almost every question he called her Mrs. Stone and more than once apologized in advance if what he asked might distress her and just as frequently said they could stop, to rest, whenever she wanted. And as she had the previous day in Beirut—could it really only be the previous day: it seemed like weeks ago!—Janet thought how unusual it was to be treated with anything approaching sympathy or understanding. It became a very long interview. Baxeter took her back even to before she and Sheridan met, to her time at Oxford and her marriage to Hank, and appeared particularly interested in her position in Middle Eastern studies at Georgetown University: he changed the tape twice before even reaching the time of Sheridan's posting to Beirut. When the third tape was nearly exhausted Baxeter said, solicitous as ever: "I must be tiring you?"

"I've nothing else to do," Janet said and thought it sounded rude. "I mean, I'm quite happy to go on as long as you want."

"It's lunchtime," Baxeter announced. "Why don't we take a meal break?"

She really didn't have anything else to do, Janet thought. "Sure you can spare the time?"

"It's a monthly magazine," Baxeter said. "I've got a long lead time."

"Then lunch would be fine."

It was Baxeter who suggested going away from the hotel, to the Tembelodendron, where he diffidently suggested he order for both of them. Janet agreed, disinterested in food but enjoying being fussed over: he got into a discussion with the waiter about how to cook the lamb and when it was served it was delicious. Baxeter took as much trouble over the Afames wine, and that was just as good. The thought came to her that there were things about the man that reminded her of John: the reflection passed as quickly as it came.

He said he had not been born in British Columbia. He had been in England when the magazine hired him as their Middle East correspondent and chose to live in Cyprus because it seemed the most convenient jumping-off spot, although he had considered moving to Rome. He knew Cairo and Amman better than she did, and Janet had to apologize that it had been years since she'd been to either capital and that when she had she had been a schoolgirl anyway. She guessed both places had changed. Baxeter said Amman maybe but not Cairo.

"The traffic's just as bad and the sewage smell is awful."

"I remember the smell." Janet smiled.

"Who could ever forget it?"

"Do you think I've been ridiculous?" Janet blurted abruptly.

"What!" he said, startled.

"Me. Ridiculous. Coming here as I did and doing what I have done. Everyone says I've been stupid, getting in the way."

Baxeter did not immediately reply. For several moments he gazed not at her but at the wineglass he held before him in both hands and then he said: "I think you've been naive, certainly. And you've been as lucky as hell. But no, not ridiculous. You've definitely made it so that people can't forget the plight of John Sheridan. That, surely, has got to be an achievement."

"I'd like to think so."

"It is important to you, what people think?"

Janet shrugged. "I'm sorry. I didn't intend to be self-pitying. I guess a lot of things have gotten on top of me."

"It's understandable," Baxeter said. "Quite a lot of things have happened to you, after all."

"All to too little purpose."

"That *is* self pity," he said, gently.

Janet smiled. "I was thinking of John more than myself."

"What are you going to do now?"

"I don't know," admitted Janet. "Get the court business over, I suppose. Hope something happens while I'm here: that there's some news, I mean."

"What if there isn't?" pressed the man.

"Go home, I guess: there doesn't seem any point in hanging around."

"Home where? America or England."

"America," said Janet. "I don't think of England as home any more. It's to America that John will come back, isn't it?"

Baxeter was slow responding to the question. "Yes," he said finally. "He'll come back to America."

"You don't believe that, do you?" challenged Janet. "You think he's dead! Or that he will be killed!"

The man reached across the table, covering her hand with his. "Stop it!" he said forcefully. "You're giving up. And you *are* letting yourself go into a trough of self-pity."

He was right, conceded Janet: despite all her attempts to think otherwise, that was exactly what she was doing. "Thanks for the warning," she said.

Baxeter took his hand away, shrugging. "And to answer you I don't know. The Hezbollah can't be anticipated, second-guessed. You know the Shia tradition of *taqqiyah*."

"'Approving of something contradictory to your faith if the need arises,'" Janet translated literally.

Baxeter nodded. "It's the catch-all," he said. "Provides a religious excuse for anything."

"So you *do* have an opinion," Janet said. "OK, so you don't know but you think it could happen? That they'll kill him?"

"I'd like to think more was being done to make contact. To negotiate," he said, not really answering.

"Exactly! That's what I can't stand . . . what infuriates me. There's been a demand! Why the hell can't America pressure Kuwait into releasing the people it's holding?"

"Kuwait never has," Baxeter pointed out.

"So why don't they establish a precedent!" said Janet, irrationally. "America sailed protective convoys around Kuwaiti tankers during the Iran–Iraqui war protecting the Kuwaiti economy. So why can't the State Department tell them that unless they release the prisoners they're holding Washington won't help in future!"

"I would have thought that an option," agreed Baxeter.

"They tortured the other CIA man to death, you know," Janet said.

"I know."

"That's what I think about sometimes," Janet said. "What's happening to him: the awful things that are happening to him."

"Welcome back," Baxeter said.

Janet frowned. "What do you mean?"

"You're fighting again," Baxeter said. "Not giving up or feeling sorry for yourself."

Janet smiled, slowly. "You manipulated the conversation very cleverly."

"I want a story on Janet Stone the fighter, not Janet Stone the quitter," he said.

"And have you got it?"

"Not yet," the man said. "I'd like to continue the interview this afternoon."

They returned to the hotel, but as soon as Janet entered she was paged for messages. She accepted them in the foyer, Baxeter beside her. There had been a telephone call from Partington, who asked her to call back, and another from her father, with the same request. The third note had no name, just a Nicosia telephone number with the suggestion she ring it to learn something to her advantage.

"What could that mean?" she asked Baxeter.

"Any one of a dozen things: it's practically cliché."

"I'll call it, of course."

"After what's happened so far don't you think you should be careful?"

"By doing what? You surely don't expect me to ignore it!"

"No," he agreed. "I don't expect you to ignore it."

"So?"

"Couldn't you do with some help?"

"I thought we'd already talked about how little of that there was around."

"Why don't we suspend the interview, until tomorrow? And why don't you let me try to help you?"

Janet stood looking at the man. "For a story?" she asked, suspiciously.

"If it leads to anything worthwhile, then yes: what else?" Baxeter answered honestly. "But I promise that if it does look good I won't publish or do anything that would endanger John, until he's got out."

Janet felt a sweep of relief at the thought of there being someone at last with whom she could at least discuss things. She said: "You really mean that?"

"My word."

"I'd appreciate your help very much," accepted Janet, meekly.

·21·

J anet felt no intrusion having David Baxeter in her room.
Rather she felt a continued relief at having someone to
do something for her. She sat in the only easy chair while
he perched on the edge of the bed, which was conveniently near the
telephone. The man appeared to be switched through several different numbers and extensions at the main telephone exchange, sometimes announcing himself to be a journalist and other times not, as
he sought to trace the anonymous number. It was an hour from the
time he started when he smiled up towards her.

"A public kiosk on Ayios Prokopios: it's the road that leads towards
the Troodos Mountains," he announced.

"Oh," Janet said.

"Why disappointment?"

She shrugged. "I don't know: I was just expecting something
different."

"If whoever it is really knows something, they're hardly going to
deal from their homes, are they?"

"No," Janet said, cheering up. "I wasn't thinking."

"Call it," Baxeter insisted. "There's got to be some demand, obviously. Say you need time to think about it and that you'll ring back. That'll give us time to talk it through."

They exchanged places and Janet dialed, feeling for the first time vaguely self-conscious at getting involved in a negotiation in front of someone else. She sat looking directly at him while the number rang, without any response. After several minutes Janet said, hand cupped unnecessarily over the mouthpiece: "No reply."

"Put it down," he suggested.

Janet did so and said: "What now?"

"Wait a few minutes: then we'll try again."

It became very quiet in the room, and Janet wished there were something else she could do. There were the calls to her father and Partington, she remembered: and at once decided against making them in front of the man.

"Now?" she said, finally.

"It's been less than five minutes," Baxeter said. "But OK, try it again."

This time the receiver was lifted on the third ring. A voice, in English, said: "This is a public telephone box."

"I was told to call it," she said.

"Janet Stone?"

"Yes."

"Glad you called."

"The message said you knew something to my advantage."

"We do."

"What?"

"We know where to look."

"Look where?"

"Here, in Cyprus. And from there where to look in Beirut."

It was all so familiar. She said: "What do you want?"

"A thousand."

At least the rate was going down, she thought wearily. Following Baxeter's suggestion she said: "I want to think about it."

"No tricks."

"What do you mean, no tricks?"

"We're not dealing with the police."

"No police," she promised.

"How long?"

"Thirty minutes."

It took much less than that for Janet to recount the complete conversation to Baxeter, who listened with his head intently to one side. As she finished the account Janet said: "It's a con, isn't it? It's got to be."

"It sounds like it," agreed Baxeter. "And I supposed you had to expect it, after all the publicity and the fact that a lot of people now know you're at this hotel . . ." He hesitated. "On the other hand, can you afford to ignore it?"

"Can I afford, literally, to try to negotiate?" came back Janet. "I know Zarpas has my bank account under permanent watch. The counter clerk would keep me waiting, and by the time I got the money he'd be behind me, asking what I was going to do."

"Yes," Baxeter said. "He would."

"So it's pointless: the whole thing's pointless."

"Why don't I let you have the money?"

"You!" echoed Janet.

"The magazine then."

"But why should you!"

"Magazines and newspapers pay all the time for stories and articles," he pointed out. "And we already agreed that if this came to anything I'd be able to write exclusively about it after John got out . . ." He smiled. "Actually," he added. "At the going rate, £1,000 is very cheap."

She'd been offered much more in Washington, at the beginning, remembered Janet. "But what if it is a con and you lose your £1,000?"

"I can't," said Baxeter, simply. "When you call back say that you'll need time to collect the money. Ask for . . ." He paused, trying to decide upon a period. ". . . ask for three hours. In that time I can ensure that all the bank note numbers are recorded. If it's a genuine call, leading to something, I'll have wasted a cashier's time. If it is a fraud, then I report it to the police, with the numbers, and the money becomes valueless. Where's the risk?"

"It seems almost easy," Janet conceded, reluctantly.

"Where can it go wrong?"

Janet thought for several moments, wanting to find the flaw. Eventually she said: "I can't find one."

"Remember," Baxeter urged. "Three hours. Agree to whatever hand-over arrangements they want: it doesn't matter." He got up and left.

There were still a few minutes before the second call, and Janet remained staring at the door through which Baxeter had gone. She supposed a lot of people would have sneered at the professional cynicism of his becoming involved but Janet couldn't be one of them. She sincerely believed he would hold back on the publication of anything that might endanger John, and Baxeter seemed able to think quickly and clearly about possible pitfalls. At the moment, it was an incredible comfort to have someone upon whom she felt she could rely: someone who didn't react to everything she did as if she were mentally defective. OK, so maybe that was just more professional cynicism, someone behaving as he had to behave to do his job. Janet decided she couldn't give a damn. It was just good not to be entirely alone any more.

Her call was answered on the third ring.

"I agree," she said.

"You didn't have any choice, did you?" the man said.

"No," Janet said. "No choice at all." There was a satisfaction in knowing there was no way the gloating bastard could cheat her: or rather, cheat David Baxeter.

"Do you know the walled part of Nicosia?"

"No."

"To the west there is the Paphos Gate. That's where we want the money brought."

"I need time to get it," Janet said.

"Two hours."

"Not enough. I need three."

"That's too long."

"I can't do it in two."

"The deal's off then."

"All right, it's off."

"You don't mean that."

"Goodbye."

"Wait!"

Janet believed she detected a muffled conversation with other people around the man to whom she was talking.

The voice returned to the line. "Three then."

"What do I do when I come to the Gate?"

"Nothing. We'll recognize you: you're a well-known lady."

"I want to know what I'm getting for my money."

"I told you before, where to look."

"I'll want proof."

"There'll be a photograph. And remember, no tricks."

Janet thought again of the other calls she had to make but she did not immediately redial. Who to call first? She decided upon England. Her mother answered, gabbling off the moment she recognized Janet's voice. The woman complained that the television and still pictures from Beirut had made her look simply terrible, as if it had been a long-arranged photocall for which Janet had days to prepare, and demanded to know what Janet imagined she was doing getting on a boat with such men in the first place. It took Janet several attempts to cut across the babble and get her father to the telephone. He began in much the same way as her mother, and it was difficult again to stop him.

In the end she shouted. "I know what you did!" she yelled.

"What?" her father said.

"You telephoned Partington and told him you wanted me stopped, any way that was possible," said Janet, still shouting. "You want to know how it happened! That's how it happened. Partington and the local CIA man set me up to be robbed and cheated and made to look stupid, so I'd have to come home like the silly little girl you think I am. You happy now? You happy that I almost got raped and that the man I stabbed might still die: that I was being shipped off to become a gang-banged whore in some back-street shed . . . !" The fury was pouring out of her, and she had to stop, breathless. When she did so it was very easy for her to hear that her father was crying.

". . . Love you," he sobbed. "Did it because I loved you . . ."

The answer—a lot of answers—came to Janet but she didn't bellow them back at the man because there wasn't any anger, not any more. Instead, quiet-voiced now, she said: "Just leave me alone, OK? Don't interfere any more."

"Come home!" he pleaded. "Please come home."

"I can't now," Janet said. "There's the court hearing."

"You're only a witness: you could come back and then return to Cyprus when it was necessary for you to give evidence."

"I don't want to come back, not yet," Janet said stubbornly.

"Don't try to do anything else," her father said, still pleading.

"I am not going to try to do anything else," Janet lied. Would Baxeter want to come to the Paphos Gate meeting with her? She was at first surprised at the thought but then accepted it because it wasn't surprising at all. She would have some protection, some safety, if he did.

"I'm sorry," her father said. "So very sorry. I didn't know how . . ." He stumbled to a halt. ". . . couldn't have . . ."

"Stop it, Daddy," said Janet, knowing the blur of tears herself now. "I'm OK. The police accept the stabbing as justifiable self-defense and say that it didn't happen in their jurisdiction anyway. I'm not hurt: not physically anyway."

"Can you forgive me?"

No! thought Janet at once: not completely, she could not forgive him. Didn't know if she ever could. She said: "Of course I forgive you."

"I really am . . ."

". . . You told me that," Janet stopped him. "Look after mummy."

"Please come home," he said.

"We'll talk about it another time."

"Do that!" her father said. "Keep in touch. Don't stop keeping in touch!"

"I said I've forgiven you." She felt no difficulty, no discomfort, in lying to her father, even though she could not ever recall lying to him before. She decided that everyone was cynical to achieve a purpose when the need arose.

"I love you," he said again.

"I love you, too," Janet said. Was that a lie, too, a response fitting the circumstance of the moment? Of course not. She'd have to be careful not to become too cynical, naive though she'd been until now.

She should have done it differently, Janet knew at once. The confrontation and the anger should have been directed at Partington, who'd triggered everything, and not at an old man whom she loved—of course she loved him—who'd done something he thought was best without any idea of what his action might bring about. Could Partington have had any conception, either? No matter. She should have vented her anger upon the embassy official and not her father, because now she felt drained, too drained to shout at anyone else. She wouldn't bother with Partington until the following day.

Where was Baxeter? Janet realized she was anxious for the man to get back and was at once surprised at the awareness. Why the hell should she worry about the return of a man she hardly knew! Because of John. The answer presented itself at once, and Janet openly smiled at it. Of course that was the reason. Despite her apprehension about the Paphos Gate meeting there was always the chance that it might—just might—be genuine, and so the sooner Baxeter came back the sooner they would discover whether or not it was worthwhile. That was it.

Janet hurried to the door when he knocked. She smiled and Baxeter smiled back: one of his teeth, to the left, was crooked, but not unpleasantly so.

He put a carefully wrapped bundle on the side table and said: "Well?"

"They didn't want to agree to three hours but finally they did," reported Janet. "The Paphos Gate. He promised there would be a picture."

"Of what?"

"He didn't say."

"Easy to get lost inside the walls," Baxeter said, reflectively.

"It's the divided sector," Janet said. "Arabs would not be able to move freely inside, would they?"

Baxeter shrugged his shoulders. "Depends on how well they know their way around."

"What about the money?"

Baxeter nodded towards the package and at the same time took a long, narrow strip of print-out paper from his inside pocket. "Every number carefully recorded," he said.

"I really am most grateful for everything you are doing."

"I've got a professionally vested interest: if this leads to anything it will be as much to my advantage as to yours," he said.

"I actually think I've got more to gain than you," disputed Janet. "And I'm still grateful."

"We've time for a drink downstairs before we go," said Baxeter. "That OK with you?"

"You're coming with me, then?"

"Didn't you expect me to?"

Janet let her hands come up and fall in uncertainty. "I didn't know," she said.

"Let's talk about it downstairs."

Janet brushed past the man as she left the room and she was aware of his cologne. It was strong. John had never gone in for things like that, Janet remembered.

Janet asked for coffee. Baxeter chose scotch. Janet watched the barman pour, caught by a familiarity but unable to think what it was. Glenfiddich, she saw, remembering: she and John had drunk Glenfiddich that first night, in Nathan's. She physically shifted in her seat, uncomfortable with the memory. Somehow it seemed wrong when she was with another man, which she acknowledged to be a stupid feeling but one she had, nevertheless. She said: "The person I spoke to kept on about not involving the police: no tricks was how he put it. I asked how I would recognize him and he told me I wouldn't. That he'd recognize me."

"You'll have to make the actual meeting by yourself," agreed Baxeter. "They'll be watching, obviously. They won't approach if I'm with you."

"Where will you be?"

Janet hadn't intended to sound nervous. Baxeter became serious and reached across the table for her hand, as he had over the luncheon table. "Don't worry!" he said. "I'll be right there, very close. Nothing bad is going to happen to you, not this time."

"Thank you," Janet said, not looking back at him. She shifted her fingers away from his touch.

"Sorry," he said, withdrawing his hand.

"There's nothing to apologize for."

"The Paphos Gate is a clever choice," resumed Baxeter, briskly. "There's a main highway directly outside, and three other major roads forming other good escape routes. I'll stay in the car directly opposite the Gate, so I'll be able to watch you all the time."

"What if . . ." Janet straggled to a halt. Forcing the question she said: "What if they *do* make a grab at me?"

"Scream," said Baxeter at once. "Scream and run back towards me. They'll want to see the money, so we'll loosen the package. If they go for you, drop it so the money breaks out: it'll deflect them."

"But they'll get the £1,000!"

"But they won't get you," said Baxeter. "And the money's useless anyway."

"I . . ." Janet stopped again.

"What?"

"Nothing," Janet said, brisk herself now. "We'd better get going."

They had driven to lunch in Janet's hired car, but this time Baxeter led the way to his vehicle. When Janet saw it she faltered, glad he was slightly in front and didn't see her reaction. It was a Volkswagen. Unlike John's, this one was dirty and there was a dent in the rear wing: it must have been a long-ago accident because it was already rusting. Baxeter let her in before walking around to the driver's side and while he was doing so Janet saw that the car was uncared for inside, as well. A sweater and some very old newspapers

were discarded on the rear seat, and the ashtray overflowed with
chocolate bar wrappings. Baxeter saw her looking when he got into
the car and said: "I gave up smoking six months ago. Now all I do is
eat sweets: the risk isn't lung cancer any more, it's diabetes."

The man drove familiarly towards the old part of the capital, joining up with the road system that looped entirely around the walls.
"That's the museum," Baxeter identified, as they went by the building, "and up ahead is the Post Office block. That's where I'm going
to park. The Paphos Gate is right opposite . . ." He hesitated, looking sideways at her. "I won't be more than twenty yards away at any
time."

"I wouldn't have thought it would have affected me so much as
this," Janet said, embarrassed.

"I would have been surprised if it hadn't," said Baxeter. He
stopped outside the telecommunications complex and pointed
across to the meeting place. "There," he said. "I'm very close."

"Yes," Janet agreed.

"You all right?"

"Fine."

Baxeter had driven with the parceled-up money on the floor beneath his legs. He lifted it on to his lap and peeled away the tape
holding the package together. He offered it to Janet and said: "Pull
the paper back from the top, like that. Then they'll be able to see the
money."

Janet took it: "Wouldn't it be wonderful if it worked! If this really
were something!"

"Wonderful," Baxeter agreed.

Janet got out of the Volkswagen and wedged the parcel under her
left arm: with the tape loosened the package felt unsteady and she
put her other hand across her body, frightened of dropping it and
scattering money everywhere. She had to time her crossing of Egypt
Avenue to dodge the approaching cars. People thronged the area
directly in front of the Gate and Janet hoped she would not be lost
from Baxeter's view among the crowd. Although it was mid-evening
there were still some fruit stalls loaded for business and groups of
souvenir vendors and postcard sellers stood at either side of the Gate
itself. Janet slowed when she reached the Gate, standing first to the
right and then crossing over to the far side. She pretended interest in
a copperwork stall, which was a mistake because the bent, claw-
fingered man began trying to thrust bracelets and necklaces upon
her. To escape Janet went across to the other side of the Gate. She

wanted to check the time but didn't because it would have meant turning her arm to see her watch and risking dropping the money. She wished she had gone to the toilet before leaving the hotel. She looked back towards the Post Offfice complex: she could make out the Volkswagen, but not as clearly as she would have liked. Baxeter would be able to see her, Janet thought, in self-assurance: she was sure he was absolutely dependable.

"Right on time."

Janet gasped in surprise, half turning. Illogically Janet had expected the man to come from outside the old part, towards her, but he had emerged from the inside, through the gate. He wore a loose *qumbaz*, a robe going right down to the ground and so voluminous it was impossible to tell if he were a thin or fat man, and around his head and concealing his lower face was wrapped a red and white Bedouin *kaffeyeh*. He'd spoken English, and Janet could not detect the sort of intonation she would have expected from an Arab. "What is it you have?" Janet demanded.

"That the money?"

"Yes."

"Let me have it."

"I want what you have first."

"Let me see it."

Janet parted the wrapping as Baxeter had shown her, determinedly closing it after a few moments. "Now you."

From beneath his robe the man brought an envelope, holding up but away from her. "Here!" he said.

"All I can see is an envelope."

Still keeping it away, the man reached inside, half pulling out what appeared to be some sheets of paper and a glossy print. "It's all here."

Janet felt the jump of excitement deep in her stomach. "What's the photograph of?"

"The house."

"What house?"

"Where he is, in Beirut."

The excitement grew, flowing through her. Trying to control it she said: "What else?"

"The address, where to go here. Where you'll get the address in Beirut."

"I don't understand why you're doing it this way," she protested.

"No tricks, remember," said the man. "If you've involved the police—if I'm jumped upon—then I won't telephone the house where I'm sending you, to say everything is all right. If they don't get a call within five minutes, they're going to leave. The same if the money is phony, when I've a chance to look at it closer. Cautious, eh?"

"Very," Janet agreed. It seemed a reasonable explanation for what the man was doing.

"Give me the money," the man demanded.

"The envelope," Janet insisted.

He offered it, tentatively, and Janet matched his movement, holding out the package, but to receive it he had to give her the envelope, freeing both his hands. He grabbed at it, turning as he did so, scurrying back into the walled city.

Janet was moving fast, too. She ran back across Egypt Avenue, careless of the cars this time, and darted inside the Volkswagen.

"Let me see!" He tugged the material from inside the envelope, spreading it out on his lap, nodding but not looking at Janet as she recounted the conversation. He studied the map and the directions more than the photograph. "It's right around the other side of the citadel," he said. "In the Palouriotissa district . . ." He handed the map across to her and said: "I'll drive, you map read."

Janet held everything up close in front of her face, trying to work out where they were going, as Baxeter turned the car, reached the junction, and began skirting the walls along Stasinos Avenue. "It says it's a two-story house," she read. "Number 11, in the cul-de-sac off Mareotis."

"I know Mareotis," said Baxeter.

"I think this really is something!" said Janet. "I've got a feeling about it!"

Traffic clogged ahead of them. Baxeter pumped the horn and said: "Come on! Come on!"

It took almost thirty minutes to complete the loop and come up to King George Square, from which Mareotis fed off. Baxeter slowed now, traveling the entire length until he reached Kapotas, where he said: "Damn!" and jerked the car around, to retrace their route.

"There!" pointed Janet, head close to her map again.

It was a narrow, rutted spur of an alley, without any proper lighting. Baxeter had to stop the car and get out to calculate the consecutive numbering. Back inside the car he edged slowly forward, counting off the houses as he did so.

". . . Seven . . . nine . . ." His voice trailed off and he stopped the car, not saying anything.

"It's a mistake: it's got to be a mistake!" Janet said, gazing at the completely empty lot where number eleven would have had to be. "We've miscounted. Let's do it again."

Baxeter got out of the car to check the numbering on both sides and then knocked at the entrance to nine. In the light behind the occupant, a fat, sag-busted woman, Janet was able to see a lot of gesturing although she could not hear what was said. There was a slowness about Baxeter's return to the car.

"I'm sorry," he said. "Really sorry."

"Tell me!"

"There isn't a number eleven: there never has been." He switched on the interior light, looking closely at the photograph. He said: "I don't even think this is Beirut. The background looks far more like Cyprus than Beirut."

Janet broke down.

The weeping this time was different from the way she had cried in Beirut. This time there was a mix of emotions, of regret and of disappointment and of frustration. She felt Baxeter's arm around her and she allowed herself to be pulled into his shoulder and she sobbed against him, letting it happen. There was some relief in weeping.

"Why!" she said, her voice unsteady. "Why does it always have to be like this!"

"Easy," he said. "We always had our doubts, didn't we?"

"I wanted so much for it to be right this time!"

"Something could still come up."

Janet pulled away from him but only slightly. She said: "Your money's gone."

"You know that's protected."

"I still feel responsible."

"Don't be silly."

·22·

axeter insisted upon going alone to the police to report the incident and freeze the money and Janet was grateful. Baxeter dropped her off at the hotel on his way, reminding her of the postponed interview the following day and Janet assured him she would not forget.

Another stupid episode, Janet thought, lying unsleeping in her darkened room. Which she'd suspected before she'd started. But she'd had no choice but to go through with the charade, so it was even more stupid to spend time on recriminations. Oddly, one of her biggest regrets was breaking down and crying like that in front of Baxeter, showing herself up. He'd been very understanding: kind and gentle and understanding. She did not think it was any professional cynicism: she was sure it was genuine. She was glad he'd been with her. There'd been some apprehension, particularly when she stood by the Paphos Gate, but the knowledge of his being so close at hand—of protection being only yards away—had made everything much easier. He really was . . .

Janet stopped the drift, determinedly, and then demanded the reason from herself. There was nothing wrong, nothing at which to feel ashamed, in reflecting on a man who was kind and considerate and had actually gone to a great deal of inconvenience—the sort of inconvenience he would be undergoing now, at the police station—on her behalf. She was not indulging in any schoolgirl romantic fantasy: that would have been absurd, unthinkable. She was merely looking back over the events of the day that she'd shared with someone. The word shared stayed with her. That's what she'd done: shared something. Not been alone. After all that had happened, the near-disasters and the humiliations, it had been nice for a few brief hours not to be alone any more. Just as she hadn't been alone after John Sheridan came into her life. Janet frowned at the comparison. Not the same, she thought: not the same at all. It would be quite wrong for her to combine—to confuse—the two.

The following morning Janet telephoned the British embassy, but without any of the anger she was now sorry at having directed at her father. In contrast, she was chillingly cool. She told Partington at once that she was aware of his role in what had happened to her, talking down his weakly-begun protest by telling him that her father as well as Hart had confirmed it. As she mentioned the American, she remembered the still-unreturned clothes. Deciding now against any more contact with the CIA man, Janet demanded—rather than requested—that the embassy help return them to the woman in Beirut. Partington, flustered, promised that he would, of course, take care of it.

"I couldn't have known how it would turn out," said the diplomat. "Not what they intended to happen to you in Beirut."

"Robbery but not rape, eh?"

"Your father said the money didn't matter: that without it you wouldn't be able to do anything."

"I don't want to talk about it any more," said Janet. It was difficult for her to accept but she really did feel bored by it now.

"I really am very sorry."

"That's what people seem perpetually to be, very sorry."

"Apart from returning the clothes, is there anything else I can do?"

"No," Janet said, careless of the rudeness.

"You will call me again, if I can help, won't you?"

"No," Janet said again. "If I thought I needed any sort of help I don't think I would come to you, Mr. Partington."

Janet was ready, waiting, for Baxeter's arrival, and picked up the telephone on the first ring when he called from the downstairs house phone. They met in the lounge overlooking the swimming pool again, although he did not at once turn on the tape recorder. Janet asked about his meeting with Zarpas, and Baxeter said he had not seen him. A subordinate officer had promised to put a stop on the money and circulate all banks, credit exchanges, and hotels. As an additional precaution, Baxeter had told his own bank to duplicate the warning through all its branches. He agreed with her that he supposed there would be a prosecution if whoever had the money attempted to pass it, but he assured Janet the policeman who had taken his statement had not talked of needing one from her.

"What about your magazine?"

"They cleared it before I started, so they knew the risks," Baxeter said, casually. "There's no problem."

"I still wish it had been my money."

"It's over, finished," said Baxeter, even more dismissively.

Janet found the resumed interview difficult, and could not at first understand why. It was because she did not think of him as a stranger any more, she decided finally. At the first encounter, their roles had been clearly defined, interviewer to interviewee, but now it didn't seem like that any more. Baxeter appeared to find a similar problem, posing his questions over-solicitously, frequently apologizing in advance for what he was going to ask and several times abandoning a query in mid-sentence, saying that it didn't matter and twice that it was too personal. It was late afternoon before Baxeter turned the recorder off.

"You must know more about me now than I do about myself," said Janet, trying to lighten the mood.

"You don't mind?"

"Not if it helps John."

"No," he agreed, looking directly at her. "Not if it helps John." Janet looked away. "Sure you've got all you want?"

"Not quite," he said. "There are still the photographs."

"Of course," Janet agreed at once. "Who'll take them?"

"I will."

"You do both?" questioned Janet, not expecting that he did.

"They get good value out of me," smiled the man.

"When?"

Baxeter looked beyond her, to the grounds outside. "The light's gone now," he said. "Are you free tomorrow sometime?"

It would fill in part of another empty day, Janet thought: which is all it would be, just occupying part of a day. She said: "Sure. What time?"

"Your convenience," he said.

"We really are being most polite to each other, aren't we?"

He was looking directly at her again but did not immediately reply. "Yes," he said. "Very polite."

"What time is the light best?"

"Mid-day, usually."

"Why not make it mid-day then?"

"Could we make it a little earlier?" he asked. "I thought we might drive somewhere for better backgrounds. The Troodos Mountains, perhaps?"

"Of course."

When Janet emerged from the hotel the following day she saw he'd had the Volkswagen cleaned, which made the rusting dent in the wing look worse than it had when the car had been dirty. It was clean inside, too, and between the two front seats there was a large carton of sweets and chocolate bars.

"Help yourself," he offered.

"You really eat these all the time?"

"I'm getting better. Down to a pound a day."

As they drove towards the mountains Baxeter maintained a constant chatter about the island, pointing out monasteries and medieval and Roman historical sites. He talked about the Crusaders and told the story of Aphrodite, whose temple, he said, was on the far side of the island. Janet listened politely, conscious of the effort he was making. He'd dug deeply into the sweet bag by the time they reached Troodos. The mountains were larger than Janet had expected them to be, mist-clouded at the summits and heavily cloaked in firs and pine. They stopped at a roadside tavern with an outside area ceilinged with vines and Janet shivered involuntarily. When he asked why she confessed that it had briefly reminded her of the sour-oiled cafe on the road to Dhekelia where she'd been taken to meet the Fettal family. Baxeter rose at once, saying they should go, but Janet insisted on staying, determined to exorcise the ghosts from her mind. She let him order the fish kebabs and he photographed her at the table and took more pictures after their lunch, Janet standing against the trellised vines and then against the verandah rail, gazing out over a deep and thickly wooded valley.

They climbed higher in the early afternoon and Janet suddenly saw the huge white globe, like a giant tennis ball, which Baxeter identified as one of the listening stations maintained by the British on the island. Janet actually opened her mouth, to speak of the eavesdropping cooperation that Willsher had told her about, but quickly shut it again. Throughout every interview she had given, and certainly during the two-day session with Baxeter, Janet had held back from disclosing anything of that conversation, determined to keep her side of the bargain with the CIA man. Did it matter any more? she wondered: that meeting in Washington seemed a very long time ago.

Baxeter took more photographs at another verandahed vantage spot, then came close beside her to point in the direction of Aphrodite's temple. Janet was once more aware of his cologne. The continual sweet-eating seemed to have scented his breath, too.

"I think I've got all the photographs I need," he said.

"Time to go then?"

"I guess so."

As they made their way unhurriedly towards the Volkswagen, Janet said: "I've enjoyed the day."

He held open the door for her to get into the vehicle and as he entered from his side Baxeter said: "I've enjoyed it too. Very much." He twisted in his seat, so that he could look directly at her. He didn't try to start the car.

"We'd better be going," said Janet.

"I . . ." he started, then stopped.

"What?"

"Nothing." Baxeter started the car and ground the gears when he engaged them.

The road snaked downwards in a never-ending loop of hairpin bends and Janet began to feel vaguely nauseated from constantly turning back upon themselves. The silence lasted for a long time. To break it she said: "What happened to the car?"

"What car?"

"This one. The dent in the wing."

"Don't know: it happened in a car park. Have to get it fixed one day."

It was not something she had ever discussed with him, but Janet was sure that John Sheridan would have repaired a damaged wing— or for that matter damage to anything else he owned—within an hour or two after he discovered it. She became instantly irritated with herself: linking them together in her mind again, she thought. She said: "Could you slow down a little? I'm beginning to feel slightly carsick."

"Do you want to stop?" he asked, solicitous again.

"No. Just go slower."

Baxeter did, markedly, and said: "Have you been to Limassol?"

"No."

"There are some good restaurants along the coast from there."

"Really?"

There was another silence, and then he said: "Would you like to eat dinner . . . ?" He hesitated. "Not immediately, I don't mean. Later, when we've got off the mountain: you'll only feel discomfort while we're going around these bends."

"I don't feel sick any more," Janet said. "But no. Thank you for asking but no."

"Of course not," he accepted at once.

"I don't want to sound rude."

"I understand."

Janet wished she did. What would be wrong with having dinner on the way back to Nicosia? She said: "Maybe another . . ." and came to a halt herself, wishing she had not begun the sentence. "I'm feeling rather tired," she finished, fatuously.

"I'm concerned," he announced.

"What about?"

"Your getting mixed up in any more nonsense like that business at the Paphos Gate. And before."

"I'm learning with experience," said Janet, bitterly. What, exactly, was she learning, she wondered.

"Can I make a suggestion?" Without waiting for an answer he continued on. "Please let me give you my phone number. There's an answering machine, so I get messages even if I'm not there. If you get any more approaches—anything at all—don't try to handle it by yourself. Let me be involved . . ." He risked a glance at her across the car. "I don't mean for a story: not primarily, anyway. Let me help you first and we'll work out the rest later. I just don't want you to be hurt."

Janet could not find the words to describe how she felt but certainly her eyes were clouded and when she started to speak her voice was jagged. She said: "That's very kind of you . . . generous . . . but what about your other commitments?"

"I can be as flexible as I like, working with the magazine."

"I was not thinking particularly about the magazine," corrected Janet. "What about girlfriends, wives, and children?"

He looked across the car again, grinning. "There are no girlfriends, wives, or children, in that or any other order."

She smiled back, grateful he was making a joke of the question. "As I said, it's a very generous offer. Thank you."

"So will you?" he pressed.

"Yes."

"Promise?"

"I promise."

Outside the hotel he made a groping, haphazard search through the pockets of his jacket and then the glove compartment and withdrew triumphantly from there with a crumpled and bent piece of pasteboard in his hand. "Knew I had one somewhere!" he said, offering her the visiting card with his number printed upon it. "And this!" he added, snatching into the carton and proffering the wrapped pastille. "It's strawberry flavored, the best. I always save it until last."

She laughed openly, unoffended by the flirtation. She was enjoying herself and it hadn't happened for a long time: not since before John had been snatched. "All I seem to do is thank you."

"Will you?"

"Will I what?"

"Come out to dinner with me some other time?"

Janet felt herself coloring and hoped he wouldn't notice in the fading light. She said: "I don't know. Maybe."

"When?"

"I said maybe!" said Janet, as unoffended by his persistence as she had been by the earlier flirtation.

"Can I call?"

"Of course you can."

"And you'll get in touch with me, if there are any more approaches?"

"I promised I would. So I will."

Baxeter did not call the following day. Janet sat around the pool in the morning and went into the city in the afternoon and checked her messages when she got back, acknowledging the disappointment and becoming unhappy at feeling it. That night, eating a solitary dinner, she kept remonstrating with herself and was convinced by the time she went to bed that her attitude was in no way unfaithful to John. After so much hostility and rejection and drama, what could be more normal than responding—properly responding—to a gesture of friendship? And that was all it amounted to, Janet was equally convinced: a gesture of friendship, nothing more. Certainly nothing more on her part.

The next day Zarpas gave her the date of the first hearing against the Fettal family, cautioning her it was only a remand appearance but warning her that the magistrates would expect her to attend. And within an hour Partington telephoned to say the borrowed clothes had been returned to Beirut and ask if she had changed her mind about his offer to help, which she hadn't. She caught a reflection of herself leaving the by-now-familiar pool, abruptly aware just how deeply tanned she had become. And at this rate, she guessed, she would become more so.

Janet tried to suppress the sound of any pleasure in her voice when Baxeter called on the Friday and was sure she had succeeded, but a brief and unsettling feeling, a kind of numbness, briefly swept her body.

When he invited her to dinner, she managed, too, to seem unsure in advance of accepting it and felt after replacing the receiver that the conversation had been maintained on precisely the necessary level of friendship. He assured her the Orangery at the Hilton was good for nouvelle cuisine, and it was, and afterwards they went to a bar on the Famagusta Road where there was good bouzouki music. He said the article and photographs had worked out very well and that his Vancouver office was pleased. She told him about the initial court appearance of the Fettals, and he at once offered to accompany her if she would like him to. Janet, surprised, accepted. Baxeter asked what she was doing on the weekend, and Janet blurted "nothing" before thinking what she was saying, so he invited her to Paphos, and she accepted. Baxeter made no attempt to kiss her—no attempt at any physical contact at all—when he took her back to the hotel and neither did he the following day, which she enjoyed as much as she had their first trip to the Troodos Mountains.

There were three outings in the succeeding week, one lunch and two dinners, and that weekend he suggested going through the Turkish-held area in one of the United Nations-escorted convoys to Kyrenia, which he assured her was possible.

Janet made the journey curiously, saddened by the occasional protest sign and the indications of squalor, compared to the Greek-held sections which were all she had previously encountered.

Janet thought Kyrenia was one of the most attractive cities she had visited on the island and Baxeter, as usual, was an enthusiastic guide. He made her climb all over the ochre and yellow castle and in one comparatively small room pointed to a small circle in the middle of the floor.

"This was the officers' mess hall," he explained. "In medieval times prisoners were sentenced to be pushed down that hole: it opens into something like the shape of an upside down light bulb. There's one in the ordinary soldiers' mess, as well. They're called oubliette holes because once put in there the prisoners never got out: they were forgotten. All they had to eat, apart from themselves, were the scraps that the officers and men used to throw them, for amusement . . ." Baxeter's voice trailed off, at the look on Janet's face. "Oh Christ!" he said. "Oh Christ, I'm sorry . . . ! What the . . . oh shit!"

"It's all right," she said, stiffly.

"It's not," he contradicted. "I don't know what to say! Jesus Christ!"

"Just don't say anything."

·23·

Mustafa Fettal died without recovering consciousness early on the day of the remand hearing, three hours before the court convened, and it was not until she arrived at the magistrates' building that Janet learned of the death.

Chief Inspector Zarpas was waiting anxiously on the court steps when she arrived with Baxeter, looking with passing curiosity at the journalist when Janet got from the car. The steps were jammed with reporters and cameramen and there was an abrupt flare of lights: there were a lot of shouted questions, too, which at the time Janet did not understand. Zarpas said: "Don't say anything: there's something you've got to know," and started to hurry her away. Janet looked around for Baxeter but couldn't see him. Zarpas took her into a side office, off the main courtroom corridor, and told her there.

"Dead?" she said, disbelieving.

"I warned you it might happen."

"Somehow I just never imagined it would."

"Well, it has," the policeman said harshly. He had probably the most important court hearing of his career about to begin, and he wanted to break the mood into which he believed she was retreating.

"What must I do now?" asked Janet, numbly. I've killed a man, she thought: taken a life.

"Do . . . ?" frowned Zarpas and then understood the question. "I've already told you that I don't intend to recommend any proceedings, because of the circumstances of the stabbing. But you've made a confession, so I must officially inform the Lebanese authorities, because of their jurisdiction. But as you already told them and they released you once, I don't imagine they'll want to proceed either."

That wasn't right, thought Janet: it wasn't right to be able to kill somebody and escape any penalty whatsoever, irrespective of how extenuating the circumstances might be. She said: "How will it affect today's hearing?"

"I don't know," admitted Zarpas. "The other two have been in conference with their lawyers for over an hour now, ever since I told them."

"I didn't mean him to die, I just wanted . . ."

"Stop it!" Zarpas said, harsher still. "Stop it right now! It happened and we know how it happened and no action is going to be taken. What you did was justified. Don't collapse into a lot of unnecessary recrimination. Let's try to make sure the other two don't walk away."

Janet nodded but didn't speak.

"Sure you're all right?" demanded the man.

"I think so," Janet managed, although it wasn't true. She didn't think she was all right: at that moment she didn't know what she was.

"You won't be required to give evidence today," Zarpas assured her formally. "I just wanted you here for any eventuality."

"When?" asked Janet.

"That depends on whatever the defense say today. And then what the court decides."

"I want to get it over with!" said Janet, too loudly.

The concern filled Zarpas's face at Janet's unsteady reactions and he thought how fortunate it was that she was not being called today. She'd be all right when the shock wore off: that was all it was, understandable shock. He said: "Let's get on inside."

The courtroom was comparatively small and it was already crowded, expectant. Zarpas led her to a reserved area deep in the well of the court and sat her down. At once Janet looked around for

Baxeter, worried when at first she couldn't see him. And then she did, inconspicuous at the side away from the main press bench. He smiled, faintly, and gave a head movement she could not fully understand but which she inferred to mean that he had heard about the death. Quite near to Baxeter she located Partington. When he realized she'd seen him the diplomat nodded too, without any facial expression. Janet looked away, not responding.

The clerk demanded that the court stand, for the entry of the magistrates, and Janet dully took her lead from what people did around her. There was a shuffle of interest when the Fettal brothers were called into the dock. Janet forced herself to look, aware that the attention of almost everyone in the court was upon her as she did so, and she made a determined effort to show no emotion.

The one who had acted as captain wore the same suit and tie as he had in the Dkehelia road cafe but his hair had been slicked back in an attempt at neatness. The other wore no jacket and hobbled with difficulty into the dock. Neither man looked at her.

The charge, that they had jointly attempted fraudulently to covert a money draft in the sum of £10,000 by purporting that they had the right to such monies, was formally delivered and at once the prosecuting solicitor asked for a remand in custody to enable the prosecution to prepare its case.

Then the defense was formally invited to respond.

The Fettals' solicitor was a fat, confident man who appeared to enjoy the theatrics of a court of law. He smiled indulgently around the room and made much of arranging before him his already perfectly arranged papers.

"Your worships," he began, still bent over his files. "My clients utterly refute this accusation and I intend to prove absolutely their innocence, although unfortunately someone associated with them who would have been called to prove that innocence has, regrettably, died this very day . . ." The man paused, as if a moment's respectful silence were necessary, and then continued: "My clients have no knowledge whatsoever of the original acquisition of the bearer letter of credit in the name of Mrs. Janet Stone . . ." The man turned and looked fully at Janet. There was no self-satisfied smile now. "They have never met Mrs. Stone nor traveled with Mrs. Stone on any vessel plying out of this island, to the coast of Lebanon . . ."

There was a bustle of surprised reaction around the room. Zarpas was sitting just two rows away and in front of her and Janet saw him lean towards the prosecuting solicitor and then pull back, nodding in apparent anticipation.

". . . My clients shared with a cousin of theirs, Mustafa Fettal, the use of a sailing boat, a general-purpose craft in which they pursued various activities, sometimes fishing, sometimes coastal trading," resumed the lawyer. He was now looking intently at the magistrates, wanting them fully to take the point he was about to make. "But the three of them did not constitute a permanent crew. Sometimes all three of them sailed it, sometimes only two . . ." A further pause identified the moment. "And sometimes, your worships, it sailed with one man! I repeat, with just one man! The day before that stipulated in the charge before you, Mustafa Fettal informed his relations, the two accused now in the dock, that upon that evening he wished to use the boat alone. One of my clients could not have sailed that night anyway: he had suffered a grievous wound to the foot, an injury involving a broken bottle, and was quite incapacitated. Neither saw anything unusual in their cousin's request; it was an arrangement each had known and used many times in the past. They of course agreed. It was then that Mustafa Fettal produced the document which is the subject of the charge before you today. He asked these two to go to a bank to negotiate the order for him and arranged that they should meet the following day for him to receive the money . . ."

Janet was conscious of more attention upon herself and knew her face was blazing with indignation at what was being said. The court couldn't accept it! she thought. They just couldn't!

". . . It is surely an indication of their innocence . . . their unawareness of what they were being asked to do . . . that they quite openly entered a branch of a local bank in Larnaca and offered the document not realizing it had to be endorsed by the person in whose name it was issued before any monies could be handed over!" said the man. "Surely, sirs, this is the innocent action of ordinary men, not the conniving behavior of villains intent to defraud!"

Ahead of Janet there was another muffled consultation going on between Zarpas and the prosecutor and more head nodding.

The lawyer concluded: "This, sirs, is the basis of the defense I shall be calling—a defense I am confident will result in their immediate acquittal without any reference to a higher court—and in the circumstances I confidently apply to you today for them to be permitted bail, to enable them to continue about their lawful duties."

The prosecutor was on his feet before the other lawyer was fully seated. The bail objection was very forcefully put. It was pointed out that the two had access to a boat, and Zarpas was formally sworn to give evidence that the police had serious doubts of either appearing at another hearing if they were allowed out of custody. The magistrates did not need to retire to reject the bail application.

When the Fettals were taken down from the dock and the magistrates retired, Janet remained where she had been seated, unsure what to do. In the brief moments of hesitation Zarpas reached her and said: "Let's go back to that office and talk again."

The policeman shielded her against the crush of question-shouting reporters in the outside corridor. Once inside the office Janet wheeled upon the man and said: "That was preposterous! Absolutely preposterous!"

"Of course it was preposterous," Zarpas agreed, mildly. "With the man dead they're able to change their story: say they knew nothing about your being taken to the Lebanon as a whore."

"It makes nonsense of everything that really took place!" said Janet, still outraged.

"That's what the defense tries to do in the majority of cases," Zarpas said. Deciding she was sufficiently recovered, he said: "But it tells us one thing. You're going to be in for some pretty tough cross-examination. You'll have to be ready for it."

"But there's proof!" insisted Janet, trying for some reality against the exasperation that burned through her. "The Arab engineer, Haseeb, at Larnaca marina! And the cafe owners on the Dhekelia road." She groped for the recollection and said, excitedly: "We were served by a young boy: obviously the son of the owner."

Zarpas moved his head sadly from side to side. "You told us all that in your statement. We haven't been able to find anyone named Haseeb working around Larnaca marina . . . or anyone who knows him by that name. No one at the Dhekelia road cafe remembers anything."

"I don't believe it!" said Janet, aghast.

"There's no one reason," shrugged Zarpas, resigned. "There's family loyalties . . . race loyalties. There's people with things themselves to hide who don't want to get involved . . . *just* not wanting to get involved is enough, more often than not."

"I really am going to be made to look the complete fool, aren't I?"

Janet said, crushed by the recollection of why she had been entrapped into the situation in the first place.

"No," Zarpas said. "You did silly things . . . unthinking, ill-considered silly things. But everyone can understand and feel sympathy with *why* you did them: what you hoped to achieve. Complete fools behave without any logic or reason. So you're not a complete fool. Just a determined lady who made mistakes."

Janet smiled at the policeman against whom she had felt antagonistic but didn't any more. She said: "I appreciate that, very much. That makes it seem right . . ." She stopped and at once blurted: "No! I didn't mean that! Not that killing. That could never be right, not completely, whatever the circumstance. But everything else."

"The legal process has begun now," Zarpas said.

"I know," Janet said, curious at the reminder.

"There's a mob of pressmen outside," warned Zarpas. "You mustn't give interviews or say anything that is likely to affect the outcome of any hearing. I don't want to give the Fettals any more loopholes through which to crawl back into the sewer."

"I won't," Janet promised.

"Would you like me to lay on a car?"

"I came with someone. I'll be all right."

There *was* a mob. Two uniformed constables had to run interference to get her to the exit. Throughout Janet shook her head against the cacophony of demands and repeated: "Nothing to say," and guessed that the photographs and the television footage would be as awful as they had been in Beirut, except that here she'd look as if she were trying to get away from the attention instead of cooperating with it. Every step of the way she searched against the glare for Baxeter's face in the crowd but couldn't see it. By the time she reached the steps the panic was beginning to well up, the fear that for some inexplicable reason he wasn't there to help her and that eventually she would be abandoned to be tugged and gnawed at by the pack around her.

And then she saw the car with its rusty dent and felt a surge of relief. He was waiting directly at the bottom of the steps, carelessly in a prohibited parking zone and with the engine running, and when he saw her emerge he leaned across to open the door for her to enter.

There was a grabbing struggle as she tried to enter the car and Baxeter pushed the throng back with the door edge. Someone yelled "Bastard!" and another voice said "Son of a bitch!" and as he took the car away from the curb, scattering them, Baxeter shouted back: "Fuck you!"

He made two very tight turns, an obvious attempt to lose any pursuit, and said: "I'm sorry."

"What for?"

"Swearing like that."

"I didn't notice," Janet said. Wanting at once to get it out of the way between them she said: "He's dead."

"I heard."

"I can't accept I killed somebody!" she said, edging back to the disbelief of the first few moments with Zarpas. "I can't conceive the crap that the defense lawyer served up, either."

Baxeter kept twisting and turning the tiny car around the central part of the city, using the ancient, difficult-to-negotiate streets. He said: "Some tried to follow. I think I've lost them."

"What the hell did they hope to achieve!" she demanded, wanting to be angry at something positive.

"That you'd break down: say something that could be expanded into a bigger story," said Baxeter. "And I've never encountered a photographer yet who's satisfied with the last picture he took."

"They'll be at the hotel," Janet realized.

"I'm afraid so: that's the obvious place to wait for you."

"I don't think I could face it," Janet said. She actually did feel physically—or was it mentally?—strange, her awareness of everything around one moment definite, the next receding almost foggily, then becoming definite again.

"Do you want to go to a restaurant? Or a bar?"

"Good God, no!" Janet said at once.

Baxeter turned away from the walled part of the town but Janet was unaware and uncaring, slumped in the Volkswagen with her head forward against her chest, playing Zarpas's reassurances over and over in her mind, like a child with a favored pop tune, but still unable to avoid the burden of guilt. Against every reassuring phrase or argument the policeman had provided, Janet put the contradicting litany of her own, I've killed, I've killed, I've killed.

"We're here," he said.

Still unconcerned at her surroundings, Janet let herself be helped from the car and followed him up the outside steps of a two-story, flat-roofed house, not aware until she was inside the room that she was in somebody's home.

"Where is this!" she demanded.

"My flat," said Baxeter, simply. "I'm sorry. It's not very tidy."

It wasn't.

It appeared to be a workplace on to which living accommodation had been added as an afterthought. By the window was a cluttered desk dominated by a word processor with an umbilical cord between two screens, not just one. Above the desk, do-it-yourself shelves held uneven walls of reference books and on a small side table there were three separate telephones. Between the shelves and the window was a drying line from which strips of undeveloped negatives hung from pegs and immediately below, a photograph's magnifying stand stood ready to examine the tiny exposures. Two filing cabinets, with gap-toothed drawers, delineated the work space from where Baxeter lived. The living area was surprisingly expansive, easily able to accommodate two couches covered with garishly-colored Arab blankets, as well as easy chairs. Newspapers and magazines overflowed from a center table onto another brightly patterned Arab rug, and a television set stood in a corner, near a floor-to-ceiling wall cabinet which housed crockery and glasses. The bottles were on a central, flat shelf.

Seeing her look, Baxeter said: "Would you like a drink?"

"I actually think I need one. Brandy would be good."

He poured for both of them, heavily, and when she took the glass Janet saw just how badly her hand was shaking.

He said: "There really is space to sit, on the couches."

Janet did so and said: "It seems to be becoming a habit for me to break down in front of you."

"It doesn't cause me any difficulty."

Janet clamped her lips between her teeth, determined against any more nonsense, waiting until the sensation passed. She still didn't risk talking immediately, covering the moment by bringing the glass to her mouth.

"So much!" she said at last. "There's been so much!"

"I know," he said, softly.

"I thought I could cope . . . was sure I could cope . . . that's one of the upsets, I suppose. Not believing any more that I can." Janet felt his arm around her, pulling her against him, and let herself go: it was much more comfortable than it had been in the Volkswagen. The smell of his cologne wasn't really too strong at all: in fact it was rather nice, an indication of how personally clean he was.

"There was bound to be a reaction," he said. "Of course you can cope."

His hand was soothingly against her face, gently rubbing her cheek and up into her hair and Janet was aware of herself sighing, of letting herself go. She said: "When my husband died I curled up into a ball and never wanted to go out again. That's what I feel like now. That I want to hide away forever."

"That's what we're doing," he said. "Hiding away where no one can find us."

Janet felt something else against the side of her head, near her hair, and could not at once decide what it was. Then she realized his lips were there, kissing her. She shifted but not away, bringing her legs up beneath her better to lean against him. She said: "That's where I want to be: hidden from everyone and everything."

She brought her head around as she spoke. His kiss, like everything else about him, was gentle, and Janet responded just as softly, so that their mouths remained close together, exploring between quietly snatched breaths. Janet felt his hand upon her and momentarily stiffened but then eased again, not wanting to stop him, and the buttons parted and the clasps unsnapped. He explored with his fingers now and Janet didn't object, letting her mind stay in that fogged part of reality where she refused to think or to rationalize or to equate, just to feel. She felt him move again and raise her up with him and walk with his arm around, supporting her, to the bedroom where she was practically unaware of her clothes coming off. It was his mouth as well as his fingers that moved over her now and Janet reached out for him, sighing with the greatest relaxation of all when he entered her. They moved perfectly together, unhurriedly, and it was ecstasy and she cried out at the moment of bursting excitement, clinging to him and knowing his explosion too.

The pain of physical release brought her shudderingly back to the reality she had briefly refused to confront, and Janet did stiffen this time, hands gripped at her sides, making herself think of what she'd done. Betrayed, she thought: she'd betrayed—humiliated—a man she loved and whom she'd postured and posed and pretended to be trying to rescue. It didn't matter that John would never know of the betrayal or the humiliation. She'd know. Always. Carry it with her like a stigma, a constant weight. A thought began but Janet refused it. There couldn't be any excuse, any escape. She'd been betrayed and humiliated and battered and frightened but the need, for a few moments, to hide and forget wasn't an excuse. There wasn't even an equation. She paraded all the words in her mind, mentally shouting the accusation: whore and tart and prostitute and slut. And they weren't bad enough, cruel enough, to describe what she'd done.

She felt Baxeter's hand upon hers, on the fist she had created, and kept it tightly shut, refusing, too, to look sideways at him.

"I am not sorry," he said.

"I am."

"It happened."

"It shouldn't have done."

"Why not?"

"Don't be so bloody stupid!" she said. "You know why it shouldn't have happened!"

"It needn't complicate anything."

"It will, won't it! You think I'll be able to forget!"

"It will only become a complication if you let it."

"You think I'm a whore?"

"Now you're being bloody stupid," he said. "I knew the situation. Do you think of me as a whoremonger or a lecher?"

The rejection quietened her. "No," she said. "I don't think of you like that."

"It hasn't hurt John: needn't hurt John."

"How do you think of me?" she said, needing an answer.

Baxeter raised himself on one arm and moved over her, so that she was forced to look at him. He said: "I think you're very beautiful and I wanted almost from the first moment to take you to bed and I think you realized what was growing up between us just as much as I did, didn't you?"

"Yes," Janet agreed, in a whisper.

"And didn't want it to stop?" he pressed, determined upon the complete catharsis.

"No," she said, in further admission. "But I still love John."

"I didn't ask you to stop: expect you to stop."

"It *is* a complication!" she insisted, angrily. "It's a bloody mess."

"It's an adult situation and we're adults."

"I don't feel like an adult. I feel like an idiot child."

"Stop it," he warned.

"What are we going to do?" she asked.

"What do you want to do?"

"I don't . . ." she began and then stopped. "Yes I do," she said. "I want us to forget about it: not forget but put it in the back of our minds like the mistake it was and . . ." she trailed off.

"And what?"

"I don't know."

"I don't think it was a mistake. I knew what I was doing. Like you did."

"Let's not start using words like love!"

"Not if you don't want me to."

"My father wants me to go back to England in between the court hearings. I think that's what I'll do. The difficulty won't exist if I do that."

Baxeter lowered himself off his arm and lay like Janet, on his back looking up at the ceiling. He said: "If you don't want to go, it won't be necessary for you to make the separation. Not for a week or so at least."

"I don't understand," she said, turning to him at last.

"I've got to go away," said Baxeter. "I was going to tell you earlier."

Despite the guilt and the resolutions Janet felt her stomach dip, at the thought of his not being near. She said: "Just for a week or so?"

"It shouldn't be any longer. It's just a quick in-and-out assignment."

"Where?"

He was silent for several moments. Then he said: "Beirut."

"What!"

"A situation piece," said Baxeter. "It'll probably accompany the article I've written about you."

"Don't go!" she blurted.

"Don't be silly," he said. "I've got to go."

"Be careful, darling. Please be . . ." said Janet and then stopped, realizing the word she'd used.

Baxeter smiled back but didn't pick up upon it, further to embarrass her. "I'm the sort of guy who does his reporting from the bar of the best hotel."

"I'm serious," Janet insisted. Unashamedly she said: "I don't want to lose anyone else."

Serious himself, Baxeter said: "Do you want me to find out what I can about John?"

Janet held his eyes. "Yes," she said. "Please find out what you can about John."

·24·

J anet slept at Baxeter's flat that night and in the morning
they made love again and it was as good as the first time.
She insisted upon returning alone to the hotel, which
was still besieged by reporters. On Baxeter's advice Janet did not try
to avoid them, which he argued would merely prolong the pressure,
but agreed to meet them all at once in a small conference room the
hotel made available to them.

When everyone was seated and the lights were on, a cacophony of
questions erupted. Janet held her hands up to stop the babble, not
bothering to speak until the sound lessened. Then she said, simply,
that she was unable to answer any questions because she had been
legally advised that having come before a court everything was now
sub judice until a verdict.

She was ignored.

"What's your reaction to the defense assertion which would appear to make your story complete fabrication?" called an American
voice, from the rear.

"The truth will come out during the court hearing," refused
Janet, doggedly. I hope, she thought.

"Mrs. Stone, has this whole episode been an exercise to achieve personal publicity?" An English voice this time, a man in the front, balding and bespectacled.

The demand unsettled and to an extent bewildered Janet. Until now—particularly in Beirut—she had been treated sympathetically by the media, but she recognized that the attitude had shifted. Now it was suspicion, actual hostile suspicion. "From the time of my fiancé's abduction I have cooperated with the press for only one reason, to maintain public interest in his plight," she retorted angrily. That anger was primarily at the assembled journalists but there was a subsidiary reason for her flushed face. When she got to the word fiancé her mind had filled with what had happened during the previous twenty-four hours between herself and Baxeter and she'd almost stumbled to an awkward halt.

"Do you intend staying in Cyprus throughout all the hearings, right up to a higher court if the case is committed there?" asked a woman.

Dear God, I wish I knew what I was going to do about anything, Janet thought. She said: "I have not yet decided upon that: it depends how long it takes."

"You didn't come back to the hotel last night, Mrs. Stone?" It was the balding Englishman in front again.

"No," said Janet and stopped. She could physically feel the flush firing through her cheeks.

"Where were you, Mrs. Stone?" A woman, somewhere in the middle of the pack.

"I . . ." groped Janet but another voice talked over her and she saw Partington walking down the side of the group to where she was sitting. "Partington, British embassy," said the diplomat. "As Mrs. Stone has already made clear, there was the need for extensive legal discussion after the initial hearing. Those discussions lasted late into the evening and it was decided by the embassy that she needed some uninterrupted time to rest . . ." He bent, cupping Janet's arm, but went on talking: "It's also been made clear that there is no further comment Mrs. Stone can make until the conclusion of the legal processes here on the island so you will have to excuse her . . ."

There was a surge of protest. Partington ignored it. Janet, relieved, let herself be guided from her chair and out of the room: Baxeter was standing right at the back, near the door. He gave no facial reaction and neither did she.

"I'd better escort you to your room," suggested the diplomat.

"Please," accepted Janet.

They remained unspeaking in the elevator. In her room Janet said: "Why did you do that down there? Say what you did?"

"From where I was sitting you looked like someone who needed rescuing."

"What about from where everyone else was sitting?"

"Maybe," said Partington, unhelpfully.

"Why were you there at all?"

"Same reason why I was in court yesterday," said Partington. "London still considers you a British national, irrespective of your American marriage. And particularly because of the high profile you've achieved. I was holding a watching brief, if you like. And to decide for myself whether you need help, despite what you told me."

Janet experienced a jolt of embarrassment at the reminder, after what the man had just done. She said: "Thank you," and decided it was inadequate.

"So do you?" pressed the man.

Yes, but not the sort you could give, Janet thought. She said: "I'm all right."

Partington remained looking at her, waiting, and Janet guessed he was expecting her to tell him where she'd been the previous evening. She stared back, saying nothing. The man said: "Please, no more escapades."

Janet realized that the man believed she had been attempting something else involving John Sheridan. She said: "Don't worry: I won't do anything silly," and thought at once it was a ridiculous statement.

"I spoke to Zarpas," Partington said.

"What about?"

"Your going back to England, during the hearings. He said that after you'd given your evidence you wouldn't be required until any higher court hearing: the gap could be several months."

"That was thoughful of you," said Janet.

"Think about it," urged the embassy official.

She had to, Janet acknowledged, after Partington had gone. But not yet. Not until . . . She didn't know until. Or when. Or how. But she certainly didn't want to make any decisions yet. She looked at her watch and then the telephone, impatient for Baxeter to make contact. They hadn't talked about when they would see each other again. Janet was shocked at her sudden doubt, trying to rationalize it. He didn't need anything more, for whatever he was writing. No further reason then, professionally. And he hadn't acknowledged her downstairs, when she'd left the press conference. She'd thought at the time that he was being discreet, disguising any association between them, but recognized there could be other reasons. What if he hadn't meant what he said? That it had all been a come-on, to achieve a one night stand. Wasn't that what Harriet and her Washington group did all the time, mouth the expected words and pleasantries to get each other into bed and have to strain the following morning to remember each other's names? It would actually be better that way: easier to lock it away in her mind—lock it away and never ever turn the opening key—if they didn't see each other again. It wasn't so difficult alone in her hotel room (and fully dressed and out of bed) to make the resolve. That was definitely what she had to do. She had . . . The telephone shrilled and Janet snatched it up on the second ring.

"How are you?" he asked.

"I hoped it would be you," said Janet. "All right, I guess."

"I'm downstairs."

"What took you so long to call?"

"Reasons," he said, enigmatically. "There's a lot of guys still hanging around. Photographers, too."

"What the hell for?"

"In the trade it's known as doorstepping," he said. "It literally means what it says. You're a running international story so they've got to stay on your doorstep to be ready if anything develops."

"I want to see you."

"I'll come up: be ready to let me in the moment I knock."

She was and immediately he thrust through the door Janet put her arms out to be held and he brought her close to him, soothing his hand through her hair, curious at her obvious need.

"I thought you said you were all right?"

"They attacked me at the conference," protested Janet. "Why did they do that? It hasn't happened before."

"Only one or two," Baxeter said. "The majority are still on your side."

"Why the change at all?"

"Stories like yours, stories that keep going over a long period of time, develop a kind of cycle," Baxeter tried to explain. "A person is built up into a hero—or in your case heroine—and for a long time everything goes their way. Then, at the slightest whiff of doubt, some change. Having created their pedestal, they start trying to knock it down and their hero with it."

"That's stupid!"

"That's the way it is." Baxeter smiled. "But it's nothing for you to worry about. Like I said, it's only one or two. It'll all be OK after the full hearing."

"Zarpas virtually told me it's my word against theirs. He can't find Haseeb, and the people at the cafe say they don't know anything about it," pointed out Janet.

"The evidence will be found," promised Baxeter.

"You were a long time calling," Janet said, again.

"I had something else to do after your conference."

Janet had become to feel warm, protected once more, in his presence, but it was washed chillingly away by the tone of his voice. "What?" she said.

"My visa's come through."

"When are you going?" asked Janet, heavily.

"Tomorrow."

"I don't want you to go."

"We've been through that," he reminded her. "We've been through it all."

"If they're watching downstairs I can't stay away from here again tonight."

"And I can't stay all night here, either."

They abandoned themselves to an afternoon of absolute love, unthinking, uncaring, unaware of anyone or anything but themselves and the cocoon of Janet's room. Four times the telephone rang without her answering and once they held each other, laughing silently, as they tried to pick out a muffled conversation outside the repeatedly knocked-upon door. Minutes after the knocking ceased a note was pushed beneath the door but neither was sufficiently interested to get out of bed to see what it said.

The encroaching blackness of evening, the time he had to leave her, darkened their mood. And they were exhausted anyway by the lovemaking which had left them damp and physically aching.

"Can I say something?" asked Baxeter.

"What sort of question is that to ask me?"

"It's been wonderful," said the man. "But for one thing."

"What?" she said, guessing that she knew.

"It was the same with both of us: the frenzy. It was like we were desperate; that it would never happen again."

"Don't: there's no point!"

"It will."

"I said 'don't.'"

"Last night you asked me not to say something else," he remembered. "That I couldn't tell you I loved you. Which I do."

"Come back!" said Janet. "Please come back."

"I will," he said. "I know I will."

"How can you *know*!"

"I just know."

Two hours earlier there would have been hilarity in the cautious way they checked the corridor before Baxeter left, but now there wasn't. He did it mechanically, ducking back once because of a passing guest, and was then gone without any farewell. Janet stood directly inside the door, head pressed against the wood, and it was several moments before she moved away. The room was completely dark but she didn't bother to switch on a light: didn't bother to do anything. She just climbed back inside the wrecked bed and begged for sleep to come, to blot out everything. Which surprisingly it did, very quickly. She was conscious of stirring twice during the night but it was not abrupt wakefulness and she drifted off again.

It was brightly light by the time she fully awoke. Beside the bed the message light on her telephone was blinking redly and she remembered the pushed-under-the-door message. She retrieved that first, smiling down at the request from Germany's *Der Spiegel* for an exclusive, in-depth interview. There were four telephone messages being held for her by the switchboard. All were from newspapers, all seeking the same. She decided to reply to none of them.

She escaped by going down the fire stairs to her hire car, which had not been identified, and drove into Nicosia for a breakfast which she needed, not having eaten at all the previous day. Afterwards she lingered over coffee, not knowing what to do next. Alone again, she acknowledged.

Without any positive intention Janet drove towards Troodos, retracing the route along which she had gone with Baxeter. It had been, she admitted to herself, that day when she'd realized—although refusing to realize it at the time—that she loved him. No, not love! It hadn't been that quick: that positive. That she was attracted to him and that there was a possible danger, she corrected.

Sensible people who recognized danger avoided it. So why hadn't she? Janet didn't have logical, easy answers to the logical, easy questions. Everything was mixed up, not confused but differing factors interlocking to make some sort of (although not entirely satisfactory) explanation. She had been alone and fed up with being alone. Frightened and in need of someone. Vulnerable. And Baxeter had been kind and understanding. Janet stopped the mental examination, curious. Why did she think of John as John and Baxeter as Baxeter? Subconsciously, she supposed, she was trying to separate them, accord one greater intimacy (and greater love?) than the other.

Was it possible to love two men at the same time? It was an uncertainty Janet had never before had to consider. There had been a passing affair at university before she'd met Hank, but once they'd established their relationship it had been enough for her. There'd been approaches, of course. In England, and later in Washington: approaches almost every time they had attended one of Harriet's parties. She and Hank had laughed about it, absolutely sure of each other, neither feeling threatened.

Was John threatened by what had occurred between herself and Baxeter? The automatic mental division, she recognized again. And there *was* a division. Groping for a way to rationalize it to herself, Janet thought that it was practically as if she were thinking of herself as two women, one in love with John Sheridan, the other in love with David Baxeter. Hardly rational: positively irrational. Nevertheless it was how it settled in her mind. She accepted it was still not a resolve: not even a proper explanation. Little more than a weak attempt at easing her conscience. Sufficient, though, for the moment. That's all she really wanted to do, go from moment to moment, hour to hour, unwilling to make plans for the next day or the day after that because there was nothing sure enough to make plans about. Wasn't that just another attempt to avoid the most difficult question of all, the one she had adamantly refused even to bring to mind? She did so now, making herself consider it. Whom would she choose, if it came to the choice?

Janet was sitting on the tavern verandah from which Baxeter had photographed her looking out over the thickly wooded valley. She shook her head, refusing to answer. Moment to moment, hour to hour, she thought.

She drove aimlessly and slowly back to Nicosia, regretting the trip because it had not been the same without Baxeter and she'd become further depressed by her failed attempts at personal honesty.

She was surprised by the amount of mail awaiting her back at the hotel. There were three more written requests for interviews from journalists and in addition two airmailed letters both postmarked from the United States. The first she opened was from the talk show agency in Atlanta, increasing from $5,000 to $10,000 their offer for a country-wide tour for after-dinner or lunch talks. The second was from a New York publishing house proposing a $100,000 advance for a book which they had tentatively entitled *The Love of Janet Stone*. If she cabled her acceptance, they would fly an executive to Cyprus to finalize the details and discuss whether she felt able to complete a manuscript herself or would like to work with a ghost writer.

Janet's vision blurred at the suggested title. She threw everything angrily into the wastebasket and stood at the window gazing out over the city and its sun-bleached, dun-colored outskirts, arms rigid by her side, both hands clenched into fists. Fuck it! she thought, not even sure at what or at whom she was swearing. Fuck it! fuck it! fuck it!

The following day Zarpas called: there was no necessity for her to attend the next remand hearing unless she wanted to, because it would be even more of a formality than the initial appearance. There was a follow-up call from the New York publisher which she refused to accept.

She let another twenty-four hours pass before calling England. Her mother, as always, answered the telephone and announced at once that she had very bad news.

"What?" demanded Janet.

"George is dead. I am so sorry, my darling."

"George?" Janet could not think what her mother was talking about.

"Your cat: Harriet telephoned last night."

It struck Janet as bizarre and she snickered. "Oh," was all she could manage.

"I knew you'd be upset," said her mother. Janet realized her instant reaction would have sounded like a sob.

She said: "Quite a lot has actually happened since I was last with George, Mother. And I've kind of been expecting it."

"Still a shock."

Could people think of animals dying as a shock? Janet guessed she would have known that—felt more than she was feeling at the moment at least—if she'd never met John Sheridan and never done what she was doing now but remained in the Rosslyn apartment with George. She said: "Thank Harriet for me, will you? Say I'll settle the vet's bills when I get back."

"She wanted to know that," the older woman said. "When you're getting back, that is."

Janet sighed, not responding. "Should I speak to Daddy?"

"He wants to speak to you."

He must have been standing next to her, because he came on the telephone at once. "There was a lot of publicity about that remand hearing."

"I didn't bother to read any of it," said Janet, who hadn't.

"No definite date for a full hearing?"

"Not yet."

"You could come home in between times, couldn't you?"

So Partington and her father were still in close contact. Wearily Janet said: "I haven't decided yet." And don't want to decide, she thought.

There was desultory talk about the cat, which Janet found utterly inconsequential, and an attempt to bring the conversation back to her return, which Janet ignored. He told her, as always, to call again soon and Janet, as always, promised that she would, gratefully replacing the telephone and deciding upon at least a week's interval. Poor George, she thought, trying but still failing to feel more. Had she changed so completely, about everything and everybody? She didn't want that to happen: not to become so hardened that nothing mattered or moved her any more. She'd known women like that—she supposed Harriet was close to being one—and thought it was ugly.

She started going back to the pool again and on the second morning realized from a faraway bustle that she was being photographed by cameramen using long focus lenses. Her immediate reaction was to feel indecent and she moved to cover herself in a wrap but then she stopped, lying back on the lounger. So what? she thought. What the hell did a picture of her in a swimsuit matter! If it made them think they were doing their job—made them think it was important—it was all right by her.

It was ten days after Baxeter's departure, in the late afternoon when she was returning sun-throbbing and still oiled from the pool, the room key slippery in her hands, that she heard the room telephone ringing. The key slipped further and she almost dropped it, running anxiously into the room when the door finally opened.

"I'm back," he announced.

Janet closed her eyes, swaying.

"Thank God!" she said. "Oh, thank God!"

"You OK?"

"Yes," she said, feeling strangely breathless. "Where are you?"

"My apartment. The pack still there?"

"Some."

"Could you get here?"

"Of course. An hour."

"Make it thirty minutes."

Janet showered and changed and didn't bother to dry her hair, so eager was she to get to him. She used the fire escape stairs again and was sure she reached the hire car unobserved. She was still cautious, driving not straight to Baxeter's home but into Nicosia, parking the car near the Paphos Gate where she had been cheated of Baxeter's money. She entered the walls through the Paphos Gate, twisting at once through the narrow alleys of the oldest part of the city, constantly looking behind in an effort to detect anyone following. She couldn't see anyone: certain not an obvious camera-hung photographer. She emerged from the citadel at Eleftheria Square, where there was a taxi rank, and rode away staring through the rear window. Again there was no indication of pursuit.

Baxeter snatched at her without speaking and Janet didn't need any words either. They made love hurriedly, hungrily, and it was much too quick, but the second time was slower and better.

"I've missed you so much," said Baxeter.

"I've missed you, too."

"You're going to hate me," he announced, abruptly.

She pulled away, staring curiously at him. "Hate you?"

"For cheating you: making love like this without telling you first."

"Telling me what?" Her stomach dipped.

Instead of replying Baxeter reached sideways for an envelope, taking out a photograph. John Sheridan looked older and grayer than in any previous prints, sagged against a wall. He was being made to hold up a copy of the *New York Times* to show the date, just a week earlier.

"Do you hate me?" said Baxeter, beside her.

"No," said Janet. "I don't hate you."

·25·

J anet became aware that she was upright, naked with her
legs splayed for support and sitting directly in front of
him: despite their having made love every way that love
could be made and the fact that there was no secret about either of
their bodies that the other had not explored and discovered (and
delighted in exploring and discovering) she snatched—immediately
regretting the haste—at the crumpled top sheet to pull it up over
herself.

"I thought that was how it might be," he said and Janet regretted
the haste even more.

"He's alive!" she said. It was not until now, this precise moment,
that Janet had opened another locked and sealed compartment, that
most secret part of her mind in which she'd believed John to be
dead. Now, abruptly, unexpectedly, incredibly, she had proof—that
he wasn't dead! That he definitely hadn't been dead, as of just one
week ago. And Janet knew—just knew—that if he weren't killed by
now, he wouldn't be. That somehow, somewhere, she would be
reunited with him. The awarenesses rushed in upon her, a tidal
wave, and Janet was swamped by it, tumbled head-over-heels upon a
bruising, scratching mental shore. For a long time she just sat, the

creased sheet like a toga held with increasing tightness before her, gazing at the stained bed upon which she had just made passionate and uninhibited love to one man while she thought about another. "Alive!" she said again, empty-voiced.

"There isn't any doubt," confirmed Baxeter.

"I want to say . . . I want to say . . ." stumbled Janet, looking down at herself and then across at his nakedness. "I want to say thank you but that's bloody ridiculous, isn't it?"

"Yes," Baxeter agreed. "Bloody ridiculous."

"You know what's even more ridiculous!" she said. "It makes me love you even more."

Baxeter shook his head, becoming aware of his own nakedness and pulling part of Janet's sheet over himself. "I don't know what to say to that."

"No." Janet made a sound halfway between a sad choke and an excited laugh. "I don't either."

"I'm glad," said the man. "However it affects you and me, I'm glad . . ." There was a gulped pause. "No, I don't mean that at all. I'm glad he's alive, certainly. I mind very much how it affects you and me. Very much."

"I don't know how it affects you and me," admitted Janet, with matching honesty.

"I want to tell you something," said Baxeter. "Even if it resolves the uncertainty about what happens between you and me, I want to tell you something . . ." There was another hesitation. ". . . I thought he was dead."

"I did, too," said Janet, quietly.

He stared at her, twisted-faced. "But then why!"

"I thought it, but I wouldn't accept it," said Janet. "And I was right, wasn't I?"

"So what's the answer?" asked Baxeter.

"Answer?"

"About you and me?"

"Darling!" implored Janet. "How can I tell you that? I secretly thought that a man I was engaged to marry was dead. You give me confirmation that he's not and within minutes want me to make decisions like that!" Would it be an easier decision weeks or months or years from now? she asked herself.

"I'm sorry," he said, at once. "It was something I shouldn't have asked."

"How did you get the photograph?" demanded Janet.

"Luck, really," Baxeter shrugged. "The simplest luck. In Beirut we have a stringer—someone who works for us on a freelance basis—naturally I've been plaguing him with demands about hostages ever since the kidnappings began in the Lebanon, years ago. He's a Shia. When I told him about the piece I had just done here on you, he said he knew where Sheridan was and I challenged him to prove it . . ." Baxeter jerked his head towards the photograph still clutched in Janet's hand. "And he did," the man finished, simply.

"What are you going to do with it?" asked Janet.

"Nothing," said Baxeter, more simply still. "Not yet, at least. I made you a promise about printing nothing that would endanger John's life. I meant it."

Janet swallowed and looked away, hoping he had not seen her reaction. "I think you're wonderful," she said. "Absolutely wonderful."

"No I'm not!" he said, almost too loudly.

"So what are *we* going to do with it?"

"*You*," Baxeter said. "I brought the proof back for you: you've got to decide what to do with it."

Janet shook her head. "I need you," she said. "You know I need you: *how* much I need you. You tell me what to do: I don't want to try anything else by myself. Do anything else by myself. I'm too tired; too beaten."

"Tell the Americans," advised Baxeter, simply again.

Janet blinked at him. "After everything that's happened, they won't even let me through the embassy door!"

"They will," disputed Baxeter. He indicated the photograph. "Look at it!" he instructed. "That's only a week old: eight days. No one has seen any proof whether or not John Sheridan is alive or dead for months. This *is* proof. They won't dismiss you this time: they can't."

"I'm not sure," said Janet, still doubtful.

"It's *got* to be the Americans," argued Baxeter, with irrefutable logic. "John Sheridan is an American citizen: an operative of the Central Intelligence Agency. Who else has the resources—the ability—to do anything but the American government?"

Janet gazed at her lover, not speaking for several moments. Then she said: "I want to say something but I don't want to hurt you, OK?"

"OK," he agreed.

"The Americans—the CIA—have had this sort of stuff

before . . ." Janet picked up and then dropped the photograph. "He's still somewhere there, in captivity. I want a guarantee that this time they'll do something!"

"Blackmail them, then," said Baxeter.

It seemed to be a day of simplistic answers, thought Janet. She said: "Blackmail them!"

"You're the media manipulator, right? Tell whoever you see at the embassy here . . . what's his name?"

"Hart," supplied Janet. "Al Hart."

"Tell Al Hart that unless you're sure—unless you *know*—that they're going to do something you're going to have copies of this photograph—copies that you'll make, before you hand this original over—made available to all the press hanging around the hotel. And that you'll give a press conference complaining that Washington are doing nothing, yet again."

"All right," acknowledged Janet, still doubtful. "But what *can* they do, just from a photograph?" She picked it up. "It doesn't show where he is: give any sort of clue how he could be got out, does it?"

"It'll prove you're someone to be believed: taken proper notice of," said Baxeter.

"So?"

"So they will *have* to do something when you provide an actual address."

"An address!" In her excitement Janet came forward and the sheet fell away but she didn't bother to pick it up again. "You have an address!"

"No," Baxeter said. "Just the promise of one. But the promise is from the same source and I think it's reliable."

"They're going to ask me about a source, aren't they?"

"Yes," said Baxeter.

"So what do I say?"

"Nothing," advised the man. "Refuse to say where anything comes from as a further guarantee of their cooperation."

"Aren't you taking a risk!" pressed Janet.

"What risk?" Baxeter smiled back. "If I were asked about it I would deny everything."

"Do you *really* think your man can find an address?"

"He found the photograph."

"You really are . . ." started Janet but Baxeter talked her down.

"No. Don't say it. There's no need."

"This hasn't made anything easier: more difficult, in fact."

"I know."

"I want to stay with you tonight," said Janet. "But I don't . . ."

". . . I know that, too," he stopped her again.

"I love you," she said.

"I love you, too."

·26·

Janet hesitated outside the American embassy at the corner of Therissos Street, caught by the irony that it was one of the feed roads on the way to Larnaca, where so much had happened. And where they'd all laughed at her: the bastards who'd tricked her and the bastards who were supposed to help her. They couldn't laugh any more; she had what she'd come to Cyprus to get and, like Baxeter said, they had to take her seriously from now on. And by Christ she was determined they were going to take her seriously!

The embassy was quite heavily fortified and Janet had to prove her identity at a guard house before being allowed to approach the main building. By the time she reached it, her arrival had been telephoned through. She asked for Al Hart. The receptionist asked if she had an appointment and Janet replied that she'd telephoned, to say she was coming. Which she had. Hart had refused to take her call.

There was a muffled conversation and the woman smiled, embarrassed. "I'm sorry," she said. "Mr. Hart isn't available."

Janet took the Beirut photograph from her handbag, holding it out and displaying it to the woman. "Tell Hart that I'm showing you a photograph of John Sheridan taken a week ago. And tell him to get his ass out here!"

Hart was in the vestibule in three minutes, face blazing, eyes bulged with anger. "What the hell's going on!" he demanded, at once.

"I want to talk," said Janet. "Politely and sensibly. I want to talk."

The man's effort at control was discernible. "Where's the photograph!" he demanded.

"Where's your office?" said Janet. It hadn't occurred to her to gloat and she was not really gloating now, but there was a satisfaction in being in control—in being the teller, not the told—after all the bullshit that had been dumped upon her.

Hart hesitated and then turned on his heel, leading her deeper into the embassy. The CIA section was at the rear and to reach it they had to pass through a ceiling-to-floor barred door like the sort Janet remembered from movies about prisons. There was a Marine on guard outside and Hart had to authorize Janet's entry in an official, signed log.

His office was a bare box of a place very similar to that of George Knox, the CIA man in Beirut: a standard design, thought Janet.

"The picture!" Hart demanded.

"I think we should set out some ground rules first," said Janet. "So OK, you don't like me. You think I'm a pain. I don't like you. I think you're a jerk. But I've got proof that John is still alive: proof you, none of you, could get. There's a possibility of my being able to get more. So we've got to work together, be together, whether you like it or not. So let's at least be civil, OK?"

Hart sat looking at her across his clean desk, a vein in his forehead throbbing in time to his annoyance. With difficulty he said: "I'm sorry. I didn't mean to be rude."

On the apology scale of ten Janet scored that at about two but decided that it was a concession. Without speaking she dug into her handbag again and offered the photograph across the desk.

Hart snatched it. For a long time he stared down and when he looked back to her all the dismissive aggression had gone. "Jesus!" he said. "Jesus H. Christ!"

"So?"

"I'm sorry," said Hart, sincerely this time. "I really am sorry."

"That wasn't what I meant," said Janet. "He's alive, isn't he? John's alive!" And so, she thought, was David Baxeter.

Hart was back over the photograph, moving it flatly against the light. He said: "It looks OK."

"What do you mean?"

"It's possible to fake photographs: superimpose things, like a newspaper with a date on it, over a picture taken earlier," said Hart.

Janet felt a plunge of despair. "But the picture itself!" she argued. "That picture hasn't been released, has it!"

"No," agreed Hart. "Like I said, it looks OK. It can be checked by experts: *will* be checked."

"It's genuine," Janet insisted, needing the assurance.

"I'm prepared to go with it right away," said Hart, smiling for the first time.

The expression was sincere, like the second apology, Janet decided. "You'll tell Washington?"

"Of course I'll tell Washington. Beirut, too," said Hart. He rubbed his hands together, as if he were warming them, and went on briskly: "OK, so where did you get it? Where do we go from here?"

"No." Janet shook her head.

Hart's smile faltered. "What do you mean, no!"

"It's my source. It stays that way."

Hart leaned across the desk, hands together now as if he were praying. "Ms. Stone," he said, controlled. "Don't you think you've been involved in enough screwups already?"

"Yes," concurred Janet at once. "Far too many screwups. And I'm not going to get involved in any more. Neither am I going to be shunted aside, as I've been shunted aside almost always since this thing began. I want guarantees and I want to remain the conduit, to ensure that they're being kept."

The vein in Hart's forehead began to dance again. "What sort of guarantees, Ms. Stone?"

Named courtesy every time now, Janet noticed. Instead of directly replying Janet said: "What if I could get a location to go with the photograph? Maybe even an address?"

Hart stared at her for a long time. Then he said: "You think you could get something like that?"

"Maybe," hedged Janet. "What if I could? If I could tell you a street where John Sheridan is being held? Will you—some American group or force or whatever—go in to get him out?"

Hart nodded, understanding the demand. He said: "I can't answer that, not right now."

"I don't expect you to answer it right now," said Janet. "What about after you've been in contact with Washington?"

"Maybe not then, either."

"I need to know," Janet said. "I told you I won't be shunted aside any more."

Hart looked down again at the photograph and said: "This isn't the only copy, is it, Ms. Stone?"

"No," said Janet. "I've quite a lot more."

"So it's an ultimatum?"

"A request," corrected Janet.

"You know it's John's life you're risking, if you release this?"

"I've had this conversation so many times I can recite it backwards," said Janet. "I'm not risking John's life. I'm trying to save his life by getting some fucking action!"

"Quite a lot about this conversation is familiar, isn't it?" said Hart, unmoved by the outburst. "You sure of your source, Ms. Stone?"

Janet indicated the picture: "It produced that, didn't it?"

"And promises an address," mused Hart. "I know what Willsher told you, in Washington. About all the professional efforts that we've made: the cooperation we've had from other countries, other agencies. To come up with nil. And now you've got a picture taken a week ago and expect more."

"Yes," said Janet.

"That's impressive!" said Hart. "The lone amateur showing all the professionals how to do it!"

"Does it matter, if it gets John out?"

"I don't know, Ms. Stone. I really don't know."

"I can't see any direction in this conversation," said Janet, uneasily.

"At the risk of further repetition," said the American. "You will be careful, won't you?"

"I've learned the hard way how to be," assured Janet. "That's why I'm trying to establish more ground rules."

"So I'll play to your game plan," accepted Hart.

No he wouldn't, Janet recognized at once. He was just stringing her along until he thought he had everything and then he'd dump her. She said: "How long before you'll get a playback from Washington?"

"Your rules," reminded Hart. "How long before you get something more?"

"I don't know," admitted Janet.

"Why don't I wait for you to make contact when you've got something?"

Already being pushed aside, judged Janet. Patronized, too. "No," she said. "Why don't you make contact when you hear from Washington?"

The American capitulated. "You're calling the shots."

Driving away from the embassy Janet tried to analyze the encounter. Good enough, she supposed: certainly the official door had been opened to her. But for their advantage, not hers. But then, objectively, what else could she expect? Their job—the CIA's job anyway—was collecting information, not imparting it. It was unrealistic for her to expect anything like complete admission, complete access, to whatever they might do. At very best all she could expect was to be allowed on the sidelines, where she wouldn't get in the way.

Janet and Baxeter had arranged to meet at the Tembelodendron and as she entered the restaurant Janet wished they had chosen somewhere else because it was where she and Baxeter had lunched the first day they met, and she was unhappy at it becoming a romantic shrine the way the Virginia inn had become *the* place for her and John. Why? she demanded of herself. Didn't Baxeter (when would she think of him in given name terms!) deserve some sort of special romantic place, as well? Janet became impatient with the constant internal argument. It was arrogant—conceited even—this perpetual effort to maintain a balancing act. And what a balancing act! She could think rationally and behave rationally and make all sorts of sensible, rational decisions—for Christ's sake she was an aloof academic, wasn't she!—but the bottom line came down to choice and she knew she couldn't choose: wasn't able to choose.

Baxeter rose to meet her. He held out his hand and she took it. He said: "Guess how much I missed you?" and she said: "I don't need to be told because I missed you that much, too."

"If I read this in a book or saw it in a movie, I wouldn't believe it!" he said. "You know what I feel when I don't know where you are: what you're doing? I feel lost: lost like one of those poor bastards will be in space one day when the survival cord linking them to their spacecraft snaps and they float away into the blackness."

Janet sat down and said: "Have you been drinking?"

"Yes," Baxeter admitted. "But it doesn't affect—doesn't minimize—what I've just said. That's how I feel."

"That's funny," said Janet. "No, not funny. Wrong word."

"What's the right word?"

"Yours," Janet said. "Lost. You wouldn't believe how long I've felt lost: been lost."

A waiter intruded into their impenetrably private world, and they ordered without thought or consideration, wanting only to get rid of the man. As the waiter left Baxeter said: "It wasn't meant to be like this."

"I don't understand," said Janet.

"No," agreed Baxeter, obtusely.

"You *have* been drinking!"

"I told you that already."

"But why!"

"Lost," he said. "Lost and lonely, like you."

"I don't want any wine," Janet announced, positively. "Nothing to drink."

"Is that how it would be?"

"I don't understand that, either."

"If we were married, would you nag me like this: decide when and when not I should drink?"

"Stop it!" said Janet, irritated.

"Just asking."

"You're ratfaced!" she accused. "Pissed out of your mind!"

The transformation was startling. Baxeter seemed to expand and grow in front of her very eyes, like a balloon being filled for flight. He straightened in his chair, adding to the impression, and jaggedly but no longer with any slur in his voice said: "Relaxing, just for a moment. Thinking. Sorry. So what happened?"

The question coincided with the arrival of their lamb and the waiter asked about drinks and looking directly at Janet, Baxeter said: "Nothing, thank you."

"Was that refusal difficult?" demanded Janet.

"Yes," said Baxeter. "Very."

"Why?"

"I asked what happened," reminded Baxeter, ignoring her question.

"Answer me first!"

"Tell me what happened!"

It was belligerence—persistence—but not drink-inspired, Janet decided. She remained off-balanced, inexplicably and uncomfortably feeling herself to be with a man whom she no longer knew. Which was disorienting. And nonsensical. She sloughed away the impression and tried to clear her mind by recounting in as much detail as possible the encounter with the Cyprus CIA officer-in-charge.

Throughout Baxeter listened, utterly intent, hardly bothering with the delivered meal. When she finished he said: "Hostile?"

"Just short of."

"So?"

"They'll take everything for nothing," said Janet.

"Getting John out won't be for nothing," halted Baxeter.

Janet dipped her head, accepting the correction. "Any promised cooperation will be minimal," she qualified. "They'll use me."

Baxeter did not react, stabbing at his food without eating it. "Yes," he said, detached.

"Hart said something odd," Janet announced.

"What?"

"He asked me if I trusted my source," Janet said. "Reminded me of the cooperation that the Americans had had from friendly countries, friendly agencies, and remarked how surprising it was that an amateur could do better. Told me to be careful."

She spoke looking fully at him and Baxeter looked directly back. He said: "I told you how it happened."

"I know word for word what you told me," said Janet. She stopped and then said: "You're not using me, are you? Not using me like all the rest?"

"Did any of the rest produce the evidence of John being alive?" came back Baxeter.

"That's not an answer to my question."

"You know the answer to your own question," said Baxeter, loudly. "I *am* using you. I am using you ultimately to get an exclusive story that no one else has a chance of getting . . ." Baxeter paused, raising his hands between them. "Which is quite different—quite separate and apart—from what else has happened between us. I'm not using you that way, certainly. My love—our love—is boxed: compartmented from anything else. Uninvolved."

Janet felt a glow at the assurance, somewhat convoluted though it was. "I wasn't really doubting you," she said.

"Then why did you question me!" persisted the man. "What else could I be than what I am!"

Janet wished the insistence were not quite so fervent. She said: "We're arguing: we're arguing about nothing."

Baxeter appeared to deflate, the balloon going down. Much more quietly he said: "Do you think Hart will stay with his promise to keep you in touch?"

"Definitely, at this stage," Janet said at once. "They want an address, don't they?" She allowed the time for him to speak and when he didn't she demanded: "So what are the chances of getting that address?"

There was an uncertain shoulder movement. "Maybe there isn't any possibility."

Janet realized, abruptly, that so completely had she begun to rely upon Baxeter that she'd never doubted he would come up with a location: the idea that he might not be able to shocked her in further disorientation. "But you said . . . ?"

"Just a promise," stopped Baxeter.

"Would it mean your going back to Beirut?"

"Yes."

"Oh shit!"

"How else could I get it?"

"I don't know . . . I hadn't thought." Everything was becoming frayed again: fragmented. It was like a smoke cloud, a mass with an apparent shape and form that was impossible to reach out and touch. Pushing herself on, Janet said: "So how do you know when to go back?"

"You want me to go back?"

"Yes. No."

"That doesn't make sense."

"It makes every sense."

"He said—the Shia—that he knew the man who took the picture: that from him he could learn the location of the house," said Baxeter. "All he had to do was to find him and ask."

"That sounds simple: a conversation of minutes."

"Yes," agreed the man. "That's how it sounds: I don't think it's quite as easy as that."

"*Will* you go back?"

There was a long silence between them. "Yes," he said. "I'll go back." There was another, shorter silence. Then Baxeter said: "Does that mean I've lost out?"

"It's too soon for a question like that!"

"Why?"

"Because it is," replied Janet, in childlike repartee.

"I want to know!" he persisted.

"No!" Janet said, desperately. "How could you have lost out, after what's happened!"

"So where does that leave John?"

Janet had not eaten her meal either. She pushed it aside, reaching across the table for his hand, kneading his fingers. "Stop it!" she demanded. "Stop trying to get inside my head! Can't you understand I've been thinking about—torn apart about—nothing else!"

"And I'm not helping?"

"No," Janet said. "You're not helping at all."

"How was it left at the embassy?" asked Baxeter, changing direction to defuse the tension.

"That Hart would call me, as soon as he heard something back from Washington."

"You'll never know, of course, whether he's telling he truth: whatever he says and however he says it."

"I accept that," Janet said. "Where does it say I've got to believe him?"

"You're becoming cynical: don't become cynical."

"You're becoming protective."

"That's what I want to be."

"Don't press: not at this time don't press."

"OK," he accepted. "Your speed; your decision."

"I don't need reminding."

The returning waiter asked if there were anything wrong with the meal and Baxeter apologized that they were not hungry and without any discussion between them they went back to his apartment. Where for the first time their lovemaking wasn't good. They coupled and came but there was a tension between them, a block. Janet waited for Baxeter to refer to it but he didn't so neither did she, telling herself she was imagining it.

"It's a multi-entry visa," announced Baxeter, beside her.

"So you could go back any time?"

"Yes."

"This Shia? Is he a member of one of the groups?"

"Connections, obviously."

"What if it's a trap: that they're setting you up to be snatched? There are journalists in captivity."

Baxeter considered the question. "They could have snatched me receiving the photograph: there wasn't any need to wait until I came back a second time."

"Don't go!" insisted Janet. "You've got a photograph and we've given it to the Americans and that's enough: let them take over from here."

"But that means John . . ." he started.

". . . I know what it means," broke in Janet, sharply.

She sensed rather than saw him shake his head. Baxeter said: "The Americans won't move—if they'll move at all—just on a picture. They've had pictures before."

Janet turned away from him, pushing her face into the pillow, not wanting him to see her cry. Trapped, she thought desperately: she always felt trapped. His hand was on her shoulders, gently massaging, his fingers soothing up into her hairline.

"It's all right," he said. "I'll be all right."

"No!" she said, muffled.

"Yes," he said, with determination.

Baxeter asked her to stay the night but Janet suggested there might be a call from the embassy, which was only part of the reason for her refusal: she still felt the barrier between them that she'd known when they made love and decided she needed to get away for it to disappear, as it had to disappear.

She regretted leaving as soon as she reached the hotel, sure she *was* imagining the barrier, but willed herself against telephoning to say she was coming back. She rang the following morning, intending to apologize, but there was no reply. She waited until mid-afternoon for him to call her and when he didn't she dialed his number again. There was still no reply. She started calling every half hour and then reduced it to the quarter hour and at six drove back to his flat. It was locked and the window shutters were closed and bolted.

Janet returned angrily to the hotel. He'd told her he was going, of course. But there should have been some talk between them before he left: some time together. Just taking off without any contact was . . . Janet's thoughts faltered, seeking the word. The only one she could think of was inconsiderate, which was ridiculous: he was going to Beirut for her, to help her locate a fiancé, so what could be more considerate, more selfless, than that? Whatever, he should still have said goodbye: it made it appear as if he didn't care and she knew that wasn't true.

Hart did not telephone but came personally to the hotel the following day and Janet felt embarrassed at his finding her predictably by the pool. The American seemed more subdued than usual, although there was no hostility: when she asked eagerly if there had been any developments he said they couldn't talk where they were and she agreed at once to accompany him to the embassy. It was a chauffeur driven car with darkened rear windows and a division between the driver and the rear-seat passengers but the CIA officer still refused to divulge anything until they reached the U.S. compound.

They went again to the rear of the building, through the barred gate, but into a larger pine-paneled and pine-furnished office. Janet came to an abrupt stop in the doorway, so that Hart almost collided into her. Robert Willsher rose first to greet her, immediately followed by George Knox, the other CIA man she'd met in Beirut. Both men were smiling, Knox more broadly than the Washington official.

"Good to see you again, Ms. Stone," said Willsher.

"Is it?" said Janet, cautiously.

"Why not come on in, so we can talk?" invited the man.

Janet continued on, going to the chair that Knox was holding out courteously for her. As she went to sit he winked at her. From the way the men arranged themselves at the table, all facing her, it was obvious that Willsher was the senior officer.

"Looks like we've got a chink of light here?" began Willsher.

"I hope so," said Janet.

Willsher nodded sideways, to the Cyprus-based agent, and said: "Al submitted a full report of your meeting. I've got to tell you it caused quite a flap at Langley."

"I'm glad there's some reaction at last."

Willsher appeared not to notice the sarcasm: if he had, he was unoffended by it. He said: "You must understand that what I am going to tell you is in the strictest confidence: if you had not kept so positively to the agreement we made in Washington, I wouldn't be telling you at all. There's been a policy decision taken, at the highest level. That photograph is absolutely genuine. If we can get a location for John it'll be the first time, in all the kidnappings, that we've something *positive* to act upon. And we're going to do just that. If we can get a location for John, we're authorized to go in and get him!"

For a moment the three men blurred before her and the room spun: hoping they would not notice, Janet actually gripped the edge of her chair, physically holding on. "Thank you," she managed. "Thank you so much."

"Which is why we must have access to your source," completed the man.

It was like being doused in cold, reviving water. "No," said Janet, as adamantly as Willsher had spoken.

"Ms. Stone," said Willsher, level-voiced. "This is foolish. We're planning an incursion into another country. OK, so it's a pretty screwed-up country but by international law it's still sovereign territory. If we do it there's going to be hell to pay. That's been allowed for: to stop being shoved around by any bunch of bums who think they can take a pop at us. Washington—the President—is prepared to take whatever flak is thrown afterwards, at any international forum. But we've got to get it right. If we lose too many men . . ." The man stopped, awkwardly. ". . . and I've got to say it, if we lose John, in the attempt, then it's all going to blow right up in our faces. You understand what I'm saying?"

"Yes," said Janet. "I understand what you're saying."

"We've got to plan, to get as much detail as we can. Rehearse, if possible, in some sort of mock-up: outside of Washington we've a training facility, at Fort Pearce. We can have a street re-creation ready there in twenty-four hours and we've got men standing by to build it. This has got to go as clean as the Israeli rescue did in Entebbe. So we must have access to your source."

"No," said Janet again. Willsher was right, of course: by telling her of the rescue operation being considered they'd met her demand for action—the reason she'd put forward before for refusing—so to go on refusing *was* foolish. But her possible access to the knowledge—through Baxeter—of where John might be was her only bargaining strength. So she wouldn't surrender it: wouldn't be cut out and discarded, yet again.

"Janet!" pleaded Knox, familiarly. "You've got to!"

"It won't work," improvised Janet. "I asked, after bringing the photograph here . . . after talking to Hart. They said no: that they won't cooperate directly with you. They'll only pass the information through me."

The three men stared at her, the skepticism obvious.

"'They'?" isolated Hart. "More than one person then?"

"Yes," floundered Janet.

"Why won't they trade direct?" pressed Hart.

"I wasn't told, not openly. There was some talk about not trusting you."

"You think it's a group with which we've worked before?" said Willsher.

Janet thought she was sweating and that it would be noticeable to them. "I don't know what to think," she avoided. "Like I said, I wasn't told directly: it's an inference."

"What nationality?" said Knox.

"They speak Arabic," Janet tried to sidestep.

"Syrian Arabic, Lebanese Arabic, what Arabic?" insisted the Beirut officer.

She was out of her depth, Janet decided: out of her depth and sinking, without any means of support. "Syrian Arabic," she said.

"What's the deal?" demanded Willsher. "What are they getting out of it?"

Thinking desperately Janet realized the Americans would probably have access to her account, through Zarpas. "Money," she said. "I've agreed to pay £20,000. But since being conned like I was before I've said I won't pay anything until *after* John's got out." She thought it had sounded all right: she wished she were able to tell more from the expression on their faces.

"And they've gone for that?" asked Hart, doubtfully.

"They gave me the photograph, didn't they?"

"How can you contact them?"

"I can't," said Janet, vaguely aware of firmer ground underfoot. "They've got to contact me."

"No planned dates then?"

"No planned dates."

"I don't like this," said Willsher. "I don't like this at all."

"I don't like it either," said Janet, aware they were the first honest words she had uttered for a long time. "This is the way they insist it has to be."

"You think you'll get a location?" said Knox.

"I've no way of knowing." Honest again, she thought, gratefully.

"So we just sit and wait?" said Willsher.

"And hope," Janet said.

"You think some sort of personal protection might be a good idea?" Hart suggested.

"No!" Janet said, too quickly, frightened of what surveillance might disclose—Baxeter. "I'm sure they won't come near me if they see any sort of official escort."

"Let's not take the risk of blowing it," Willsher said.

"You will tell us!" Knox said. "You won't try anything like before: try to do something yourself?"

"I brought the photograph here," reminded Janet. "If I had intended doing anything myself I would not have done that, would I? I recognize well enough that you're the only people with a chance of getting John out."

"Just don't forget it," Willsher cautioned. "This is big league stuff now: the biggest."

"Let's keep in daily contact," Hart suggested. "Just to keep the lines open."

"Of course," Janet agreed.

"And don't forget what I said before, will you, Ms. Stone?" Hart said. "Be very careful."

Despite the apparent assurance Janet expected them to attempt some sort of surveillance and over the following days she tried to detect it. She actually set her idea of traps, staying entire days in the hotel and around the pool, alert for obvious attention, and at other times going for long drives through the Greek parts of the island where there were tourist spots and lingering at them, intent for a familiar face following her. Not once did she detect anything. She maintained the daily contact and once accepted Willsher's invitation to dinner, which was an appalling mistake. The Washington officer resumed the embassy interrogation and Janet sweated and lied again, sure by the end of the evening that Willsher knew she was lying.

It was a fortnight before Baxeter returned. So resigned had Janet become to his absence that she did not expect the call to be from him when she lifted the receiver. As soon as she recognized his voice she erupted in a babble of questions and he had to shout her down to be able to speak himself.

"I've got something," he announced, simply.

Janet swallowed, unable to respond. Or think clearly—properly—how she should have thought. Her immediate impression was that the moment of decision was drawing inexorably nearer, like a noose tightening. She said: "I'll come to the flat."

She used the same avoidance technique as she'd tried before, driving openly to the communication complex and even more openly parking the car, then hurrying into the walled section of Nicosia to come out again by the rank on Eleftheria Square. Like before she drove away straining through the rear window: there was no indication of pursuit.

They thrust into each other's arms, neither speaking for a long time. Then Janet said: "I don't ever want you to go away again," and Baxeter said: "I won't."

They separated at last and Janet said: "You've got an address?"

Baxeter nodded and said: "It's in the Kantari district."

"Genuine?"

He shrugged: "Who knows, until someone goes there?"

"Someone is going there," disclosed Janet. She told him everything about the encounter at the American embassy and the assurances from Willsher and how—and why—she'd refused to disclose Baxeter's identity to the Americans. Throughout Baxeter sat nodding, not looking directly at her but slightly to one side, deep in concentration.

"And they agreed to it?" he demanded as soon as she finished. "You're still the conduit?"

"Yes."

Baxeter nodded in further contemplation and said: "And they must continue to do so."

Janet thought the tone of his voice was strange. "Why?"

Baxeter blinked out of his reverie. "The address could change," he said. "You must tell them that. Let them rehearse the Kantari rescue but make them understand they can't exclude you because John might be shifted at the last moment."

Janet stared curiously at him, aware of that sensation of a barrier arising between them again. She said: "And you would know, if there were a last minute change?"

"I have a promise," he said.

Abruptly Janet recalled Hart's remark that day at the U.S. embassy when she produced the photograph of John, in captivity. *The lone amateur showing all the professionals how to do it,* she remembered, the words echoing in her head. Very quietly she said: "David, what do you do? Really do?"

"You know what I do."

"Tell me," she insisted.

"I'm genuinely employed by a Vancouver magazine," he insisted.

"But that's not all, is it?"

Baxeter stared back at her for several moments. Then he said: "No, that's not all."

·27·

J anet felt naked—like she had been literally spreadeagled, naked, at that earlier revelation—although now
she was wearing clothes. And this time the exposure was
worse, far worse: not just clothes stripped off. Skin too. A moment of
flagellation. She sat scooped up in a leather-backed bucket chair,
her arms encompassing her legs, her head virtually against her knees
like a mollusk ready at a moment's notice to retreat into its shell,
never to come out again. She did not catch every word he said: every
sentence even. It wasn't necessary. The mentally chafing parts—the
lump-in-the-stomach uncertainties—were finally fitting into the jig-
saw: an incomplete outline was becoming a more tangible image.

"The Mossad!"

"Yes," said Baxeter, an unfettered admission.

"Why does Israeli intelligence want to become involved?"

"Policy, from on high," said Baxeter.

Almost a paraphrase of Willsher; Janet supposed there were a restricted number of ways an idea could be expessed without repetition
or cliche. She said: "I want to know! Everything!"

"What?"

"Your approach, that first day? Journalism? Or intelligence?"

"Both."

"No!" Janet said. "I don't believe you!"

"All right!" Baxeter said. "It was to see."

"See what?"

"If there were an advantage."

"Jesus!"

"This isn't easy for me."

"How the fuck do you think it is for me!"

"Do you have to swear?"

"Yes, I fucking well have to swear!"

"Don't!"

"Shit!" she snarled. "What about your getting involved in that demand for £1,000! That was a setup, wasn't it! Your people!"

"Yes," he admitted.

"Why!"

"To get closer to you."

"To make me feel dependent, you mean! To come to rely upon you?"

"Yes," he said, admitting more.

"You bastard! All of you. Bastards!"

"Have you any idea what I'm doing? What I'm disclosing! The rules I'm breaking?"

"I don't give a fuck about your rules!"

"I love you."

"Stop it!" Janet cupped her hands over her ears to close out what he was saying.

"I'm trying to get through to you," he said. "Make you understand. I was told to get close to you . . . OK, to see if you could be used. I wasn't told to fall in love with you. Which is why I am being honest now: telling you truthfully. I came near to doing it before . . . thought you'd guessed that day at the Tembelodendron . . ."

Janet still had her hands up to her head. She moved it, jerkily, from side to side in refusal. "I don't want to hear! Don't want your lies!"

"That isn't a lie," Baxeter insisted. "Listen to me, for Christ's sake!"

"He's not your God."

"Don't be facile."

"What do you expect me to be!"

"Sensible."

"Go fuck yourself!"

"Go ahead," Baxeter said. "Why don't you go ahead and mouth off every swear word there is and get it out of your system?"

Janet took her hands from her head. "I'm not sure that's what I need to get out of my system."

"Are you going to listen to me?"

Janet sat with her arms around her legs again, staring at him, wanting to feel hatred—something like it at least—but nothing would come.

Baxeter waited but when he saw she was not going to speak he said: "Journalism is the cover, like the passport. It enables me to travel all over the Middle East. My first meeting with you was exactly what I told you: exploratory. How did I know how it was going to work out!"

"What about John?" Janet demanded. "The photograph and the address? Did you really go to Beirut to get them?"

"Collect them," corrected Baxeter. "We've got a lot of sources there: a lot of operatives. We've got to have."

"But why?" she pressed. "Why get involved? Is there an advantage there, too?"

"It would be a humiliation to the terrorists, if America were able to get in and get out one of their people," said Baxeter. "And I hope there could be a personal advantage, too."

"I don't understand that last part."

"You're never going to be able to choose with John still in captivity, are you?" he said, simply.

Why couldn't she hate this man! Janet asked herself. Why couldn't she despise and detest him for using her like everyone else had used her! "No," she said, almost to herself.

"Forgive me?"

"I don't know."

"I haven't hurt you."

Janet supposed he hadn't, but it was difficult for her to work out. "I don't know that either," she said.

"I obviously couldn't tell you in the beginning," he said, trying to convince her. "And afterwards it was too late. Now it means there's a chance of rescuing John!"

It was convoluted but true, she recognized. "I suppose you're right," she conceded.

"So you forgive me?" he asked again.

"I said I don't know. I need to think: understand everything."

Would she ever understand everything!

"I want you to stay tonight."

Janet realized, despising herself, that she wanted very much to stay. "No," she said, as strongly as she could. She accepted—just—his explanation but she'd still been used and couldn't dismiss it as lightly as this, as if it hardly mattered.

"I guess it was too much to ask."

"Too much to expect."

"That too," he agreed.

"Was it true what you said, about the possibility of John being moved?"

"That's the way they operate, precisely to prevent rescue."

"Why me!" demanded Janet abruptly, as the query occurred to her. "Why bother to use me as a conduit? Israel and America are allies: you rely enormously on Washington. Why not deal direct, agency to agency?"

Baxeter nodded, acknowledging the question. "Ready for the cynicism?"

"Yes."

"Damage limitation," said Baxeter. "This way it remains entirely an American operation. They get the credit if it goes right, the criticism if it goes wrong. We're prepared to sacrifice one to avoid getting caught up in the other."

"How do you learn to think like that!"

"Years of practice," Baxeter said.

Janet shuddered, involuntarily. "It's creepy."

"Sure about not staying?"

No, she thought. "Positive," she said.

"You know everything you have to tell the Americans?"

Janet wished he had tried harder to persuade her. "Yes," she said.

Hart was at the hotel to collect her in the chauffeur-driven limousine within thirty minutes of Janet's call. They assembled again in the pine-paneled conference room and the three men huddled excitedly around the paper that Janet offered, with the Kantari address.

"Know it?" Willsher asked.

The Beirut agent nodded. "We've more than enough photographs and plans of the street for the mockup at Fort Pearce," he promised.

"What about checking it out ourselves on the ground: trying

to establish if it really is where John's being held?" came in Hart.

Knox made an uncertain movement with his hand. "We could try, I suppose. But what if we're spotted?"

They seemed to have forgotten her presence, thought Janet. She said: "Don't forget the possibility of his being moved."

Willsher looked back to her.

Janet repeated the warning that Baxeter had given, together with the assurance of her being able to learn any new location.

"Sure you'll be able to find out?" Willsher asked.

"Yes," Janet said. She was now, she thought: now that she knew what Baxeter really did. She supposed she should feel reassured and wondered why she didn't.

"We'll have to build that contingency in, of course, through every stage of the planning," Willsher said, to the other two men. "And blanket Kantari with every sort of listening device that's been invented, as a backup." The man turned back to Janet. "Looks as if you're going to remain an important part of the team," he smiled.

"It's good to be involved," said Janet. Should she feel a hypocrite? Only about her romantic involvement with Baxeter, she decided: everything else was being moved along the labyrinthine paths that Baxeter and these three men trod all the time. If it had not all been literally in such deadly earnest—so important—Janet could imagine laughing at the absurdity of it.

"Still keep in daily contact," Willsher told her. "There've been more thoughts from Washington, too."

"What?" she asked.

"We've decided to maximize the impact of getting John out," said Willsher, confidently. "I'm to ask you if you'd agree to reunion publicity?"

Janet swallowed, not able immediately to respond. What would that moment be, the ultimate hypocrisy or the ultimate, inevitable choice? "Aren't you planning ahead a little?" she said.

"That's exactly what we're doing." Willsher chose not to acknowledge her caution. "Everything that can be planned for is being planned for."

"Of course I agree," she said. Hypocrite, she thought: what right did she of all people have to criticize Baxeter or anyone else for lying and cheating and being labyrinthine?

"We're not going to fail," Willsher said confidently. "This isn't going to be another Iran hostage screwup. We're going to get John out and leave an awful lot of bloody noses behind, believe me!"

"I'd like to," said Janet. "I'd like to believe you very much indeed."

"Perfect!" said Baxeter enthusiastically, an hour later.

"Is it?" said Janet.

The Israeli became serious, matching her mood. "There always had to be a decision time, sooner or later."

"I know."

"So this is it."

"Not quite," she said.

·28·

It would have been fatuous for Janet not to think about the choice she had to make: it was constantly at the forefront of her mind. At best she could refuse to consider it, with any finality, which was how she went through the succeeding days: aware but uncommitted. If she could remain uncommitted, that is, spending every available moment with Baxeter and making love every night—and sometimes during the day—and feeling content only in his presence or when he was near. They drove to the mountains again and this time there was none of the aching nostalgia she'd experienced when she'd made the journey alone, and he took her to a production of Shakespeare's *Much Ado About Nothing* at a restored Roman amphitheater in the low seacliffs near Limassol: the backdrop was breathtaking, the performance magnificent and the irony of the title not lost on them. After the play they went to a restaurant near Lady's Mile. Baxeter said it was the one he'd had in mind after the photographic session in the mountains when he'd asked her to dinner.

"That was the first time I knew," he said. "Thought I knew, anyway."

"Me, too," said Janet.

Janet maintained daily contact with the CIA group at the American embassy and on the fifth day, at Willsher's invitation, went to the legation, intrigued by what she found. The room in which they had always met had been transformed into what she could only think of as a war room. There were three separate blackboards on their easels—two draped with maps with blown-up inserts of Kantari, the third covered with ground and aerial photographs—and an additional cork pinboard upon which photographs had been given map references. Neither Hart nor Knox were present, but during their meeting a hard-boned, crewcut man in unmarked jungle camouflage fatigues came into the room, consulted an index on the pinboard and withdrew. He paid no attention whatsoever to either of them and Willsher made no effort to introduce him.

"It looks positive," Willsher said. "We've had lots of image-intensified pictures—movie as well as still—blown up to their maximum enlargement of the area and particularly the street. Under analysis there seems to be a lot of activity. We've identified Amal militia groupings: weaponry, stuff like that. Also there is some indication of a radio installation. The British are giving us a tremendous amount of cooperation: we think we've isolated their wave band and we're backing up with our own satellite intercepts, as well."

"What about Fort Pearce?" asked Janet.

Before replying Willsher looked towards the door through which the soldier had just left the room. "Why I asked you to come today," he revealed. "They've finished the mockup exercises. They're here."

"Here!" echoed Janet, surprised. Nearer and nearer, she thought.

"We're on countdown, Ms. Stone. Which is where you come in. We want to hear from you that John's still there: that we haven't got to re-direct."

"Yes," Janet accepted, emptily.

"How long?"

"I don't know," answered Janet, honestly. It seemed absurd, but it was something she had not discussed with Baxeter.

"Could you give me some idea tomorrow?"

"I hope so," said Janet. "What's the plan?"

"That's classified," refused Willsher.

"I didn't mean the details of the incursion," elaborated Janet. "What about afterwards? If you find John where are you going to take him?"

"Here," said Willsher. "The British are making their air base at Akrotiri available. Already on its way towards the Lebanese coast is a major part of the Sixth Fleet, including the aircraft carrier. They won't enter territorial waters but there'll be blanket air support. John will be helicoptered here to undergo medical checks while we set up the press briefing."

The planning appeared to be absolute. "Where you want me to be present?" she said.

"Right alongside the man you love," smiled Willsher.

It felt like a physical blow, a punch low in the stomach. She managed a smile and said: "It should be quite a media event." Would Baxeter attend, as the journalist he was supposed to be?

"And show these fanatic bastards up to be the useless idiots they are," said Willsher, with sudden vehemence.

What else would it show up? "It could all be over in days?" she said, distantly.

"That's the scale we're working to," Willsher confirmed. "Over and finished in days." He smiled. "All we're waiting for is the word from you."

Once again Baxeter heard her out with the distracted attitude she found disconcerting, concentrating upon what she was saying but not upon Janet herself.

"Days?" he queried.

"That's what Willsher said: all they're waiting for is my confirmation."

"I'll need their definite date," said Baxeter.

"Why?" asked Janet.

"It's important."

"Why?" she repeated.

"Trust me."

"Will you have to go back to Beirut?"

"Maybe not this time."

"How long?"

Baxeter pulled down the corners of his mouth. "Maybe forty-eight hours."

Over and finished in days, she remembered. What, exactly, would be finished? Baxeter left early the following morning, but this time there was none of the earlier emptiness because her mind was in a turmoil of indecision. How could she dispassionately pick one against the other! The very word was a mockery: passion had every thing to do with it. Uncomfortably, her mind held by it, Janet decided that if she were making a comparison, which was what she had to do, then Baxeter was a better lover than John. But that was only a part of it. She knew she loved Baxeter because she'd been with him: practically lived with him. It seemed so long ago with John: almost difficult to remember. So she had to have time with him again. Not for herself, she thought quickly. To be fair to John, that's all. Was she capable of that sort of hypocrisy, going through the charade of the media reunion and all the time conducting some sort of mental trial? She didn't think she was: *couldn't* think, properly, of anything.

Baxeter wasn't away the forty-eight hours he'd estimated. He called on the evening of the second night and met her in a restaurant in Ayios Dhometios they had not used before. He was there before her, and as Janet sat down the man said: "John is still there."

Janet tried to think of something appropriate to say but couldn't. "Good," she mumbled.

Baxeter leaned intensely across the table towards her. He said: "It's vital you understand the importance of learning the precise day the Americans are going to go in!"

"Why?"

"I've been to Tel Aviv," disclosed Baxeter.

Janet frowned over the table, trying to understand the significance. "So?"

"From what Willsher told you is it obvious the Americans are planning a frontal assault, backed up by air support and whatever else from their fleet?" said the Israeli.

"I guess so," agreed Janet. "I hadn't thought about it to that extent: Willsher said they were prepared."

"It won't work," declared Baxeter, flatly. "It can't work."

"Can't work!" The anxiety flared through her.

"Even if they achieve complete surprise there'll still be some resistance," predicted Baxeter. "Our military people in Tel Aviv estimate that moving at the maximum possible speed—night is the logical attack time, which is going to cause further hindrance—it will take an hour from the moment they hit the beach to get to where John is, in Kantari . . ." Baxeter stopped, hesitating at what he had to say. "By which time John will have been moved," he said. Bluntly he added: "Or killed!"

"No!" moaned Janet, softly. "It can't go on like this! It just can't. It's got to stop!"

"That's why my knowing the actual day is important."

"Why?"

"We've decided to use the American landing as a diversionary tactic," said Baxeter. "We're going to send a commando team in ahead of them. We'll get John out."

·29·

Janet sensed the atmosphere the moment she entered the map-strewn room, the sort of solemnity that remains after a disagreement or a dispute, except no one looked as if they had been arguing. Willsher was in his preferred chair, at the center of the table, and the soldier who had interrupted them on the previous occasion was by the furthest blackboard, where the maps had been coordinated with photographs. He still wore his unmarked fatigues. Knox was at the window. He gave Janet the briefest welcoming smile and then looked back at the fourth man in the room, who was sitting alongside Willsher. He was elderly, with a hedge of straggling white hair around a bald dome. He wore half-rim spectacles low on his nose and a crumpled, neglected sports jacket over an equally crumpled and neglected checked sports shirt, without a tie.

The man stopped talking when Janet entered the room, looking expectantly towards her. Willsher stood, holding out his hand in invitation towards a chair opposite them and said: "I'm glad you're here, Ms. Stone: seems there is something we haven't allowed for." The CIA official half-turned to the man beside him. "Professor Robards," he said in introduction.

"What hasn't been allowed for?" asked Janet, not sitting.

"John's mental condition," announced Willsher.

"His what!"

"My specialty is the psychological affect of long incarceration," explained Robards. "I've worked with some of the men imprisoned by the North Vietnamese during the war. And latterly tried to expand it to include the traumas likely to be suffered by kidnap victims such as John: people who've spent time possibly in solitary confinement, possibly experiencing some degree of torture and certainly with captors they identify as enemies, not knowing if at any moment they are going to be killed."

Robards had an unemotional, scholarly delivery, talking as if to a class of students. Janet considered it altogether too sterile and distant. She said: "You think John will be traumatized?"

"It's inevitable," said the psychologist, flatly. "The only uncertainty is to what degree. He could have the mental strength to recover in a day: alternately it could take months and maybe even require psychiatric treatment."

Janet looked at Willsher, remembering. "You told me he could stand it!" she said.

"I thought he would be able to," said the man, apologetically. "I didn't know."

"No one knows," reiterated Robards. "I've encountered men built like trees whom I would have bet could withstand any sort of stress, but who have collapsed almost at once and taken years to recover. And wimpy little guys weighing ninety pounds who've taken everything and walked away without a mental mark."

"Is that why you're here, to treat him?" Janet asked.

"Langley thought it might be a precaution," said Willsher, answering for the man.

"And I'm glad you're here, too," Robards said to her.

"Why?"

"Like I told you, John's spent quite a lot of time not knowing what to expect from one minute to the next. He's going to be rescued by a commando group making a sudden assault: there'll be a great deal of noise: explosions, shooting, stuff like that . . ."

". . . A great deal," endorsed the unnamed officer. "A primary tactic is to disorient with as much noise as possible."

What was she doing! Janet demanded of herself. What was she doing sitting here, listening to these people talk about rescuing John when she already knew they weren't going to rescue John at all! Tell them, she thought at once. Tell them and . . . and what? How could she tell them without exposing herself and Baxeter? And John: John too. John wouldn't survive the frontal assault, Baxeter had told her. And Baxeter was an Israeli. Hadn't the Israelis done in Entebbe exactly what was being planned here: hadn't the Ugandan assault been used by Willsher himself as a role model? Weren't they experts, the people who knew best? The American attempt to rescue the Iran hostages had been a disaster. She had to leave it to the experts. Janet felt constrained, straitjacketed by the conflicting demands: and she felt something else, a rumbling churn of nausea deep in her stomach.

". . . John won't know what's happening," the psychologist was saying. "It won't initially occur to him that it's a rescue. He'll think it's what he's been threatened with, ever since he was seized. It will be the moment of maximum pressure, maximum terror. And then there'll be the pendulum swing, from terror to relief when he realizes it's the Americans coming in: that's the likeliest snapping point, that swing from one extreme to the other . . ."

Stop! thought Janet: stop! stop! stop! She said: "Why is my being here important?"

"Because yours is the face he'll recognize," said Robards. "People held like John seize upon images that mean the most to them: that's how they cling to reality. How John will have clung, thinking of the person closest to him in the world."

Janet closed her eyes, swallowing against the sickness bubbling up through her. Why, of anything she could have asked, had she posed a question to get an answer like that? She was only vaguely aware of Robards's voice, talking on.

"I'm sorry to have been so blunt," apologized the man, misconstruing her emotion. "It's important you know how difficult it might be."

Janet opened her eyes, forcing the smile. "Thank you for setting it out as you have."

"I'm sure it's not going to be like that!" tried Knox, from near the window. "I'm sure it's all going to work out great!"

"It won't fail from lack of preparation," came in the commando officer, joining in the encouragement. "We're as ready as we're ever likely to be."

"Which brings us back to you, Ms. Stone," said Willsher.

Janet stirred, gratefully. She had to get out, she thought. The constricted feeling had gone beyond a mental impression. She felt the room closing in upon her, walls and ceiling pressing around her, squeezing her breathless. She said: "It's the same location. John hasn't been moved."

"Son of a bitch!" said the soldier, driving a fist into the palm of his other hand in satisfied excitement. "Just what I wanted to hear."

"We can go then," said Willsher. It was not really a question, but the soldier responded.

"Two ackemma tomorrow," he said.

She had it, Janet accepted. She had the precise information required by one man she loved to free the other man she loved. Jesus! she thought, despairingly.

Knox offered to accompany her back to the hotel but Janet said she wanted to be alone and the CIA officer withdrew at once, imagining her need for solitude to be caused by the nearness of the operation, with no way of knowing the proper reason. Or the seed of an idea germinating in her mind.

She had the limousine drop her by the old city, and wended her way completely across the Greek-held section to emerge by the Famagusta Gate. Baxeter was waiting as he'd promised he would be, parked in Themis Street. The Volkswagen was dirty, as it had been the first time she'd ridden in it: why did such inconsequential things register?

He drove off as soon as she got in. "You were much longer than I expected," he said.

Janet didn't bother with an explanation. The determination that had started to grow on her way from the embassy was hardening within her. She said: "Are you to be part of the commando assault?"

Baxeter glanced quickly across at her and then back at the road. "Yes," he said. "I'm trained."

"I want to come," announced Janet.

"What!" Baxeter had taken Kennedy Avenue, driving without any particular intention towards Famagusta. He jerked the car hurriedly into the side of the road, cranking on the handbrake.

"I want to come," repeated Janet.

"That's absurd! Utterly absurd! Laughable!"

"Not to me," she said. "Nothing seems laughable to me: absurd a lot of the time but never laughable."

"Why!"

"I've just had a long lecture about John's needs," said Janet. "It was very convincing. I think it's about time I started doing the right thing and considered John's needs, don't you? John's needs rather than my needs or your needs."

"I promise you he will be gotten out," said Baxeter.

"I know the time," said Janet. "The precise hour and the precise day. Unless you agree to my coming I don't intend to tell you."

"Darling, this *is* ridiculous. How can you expect us to take you? You're an . . ."

". . . Amateur," finished Janet, for him. "I won't get in the way. I'll do exactly what I am told, when I am told. I must be there, when John is freed. He's got to see my face."

"No."

"I mean what I say."

"It's not my decision."

"Then I'll rely on the Americans," said Janet. She stopped, breathing in courage for the final, determined ultimatum. "And I'll tell them what you intended to do: how you intended to use their assault as a diversion. I know what that will mean: for me personally. What they'll learn. I don't care, if it'll help what they're trying to do. They might need to alter their planning. It's got to work: that's all that matters. That John is freed."

·30·

I t was a fishing boat again: in the darkness it seemed to have the same mid-section construction and be about the same size. Janet waited, expectantly, for the revulsion, but nothing came. This boat was cleaner, although there was still the stink of fish. The muttered challenge came as soon as Baxeter hauled her inboard from the rowboat which had ferried them from the bay near Cape Pyla. Janet guessed the mutter to be Hebrew, a language she did not understand. Baxeter's retort was brief but sharp, in the tone of a superior to subordinates, and the challenge stopped abruptly.

"There's shelter in the wheelhouse," suggested Baxeter.

"No!" Janet said at once, remembering the last time. Baxeter had retreated from her, in attitude and mind: he had agreed that she should come as soon as she threatened going to the Americans, but he clearly begrudged the concession.

"It won't be long: a mile or two," he said.

"What then?"

"Transfer to a proper patrol boat."

Until now Janet had not considered how they were going to reach the Lebanese mainland: it was going to be a great deal different than before. Trying to rebuild bridges between them, she said: "Now that I've explained what Robards told me, don't you understand?"

"No," rejected Baxeter. He was actually standing away from her, his gaze towards the open sea where he expected the Israeli patrol boats to be laying off.

Was it his reluctance to accept her presence? wondered Janet. Or was this a side of Baxeter she had not experienced before, the man's ability to compartment himself, concentrating upon something or someone absolutely essential at that particular and absolute moment and able to relegate everything or everyone else of subsidiary importance? "It's necessary that I come," she insisted.

"You made that clear."

There was a call, a single word in Hebrew, from the wheelhouse and Baxeter slightly changed the direction in which he was looking. Janet followed his gaze, hearing the patrol boat before she actually detected it: a throaty, heavy, bubbled sound of very powerful engines throttled back to minimal tick-over, practically a protest at the waste of such power.

The seamanship was superb. Without any obvious signals the captain of the fishing boat brought his vessel softly against the side of the matchingly maneuvered patrol boat and the two sides kissed the hanging fenders with the merest jolt.

"Step across: follow me," ordered Baxeter.

Janet did as she was told without any stumble or uncertainty and was glad, anxious not to indicate this early that she might become an encumbrance. Despite the darkness she was immediately noticed. There was an eruption of babbled Hebrew against which Baxeter argued, and then started to shout: unseen, black-garbed figures whose faces and heads also seemed blackened shouted back, milling in front of them and gesticulating wildly. Some of the shouts were to the fishing boat that was easing away, and it at once reversed its engines. Janet guessed the instruction had been to return to take her off. The argument became a violent, yelling row, with Baxeter standing in front of her in the manner of a protector. Gradually Janet recognized a sameness in the gestures, and as she did Baxeter said to her over his shoulder: "They are insisting I talk to Tel Aviv."

He reached protectively behind him and seized her arm to guide her towards the darker superstructure.

Once she entered the radio shack Janet understood where she was—on a very special custom-built vessel created for a very special function. Everyone wore black, one-piece boiler suits—even the zips were black—without any insignia of rank, fitted with push-back hoods that could be pulled up entirely to cover the head. There was no white light, just red, but despite the dullness Janet could make out that all the internal fittings were black, not a single item risking the reflection of any sort of light and that beyond, on the open deck, all the metal was blackened too, covered by some plastic or bitumen coating.

A fair-haired man insisted upon using the radio first, yelling into the mouthpiece as loudly as he had upon the deck, and then Baxeter snatched it away from him but spoke in more controlled tones than the other man, forceful reason against inconsiderate anger. From the transmitter came a flurry of questions and although she could not understand the language Janet was able to discern three different voices and guessed the concern would be as great in Israel as it appeared aboard this bizarre boat. First Baxeter responded, then the fair-haired man, then Baxeter again: the transmission ended with the fair-haired commando throwing down a pencil in disgust and stumping past her. Janet was near the doorway and he actually attempted to collide with her but at the last minute she went further sideways into the shack and he missed. Janet, who was pleased, hoped Baxeter had seen.

"You won?" guessed Janet.

"You can come," agreed Baxeter. "I have to face an internal inquiry when it's all over."

"I'm sorry."

"I hope I'm not."

The engines' heavy bubble became within moments the roar of throttles being opened as the patrol boat unexpectedly lifted on its stern and hurtled forwards, smashing through the water. There was no warning of the acceleration and both she and Baxeter stumbled backwards: he managed to grab a support rail and then snatched out for her, stopping her falling.

"An expression of displeasure," said Baxeter. "You're very much resented."

"I'm an expert at resentment," said Janet. She had to shout to make herself heard over the engine scream.

Baxeter did not try to talk. He pulled her from the radio room out on to the deck and then through a small housing covering some steps. He went down ahead of her, calling out in advance what she guessed to be some sort of warning of their approach. There were about eight men below, in the mess area: it smelled of stale cigarette smoke and bodies too close together for too long. The men regarded them sullenly, without any greeting: the vehement radio protestor was not one of them.

Baxeter went through the mess to a bunk area further back, groped in a locker and handed her a pair of the black coveralls that were clearly the regulation dress. He said: "I think they're the smallest."

Janet stood looking uncertainly down at the suit. It felt like a rubberized material, tight at the wrists and ankles, and lined with a silk-like material: closer she saw that the hood was wired, with earpieces inside, so that the wearer could be linked up to a communications system.

"How do I wear it?" she asked Baxeter. "Over my own clothes?" She had on her much-worn jeans, shirt, and sneakers.

"You can try but you'll be damned hot," said the Israeli. "If you take them off don't expect the courtesy of their turning their backs; it'll be part of making you feel unwelcome."

Janet stripped to her pants and bra, not brazenly but not embarrassed either, her back defiantly to them: the overalls were big but wearable. Baxeter changed too, facing her with seeming indifference to her taking off her clothes. Baxeter indicated a seat at the far end of the table around which the other men sat and said: "It'll be better if you get off your feet: you can very easily become exhausted constantly bracing yourself against the pitch and roll of this thing."

She said: "How long?"

"Not more than an hour," assured Baxeter. "This is the fastest incursion boat we've got."

"What about the American fleet?" asked Janet. "Won't they be between us?"

"They're further north, nearer the Turkish coast."

"What about their radar?"

The Israeli smiled at her naivete. "There are more baffling and confusing devices aboard than most other countries, including those in the West, know we have invented."

Janet looked along the table. "Isn't this division a bit unnecessary?"

"Not to men like these," said Baxeter. "They work in groups, teams that take months to train together. They think like each other, react like each other, know each other. That way they stay alive. An intrusion, like you, throws the synchronization out. Because you're here they think they might get killed."

"I didn't understand," said Janet, deflated.

"That's why they're not accepting you: won't accept you."

"What about when we get ashore?"

"You're my responsibility," said Baxeter.

"Your burden?" suggested Janet, trying for a more accurate word.

"You speak Hebrew?"

"No," she said.

He smiled, briefly. "That was the word Tel Aviv used to describe you."

There was the soft noise of muffled descent on the rubberized companionway and the fair-haired man came into view, carrying a snakes' nest of radio links. He handed them out individually to the waiting men and then stayed by them, staring down at Baxeter and Janet. There was a curt question to which Baxeter replied with equal curtness: two of the seated men sniggered and Janet guessed Baxeter had scored with his retort because the man flushed, slightly, and tossed one of the connectors towards him. Baxeter caught it easily.

"There's no purpose in your having a headset," said Baxeter. "It's minimal communication anyway, it's in Hebrew and it's coded. Just understand one thing. Don't ever lose me. Don't get separated, and don't fall back into one of the other groups: they'll either intentionally abandon you—or kill you."

"You're joking!"

"That's their training, to kill or be killed," insisted Baxeter. "You're as near to being an enemy as makes no difference."

Janet tried to subdue her shudder but couldn't: Baxeter was connecting his radio links, intent on the hood of his uniform, and Janet did not think he'd seen her reaction. In case he had, she said: "It frightens me, this matter-of-factness."

"It's meant to."

There was a perceptible reduction in engine power. Baxeter called out to the other end of the table and one of the men replied, in agreement. Baxeter said: "We're getting close: they'll be putting out a lot of deceptive electronics now and transferring to a much quieter engine. We'll do the last mile by rubber dinghy."

There was a curt, tin-voiced order over the tannoy and the men began to assemble, picking up weapons and multi-pocketed rucksacks. There were eight of them, and Janet watched fascinated as they formed up in two lines of four, one man facing another, each reaching out and touching the one opposite, checking off equipment and packs, each ensuring that the other had overlooked nothing. Synchronized teams, she remembered. Baxeter had to prepare himself alone and Janet wished she could have helped him: closer she saw all the buckles and fastenings were rubber that would make no noise under movement.

By the time they reached the deck the dinghies had been dropped overboard, six of them, trailed by short lines along the sides of the now barely moving patrol vessel. Janet made out eight men additional to those in the mess from which they'd just come. Again the entry was perfectly coordinated. Groups of four dropped without any apparent instruction in perfect order into their boats—eight commandoes to each boat—and towed off the one behind them, empty, to make room for the next entry. Janet and Baxeter were allocated the last boat: everyone else was inboard and she felt them watching for her to stumble and make a fool of herself. She hit the slatted bottom unsteadily but retained her balance and managed to sit without any need for help. She would have liked to see their disappointment, but it was too dark.

The dinghy churned away from its mother ship and Janet looked curiously to its stern, where a single coxswain hunched at the tiller. There was the foam of a wake but hardly any noise at all. She decided the engine had to be electric, so quiet was it: a line of propellers dropped straight into the water from a straight-bar assembly, and Janet was reminded of the food blender in the kitchen of her Rosslyn apartment.

She felt a demanding tug and leaned towards Baxeter. His mouth directly against her ear, he said: "When we're ashore don't try to talk: whatever the circumstances, don't say anything to make a sound that will carry. If you want to communicate with me do what I've just done, so that we can get as close together as this. Understand?"

Janet nodded, without trying to reply even here. From the wind on her face she could tell it was cold, but she was perfectly warm otherwise inside her special suit. Her mouth was unnaturally dry and she would have liked a drink. She hadn't used a toilet—hadn't thought of it—before she'd left the patrol boat, and hoped there would not be the need. Ahead she could make out the lighter glow of land and habitation although they did not seem to be coming as

close to the city itself as she had on the fishing boat. She turned to
Baxeter to ask before remembering the injunction against unnecessary noise. She turned back, to look ahead, saying nothing.

Directly in front of her in the dinghy the commandoes were putting on night goggles: they made their faces look frog-like. Beside her
Baxeter did the same. Baxeter handed her a set, which she fitted on
awkwardly.

They were close enough now to hear the surf against the shore
over the hardly audible pop of their engine. Beirut was definitely
away to their left but so dark was it, even with the benefit of the night
vision equipment, Janet found it impossible to judge how far.

Baxeter tugged at her again, indicating that she would soon have
to go over the side to wade the last few yards through the water. The
men began to leave the dinghy, once more in perfect unison, first
port, then starboard, then port again, with scarcely a disturbance of
the craft to show their departure. Baxeter prodded her and Janet
edged doubtfully over the side, apprehensive of dropping into water
she couldn't see, not knowing what she would encounter underfoot.
There was another shove, harder this time, which actually propelled
her over the edge. She tensed for the shock of coldness but there
wasn't any because the suit was completely waterproof: nothing
brushed against her in the waist-high water and hard-packed sand
was even underfoot.

She stood there, knowing a surge of uncertainty, and then felt
Baxeter's hand upon her arm, guiding her towards the shore. She
tried to wade like him, with slow, long strides, so that there was no
sound from the water.

When they reached it the beach was deserted. Baxeter urged her
forward more quickly. Janet stumbled once because the beach had
patches of shingle and rock outcrops. Impatiently, Baxeter got directly ahead and felt backwards with his hands, showing her where it
was safe to walk. Janet was conscious of ascending a rising slope and
as it became lighter she realized they had climbed an incline to a
shore-road. Ahead was the uneven outline of vehicles, three or four
quite low, jeep-like, then a higher-sided lorry and more jeeps. It was
a considerable convoy and Janet wondered how they had managed
to get a fleet that size undetected across the border and up through
Southern Lebanon.

Baxeter led her to the last jeep and they sat in it alone, apart from
the driver. Baxeter was leaning forward but not too close to the
driver, his head automatically bent as he whispered into the throat

mike that formed part of his communications set. They moved off at staged intervals and Janet very quickly lost sight of the leading vehicles.

They traveled only briefly, not more than fifteen minutes, before pulling into a walled yard in what had to be the southernmost suburb of the city. As their jeep, the last, went through the gate, shadowy figures closed it immediately behind them. Janet squinted around the parking area, sure there were not as many vehicles now as there had been when they set out.

Groups of men were assembled in absolute silence and in marked separate units. She could make out heavier equipment she guessed had been hauled ashore in the supply dinghies: there were two long-barreled guns she thought must be rocket launchers and quite near a man was harnessed into a cumbersome tank from which a nozzle led. A flamethrower, she supposed.

They exited on foot at timed intervals, with her and Baxeter bringing up the rear. There were city sounds now: music strained through walls and windows, the occasional headlight glare of a car, people huddled in cafes they were careful to skirt, always getting past by going around and keeping the block of the building between them. At first Janet had been able to make out quite a few of the commandoes, but it became increasingly difficult and then Baxeter pulled her away from the direction they had been following up a very narrow, darkened alley, little more than a footpath between two buildings.

Janet followed dutifully, conscious once more of a slope underfoot and bending forward to climb it. Once again the devastation was all around, as it had been when she'd fled her attackers: Janet supposed they would have not have been able to move around the city with such comparative ease unless the lighting had been practically non-existent. The chief danger of attention came from foraging dogs which barked and snarled and sniffed after them: twice windows above opened and there were Arabic shouts for the animals to be quiet. Each time Baxeter was ahead of any movement, moving her quickly into the shadows of a doorway.

She and Baxeter had been moving apparently alone for longer than Janet had expected and she wished she knew Beirut well enough to know when they actually got into the Kantari district. She should have asked to look at the maps or the photographs in Willsher's room in Cyprus: the Americans had relaxed sufficiently in her presence and she was sure they would have allowed it. She longed to stop Baxeter, to ask him, but recognized that the question did not constitute the sort of emergency he'd stipulated.

They came to an intersection with a wider, better-lit thoroughfare and once more Baxeter pulled her into the concealment of a doorway while he edged forward to reconnoiter their crossing. It gave Janet the opportunity to look around, particularly behind her. She did so, frowning. She made out the glint of the sea and the brighter harbor area (was that the area through which she'd fled, in gut-tightening fear of being caught?) and even the faraway bright normality of East Beirut. Was Kantari on a hill? She had imagined it to be further down, in the flatter part of the city.

Baxeter was back beside her, sign-languaging an occupied cafe to the left on the main road, where it sloped back down towards the waterfront, and gesturing for her to move at once and hurriedly when he gave the signal. Janet nodded her understanding, pushing away from her concealment and going head bent, looking neither left nor right, across the road. The illumination was still comparatively low and the highway deserted but Janet walked with the feeling of scurrying beneath an inquiring spotlight, tensed for a shout of challenge. Nothing came. She was panting, more through apprehension than effort, when she reached the other side, finding her own concealing doorway. She looked back, trying to locate Baxeter but couldn't. She checked her watch. One-thirty: thirty minutes to go before the American assault. Why had they split from the rest of the group?

Janet did not see Baxeter start out. He was suddenly in the street, moving low and very fast. Janet actually held her breath, waiting for the challenge that had not come when she crossed, but once again there was nothing. She gestured as he pushed into the alley and he halted, close against her in the doorway.

Seizing the opportunity Janet gestured him even nearer. He eased the hood away from the side of his face and she heard a staccato spurt of Hebrew from the headset. She hissed: "Why have we separated from the others!"

"Safer," he whispered back, closing off the exchange by pulling the hood back into place.

Baxeter led off again, going to the end of the alley and then breaking to their right, running parallel with the road they had just crossed. From the camber Janet knew they were still climbing.

They made a detour around another coffeehouse from which there was thin music and the mumble of conversation and once had to pull, unmoving, into a rubble-strewn courtyard to evade a sudden gaggle of men who appeared ahead of them, walking in their direction. The group passed, unaware. Janet expected she and Baxeter to move out at once but Baxeter held her back. She thought it was to let the men get further away but then realized Baxeter was re-holstering into his backpack a short hand-weapon that bulged with a fat-nosed silencer. Just innocent men, merely walking home from some late-night outing, Janet thought: it would have been murder.

He urged her on until they reached the junction at which they'd first seen the approaching men. Baxeter hesitated for a moment, orienting himself, led her about ten yards to the left and then stopped, hunkering down against a large, deserted building beside which there was a completely open space, pulling her down to his level. Across the open space there was a perfect view of the entire city, much better than when she'd first looked down, laid out for inspection in the sharp moonlight.

She indicated she wanted to speak again and he pulled aside his cowl. Janet said: "I don't understand what's happening."

"Wait," he said, brusquely.

The explosions split the night open, appearing to be all around her, so near and so loud that the pain seared through her ears. She was partially deafened but still able to hear the sudden roar of aircraft and then everything became fiercely white—lighter than the brightest day—as dozens of phosphorus illuminating shells burst from what seemed every point in the sky. Janet blinked against the glare, able to see everything. There was a fresh eruption of noise, of machine-gun fire and the slower-paced crack of rifles and handguns and the crump of shells: there were spurts of flame where the shells landed. All along the waterfront landing craft were spewing men ashore: they emerged firing from behind the drop-fronted ramps and several fell almost immediately. Janet recognized that the overhead roar was not that of aircraft but of helicopter gunships. They hovered all along the waterfront, continuous streams of flame coming from their Gatling cannons protruding from either side.

And then Janet recognized something else.

She stared wildly around, convinced she knew the imposing government building about two hundred yards away as one she had driven past on her way to the American embassy that morning after she'd toured the harbor looking for the fishing boat that had first brought her to Beirut. Then she saw the embassy itself and knew she was right.

Furious, eyes bulging in her anger, Janet snatched and tugged and Baxeter staggered sideways, surprised. He jerked the head cover off. Because noise didn't matter any more—had to be yelled over, in fact—he shouted: "What the hell's going on!"

"This isn't Kantari!" Janet shouted back. "I know this place. It's Yarzy and that's the American embassy. Why aren't we in Kantari?"

"Because it was absurd and laughable, like I told you," he said. "That *is* the American embassy and if anything goes wrong get the hell to it: you'll be safe there."

"But John . . ."

". . . Shut up and stop being a fool!" said Baxeter. He tugged binoculars from his backpack, thrust them towards her and gestured far away, to their right. "There," he said. "Focus there!"

Janet hesitated, then did as she was told. It took her a moment to adjust the binoculars, a moment in which there was a fresh spray of phosphorus. It was like a firework display, she thought: an obscene, killing firework display, and she had the ringside seat.

The enlargement was perfect. She could see the American commandoes spreading through the street, and other men, civilians, desperately firing at them as they retreated. The gunships moved with the advance, pouring down cannon shells: she saw one Arab practically cut in half by the concentration of fire and an already shattered building actually collapsed. And then she saw black-suited and black-helmeted men.

Janet tried to count but stopped at seven. They were all in one street, with two in a side alley, and all facing the direction from which the Americans were approaching, so that the Arabs were pincered in between. Twice groups of Arabs tried to get into the street and only then did the Israelis fire, blasting the entry and preventing them.

Janet turned beseechingly to Baxeter. "What . . . ?"

"Just watch!"

When she looked back the Arabs had stopped trying to get into the Israeli-sealed street and were being forced further along another road to escape. Camouflaged Americans were everywhere now, entering the street itself and moving house-to-house along bordering and parallel alleys but she could no longer see any Israelis. There was an abrupt concentration of troops around one house halfway along. She watched one man's arm move and the door was blown in and she realized he'd thrown a grenade. The house was rushed and into the street—quiet and secured now—another coordinated group moved, a stretcher between them.

And then she saw John.

He was at the doorway, supported by two American commandoes: his arms were along their shoulders and theirs were around him and he sagged between them. Janet whimpered, hearing herself make the sound, and a huge feeling of pity welled up inside her. There was an obvious indication towards the stretcher and John shook his head, trying to walk but almost at once he stumbled and allowed himself to be shakily lowered on to it. They moved off at once, the stretcher completely encircled by men with their backs to it, most literally walking backwards, forming a tight circle of protection.

"OK!" Baxeter said. "You had to be here to see him freed. And you were. Now let's get out!"

Janet did not move, still watching the progress of the rescue squad, and Baxeter jerked her upright, pulling the binoculars from her. "I said we've got to get out!"

Dully, bewildered, she stumbled after him, conscious that the night was becoming black again because no more phosphorus was exploding: there was still firing from below but it was sporadic now and the gunships had stopped blasting. They appeared to be going back along exactly the same route they had climbed but at the brighter thoroughfare Baxeter halted longer than before, head lowered as he mumbled into his throat microphone. Janet had an abrupt spurt of fear as a shadow became the figure of a man and then there were others and she realized they had linked up with some of the other Israelis. At once they moved off, in their own tight circle of protection. They were practically across the street before the shout came: at once two of the Israelis stopped, turning towards the cafe. One fired a short burst and the other hurled a grenade. Baxeter was dragging her along, her hand in his, and they were in an alley before the blast of the explosion rippled up the street.

Janet stumbled along, panting, the air burning her throat, aware that as well as being pulled by Baxeter she was being pushed by another of the men, his hand in the small of her back. A dog barked, suddenly snarling in front of them and at once there was a wailing howl as it was kicked out of the way. A challenge came, from a window above, but the head jerked back from view at a spray of automatic fire that whined off the brickwork, bringing dust raining down upon them.

"Can't keep up: got to stop," Janet groaned.

Baxeter continued pulling and the other commando went on pushing, no one slackening their pace.

"Please!"

They ran on.

The gates of whatever yard it was in which they had hidden the vehicles were open, men guarding the entrance, and as they reached it the first emerged, the lorry, closely followed by two jeeps. Baxeter had to physically lift Janet into the back of another: she rolled sideways as she went in, laid against the hard seat, and could not raise herself. She felt Baxeter behind her, his hand protectively against her shoulder.

The convoy hurtled back along the coast road and she was jolted and thrown about, scarcely aware in her exhaustion of what was happening. Twice she heard what she thought was gunfire but her ears were so dulled by the earlier attack she wasn't sure.

She was just able to straighten by the time they got back to where they beached. Surrendering herself completely to Baxeter's guidance she was led back down the incline, over the shingle and briefly out into the water. He folded backwards easily into the rubber boat, leaning out and lifting her bodily in beside him.

Behind there was the crump of yet another explosion and Janet squinted back in time to see the lorry and the jeeps burst one after the other into a solid wall of flame. It was not casual destruction, she realized: they had been arranged so that they formed a solid, blazing barrier against any pursuit. As the awareness came to her Janet saw in the light of the flames the dark outlines of pursuing army vehicles moving along the coast road after them.

The dinghy started off at once. There were far more people aboard than when they had come in from the patrol boat, and when they reached it men milled around on deck, laughing and hugging and patting each other on the back: she could see four men on stretchers but there were no obvious bloodstains to show that they had been wounded in the assault. Baxeter moved into the apparent celebration. Janet stayed by the wheelhouse, ignored.

No attempt was made to bring the dinghies inboard. A number of men threw things into them as the patrol boat surged off and almost at once there were grenade bursts and the rubber boats started to settle and sink.

Janet clung on to the wheelhouse, grateful for the wind that whipped into her face, drying the perspiration that soaked her: as close as she was, she could hear a continuous radio commentary in Hebrew and see the blips against the radar screen. The heavy concentration to one side would be the American fleet, she supposed: there were other isolated markings, one directly ahead.

She was aware of someone next to her and turned to see Baxeter. "All right?" he said.

Janet shrugged, not replying, her mind at that moment blank of any thought.

"It worked," said Baxeter.

Again Janet did not reply.

She was conscious of the obvious drop in power, knowing they had not traveled as long this time as they had ingoing from the fishing boat. And then she realized the rendezvous was not with the fishing boat but with two other patrol vessels exactly like the one on which they were already traveling. Again they came expertly together and there was a scrambled transfer, the stretcher cases going across first. Janet watched, counting. It was achieved very quickly, hardly more than minutes. There were shouted farewells and the two new vessels creamed away in convoy. Only she and Baxeter remained, aside from the crew.

"Thirteen," she said to Baxeter, as the patrol vessel climbed back on top the water again.

"What?" said Baxeter.

"Making allowances for those ashore in your vehicles when we got there I'd guess we came back with thirteen more people than when we went in."

"Actually," said Baxeter, "it was twelve. And they weren't our vehicles; they were hijacked from the Lebanese army."

·31·

Baxeter had tried to speak, to explain, but Janet had refused him, choked by this, the final betrayal, tricked by a man she thought had loved her. She spat out that she hated him. He said he didn't believe her and she screamed back that she didn't give a fuck what he believed: that all she wanted to do was get back to Cyprus. He'd reached out to touch her, but she'd shrugged him away, not wanting even the slightest physical contact.

"You're being juvenile," he said.

"*Have* been juvenile," she qualified. "Welcome to the graduation."

"You're not very good at sarcasm: it comes out wrong."

"What the fuck are you good at?"

"What I do."

"What's that?"

"John's free: you saw it happen. That's what I'm good at."

"I'm impressed!"

"You should be. And the sarcasm still isn't working."

"Go fuck yourself!"

"The barnyard language doesn't work, either. Never has."

Like everything else in the operation, which Janet now accepted

Baxeter had personally organized, the reunion with the fishing boat went perfectly and there was no difficulty landing at the shoreline break near Cape Pyla from which they'd embarked.

He did not immediately try to start the car, looking across at her. "I said I wanted to explain."

"Shut up! Just shut up and get me back to the hotel!"

"Your choice."

"I just made it."

"Sure?"

"Sure."

They drove in silence through the still-dark night towards Nicosia. They'd crossed from the Lebanon in an incredibly brief time and there wasn't yet the peach and pink tinge of dawn on the horizon: but a helicopter would have been quicker, and the American plan was for John to be helicoptered in at once to the British base at Akrotiri, she remembered. What if they'd tried to reach her at the hotel? What reason could she convincingly give for not being there? Nothing right, Janet thought, dismally: from the very outset she had done nothing right. She'd fumbled and thrashed out and made ripples—maybe even waves—but not once had she got anything right. Not once. Fucked up, all the way along. Baxeter's distaste of her swearing forced itself upon her: fucked up, she thought again, defiantly. And then again, fucked up.

Baxeter started to drive into the hotel gate but Janet stopped him there.

"We have to talk," he said, as she got out.

Janet slammed the door, saying nothing.

The skeletal night staff were still on, the clerk hastily buttoning his shirt collar as she approached the desk. When she asked, he assured her there were no outstanding messages: relief lifted Janet. She felt the physical need to cleanse herself of everything and everybody with whom she had been in contact during the previous hours. She showered for a long time, twisting the water control from cold to hot, first to chill and then to burn herself but soon became irritated at the obvious scourging, snapping off the pretense. She didn't sleep when she finally got into bed, lying wide-eyed but able to see nothing clearly as the day lightened through the window. Fucked up, she decided once more and then confronted another truism: her cursing was thought-out and artificial, words without the necessary gut-felt emotion.

The telephone shrilled at six o'clock. It was Willsher. Janet had to force the excitement befitting the announcement that John Sheridan was a free man, using words like wonderful and fantastic and agreed to be ready when the limousine arrived, in an hour's time.

Al Hart was the escort once again. He was unshaven and haggard and wore denim fatigues and Janet knew he had somehow been involved. As soon as she got into the car, Hart said: "It was a cakewalk: we annihilated them!"

Janet thought how easily Baxeter had been prepared to shoot the group of innocent men who'd almost come unexpectedly upon them. She said: "What were the casualties?"

"We lost ten men: maybe twenty-five wounded," disclosed the CIA man. "None captured, though: that would have been the disaster."

Ten men—probably with wives and kids—who this time yesterday had been alive, Janet reflected. She said: "So it's being regarded as a success?"

The stubbled man grinned at her across the car. "There's already been a congratulatory telephone call—and a follow-up cable—from the President. What do you think?"

Janet wished—as she'd wished all too often—that she knew what to think. She said: "So how's John?"

"I only saw him briefly: a few minutes," said Hart, guardedly. "He looked OK to me: bewildered, not quite able to grasp what was happening, but basically OK."

"I hope to Christ you're right," said Janet. How many more disappointments could there possibly be?

At Akrotiri, Hart actually had to get from the car to complete the necessary formalities: an armed escort entered the limousine next to the driver to take them through the military complex. The soldier pointed out the infirmary buildings when they were still some way off and Hart came forward eagerly in his seat: his leg began pumping up and down, a nervous mannerism.

There must have been the sort of warning of their approach that there had been when Janet had made her entry into the American embassy (a week, a month, an eon ago?) because Professor Robards emerged immediately from the hospital entrance when the car stopped. Janet had expected the psychologist to be wearing a white coat and maybe carrying some tool of his trade, whatever a tool of his trade was; instead he had on the same crumpled jacket and check shirt of their previous encounter. Janet wondered if the man bathed.

"How is he?" Janet demanded.

Robards smiled. "Better than I expected. I want a day or two to be sure—the damned press conference can wait—but he's better than I expected him to be."

Janet was conscious of a stir within her which she put down as relief. Was it enough? she asked herself. She said: "That's good. I'm very glad," disappointed in herself as she spoke. From the emptiness of her voice she could have been speaking about a casual acquaintance.

Robards didn't notice. He said: "It's more than good: it's astonishing. Your fiancé is one hell of a tough guy, mentally as well as physically."

My fiancé, thought Janet. Why didn't she feel any longer that John Sheridan was her fiancé? She said: "I can see him right away?"

"He's insisting on it," said Robards, smiling again.

"Is there anything I should say? Shouldn't say?"

Robards made a sharp, dismissive gesture with his head. "Don't hold back on anything. If you feel like saying something, say it. He's quite tense, coiled-up. He'd recognize in a moment any sort of hesitation: be unsettled by it."

Janet walked with the psychologist through gleaming, polished corridors, conscious of the man's crepe-soled shoes squeaking over the tiles. She expected the hospital smell of disinfectant and formaldehyde but it wasn't present and then she remembered it was not physical injury that was treated in this wing. Having posed the question she was unsure what she was going to say.

John Sheridan was in a single-bedded side ward, an all-glass cubicle where he was always visible to the nurses from their central control desk area. There were three nurses at the desk and another was leaving Sheridan's room as they approached. Through the glass Janet could see Sheridan staring directly ahead, eyes unfocused. His hair remained as thick as it had always been but it was almost completely white now. His cheeks were sunken and emaciated and his eyes were blinking. Both thin hands were outstretched, without movement, on top of the sheet, and the veins were corded black across their backs.

"Are you coming in with me?" asked Janet, suddenly needing support.

"Do you want me to?"

"I don't . . . No . . . perhaps not . . ." she stumbled, awkwardly.

"It would probably be better, just the two of you."

"Yes."

"But if you want . . . ?"

"No."

"I'll be at the desk: all you need to do is call."

"Yes," Janet accepted. So what the hell was she going to say?

"Good luck," encouraged Robards. Janet wished he hadn't said it.

She stopped in the frame of the doorway, looking in. For a few brief moments he did not appear to see her and then recognition came into his eyes and his face filled with happiness.

"Hello," he said. "Hello, my darling." His voice was thin and uneven.

"Hello," said Janet. It sounded vacuous and inadequate. Which it was. Go on in! she urged herself; go in! go in! She did at last, hesitantly, her feet sliding one after the other over the polished floor. Janet got to the bedside and smiled down, and when he smiled back she was shocked to see that some of his teeth were missing. She didn't know if she'd kept her reaction from showing. She reached tentatively out and he stretched his hand up to hers: his skin felt strange, like paper. An old person's hand, she thought. Kiss him! She had to kiss him!

Janet started to lean forward but Sheridan twitched back, turning his head away. "No!" he said.

"Why not?"

"Not clean," he mumbled. "Not clean yet."

"What do you mean, not clean?"

"Haven't washed, not properly, for a long time," said Sheridan. "They bathed me this morning but there's some skin infection, from the dirt. I hate dirt!"

He always had, thought Janet, remembering the fastidious apartment. Concentrating, she saw there was filth ingrained in the creases on his hands and beneath his fingernails: his chalk-white face was patched with pink and there were occasional grazes where the shaver had snagged. She said: "I *want* to kiss you!"

"No!" The voice was tremulous, tears close. Sheridan said: "It's nothing serious, the infection. They say it'll clear up in days."

Still with her hand in his Janet managed to pull a chair closer to the bed, to sit down. As close as this she could smell at last the disinfectant or whatever they were treating him with. She said: "It's good to see you, my darling." Vacuous and inadequate, she thought again.

"The doctor, Robards, he told me what you've done."

If only you knew what I'd done, my darling, Janet thought. She said: "I had to get you out."

"I never thought it would happen," said Sheridan. "Not really. I refused to give in, *wouldn't* give in because if I had the bastards would have won, but deep down I never thought I was going to get out alive."

"Did they hurt you badly?" asked Janet. At once she regretted the question: don't hold back on anything, she recalled.

Sheridan nodded. "In the beginning. They wanted to break me: make me beg . . ." He pulled his lips back, an ugly expression. "Lost some teeth. I think they bruised my kidneys, too. Peed a lot of blood, but it's stopped now. Robards said they'd check for permanent damage. They didn't maim me: threatened to cut fingers off but they didn"t."

"Poor darling: my poor darling!" Janet covered the bony, fragile hand with both of hers, frightened against hurting him if she squeezed too hard.

"It was you," said Sheridan, confusingly. "That's how I resisted them: thinking of you. Although, as time went on, I began to believe I'd never get out, I still kept thinking of you, knowing that you'd be waiting. That's why I begged, in the end. Didn't mean anything and it stopped me being beaten: reduced the risk of my not getting back to you."

"Don't, my love! Please don't!" said Janet, begging herself. Sheridan was a blurred outline through her tears. It was exactly how Robards had predicted he would hang on, she remembered.

"It's all right," assured Sheridan, their roles reversed. "It doesn't upset me to talk about it: they didn't really win. Just thought they did. So I'm not ashamed or anything silly like that."

"I don't think you've got anything at all to be ashamed of, my darling," said Janet, with feeling.

"We should have been married by now: I thought about that, too."

Janet swallowed. "So did I."

"Have we got the house?"

She nodded. "All waiting."

"I planned things," disclosed Sheridan. "That's how I kept my sanity, thinking about all the pictures and plans you sent and imagining how we'd fix it up . . ." The man smiled, almost embarrassed. "Every room: carpets, drapes, stuff in the kitchen, things like that.

But it was only a game for me, a way of staying sane. We needn't do any of it, of course."

"We'll fix it up however you want," said Janet. How could she make a promise like that?

"I want so much to get back," he said. His lips began to tremble and momentarily he had to stop talking, clamping them shut against a collapse. "To get back where things are familiar: where I'm sure. Don't want to be unsure again," he picked up. Sheridan moved one of his hands, to cover hers. "Remember what I said a long time ago about never going away again?"

Janet nodded once more, unspeaking.

"This time I *really* mean it," promised the man. "Never again. Ever."

"Good," she said. Was that the best she could manage?

"I've got to stay here a couple of days for tests."

"Robards told me."

"But after that we can go home, can't we?" he asked with sudden urgency. "Back home to Washington?"

"Yes," agreed Janet, feeling the pressure of his dependence. "We can go back home."

"Come and see me every day!" Sheridan pressed further. "I want to know you're around."

"I'm around," said Janet. "And of course I'll come every day."

Robards was waiting where he'd promised to be, in the desk area. He smiled as Janet emerged and said: "Well?"

Janet was unsure how to answer. She said: "He's very thin."

"A couple of weeks from now, with the proper care and diet, he'll be a different man," guaranteed the psychologist, buoyantly. "How did he seem apart from that?"

"Nervous," said Janet.

"But not unstable?"

"No," she agreed. "He certainly didn't seem unstable. He said it didn't hurt to talk about it."

"That's the most important thing," seized Robards. "We've got to get it all out: I don't want anything left unsaid which is going to stay inside his head and fester."

"Will two or three days be sufficient for you to achieve that?" What was she trying to delay? Janet asked herself.

"Here certainly," assured Robards. "We'll carry on, of course, when we get back to Washington."

"Of course," accepted Janet. "I wasn't thinking."

"Willsher's here," announced the psychologist. "He wants to see you."

The CIA official rose politely as Janet entered the visitors' room and waited until she sat down. The man didn't smile.

"He seems OK," said Janet.

"Yes," said Willsher. "We're very relieved."

"So am I," said Janet. It had been automatic to say it; the words came without thought. "Hart said there'd been congratulations from the President?"

"The outcry is what we predicted it would be, but Washington is regarding it as an unqualified success," said Willsher. "Which is what I want to talk to you about."

"Me?"

"Robards won't let us make John available to the media for a couple of days, but there's a clamor for access," said Willsher. "We want you to hold the first press conference by yourself."

"By myself!" Inconceivably, her mind blocked by other things, Janet had forgotten the media interest she had been largely instrumental in cultivating.

"You've done pretty well in the past," reminded Willsher, pointedly.

"What more is there to say?" she asked, wearily.

"Which is what I want to talk to you about most of all," said Willsher. "The discovery of John's whereabouts . . . planning of the incursion . . . everything like that, has got to remain entirely a CIA operation. You weren't involved. Understood!"

Janet blinked at the demand. "If you like," she said, badly.

"We do like," said Willsher, forcefully. "Who you humped to get what you wanted remains unsaid as far as we're concerned."

"Who I what!"

"Lady!" said Willsher, weary himself now. "You surely don't think that we haven't known what's been going on, do you? We've had you and Baxeter under wraps from the first time you jumped into the sack together: we've had a wire in your hotel bedroom for weeks. Heard every sigh and groan. Like I said, that's your business. It worked."

"Oh my God!" exclaimed Janet, coming forward with her head in her hands.

"It remains unsaid," repeated Willsher. "John will never know."

"But why didn't you . . . ?" groped Janet, through her hands.

"Didn't we what? Confront Baxeter and demand cooperation? Because we wouldn't have got it, would we?" said Willsher, as if he were explaining a simple lesson to a dull child. "Baxeter was conning you and had to imagine he was conning us, too. He'd have backed off if we'd confronted him. And we'd have lost the opportunity to get John. We just didn't see the curve until it was almost too late but we managed to minimize it: everyone got their share."

Janet didn't understand the last remark. What share had she got, out of any of it? She straightened, with difficulty, and said: "I don't know if I can do it."

"Oh yes you can," said Willsher, coming forward himself so that their heads were quite close. "We've got a success, like I told you. And it's going to end up a success, all the way down the line."

"Or else?" anticipated Janet.

"I'm not in the business of threats," said Willsher. "For the moment I'm in the business of writing happy-ever-after love stories. You go before the press by yourself and you go before the press with John, before you fly back to America, and it's going to be violin music and roses and everyone back home is going to get a lump in their throats and know an international violation was justified and think what a great and free country ours is. Whatever you personally decide is going to happen between the two of you once you get there and the press isn't looking is entirely a matter for you. For the moment what happens is entirely a matter for us."

"Just like that?" said Janet, trying successfully to match the cynicism.

"No, not just like that," offered Willsher. "The court case is still outstanding and you stand a chance of being trashed if the prosecution can't come up with that Arab engineer or get the cafe people to remember what happened."

"Yes," agreed Janet, doubtfully.

"We know where Haseeb is," disclosed Willsher. "We're going to make sure that Zarpas does, too. And the cafe owner is going to recover his memory."

"By being threatened?"

"Whatever it takes: nothing is going to tarnish this."

"Not a detail overlooked!" said Janet.

"Not a one," said Willsher, confidently.

"Satisfied!" demanded Janet, her control wavering. "Are you satisfied with what you've done!"

Willsher was quite unmoved by Janet's outrage. "Of course, I'm satisfied," he said. "It all worked out, didn't it? You wouldn't believe how unusual it is for everything to turn out as completely as it has this time."

"But what about me!"

"Your problem, Ms. Stone. Your problem," said the man. "You made it one, after all."

·32·

Later, when Janet watched a recording of the solitary press conference, it was difficult for her to believe that she was the person smiling the smiles and saying the words, a self-effacing, modest woman refusing to accord herself any special attributes (what special attributes did she have, for God's sake!) or make any particular claims. She took hardly any recollection at all from the conference room itself, a smoky, jostled, yelling chamber where she confronted more journalists and television cameras than ever before and subjected herself to an inquisition that went on for more than two hours: at the end her voice croaked with overuse and her eyes watered from the tobacco sting.

She talked of her ecstatic delight at John being freed. His apparent fortitude was staggering: he was suffering some deprivation but there were no indications of permanent physical or mental harm: yes, he had been tortured but not seriously: yes, she had always known that one day he would be freed; no, she'd never despaired: yes, she looked eagerly forward to their time together now: no, they had not yet fixed a date for the delayed wedding: yes, of course it was some-thing they would have to arrange but ensuring John was fully re covered was the first priority: no, she did not know the details which had enabled the incursion force to go into Lebanon and get him out: yes, she knew of the international furor: yes, she thought the invasion was justified because the country itself appeared willing to allow gangsterism and terrorism to continue unchecked: yes, she worried desperately about other hostages still detained whose predicament might be worsened by what had happened, but hoped it would act as a warning to the gangs and groups holding these remaining hostages that they were vulnerable, and lead to other early releases: yes, she welcomed the decision and strength of America, which she sincerely thanked, in taking the decision to mount the rescue: no, she did not regret what she had attempted, nor the difficulties she had personally experienced, in coming here and doing what she'd done: yes (a pause here because she could not help it), she had occasionally behaved stupidly and had been lucky to escape unscathed: but yes, she would do it all again, if the outcome were the same as it was today.

After the conference Janet agreed to separate, individual television interviews with the four major American networks and then the English and the French and the German until at the end she was parroting her replies, dull-eyed and dull-eared, scarcely waiting for the predictable questions to be posed before going into her prepared and rehearsed and by now practically cliched answer.

She slumped in the back of the U.S. embassy car taking her back to the hotel, limp and wrung out, her mind hardly capable of sustaining a single thought and certainly not a continuous contemplation. Incredibly, there were still more cameramen and journalists at the Churchill. Janet pushed through them, refusing another questioning session, careless of the photographs being taken as she shuffled into the elevator to go up to her room.

There were call-back messages from her parents and Partington and Zarpas. Janet let herself drop backwards on to the bed, literally prostrated by the ordeal she had undergone, relegating everything to the following day.

The exhaustion from not sleeping at all the previous night overtook her but Janet did not lapse completely into sleep. It was a suspension, halfway between sleep and wakefulness, a pleasantly light-headed sensation: she wondered if this were what it was like to be a drug addict after a fix, suspended beyond the need to reason or worry or think, wrapped in the softest, thickest, most protective cotton wool. Everything had happened to her, so nothing else could, not any more: no more hurt to feel. No more pain, not more bruising. Safe, like she'd always wanted to be.

The telephone rang, distantly, but she ignored it. It stopped and rang again at once. Stopped and rang again. Stopped and rang again. And then again, worming its way into her semi-consciousness. She lifted it at last, without identifying herself, waiting for the caller to speak.

"I want to come up."

"No."

"We have to talk."

"No."

"You *know* we have to talk."

"I said no."

"Please!"

Janet couldn't remember his pleading before. She remembered something else, though. *We just didn't see the curve until it was almost too late . . . everyone got their share.* "What about?"

"You know what about."

She had to know, completely. "Where?"

"Let me come up?"

We've had a wire in your hotel bedroom for weeks. Heard every sigh and groan. "No. Somewhere else."

"You choose."

Yes, thought Janet. She had to choose. At last. "Is your car here?"

"Yes."

"I'll use the emergency exit."

Did Willsher and his men know about her use of the fire escape stairs? wondered Janet, as she pushed against the heavy locking bar and began to descend the stone steps. What Willsher knew—what anyone knew—didn't matter any more.

Baxeter must have moved the Volkswagen because it was directly opposite the door through which she emerged. As she approached he leaned across as she always thought of him as doing and thrust the door open for her. Janet sat with her back partially against the door, determined to look directly at him.

"Do you want to drive around?" he said.

"I don't mind."

"It might be best."

"I said I didn't mind."

Baxeter started the car and ground the gears like he normally did and Janet thought, why can't I feel like I should feel! Why can't I hate the bastard instead of feeling like I do about him! He took the road towards the mountains, the mountains where they'd first realized what was happening between them, and Janet recognized it at once. Unthinking or intentional?

Wanting to unsettle him Janet said: "The Americans know."

"What!"

"About us, everything. Willsher told me today."

Baxeter drove for several moments without responding. Then he said: "Shit!"

"That fits well enough a lot of what happened."

"Everything worked out as it was planned," Baxeter insisted, almost defiantly. "You got John back."

"The psychologist thinks he's going to be OK."

"That's good."

"I'm waiting," said Janet.

They were on the central plain now, in heavy darkness, away from any street or village lights. Baxeter coasted the car into the side of the road but didn't look at her when he stopped. He said, simply: "It was an exchange."

"The twelve extra men?"

Despite the darkness she was aware of his nodding. Baxeter said: "You know what it's like in Beirut, faction fighting faction, gang fighting gang. The Shia group holding John were warring with a group holding twelve of our people . . . people we had to get safely back: Israel always gets its people back. You know that . . ."

Entebbe, remembered Janet. She said: "What was the deal?"

"We got our soldiers, the Shias got Americans delivered up to them, on a plate . . ."

"I can't believe you did that!" said Janet, incredulous. Why not? Weren't these people—all of them—capable of anything!

"Your arrival, all the publicity, was the way to do it. The idea was to leak information sufficiently accurate to persuade the Americans to go at a time and on a day when they would be expected. In return we got our hostages."

"You knowingly set the Americans up!"

"*Appeared* to," qualified Baxeter. "Half an hour before the Americans landed we broadcast as supposed Shias exchanging last minute information on the wavelength we knew the Americans were monitoring. So they were warned well in advance. It was really the Shias who got ambushed."

Janet was staggered by the matter-of-fact cynicism. *Everyone got their share*, she thought once more. "John!" said Janet, in abrupt awareness. "There was no need under that arrangement with the Shias for John to be actually gotten out!"

Baxeter looked at her at last: it was difficult for her properly to discern his features. "The Americans had to be successful, to mitigate any bad feeling between us if they discovered what was really happening. Which you tell me they have."

"If the Americans hadn't reached Kantari, you'd have got John out?"

Baxeter nodded again. "But it wasn't necessary. The American assault was brilliant: they did it."

"If you'd had to rescue John he would have been handed over at the embassy where we were, in Beirut? On the hill at Yarzy?" persisted Janet, in growing comprehension.

"Yes," Baxeter confirmed.

"But not by a group of Israelis?"

"No."

"That's why I was allowed along!" Janet said. "You didn't *agree* to my coming! You *needed* me, if the American assault didn't work!"

"It was an insurance," the Israeli conceded.

"Oh, you are!" Janet said. "You *are* a bastard."

"Everything had to be covered," Baxeter said.

At last, Janet thought: the complete, ugly, nasty, opportunistic truth at last. "Willsher said you conned me," reflected Janet, distantly. "I never guessed how completely . . ." Her voice becoming harder, she demanded: "How much did you laugh at me? How much did everyone laugh at me?"

"No one laughed at you," Baxeter insisted. "It wasn't like that."

"I deserve to be laughed at," Janet said, reflective again. "I must have been the best comedy act in years!"

"I haven't lied—I haven't conned—about one thing," Baxeter said.

"There wouldn't be any advantage left for you now, would there?" she accepted, bitterly.

"Stay!" Baxeter said.

"No," Janet said at once.

Baxeter held his hands out, another pleading gesture. "OK!" he said. "Go to America. Be with John for a while. But you'll come back: we both know you'll come back."

"No," she said again. Where did the determination—a determination she didn't feel—come from?

Baxeter did not speak for a long time. Then he said: "Don't you love me?"

"That isn't it."

"That's all it can be: all it needs to be."

"That's making it too simple."

"John more then?"

"I won't answer that."

"You love me!" he shouted.

"Yes." How could she say that, admit the truth, and feel nothing?

"Then why!"

"I don't need that: not a feeling of love. I need to feel safe. With John I feel safe. I always have. I could never feel safe, with you."

"That doesn't make sense!"

"It doesn't have to, not to you. All it has to do is make sense to me."

"You'll come back," he said again. "I know you'll come back."

·Epilogue·

Janet visited Sheridan every day, as she'd promised, and was amazed at his visible improvement. By the time of their joint press conference, the gauntness had gone from his face and he'd overcome the tendency to lose concentration, turning inwardly upon himself. The media gathering was still strictly controlled, however. Sheridan gave only a brief description of the brutality during his imprisonment, refusing to elaborate too much because of the distress it might cause relatives and friends of hostages still held in Lebanon. The focus anyway was upon them both. All the questions about their hopes and their marriage that had been put to Janet were repeated and for over an hour they strolled in the embassy grounds, hand in hand and arm in arm and embracing, for the benefit of the camermen.

They were driven directly from the embassy to the airport. On the plane a curtained alcove had been arranged in the first class section, to give them some privacy. The steward offered champagne even before takeoff and they accepted.

"Here's to us," toasted Sheridan and Janet replied: "Here's to us."

"No more upsets," promised Sheridan, as the plane climbed,

banked over the island, then set its course. "From now on it's just us, never apart. We're going to be so happy, darling."

"I know we are," said Janet. "So happy." It had been naive of her to have expected Baxeter to attend the press conference, but she'd hoped he would. She'd wanted very much to see him, just once more. That's all, though: just once more. She wouldn't come back: although she might want to, she definitely wouldn't come back.